I liked it

CRITICAL ACCLAIM FOR THE MAGNIFICENT, BEST-SELLING NOVELS OF BARBARA TAYLOR BRADFORD

EVERYTHING TO GAIN

"We genuinely root for Mal during her grueling struggle to live on."
—*San Francisco Chronicle*

"[Bradford] has a sharp eye for detail, her characters own some complexity, and there's a knowing quality to observations on how people work."
—*Phoenix Gazette*

"Bradford has not lost her touch. . . . The author brings new life to a familiar theme. . . . Persuasive and richly detailed."
—*Blade-Citizen* (Oceanside, CA)

"If you like Victorian splendor [and] long sweet passages of simple love . . . this one's for you."
—*Oklahoman* (Oklahoma City, OK)

"Moving and unforgettable."
—*Romantic Times*

TO BE THE BEST

"A novel for everyone . . . A satisfying, lushly detailed saga."
—*Rave Reviews*

A Woman of Substance

"A wonderfully entertaining novel."

—*Denver Post*

"A long, satisfying novel of money and power, passion and revenge . . . [A] dramatic and often moving story . . . Interwoven are themes of high finance, romance, and revenge, set against the sweep of 20th-century history."

—*Los Angeles Times Syndicate*

Hold the Dream

"Attractive, intelligent, and capable, Paula McGill Fairley proves a worthy successor to her grandmother's domain."

—*Booklist*

"Another instant bestseller. The men and women are all gorgeous, rich, well-dressed. There are luxurious descriptions of dinner parties, apartments and homes, food and drink, and of course jewels. . . . The perfect page-turner."

—*Philadelphia Inquirer*

"Fascinating."

—*Houston Chronicle*

VOICE OF THE HEART

"Barbara Taylor Bradford is back with a new, vibrantly characterized leading lady and a glimpse at the dazzling world of the rich and powerful. . . . [A] richly woven tale."

—*Working Woman*

"It is easy to want every item Bradford catalogues, easy to imagine wearing it, eating and drinking it, driving it, smelling like it . . . The geography of *Voice of the Heart* takes a reader to all the right places."

—*Los Angeles Times*

"Meant to be read in a peignoir on a chaise lounge whilst nibbling scented chocolates."

—*Cosmopolitan*

"A captivating work filled with glamour, intrigue and ironic reversal . . . Richly textured, highly entertaining."

—*Booklist*

"Engrossing . . . Stunning."

—*Pittsburgh Press*

"A rich tapestry of love and romance . . . the surprise ending is both poignant and fitting."

—*San Diego Union*

Books by Barbara Taylor Bradford

*Dangerous to Know**

*Everything to Gain**

*A Woman of Substance**

*Voice of the Heart**

*Hold the Dream**

*Act of Will**

*To Be the Best**

The Women in His Life

Remember

Angel

*Available from HarperPaperbacks

BARBARA
Taylor
Bradford

DANGEROUS TO KNOW

📖 HarperPaperbacks
A Division of HarperCollinsPublishers

HarperPaperbacks *A Division of* HarperCollins*Publishers*
10 East 53rd Street, New York, N.Y. 10022

Copyright © 1995 by Barbara Taylor Bradford
All rights reserved. No part of this book may be used or reproduced in any manner whatsoever without written permission of the publisher, except in the case of brief quotations embodied in critical articles and reviews. For information address HarperCollins*Publishers*,
10 East 53rd Street, New York, N.Y. 10022.

A hardcover edition of this book was published in 1995 by HarperCollins*Publishers*.

Cover art © by Pascal, *Mid-Day in Grasse*

First HarperPaperbacks printing: June 1996

Printed in the United States of America

HarperPaperbacks and colophon are trademarks of HarperCollins*Publishers*

❖ 10 9 8 7 6 5 4 3 2 1

For Bob, with all my love

Mad, bad, and dangerous to know.

—Lady Caroline Lamb, writing of her lover,
the poet Lord Byron

THE NARRATORS

PART ONE

VIVIENNE
LOYALTY

CHAPTER ONE

The first time I met Sebastian Locke I fell in love with him. He was thirty-two years old. I was twelve. I had no idea at the time that he was my mother's lover. Nor did I know then that ten years later I would marry him.

Now he was dead.

He had died in somewhat mysterious, even suspicious, circumstances. It was not yet known whether he had died of natural causes, committed suicide, or been murdered.

We were divorced. I had not seen him for almost a year, until last Monday, when we had lunched together at his request. Obviously the police hoped I might be able to throw some light on the matter of his death, but I could not. I was as perplexed as everyone else. However, they had just arrived to see me. I was appalled. That Sebastian was dead was only just registering with me. I glanced around my library. The

familiar room looked exactly the same as it always
had. The two walls of books were balanced by an
eclectic mixture of antiques, my grandmother's horse
paintings, and her Victorian lamps. But somehow it
was out of kilter. So was I. Pulling myself together, I
buzzed the intercom and told my secretary Belinda
she could show them into the library.

A split second later I was shaking hands with
Detectives Joe Kennelly and Aaron Miles from the
Major Crime Division of the Connecticut State Police.

"We're baffled, Mrs. Trent," Detective Kennelly said
as we all sat down. "Until we get the autopsy report
we're working in the dark. As you already know, the
circumstances are suspicious, so we can't rule out foul
play. But who would want to kill Sebastian Locke?
Surely such a good man didn't have enemies, did he?"

They both focused their eyes on me, and intently so.

Silently I stared back at them. I did not say a word. I
could think of several enemies, and any one of them
might easily have murdered him. However, I was not
about to mention this to the police. That was a family
matter, and, oddly enough, even though we had been
divorced for eight years, I still thought of myself as
being a member of the Locke clan, and was treated as
such by the family—what was left of it.

Clearing my throat, I said finally, "Naturally, a man
like Sebastian met a lot of people on his travels around
the world, and from all walks of life. I suppose he
might have made an enemy or two, unintentionally, of
course. Powerful men often do inspire hatred in some,
for no reason other than the power they possess."

Without shifting my steady gaze I pursed my lips,
shrugged helplessly, and finished, "But I'm afraid I

can't point a finger at anyone in particular, Detective Kennelly."

His partner said, "Was Mr. Locke in the habit of coming up to Connecticut alone?"

Genuinely puzzled, I frowned. "He was no longer married to Betsy Bethune, his last wife," I responded. "But I suppose he might have come to the farm alone. Unless he brought a friend or colleague along, or invited special guests to join him for the weekend."

"I meant was he in the habit of coming up to the farm when the servants were off?" Detective Miles clarified.

"No, he wouldn't do that . . . well, I shouldn't say that. Actually, I don't really know what he was in the habit of doing anymore. We had been divorced for a number of years, and I saw him infrequently of late."

"However, you did see him a week ago, Mrs. Trent, and only a few days before his death," Detective Miles reminded me.

"That's true. We had lunch together, as you most obviously know. From his appointment book, I've no doubt."

Detective Miles nodded. "Yes, we did see your name in his book, along with the other appointments he had that day."

"We spent a couple of hours lunching at Le Refuge on Eighty-Second Street on the East Side, just a few blocks away from my apartment," I volunteered. I had nothing to hide.

Detective Kennelly's tone was brisk when he asked, "How *was* Mr. Locke? What kind of mood was he in that day? Did he seem despondent? Troubled in any way? Worried perhaps?" The detective raised a brow quizzically.

I shook my head. "None of those things. In fact, just the opposite. He was very Sebastian Locke, very much himself . . . calm, cool, collected. That's the way I always think of him—" I broke off. I felt the tears filling my throat. *Sebastian was dead.* It didn't seem possible. I still hadn't taken it in; I found it hard to conceive that he was no longer alive.

Taking a deep breath to steady myself, I cleared my throat, and went on slowly, "That's the way he always was. Very much in control of himself and the situation. And his demeanor was perfectly normal at lunch."

As the words came tumbling out of my mouth, I realized this wasn't the truth. Not quite. Last Monday Sebastian had not been himself at all. He had been ebullient, excited, and certainly not as low key as he usually was. That somber streak of his had not been even remotely in evidence. In fact, he had actually seemed *happy,* a most unnatural state of affairs for him. But I did not confide this to the two detectives. What was the point? I was absolutely certain Sebastian had dropped dead of a sudden heart attack. He was no more the kind of person to commit suicide than I was. Nor was he a candidate for murder, for that matter. He did have a few enemies, such as political factions, at least so I believed, but looking at it rationally, I seriously doubted that anyone would go so far as to kill him.

"Yes, Sebastian was absolutely *normal,* Detective Kennelly," I reiterated, and with a degree of firmness. "There was nothing at all untoward in his behavior, and he spoke very positively about his plans for the rest of the year."

"And what were those plans?" Kennelly asked.

"He was going back to Africa again, to oversee a particular distribution of aid to the poor and the sick, and then he was going on to India. To Calcutta, to be exact. He said he wanted to pay a visit to Mother Teresa. He'd always been a big supporter of her clinic, had given her significant financial contributions in the past. He told me he would be coming back to the States in December, because he intended to spend Christmas here in Connecticut."

"And you didn't see him again that week?" Detective Miles leaned forward, zeroing in on me as he asked the question.

"No, I didn't, Detective Miles."

"What about up here in Connecticut this weekend?" he asked.

"I had a deadline to meet, and I was locked up finishing my story, first in the city and then here. In this very room, in fact, and I hardly left it for the entire weekend."

"I see." Detective Miles inclined his head in a small show of courtesy, and slowly stood up. His partner Kennelly also rose.

I said, "When actually *did* Sebastian die?"

"Time of death hasn't been determined yet, but probably some time on Saturday evening," Miles answered me.

It was Kennelly who said, "Thank you for your time, Mrs. Trent."

"I haven't been much help, I'm afraid," I answered.

"At least you've established Mr. Locke's mood for us, his frame of mind, and corroborated what everyone else has said so far, mainly that he was acting like himself right up to the time of his death," Kennelly said.

"I'm sure he died of natural causes. Jack and Luciana agree with me."

"We know that, Mrs. Trent. We've talked to them at length," Detective Miles volunteered.

I was fully aware of this, but I made no further comment as I walked the two policemen to the door of the library. "When will you have the results of the autopsy?" I inquired quietly.

"Not for a while," Detective Kennelly replied, pausing on the threshold, turning to look at me. "Mr. Locke's body hasn't been moved from the farm yet. But later, probably tomorrow, it will go to the Chief Medical Examiner's Office in Farmington. The autopsy will be performed immediately, however, the final results are not necessarily quick to come in." He gave me a faint smile that seemed somehow apologetic.

"We'll be in touch, Mrs. Trent," Detective Miles added.

Sitting down at my antique French country desk, I picked up my fountain pen but merely stared blankly at the pages spread out in front of me. Earlier, I had attempted to edit the piece I had finished on Sunday night, but without much success. The news of Sebastian's death this morning and the arrival of the police ten minutes ago had broken my concentration. I was finding it virtually impossible to get back to work. Not surprising, I suppose, under these terrible circumstances.

My thoughts were entirely focused on Sebastian; I had thought of little else but him since Jack phoned me with the shocking news of his death.

Gazing blindly into the empty room, a myriad of thoughts jostling for prominence in my mind, I put the pen down and leaned back in my chair.

Sebastian had been a part of my life for as long as I could remember, and perhaps more than anyone he had been the greatest influence on me. Even though we had had our noisy quarrels, heated differences of opinion, and stormy, emotional episodes that left both of us very shaken and upset, we had always managed to patch things up, to stick together, to remain close, no matter what. Knowing him all my life though I had, it was after our divorce that we had come to understand each other; and it was only then that our relationship acquired a certain degree of peace and serenity.

Our marriage had been tempestuous at times and short-lived; through the passing of time I had come to realize why it had been so volatile, and brief. Put simply, the forty-two-year-old experienced man of the world had not known how to cope with the twenty-two-year-old child who was his new bride. Me.

An image of Sebastian on our wedding day flashed before me, and once again my throat closed with a sudden rush of emotion. Tears were incipient, pricked behind my lids; I blinked them away. On and off, for the last few hours, I had been shedding tears . . . tears for Sebastian, dead at fifty-six, and with so much more of life to live . . . tears for myself . . . tears for Jack and Luciana . . . tears for the world.

Difficult, haunted, and troubled man though he had been, he had nevertheless been a great man. A good man. No matter what he was in his personal life, his shoulders had been strong enough to carry so many of the world's burdens, and his heart had been filled with compassion for those who were suffering and in need.

A French journalist had once written about him that he was a beacon light in these darkly turbulent and troubled times we lived in. Certainly I deemed this to be the truth. The world would be a lesser place now that he was no longer in it.

Oh Sebastian, you were too young to die, I thought, and I put my head down and closed my eyes, reliving Jack's phone call of this morning. I had been checking the facts in my story when Belinda had told me that Jack Locke was on the line . . .

"Jack! Hello!" I exclaimed. "How are you? And more importantly, where are you?"

"Here. In Connecticut. At the farm, Vivienne."

"That's great. When did you get in from France?"

"Two days ago, but Vivienne, I—"

"Come on over for supper tonight! I've just finished this long piece for the London *Sunday Times* Magazine, and it'll do me good to cook, to relax with y—"

Cutting me off in a peremptory way, he said swiftly, "Vivienne, there's something I must tell you."

I detected an odd note in his voice, and it made the hackles rise on the back of my neck. Stiffening, I clutched the phone tighter in my hand. "What is it? What's wrong, Jack?"

"It's Sebastian . . . Vivienne . . . I'm not sure how to tell you this, how to break it gently, so I'm gonna come right out with it. He's dead. Sebastian's dead."

"Oh my God! No! It can't be! What happened? When did he die?" I demanded shrilly, and then I heard myself wailing, "It can't be true. He can't be dead. No, not Sebastian." My stomach lurched, and then as agitation fully took hold of me, my heart began to pound against my rib cage.

"It *is* true," Jack insisted. "I got a call this morning. Around nine-thirty. From Harry Blakely. The tree man. The aborist who looks after the trees at the farm. You know him, don't you?"

"Yes."

"Harry called me to tell me he'd found Sebastian's body out back. Near the lake. Harry had gone to the farm as he usually does Mondays. He was heading down to cut off the tops of some dead willows. He stumbled over the body. Sebastian was sprawled face down, near those rocks at the far end of the lake. He had a gash on his forehead. Harry said he looked as if he'd been outside all night. Maybe longer. Once he'd established that Sebastian was dead, Harry went up to the house to call the State Police in North Canaan. He told them about finding the body. They instructed him not to move it. Not to touch a single thing. Then he called me at the house in Manhattan. I grabbed Luciana, who's in from London. We took Sebastian's helicopter out here. Harry was also disturbed about the mess in Sebastian's library. The room was in total disarray. A lamp was overturned. A chair was on its side. Papers were strewn everywhere. And the French doors were ajar. The glass was broken in one of the panes. Harry thought it looked as if it could have been smashed on purpose. By an intruder."

"Are you saying that Sebastian may have been *killed?*"

"It's possible. Very possible," Jack said. "The circumstances are somewhat suspicious, wouldn't you say?"

"From what you're telling me, it does look strange, yes. On the other hand, Sebastian might have had some sort of attack, a stroke perhaps. He could have staggered around the room, then gone outside to get air . . . " My voice petered out. It was foolish to speculate. But a second later I did just that again.

"Do you think he fell and hit his head, Jack? Or are you suggesting he was chased out of the house, and then struck by someone? The intruder? If there was one."

"I don't know, Vivienne. I wonder if we'll ever know."

"Oh, Jack, this is just horrendous! I can't believe he's dead. I just can't." I found myself weeping once more.

"Don't cry. Please don't. It won't bring him back."

"I know it won't but I can't help it. I've loved him for as long as I can remember, since I was a child. And I still cared deeply for him, despite the divorce."

"I know," he muttered.

There was a silence between us.

"How's Luciana?" I asked at last, endeavoring to ignore Jack's coldness, this seeming lack of feeling I was detecting.

"She's fine. Holding up. She'll be okay."

"Would you like me to drive over to Cornwall? I can be there in half an hour, in three-quarters of an hour at the most."

"No, you don't have to come. But thanks for offering. Anyway, this place is crawling with police. That's another reason I called. To alert you. They'll be over to see you. Some time today. You're in Sebastian's appointment book. They asked me who you were. I told them you were his ex-wife. *One* of his ex-wives. You were with him very recently. I guess that's why they want to talk to you."

"I understand, Jack, but I really can't tell them anything. Sebastian was in the best of spirits. And health, as far as I could tell last Monday. Oh God, it's a week ago exactly that we lunched. I can't believe this, I just can't," I sobbed.

Fumbling for my handkerchief, I blew my nose and tried to get a grip on myself and my emotions.

"It's the shock," I mumbled into the phone after a second or two, "the unexpectedness of it. How can Sebastian be dead? He was larger than life, and he seemed so invulnerable. *Invincible.* To me, anyway. I thought nothing would ever happen to him, that he would live forever. Well, at least that he'd live to be an old man. Actually, I always thought of him as being immortal, if the truth be known."

"He was only too mortal," Jack said in a low, tense voice. "Listen, I gotta go. I can see two detectives heading this way. Walking up the back lawn. Looking as grim as hell," he snapped.

"Jack, please call me later!"

"Sure."

"*Please.*"

"Okay! Okay!"

He sounded more impatient than usual.

"And please tell Luciana how sorry I am. Perhaps I ought to speak with her now."

"She's out. Taking a walk. We'll all meet up later."

He was gone without another word, without even

saying good-bye. I sat there holding the phone in my hand, as if turned to stone, listening to the interminable dial tone. Finally, I replaced the receiver.

Ever since that call this morning, I have been numb from shock, full of grief, disbelieving. Now, suddenly, I felt drained. A vast emptiness settled within me. It was as if I were quite hollow, just a fragile shell.

I have never experienced such feelings before. No, that's not true. I have. When my mother died with this same kind of suddenness, this awful abruptness that always leaves others reeling and lost. And when my second husband Michael Trent suffered an unexpected heart attack, a fatal heart attack, I was devastated, floundering, cast adrift then just as I am today.

Life is hell; no, death is hell, I muttered to myself, and then wondered why it was those I loved had always been taken from me with such breathtaking unexpectedness.

Pushing myself up out of my chair, I left the library. In the corridor, I poked my head around the door of Belinda's cubbyhole of an office, told her I was going for a walk, and pulled an old wool cape out of the coat closet.

I stood on the back step and took several deep breaths. On this Monday afternoon at the beginning of October the weather was positively glorious, and mild, like spring. I glanced up. The arc of the sky was vivid blue and clear, and everything appeared to shimmer in the bright, golden sunlight. The trees had already started to turn, the leaves changing color from verdant green to yellow, russet, and scarlet; some were a deep, plummy purple, others a mellow gold tinged at the edges with the palest of pinks. It was fall, that special time of year when tourists from all over the world came to Connecticut to see the magnificent foliage, which was so breathtaking.

Moving quickly along the stone-flagged path, I headed across the lawn toward a small gazebo that stood at the edge of a copse of trees. I loved this remote corner of the garden where everything was bosky, still and silent.

My grandmother had built this gazebo many, many years ago, long before I was born. It had been created for my mother when she was a child. She had grown up in this old colonial stone house which stood in the hills above New Preston, a picturesque little town in the northwestern highlands of Connecticut.

Climbing the three wooden steps, I went inside and sat down on the bench, pulling the cape around me, shivering slightly. Yet it wasn't cold today. The sun was a huge bright orb, and in this part of the world we were enjoying an extraordinary Indian Summer, the likes of which had not been seen around these parts for a long while. I had shivered a moment before only because I felt the presence of ghosts here in this rustic little structure, saw them all . . . all of them. I found myself falling backward in time to be with them.

Gran Rosalie, with her pretty pink complexion and snow-white hair piled high on top of her head, was sitting there so proudly, with such dignity, on the bench in front of the round table.

She was pouring tea from her old brown china pot

with the chip on the lid, which she would not throw away because she said it made the best tea. Gran was telling me stories about this lovely old house, Ridgehill, which had been in her family for generations. Built in 1799, it had been passed down from mother to daughter and had always been owned by a woman, never a man. That was the stipulation in the will of Henrietta Bailey, my great-great-great-great-grandmother. It was she who had built the house with her own money and who had been one of the most powerful matriarchs of the Baileys. My gran was a Bailey, descending directly from her; Bailey was even part of my name.

My grandmother had the most beautiful of voices, cultured, lilting, full of musicality. She was reminding me that one day the house would be mine. Carefully, she explained about Henrietta and her will, told me how my amazing ancestor had wanted the women of the Bailey family always to be protected. So the house must pass from mother to daughter, even if there were sons. If there were no daughters then the house passed to the wife of the eldest son. I loved to hear the history of my family. I cherished Gran's marvelous tales . . .

My mother was here now . . . all golden-light and brightness, a shimmering kind of woman with her abundance of red-gold hair, perfect, milky skin, and startling green eyes. His emerald eyes, my father called them.

Now he was with us too . . . the Irishman. Black Irish, Liam Delaney was, my gran told me that. Black Irish and something of a charmer, a twinkling rogue of a man, a man whom women fell for at the drop of a hat, at least so my gran said to me time and again when I was growing up.

He was tall and dark, with rosy cheeks, sparkling brown eyes, and a brogue as rich as thick clotted cream. The Black Irishman, the twinkling rogue, had been a writer. I suppose I have inherited his penchant for words, his flair for stringing them together so that they make some sort of sense. His had been a powerful gift; I'm not so sure that mine is of quite the same magnitude. Gran always said that if it wasn't, then it was only because I hadn't kissed the Blarney Stone in County Cork, as my father had claimed to have done. Gran used to say it was surely the truth, for no one else she knew had such wondrous powers of persuasion as he.

He left us, though, my father did, one day many summers ago, telling us he would be back within three months. But he never did return, and I have no idea to this day whether he is dead or alive. I was ten years old when he went off on that journalistic forage for new material, traveling into the far, far blue horizons of the world. Twenty-six years ago. Perhaps he *was* dead by now.

My mother had been sad at first; she had cheered up only when his letters began to arrive at regular intervals. She read parts of them to me as they came in one by one; but only small portions, skipping the intimate bits, I suspect. I've been brought up to believe that my father was quite a man with the fancy words, especially when it came to wooing women.

First he was in Australia, then he went to New Zealand, and finally he left the Antipodes and traveled to Tahiti. Fiji was another port of call as he wandered around the Pacific, God knows in search of what. Other women? More exotic women? Not long after

my mother received a letter from him postmarked
Tonga communications had abruptly ceased. We never
heard from him again.

When I was small I used to think that my mother
was suffering from a broken heart, that she was endlessly yearning for my father. I had not known then
that eighteen months after Liam Delaney had set sail
for those exotic isles of Micronesia, she was already
falling in love with Sebastian Locke.

Now, leaning forward on the bench, I squinted
slightly, narrowing my eyes, peering out into the sunlit garden . . .

In my mind's eye I saw him quite clearly, walking
across the lawn toward me, just the way he had done
all those years ago.

Sebastian Locke, heading in my direction, long-
limbed, slender, the embodiment of nonchalant grace,
walking toward *me*.

That summer's afternoon, the first time I ever set
eyes on him, I thought he was the most beautiful man
I had ever seen. He was far more handsome than my
father, which was saying a lot indeed. Sebastian was
tall and dark-haired like my father, but whereas Liam's
eyes were velvet-brown and depthful, Sebastian's were
a clear, vivid blue, the brightest of blues. Like bits of
sky, I recall thinking that day, and they had a piercing
quality to them. It was as if they could see right
through you, as if they could see into your mind and
heart. I really believed he knew exactly what I was
thinking; even last Monday I had thought the same
thing over lunch.

Sebastian was wearing white gabardine pants and a
pale blue shirt on that stifling July day in 1970. The

shirt was made of voile, almost flimsy in weight. I've liked voile shirts on men ever since. The shirt was open at the neck, with the sleeves rolled up, and his face and arms were tan. His body was tanned as well. I could see it through the voile. He was a lithe man, very fit, athletic.

He had leaned against the posts of the gazebo and smiled at me. His teeth were very white and even in his sun-bronzed face, his mouth sensitive, and the vivid eyes were set wide apart in that arresting face.

Those eyes regarded me unblinkingly, and with great interest for a few seconds. It was when he said, "Hello, young lady, you must be the famous Vivienne," that I had felt myself becoming hot around my face and neck. Then he had stretched out his hand toward me. As I had taken it he had nodded slightly, as though acknowledging me yet again. He held onto my hand much longer than I expected, and as I looked up into that open, clean-cut face, my own very serious in its expression, my heart had skipped several beats.

And of course I had fallen hopelessly in love with him. I was all of twelve years old at the time, but I felt much older on that particular day. Very grown up. After all, it was the first time a man had actually made me blush.

Sebastian was thirty-two but looked much younger, extremely boyish and carefree. Vaguely, I somehow knew that he was the kind of man women automatically gravitate to; somehow I understood that he had charisma, sex appeal, that *je ne sais quoi* the French forever talk about.

In any case I was all agog over him. I never did get

him to admit it to me, but I was certain he felt something special for me that day.

On the other hand, he might have liked me simply because I was the daughter of my mother, the beauteous Antoinette Delaney, with whom he was having a grand love affair at the time.

That afternoon, when he had sauntered up the steps of the gazebo and seated himself next to me, I had known he was going to play a huge part in my life, in my future. Don't ask me how the young girl that I was then sensed this. She just did.

We had talked about horses, which he knew scared me to death. He had asked me if I would like to come to Laurel Creek Farm in Cornwall to learn to ride.

"I have a son, Jack, who's six, and a daughter, Luciana, who's four. They're already astride their ponies and doing well. Say you'll come and ride with us, Vivienne, say you'll come and stay at the horse farm. Your mother's a fine equestrienne, as you well know. She wants you to ride as proficiently as she does. You mustn't be afraid of horses. I will teach you how to ride myself. You'll be safe with me." He was correct in that, I did feel safe with him, and he did teach me to ride well, showing much more patience and understanding than my mother. And I loved him all the more for that.

A long time later, many years later, I realized he had been trying to make us into a family, that he had wanted my mother for himself. For always. But how could she have been his forever? She was married to Liam Delaney, and *he* had gone missing far across the ocean. Until she got a divorce she could never remarry. Not Sebastian. Not anyone.

Still, Sebastian *had* tried to blend us into a tight-knit little circle, and in certain ways he succeeded.

That afternoon, staring up at him, I had only been able to nod mutely as he talked about horses, tried to reassure me about learning to ride. I was rendered speechless by this man, totally mesmerized by him.

I was under his spell.

And I was forever after, for that matter.

It was Belinda who broke into my memories and my golden dreams, who scattered my beloved ghosts to the far corners of Gran Rosalie's garden.

"Vivienne, Vivienne!" she called as she hurried down the path, waving frantically. "It's the *New York Times*. They're on the phone."

I leaped to my feet on hearing this and raced toward her. We met in the middle of the lawn. "The *New York Times*?" I repeated, searching her face, my heart sinking.

"Yes, they've gotten wind of it . . . wind of Sebastian's death. They seem to know that the police were called in, that the circumstances are suspicious. Etcetera, etcetera. Anyway, the reporter wants to have a word with you."

The mere thought of tomorrow's headlines around the world sent a chill surging through me. And of course there *would* be headlines. A famous man had died, a man of conscience and compassion . . . the world's greatest philanthropist. And he might have been murdered. I shrivelled inside at the mere thought of those headlines. The press would turn his life upside down and inside out. No one, nothing, would be sacrosanct.

"The reporter wants to talk to you, Vivienne," Belinda said more urgently, taking hold of my arm. "He's waiting."

"Oh God," I groaned. "Why me?"

CHAPTER TWO

"**W**hy me?" I repeated later that evening, staring up at Jack. "Why did you elect me to be the spokesperson for this family?"

He had just arrived for supper a few minutes ago, and we were in my small den at the rear of the house, a room he preferred: It was intimate, warm, with its red brocaded walls and old Persian carpet. He hovered in front of me, his back to the fire, his hands in his pockets.

Returning my stare, seemingly at a loss, he did not answer. Then shaking his head in a thoughtful way, he started to speak, stopped, frowned, and pursed his lips.

"Well, Vivienne," he said at last, "I'm not sure why." He shook his head again. "*Liar,*" he said emphatically. "I'm a liar. And a coward. That's why I sicked the *Times* on you. I didn't want to talk to them myself."

"But you're the head of the family now. I'm not," I protested.

"And you're a journalist. A *respected* journalist. You know better how to deal with the dreaded press than I do."

"Luciana could have spoken to them. She's Sebastian's daughter."

"You're his ex-wife," he shot back.

"Oh, Jack, *please*."

"Okay, okay. Look, she's been out of it all day, ever since we got here. She can barely speak to *me,* never mind the *New York Times*. You know how fragile she is. The least little thing upsets her."

"It always has. I never even expected her for supper tonight, even though she accepted. I knew she wouldn't come," I retorted. When we were children growing up together, Luciana had usually been the one to hang back, to drop out, to claim tiredness, even sickness, when she didn't wish to do something, or if she was faced with a difficult situation. But fragile she wasn't. I knew that for a fact. She was strong. And tough. Not that Luciana ever let anyone know this. Dissembling came to her readily and with great ease; she was a facile liar, an expert spinner of tall tales. Her father once told me she was the cleverest liar he had ever known.

"How about a drink?" Jack said, cutting into my thoughts about his half sister.

"Of course!" I exclaimed, jumping up. "How rude of me. What would you like? Your usual scotch? Or a glass of wine?"

"Scotch, please, Viv."

I went to the antique Georgian table near the door, which held a few bottles of liquor and a bucket of ice. I fixed his scotch, a vodka on the rocks for myself, and carried them back to the fireplace. Handing him his glass, I sat down.

He muttered his thanks, took a great gulp of the amber-colored alcohol, and stood nursing it in both hands, ruminating.

"It's been a terrible day," I said. "The worst day in a long time. I still can't quite accept the fact that Sebastian's dead. I keep expecting him to walk in any minute."

Jack made no comment, merely sipped his drink and rocked back and forth on his heels.

I regarded him over the rim of my glass, thinking how unsympathetic and without emotion he was. I experienced a little spurt of anger. Jack could be so cold, cold as an iceberg. At this moment I hated him, as I had sometimes hated him as a child. His father had been found dead this morning, and in the most peculiar circumstances. Yet he was behaving as if nothing had happened. And he certainly wasn't showing any signs of grief. It struck me as being most unnatural, even though father and son had never really been close. I had been distressed for the entire day, fighting tears, engulfed by sadness. I mourned Sebastian, and I would go on mourning him for a long time.

Suddenly, without preamble, Jack said, "They took the body."

Startled by this announcement, I gaped at him. "You mean the police took the body away?"

"Yep," he answered laconically.

"To Farmington? For the autopsy?"

"You got it."

"I really can't stand you when you're like this!" I

exclaimed, and I was surprised at the harshness of my voice.

"Like what, sugar?"

"For God's sake, come off it, you know what I mean. So cold and hard and detached. Half of it's pretense anyway. You can't fool me. I've known you for the best part of your life and mine."

He shrugged indifferently, drained his glass, went and poured himself another drink. Walking back to the fireside, he continued, "That detective, Kennelly, told me we'll get the body back tomorrow."

"So quickly?"

He nodded. "Apparently the Chief Medical Examiner will do the autopsy first thing tomorrow morning. He'll take out tissue and organs, plus blood and urine samples, and—"

Shuddering, I shouted, "Stop it! You're talking about Sebastian! *Your father.* Don't you have any respect for him? Any respect for the dead?"

He gave me an odd look but made no comment.

I said, "If *you* have no feelings for him, so be it. But just remember this, *I do.* I will not permit you to speak of him in such a heartless, cold-blooded way."

Ignoring my remarks, Jack said, "We can have the funeral later this week."

"In Cornwall," I murmured, trying to adopt a softer tone. "He once told me he wanted to be buried in Cornwall."

"What about a memorial service, Viv? Should we have one? If so, where? More importantly, when?" He grimaced. "As soon as possible. I have to get back to France."

Though he was infuriating me again, I held myself

still. Exercising great control, I responded calmly, "In New York. I think that would be the best place, certainly the most appropriate."

"Where?"

"At the Church of St. John the Divine," I suggested. "What do you think?"

"Whatever you say." Jack flopped down in the chair near the fireplace and regarded me for the longest moment, a speculative look entering his eyes.

"Oh, no," I said, catching on at once. "Oh no, no, Jack! You're not going to talk me into arranging the funeral and the memorial. That's for you to do. You and Luciana."

"You'll help, though. Won't you?"

I nodded. "But you're not going to shrug off your responsibilities, as you have so many times in the past," I warned. "I won't allow you to do that. *You* are the head of the Locke family, now that Sebastian's dead, and the sooner you understand this the better. There's the Locke Foundation to run, for one thing, and you'll have to pick up the torch he dropped when he died."

"What do you mean?" he asked quickly, sharply, his eyes instantly riveted on mine. "What torch?"

"The charity work, Jack. You'll have to carry on where he left off. You'll have to tend to the sick and the poor of the world, those who are suffering, just as he did. Thousands are depending on you."

"Oh, no! No *way*, sugar. If you think *I'm* going to hand out money like a drunken sailor, then you're crazy. As crazy and as foolish as he was."

"This family's got so much money it doesn't know what to do with it!" I cried, furious with him.

"I'm not going to follow in Sebastian's footsteps, trailing halfway round the world and back, dispensing largesse to the great unwashed. So forget it, Viv, and don't bring it up again."

"You'll have to run the Locke Foundation," I reminded him. "As the only son and heir that's not only your inheritance but your responsibility."

"Okay, okay, so I'll run it. Long distance. From France. But I ain't no savior, out to cure the world of its ills. And illnesses. Just remember that. My father was a madman."

"Sebastian did a great deal of good, and don't *you* ever forget *that*."

Slowly, he shook his head. "It's odd. It really is."

"What is?"

"The way you adore him still after all these years. And after all the things he did to you."

"I don't know what you mean by that. He treated me very well. Always."

"Better than the other wives I've got to admit. He liked you."

"Liked me! He *loved* me. Sebastian loved me from the very first day we met, when I was twelve—"

"Dirty old man."

"Shut up! Furthermore, he continued to love me after we split up."

"He never loved anyone," Jack announced swiftly, scathingly, giving me a pitying look. "Not me. Not my mother. Not Luciana. Not her mother. Not your mother. Not his other two wives. Not even you, sugar."

"Stop calling me sugar. It's disgusting. And he *did* love me."

"I told you, he wasn't capable of loving. He couldn't love anyone if his life depended on it. It wasn't in him. Sebastian Locke was a monster."

"He was not! And I know he loved me, do you understand that? I know he did," I answered heatedly, swallowing my anger, clinging to my composure.

"If you say so," he muttered, giving in to me, which he frequently did. Averting his head, he stared into the fire, a morose look settling on his face.

As I sat watching him, thinking how sad it was he was so wrong about his father, thinking how little Jack had known about him, it occurred to me that he bore a strong resemblance to Sebastian tonight. Their profiles were the same; Jack had inherited his father's strong jawline and aquiline nose, as well as his fine head of dark hair. But his eyes were a faded, watery blue, not the bright cornflower hue his father's had been. As for their characters and personalities, they were as dissimilar as any two men could be.

The moroseness stayed with Jack throughout supper. He ate sparingly, drank a lot, and said little.

At one moment I reached out and touched his hand, and remarked softly, in my most conciliatory voice, "I'm sorry I shrieked at you."

He did not answer.

"Honestly, I am. Don't be like this, Jack."

"Like what?"

"Mute. Unresponsive. And infuriatingly mule headed."

He stared at me, then he smiled.

When Jack smiled his face lit up, and he was engaging, almost irresistible to me. That was the way it had always been. I smiled back, my affection for him once more intact. "It's just that I can't bear it when you're nasty about Sebastian."

"We see him differently, you and I," he mumbled, swigging more of my best red wine, the Mouton Rothschild which Sebastian had sent me last year.

He continued, "You've always been . . . agog about him . . . so . . . so adoring and worshipful. Look, I don't wear the same kind of rose-colored glasses, Viv."

"You adored him too, when you were little."

"That's what *you* think. But it's not true."

"Oh Jack, don't lie to me. This is Vivienne you're talking to . . . good old Viv, your best friend."

He threw back his head and laughed. "Jesus, don't you ever let up? When it comes to persistence, you're like a dog with a bone."

"Only when we're discussing Sebastian Locke," I countered.

"Well, one thing is certain, your loyalty is commendable, sugar."

"Thanks. And stop calling me sugar in that awful tone of voice. You know I hate it. You do it just to get my goat."

He grinned, reached out and squeezed my hand. "Truce?"

"Truce," I agreed and as quickly as I had when we were children.

We spoke about other matters for a short while after this. About France, Provence to be exact, and our respective homes there, houses which Sebastian had given us at different times. Although I did not dare remind him of this. It was obvious to me that he was as unrelenting about his father in death as he had been during his lifetime. Jack had never given Sebastian the benefit of the doubt, nor apparently did he intend to do so now. When it was too late, anyway.

It was when we returned to the den to have coffee that Jack suddenly started to talk about the circumstances of Sebastian's death once again.

Settled in an arm chair, with his coffee and cognac on a small side table next to him, he said, "The police had me check through his things. In the library. The rest of the house. No valuables were taken. As far as I could tell."

"Does that mean they've now ruled out the possibility of an intruder?"

"They didn't say."

"It's perplexing." I sat back in my chair, my mind turning over the few facts we had. "When I lunched with Sebastian he mentioned that Mrs. Crane was away on vacation . . . " I stopped and looked at him.

"What are you getting at, Viv?"

"I guess I think it's a bit odd that Sebastian came up to the farm when there was no one there to look after him. When she was away. Even the police think that, Jack."

"He told me on Thursday that he had some work to finish. He gave me the impression he was looking forward to being alone up here, from his tone and his attitude."

"Maybe he wasn't alone, though."

Jack threw me a swift look and his brows puckered. "That's a possibility. Somebody could have been with him. Yes, of course they could."

"And that somebody might have ended up doing him bodily harm," I pointed out.

"Only too true."

"By the way, why did you and Luciana suddenly come to the States? Was there a special reason for this visit?"

"We didn't come to kill Sebastian," he said, and gave me a smirk that was oddly ghoulish.

"For God's sake, I wasn't implying any such thing. And do stop it. You know your facetious talk only infuriates me. Grow up, act your age, Jack. This is very serious . . . a serious situation."

"Sorry, Viv. Luciana and I came in for the annual meeting of Locke Industries," Jack explained in a quiet, more subdued tone, sounding suddenly and effectively chastised at last. "It was supposed to be held tomorrow. Naturally, it's been canceled."

"I should hope so! Anyway, I must go back to my original reaction of earlier today, when you first told me Sebastian was dead. I was certain he'd had a heart attack, or possibly a stroke. And to tell you the truth, I still believe, deep down, that that's what happened."

When Jack made no response, I gave him a penetrating look, asked, "Well, don't you?"

He brought his hand up to his face, rubbed his mouth and his chin, suddenly reflective. "I don't know," he answered. "This afternoon I would have agreed with you, but now I'm vacillating. Not sure of anything."

"Do you honestly think he was attacked? By an intruder?" I pressed.

"Maybe. He could have gone into the farmhouse and surprised a burglar."

"Before the burglar had an opportunity to steal anything? Is that what you think? After all, you said there's nothing missing."

"Well, the paintings and the major art objects are in place. On the other hand, Sebastian could have had something else there worth stealing, something to tempt a thief."

"Such as what?" I frowned, shaking my head. "I don't get it, Jack."

"Cash, Vivienne. You know Sebastian always carried a lot on him. I was often warning him about that. Or maybe there were some documents around."

"Documents," I said sharply, staring at him. "But if someone stole documents that smacks of premeditation, doesn't it? Listen, a thief breaking in at random, looking for loot, is one thing. A thief breaking in and stealing documents is a different thing altogether. It suggests prior knowledge to me."

Jack nodded. "You're right there."

"What made you think of documents? Are there any missing? And what kind of documents did you have in mind?"

"I don't know, and to be honest, I don't know why I thought of them. Except that Sebastian said he was going to the farm to work. Whatever else he was, he wasn't a liar. If he said he had to go over papers, then he was telling the truth. But there weren't any, at least none that he'd been working on—"

"What about all those scattered around the library?" I cut in.

"The letters on the floor and spread over the desk were just the usual things. Correspondence, bills, personal notes from people. The way he spoke on Thursday he sounded as if he had real work to do on important documents. Come to think of it, he did actually say *documents*. I guess that's why I just thought of them now." He lifted his shoulders in a shrug. "Look, I haven't been at Laurel Creek Farm in a coon's age, Viv, so how would I know if there's anything missing? Mrs. Crane's the best person to ascertain that, but then only as far as the art is concerned. Not even she would know if any papers have disappeared."

"No, she wouldn't." I let out a long sigh. "It looks as if we're back to square one."

"Yep . . . " Jack shook his head, his puzzlement surfacing again. Then he said suddenly, in a torrent of words, "Look, Viv, I disagree with you. I don't think he died of natural causes, as you do. I think he was killed. Most probably by an intruder. Sebastian surprised him. The intruder ran out. Sebastian chased him. They struggled. And Sebastian got himself killed. Sort of inadvertently."

"Or he was murdered by someone who was with him at the farm, for reasons we don't know," I remarked.

Jack pondered for a moment. Then slowly, and more thoughtfully than usual, he said, "We're speculating. We'd better stop. It'll lead nowhere." Pinning me with his eyes, he added, "Let's admit it, Vivienne, we won't know exactly how he died until the police get that autopsy report from the Chief Medical Officer in Farmington."

I could only nod. I agreed with him, at least as far as his last comment was concerned.

CHAPTER THREE

Long after Jack had left, I prowled around the house, stacking the dishwasher, clearing up, making the den and the dining room neat and tidy.

At one moment I even had another stab at my story, hoping to do the final edit, but I was not very successful. I would try again tomorrow, and if my concentration still eluded me I would have to let it go out as it was. The piece had to be at the newspaper in London by Friday at the latest, and I would have to FedEx it on Wednesday, no matter what.

The hall clock was striking midnight by the time I climbed the stairs of Ridgehill and went to my room, feeling weary and worn down.

I, like all of my female forebears, occupied the master bedroom that stretched almost the entire length of the house. Situated at the back, rather than the front, it was a charming room with rafters, many windows, and an imposing stone fireplace. French doors on either side of the fireplace opened out onto a wide balcony suspended over the garden. This was the most marvelous spot in the world for breakfast on spring and summer mornings, especially when the lilacs were in bloom.

Ridgehill stood at the top of Tinker Hill Road. Set amidst a copse of centuries-old maples, it looked out over Lake Waramaug. When my illustrious ancestor Henrietta Bailey had built this house she had thought things out most prudently, had chosen well when situating the master bedroom within the overall architectural plan. The views were spectacular from the many windows, were panoramic in their vistas.

I went and stood at one of the windows, moving the curtain slightly, staring out across the tops of the trees toward the large body of water far below. The lake was as flat and as unmoving as black glass, and above it the sky was littered with tiny bright stars. There was a harvest moon tonight, silvery and perfectly spherical, riding the black clouds. It cast a sheen across the murky waters of the lake, touched the tops of the trees with brilliance.

What a beautiful night, I thought, as I let the curtain drop and turned away. After undressing, I slipped into a nightgown and climbed into the grand old four-poster. Turning out the bedside lamp, I pulled the covers up over me and settled down for the night, hoping to fall asleep quickly. It had been such an exhausting day emotionally. A day of shock. A day of sorrow.

Moonlight filled the room. The silence was a balm. I lay there drifting with my thoughts; Sebastian was foremost in them. We had shared so much in this room. So much pleasure. So much heartbreak. I am convinced that I conceived my child in this room, his child, the child I lost in miscarriage. And, once again, I found myself wondering if Sebastian and I would have remained together if that child had been born. Perhaps.

Cradled in his arms, I had lain in this bed, weeping on his shoulder, and he had comforted me about the loss of our baby. How could Jack believe he was a monster? Nothing was further from the truth. Sebastian had always comforted and nurtured me. And everyone else, for that matter. Jack was so terribly wrong about him; his judgment about Sebastian was flawed, just as it was flawed about most things in his personal life. He had made a mess of it and he loved to blame others, especially his father. I loved Jack like a brother, but I saw him with clear eyes.

Sebastian had always been there for me, for as long as I could remember, since my childhood. I recall so well the afternoon he had come to me, after my mother had been found dead at the bottom of the cellar steps at his farm. I had just arrived from Manhattan; Jess, my mother's housekeeper, had phoned him the instant I had walked through the front door and he had rushed over to Ridgehill immediately, full of concern for me.

It had been such a warm June day, unnaturally hot for that time of year, and I had been sitting on the balcony of this room, distraught, sobbing, my heart breaking, when he had come looking for me.

Eighteen years ago.

I had been eighteen when my mother died. So long ago now. Half my life ago. Yet it might have been yesterday, so vividly did I recall it.

I found myself focusing on the past yet again, and I walked back into that June afternoon of 1976.

"Vivienne . . . darling . . . I'm here! I'm here for you," Sebastian said, coming through the bedroom and out onto the balcony like a whirlwind.

I lifted my head and blinked, staring at him, my eyes blinded by my tears and the bright sunlight streaming out behind him.

He was by my side in an instant, sitting down next to me on the long bench. Worriedly he looked into my face and his own was bleak, strained. A muscle pulsed in his temple, and his startlingly blue eyes were dulled by sadness.

Wiping away the tears on my cheeks with his fingertips, he enveloped me in his arms, held me close, soothed me as though soothing a wounded child.

"It's such a terrible tragedy," he murmured against my hair. "I cared for her too, Vivienne, so I know what you're suffering. I'm suffering myself." As he spoke his arms tightened around me.

I clutched him. "It's not fair," I sobbed. "She was so young. Only forty-two. I don't understand how it happened. *How did it happen?* How did my mother fall down the basement steps, Sebastian? Do you think she got dizzy and lost her balance? And why was she going into the basement, anyway?"

"I don't know. No one knows. It was an accident," he replied, then drew slightly away and looked down into my face. "You're aware she'd come to stay with me, whilst some of the rooms at Ridgehill were being painted, but I wasn't in Connecticut last night. I was in the city for a Locke Foundation dinner. I got up at the crack of dawn and drove out to the farm, wanting to have breakfast with her. And also hoping to go riding with her later. When I arrived, the whole place was in an uproar. Aldred had found her body earlier and had called the police. Then he'd spoken to Jess, told her to get in touch with you. By the time I got hold of her, you were already on your way to New Preston."

I nodded, and before I could say anything my grief overcame me once more, and fresh tears flowed. Sebastian continued to comfort me; he was so kind.

At last, I managed to say to him, "Jess believes my mother died instantly. Do you think she did? I couldn't bear it if I thought she'd suffered."

"I'm sure Jess is right. When someone tumbles down a steep flight of stairs I think it must go very fast . . . in a terrible rush. There's no question in my mind that she did die immediately. She couldn't have suffered, rest assured of that."

Conjuring up the image of my mother falling to meet her doom, I suddenly cried out in my anguish. He held me closer, calming me as best he could. "I know, I know," he said softly against my hair.

"You're going to miss her, Sebastian," I eventually muttered. "You loved her, too."

"Yes."

I buried my face against his chest and held onto him as if he were the only thing I had left in the world. In a way, he was; and he was my safe haven.

Sebastian stroked my hair, smoothed his hand down my arm, continuing to murmur gentle words. I pressed myself even closer, and I felt as though I were somehow drawing strength from him.

We sat together like this on the balcony for a long time, and eventually a kind of peacefulness drifted over me and my tears finally ceased altogether. But he made no move to get up, and neither did I; and so we continued to sit on the old bench.

At one moment I stiffened inside and held my breath, hardly daring to move. Something quite strange was happening to me. My heart was pumping rapidly; my throat had gone dry and was suddenly constricted.

The blood rushed up into my face; I understood exactly what was happening, understood myself only too well. I wanted him to stop kissing my hair and kiss me instead. I wanted his mouth on mine. I wanted his hand stroking my breast, not my arm. I wanted him to make love to me. Without knowing it, he was arousing me sexually, and I discovered I didn't want him to stop. When I realized how damp I was between my legs my face flamed. I was mortified.

I did not dare to stir in his arms. I did not dare to look at him. He could read my mind; he'd always known what I was thinking ever since I was a little girl.

And so I continued to sit there, waiting for these extraordinary feelings to subside, to go away. I was confused and embarrassed. How could I be experiencing such feelings, today of all days? My mother was lying dead in the morgue at Farmington, probably being autopsied by the Chief Medical Examiner at this very moment.

I shuddered inside. Sebastian had been her lover for more than six years. And now I wanted him for myself. I shuddered again, hating myself for my dreadful thoughts about him, hating my body, which was so betraying me at this moment.

Thankfully, at last, Sebastian's arms slackened and he let go of me. Tilting my face to his, he kissed me lightly on the forehead. He attempted a smile, looked as if he were about to speak, but remained silent.

Eventually, he said in a low, concerned voice, "I realize you must be feeling very much alone, but you do have me, Vivienne dear. And you mustn't worry about a thing. I will look after you. I know it's impossible for me to take your mother's place, but I am your friend, and I'm here for you whenever you need me."

"Ever since that day you found me in the gazebo, that first day we met, I've felt protected by you," I replied, and I meant every word.

Again he tried to smile, but without much success. After a brief moment, he said, "You must always come to me, whatever the problem. I won't let you down, I promise." A small sigh escaped him, and he said, almost to himself, "You were such a lovely child. You touched my heart."

And now he was dead, and no longer there to protect me, and my life would be that much poorer without him. I pushed my face into the pillow and it was a long time before I could stem the tears.

I must have eventually fallen asleep, for when I awakened with a start sunlight was streaming in through the many windows. Last night I had forgotten to draw the curtains and a new day had dawned. I could hear the chirping of the birds outside, and far away, in the distance, the *cawk cawk* of the Canada geese circling the lake.

I eyed the clock on the bedside table, saw that it was almost seven, and slid down into the bed, luxuriating for a few moments longer in the comfort and warmth. And then reality thrust itself into my consciousness, and with a rush of sudden intense pain I remembered the events of yesterday.

Sebastian was dead. I would never see him again.

I held myself still, breathing deeply, thinking about him, recalling so much about him, so many little things. We had been divorced for eight years, and I hadn't seen all that much of him in the last three. But before then he had been such an important and integral part of my life for over twenty-one years. *Twenty-one.* An auspicious number to me. I had been twenty-one years old when Sebastian had first made love to me.

His image was so very clear in my mind at this moment. I saw him exactly as he was that year, 1979. I was twenty-one. He was forty-one. Twenty years older than I, but he never seemed it, not ever.

Closing my eyes, I pictured him walking into the library downstairs. It was the night of my twenty-first birthday. Sebastian had thrown a fantastic party for me at Laurel Creek Farm, held in two flower-decked marquees in the garden. The food had been delicious, the wine superb, the band the best, imported for the occasion from Manhattan. It had been a glorious evening. Until Luciana had ruined it. She had been so nasty to me toward the end of the evening I had been taken by surprise, thrown off balance, and horrified by the mean and hateful things she had said to me. Stunned and hurt, I had fled. I had come home to Ridgehill . . .

* * *

Tires screeched, slowed to a stop on the gravel. A car door banged ferociously.

A split-second later Sebastian stormed into the library, his body taut, his face white.

Forlornly, I stood by the French windows leading out to the garden. My handkerchief was screwed into a damp ball in my hand; tears were still close to the surface.

I had never seen him looking so furious before, and as I stared at him I realized he was terribly upset.

He stared back at me, and his eyes were chips of blue ice in his drawn face. "Why did you run away like that? Like a frightened colt?" he demanded in a stern voice. Then he crossed the room in a few long strides and drew to a standstill in front of me, stood looking down at me.

I was silent.

"Why?" he demanded again.

"I can't tell you."

"You can tell *me* anything, and you know it! You've been confiding in me since you were a little girl," he said, his anger still apparent but under tight control.

"I just can't. Not about this."

"Why not?"

I continued to gape at him stupidly. Then I shook my head emphatically. "I can't."

"Come along," he exclaimed in a warmer, more cajoling tone. "We've always been such good friends, you and I. Real pals. Vivienne, please tell me what happened, what made you bolt."

When I said nothing, he went on swiftly, "It was Luciana, wasn't it? She upset you."

I nodded, but still I did not open my mouth.

"She hurt you . . . she said something . . . *contemptible*. Didn't she?"

"How do you know?"

"I know my daughter only too well," he snapped. "Tell me what she said."

"Sebastian, I can't. I'm not a snitch."

He scrutinized me a little more intently, and nodded to himself. "Integrity's bred in the bone, especially in your bones. Do you know, Vivienne, you're the most honorable person I've ever met, and whilst I understand your reluctance to tell tales out of school, I do think you ought to confide in me. After all, the party was very special . . . to us both. Certainly giving it for you meant a great deal to me, and I was startled when you ran off the way you did, looking so upset. In all fairness, I think you should tell me exactly what happened."

He was right, of course he was. Taking a deep breath, I plunged: "She said I was a problem to you. A nuisance. That you wanted to be rid of me. She said you resented me, resented having to look after me, having to pay my tuition at Wellesley. She said I was a charity case, a nobody, just the brat of one of your—" I stopped short, unable to continue, and swallowed hard.

"Go on," he commanded in a clipped, rather brusque tone.

"Luciana . . . She said I was just the brat of . . . of one of your whores," I whispered.

His mouth tightened in anger, and I waited for him to explode. But he did not. He merely shook his head, looking dismayed, and muttered in a tight voice, "She's a liar, my daughter. There are times, Vivienne, when I

believe she's the cleverest liar I've ever known. A better
liar than Cyrus, and that's saying something. But she's
very often foolhardy, stupid in the lies she tells. As she
has been tonight. Yes, Luciana is a little fool."

"I'm not a nuisance to you, am I?" I whispered.

"Of course not! Surely you must know that by now.
Haven't I proved to you that I care about you, care
about your well-being? And what about your party? I
wanted to give it for you, and I enjoyed doing so."

I nodded. I could not say a word. It wasn't that I
was tongue-tied. Rather, I was mortified and angry
with myself. I realized how ridiculous I must look to
him, how untrusting of him I must appear. He had
never let me down, and I knew him to be a scrupulous
man, a man of his word. Naturally he didn't resent me.
Nor did it matter to him what my school fees cost, or
my clothes and my upkeep. Money had never mattered to him. He had so much of it, he was almost
contemptuous of it. Or so it seemed to me. Certainly
he gave a great deal of it away. I had been an idiot, listening to Luciana. She had driven me away because
she was jealous of me and my relationship with her
father. All of a sudden I thought of her jealousy when
we were children. She had manipulated me tonight;
worst of all, I had allowed that manipulation.

He put his hand under my chin and lifted my face
to his. "Tears, Vivienne? Oh dear, what a sad ending to
such a beautiful evening."

"I'm sorry, Sebastian," I answered, sounding
choked. "I'm so very sorry."

Wiping my damp cheeks with his hand, he murmured, "Hush, darling, hush, there's nothing to be
sorry about."

"I shouldn't have listened to her."

"No, you shouldn't," he agreed. "And remember, don't pay attention to a thing she says in the future. Or anything Jack says, for that matter. He's not quite as bad as she is, and he's not a liar, but he can be devious."

"I won't listen to either of them," I promised. I took a step forward, looked up into those bright blue eyes which were so carefully regarding me. My own expression was intense. "Please say it's all right between us."

His sudden wide smile made his eyes crinkle at the corners. "Nothing will ever come between *us*, Vivienne. We're far too close, and we always have been. We're friends for life, you and I. There's a very special bond there. Well, there is, isn't there?"

I nodded. I couldn't speak. I was overwhelmed by him, by the potency of his looks, his sexuality; and I was engulfed by my own erupting emotions. I wanted him to belong to me, I wanted to belong to him in the truest sense. I tried to say something but no words would come.

Looking momentarily puzzled, he gave me a questioning glance, his eyes narrowing as he said, "You've got the most peculiar expression on your face. What are you thinking?"

I took another step nearer, leaned into him, and kissed him on the cheek. Finally finding my voice, I said, "I was thinking how wonderful you are, and how wonderful you've always been to me. And I want to thank you for my birthday party. My very special party."

"You're very welcome," he said.

Holding my head on one side, I gazed up into his face. "I'm twenty-one. I'm grown up."

"You are indeed," he said with a faintly amused smile.

"Sebastian?"

"Yes?"

"I'm a woman now."

There must have been something unusual in my expression, or perhaps it was the inflection in my voice. But whatever it was, he stared back at me in the oddest way and for the longest moment, that puzzled look more pronounced. Unexpectedly, he took a step toward me, then he stopped abruptly.

We exchanged a long look, one so deep, so knowing, so full of longing, I felt my breath catch in my throat. Before I could stop myself, and almost against my own volition, I began to move forward, drawing closer to him.

It seemed to me that he watched every step I took, and then without uttering a word, Sebastian reached out for me. He pulled me into his arms with such fierceness, I was startled. And he held me so tightly I could scarcely breathe.

And everything changed. I changed. Sebastian changed. Our lives changed irrevocably. The past was demolished. Only the present remained. The present and the future. Our future together. We were meant to be, he and I. At least, so I believed. It had always been so. Our course had long been set. Somehow I knew this. Moving his head slightly, Sebastian bent down and kissed me. When he moved his tongue lightly against my lips, I parted them quite naturally. Our tongues touched. My legs felt weak and I held onto him tighter than ever for support, as he continued to kiss me in this most intimate manner. Without warning, he stopped, held me away from him almost roughly and looked down into my face.

Again our eyes locked. I knew he wanted me as much as I wanted him. He had already told me so without uttering a word. And yet I detected hesitation in him.

I took hold of his hand and led him upstairs. Once inside the room, he let go of my hand and moved away from me, hovered in the center of the floor. I felt, rather than observed, his uncertainty. After a moment, he said in a strangled voice, "I came to take you back to your birthday party . . . " His voice trailed off.

"No! I don't want to go back. I want to be here. *To be with you.* That's all I've ever wanted, Sebastian."

"Vivienne . . . "

We moved at the same time.

We were in each other's arms, holding onto each other. Eventually we drew apart. He struggled out of his dinner jacket, threw it on a chair, undid his bow tie as he walked to the bedroom door. With one hand he locked it; with the other he began to remove the sapphire studs from his evening shirt, and his eyes never left my face as he walked back to me.

I opened my arms to him. He came into them swiftly, held me close to him. He undid my zipper and suddenly my evening dress was a pile of white lace at my feet. Drawing me toward the bed without a word, he pushed me down on it, lay next to me, took me in his arms once more. His mouth found mine. He caressed every part of me, his hands moving over me with such expertise I was soon fully aroused, spiralling into ecstasy. When he entered me a moment later, I gasped, cried out and he stopped, staring down at me. I assured him I was all right, urged him on, wrapping my arms around him. My hands were firm and strong on his broad back and I found his rhythm, moved with him, inflamed by his passion and my own urgent desire. And so we soared upward together, and as we reached the peak I cried out again, as did he.

We lay together silently. Sebastian's breathing was labored and his body was damp. I went to the bathroom, found a towel, came back and rubbed him dry. He half smiled at me, pulled me to him, wrapped his long legs around my body, and rested against me, still without speaking. But there was no awkwardness in our silence, only eloquence, ease.

I let my fingers slide into his thick black hair; I ran my hands over his shoulders and his back. I kissed him as I wanted to kiss him. It was not long before we made love again and we did so without constraint.

Satiated and a little sore, we eventually lay still. After a while, Sebastian raised himself on one elbow, looked down at me. Moving a strand of hair, he said quietly, "If I'd known you were a virgin, I wouldn't—"

I pressed my fingers against his lips. "Don't say it."

He shook his head. "It never occurred to me, Vivi, not in this day and age . . . " His sentence trickled away and he shook his head, a little helplessly, I thought.

I said, "I was saving myself."

A dark brow lifted above those piercing blue eyes.

"For you," I explained with a smug smile. "I saved myself for you, Sebastian. I've wanted you to make love to me for as long as I can remember."

"Oh Vivi, and I never even guessed."

I reached out, touched his face. "I love you, Sebastian Locke. I've always loved you. And I always will . . . all the days of my life."

He bent down and kissed me softly on the lips, and then he put his arms around me, holding me close to him, keeping me safe.

The phone was screaming in my ear.

I roused myself from my half-dozing state and my memories instantly retreated. Reaching out, I lifted the receiver and mumbled, "Hello?"

"It's me," Jack said. "I'm coming over. With the newspapers."

"Oh God, don't tell me," I groaned. "Lousy head-lines, I've no doubt. And obituaries."

"You got it, kid."

"You're going to be besieged by the press," I muttered. "Perhaps you *are* better off coming here. Maybe you should bring Luciana with you, Jack."

"She ain't here, Viv. She's skipped it, gone back to Manhattan."

"I see," I said and sat bolt upright. "Well, that's not surprising." Sliding my legs out of bed, I continued, "I'll put coffee on. See you in about half an hour."

"Make that twenty minutes," he answered brusquely and hung up.

Chapter Four

It was quite obvious that Jack was in one of his peculiar moods. His face proclaimed it to me before he had walked even halfway across the kitchen.

"Good morning," I said, carrying the coffeepot over to the table and putting it down. When I received merely a curious, gruntlike mumble from him, I added sharply, "So, we're maungy this morning, are we?"

The use of this word caught his attention at once, and he glanced at me rapidly. "*Maungy*. What does that mean?"

"You've heard it before so don't pretend you haven't. It was a favorite of Gran's. She often used to call you maungy when you were a snot-nosed little boy in short pants."

Ignoring my acerbity, he said evenly, "I don't remember," and flopped into the nearest chair. "And I don't know its meaning."

"Then I'll tell you," I answered, leaning over the table, peering into his face. "It means peevish, bad tempered, or sulky, and it's a Yorkshire word from the West Riding where my great-grandfather came from." I paused, said in a lighter voice, "Surely you haven't forgotten Gran's marvelous stories about her father? She never failed to make us laugh."

"George Spence. That was his name," Jack said, and then grimaced. "I need a life-saving transfusion. Strong coffee. Immediately, sugar." He reached for the pot, poured cups of coffee for both of us, and took a gulp of his.

"Jack, don't start the day by calling me sugar. Please. And so that's *it*, is it? You have a hangover."

"A beaut. Hung one on. Last night. When I got back to the farm."

His occasional bouts of drinking were nothing new and had worried me off and on, but I had stopped trying to reform him, nor did I chastise him anymore, since it was a futile waste of time. And so I refrained from commenting now. I simply sat down opposite him, eyeing the newspapers as I did. "How bad are *they*?"

"Not as bad as we expected. Quite laudatory, in fact. Not much muckraking. You're mentioned. As one of his five wives. Front page stories. Obituaries inside."

I pulled the newspapers toward me. Jack had brought the *New York Post*, the *New York Times*, and the *Daily News*, and as I spread them out in front of me I saw that they were more or less saying the same thing in their different ways. A great and good man had been found dead, circumstances suspicious. All three papers decried his death, sang his praises, mourned his passing. They carried photographs of Sebastian and they were all fairly recent ones, taken in the last couple of years. He looked wonderful—distinguished, handsome and loaded with glamour, dangerously so. But that had ceased to matter.

Skipping the *Post* and the *News* for the moment, I concentrated on the *Times*. The front page story by the reporter who had spoken to me on the phone yesterday was well written, careful in its details, cautious in its tone, and scrupulous in its accuracy. Furthermore, I was quoted verbatim and without one word I'd said being altered or paraphrased. So much for that. And certainly there was nothing sensationalized here.

I turned to the obituary section of the *New York Times*. A whole page was devoted to Sebastian Lyon Locke, scion of a great American dynasty, billionaire tycoon, head of Locke Industries, chairman of the Locke Foundation, and the world's greatest philanthropist. There was a simplified version of his life story; every one of his good deeds was listed along with the charities he supported in America, and there was a fund of information about the charity work he did abroad, especially in Third World countries. It had obviously been written some years earlier, as most obituaries of famous people were, with the introduction and the last paragraph left open, to be added after the death of the particular individual had occurred.

Glancing at the end of the story, I was surprised to see only four names. I was mentioned as his former ward and his ex-wife—as if the others had not existed—along with Jack and Luciana, his children, and Cyrus Lyon Locke, his father, whom I'd completely forgotten about until now.

"Oh my God! Cyrus!" I cried, lowering the paper, looking over the top of it at Jack. "Have you been in touch with your grandfather?"

"That old coot! He's more dead than alive. Rotting in Bar Harbor. In that mausoleum of a place. It ought—"

"But have you *talked* to him?" I cut in. "Does he *know* about Sebastian's death?"

"I spoke to Madeleine. Yesterday. Told her everything. The old coot was sleeping."

"Did you tell her to bring him here for the funeral?"

"Certainly not. He's too old."

"How old is he?" I asked, frowning. Cyrus's age escaped me for the moment, but he had to be in his eighties.

"He was born in 1904. So he must be ninety. And he's too old to travel."

"I don't know about that . . . look, he should come, Jack. After all, Sebastian was his only son."

"His last surviving son," Jack corrected me.

"So what did Madeleine say?"

"Not much. As usual. Gave me her condolences. Talked about Cyrus being frail. But not senile. I can't stand her. She's the voice of doom. Even when she's wishing you well."

"I know, impending disaster does seem to echo in her voice. And I'm sure what she said about Cyrus is true, that he's not senile. Cyrus Locke has always been a remarkable man. Quite remarkable. A genius, really."

The phone rang, interrupting our conversation. I went to answer it.

Picking up the receiver, I said, "Hello?" and then glanced over at Jack. Covering the mouthpiece with my hand, I murmured, "Talk of the devil. It's for you, Jack."

"Who is it?"

"The voice of doom with an Irish accent."

"Hello, Madeleine," Jack said into the phone a split-second later. "We were just talking about you. And Cyrus. Vivienne wants to invite you to the funeral, Madeleine."

I glared at him, silently mouthing, "It's not my funeral."

Ignoring me, he listened to Madeleine for a few minutes, said good-bye, and hung up. He lolled against the door jamb with a thoughtful expression on his face. "I left this number at the farm. With Carrie. Mrs. Crane's niece. She came in to help. Until her aunt gets back. Tonight."

"Thanks a lot," I said, and sighed, threw him a reproving glance. "Tell me, Jack, why is it you have the need to put the burdens of this family on me most of the time? This is not my funeral. It's your responsibility. Yours and Luciana's."

"Forget Luce. All she wants to do is run. Back to London. To that twerp of a British husband of hers."

"Isn't he coming for the funeral?"

"Who?"

"The husband. Gerald Kamper."

"Who knows. But *he* wants to come. The old coot. Grandfather." Jack made a face. "To the funeral of a son who loathed him. Can you beat that?"

"I knew he'd wish to be present."

"Merde," Jack muttered half to himself.

"It'll be all right, we'll manage well enough," I reassured him. "And it *is* only natural he wants to attend his son's burial."

"*Only natural!* Don't be so *stupid!* There's nothing

natural about Cyrus Locke. Just as there wasn't anything natural about Sebastian. He had no feelings. Neither does Cyrus. Faulty genes, I suspect. And the old coot's a monster like his son was. Better he remain in Bar Harbor. With his secretary-housekeeper-mistress-jailer. Or whatever the hell she is. I—" Jack stopped and grinned in that awful, ghoulish way of his, and added, "We won't be able to keep him away. Cyrus wants to be sure."

"Sure of what?"

"That Sebastian's really dead. That he's three feet under. Kicking up daisies."

"Oh, Jack."

"Don't *oh Jack* me in that pathetic way. Not this morning. You did it yesterday. All day. No tears either. I've had enough. You're just a sentimentalist, kid."

"And you're the most unpleasant person it's ever been my great misfortune to know. You disgust me, Jack Locke. Sebastian's dead and you act as if it's of no consequence, as if you don't care."

"I don't."

"Talk about Cyrus being unnatural. *You* certainly are."

"Chip off the old block, eh?" He laughed hollowly.

"You make me sick. Sebastian was a wonderful father to you."

"Go and tell that to the Marines! You should know better. He was never a father to me. Never cared about me."

"He did."

"I've told you before. I'm repeating myself. *He couldn't love anyone.*"

"He loved me," I announced and sat back, glaring at him.

Jack laughed harshly, and there was a disdainful expression on his face when he exclaimed, "Here we go again! He was crazy to get you into the sack. That I'll readily concede. He had the hots for you. Even when you were just a kid. He couldn't wait to get into your panties."

"That's not true."

"Sure it is. We used to call it the Gradual Seduction of Vivienne. You know, like the title of a play."

"Who?"

"Luciana and I."

"What do you mean? Why?"

"Because for years *we* watched *him* watching *you*. Fascinating. The fat cat waiting to pounce. On the little mouse. Waiting for you to get a bit older. Smarming all over you. Catering to you. Flattering you. Showering you with gifts. Softening you up. Getting you ready for him. He couldn't wait to seduce you, Viv. We knew that. Luce and I. He did it as soon as he dared. As soon as it was safe. When you were finally twenty-one. The night of your twenty-first birthday party. Jesus, he couldn't even wait until the next day. The big seduction scene had to be that night."

"Jack, listen to me, it wasn't like that, honestly it wasn't. Sebastian did not seduce me."

Jack threw back his head and guffawed. "Trust you to always defend him. No matter what."

"But it's the truth," I protested.

Shaking inside, filled with a fulminating rage, I vacated the kitchen. I left Jack sitting at the table drinking his third cup of coffee and smoking a cigarette. Seemingly he had started that bad habit again.

I went into the library and, seating myself at the desk, I began to read my piece for the London *Sunday Times* Magazine section, trying to calm myself as I did.

And then automatically I picked up a pencil and began to edit, doing the kind of fine tuning that was important to me in my work as a journalist. I was so furious with Jack my adrenaline was pumping overtime. But my anger gave me the extra steam I needed, enabled me to push my sadness to one side, at least for the time being. Within two hours I had finished the editing job. I sat back relieved, not to mention pleased with myself.

When Belinda pushed open the door a few minutes later I was taken by surprise. She was not due for another hour and I gave her a puzzled look as I greeted her.

"I'm early because I thought you might need me for something," she explained, walking over to my desk, sitting down in the chair next to it. "I brought all the newspapers, but I guess you've seen them already."

I nodded. "Jack arrived with them three hours ago. By the way, is he still occupying my kitchen?"

"No, he's set up camp in my office, where he's talking on the phone, making the arrangements for the funeral and the memorial service."

"I'm glad to hear it. I had the dreadful feeling he was going to start acting like the flake he can be at times. That he'd goof off, leave everything to me."

"He's speaking with the pastor of the church in Cornwall right now," Belinda explained. "Talking about Friday for the funeral."

"We agreed on that last night. And he wants to have the memorial next week. On Wednesday, to be exact."

Belinda looked at me askance. "I wonder if that gives us enough time? I mean, to inform everybody."

"Honestly, Belinda!" I shook my head, smiling faintly. "The days of the carrier pigeon and the tribal drum are long gone. They're extinct. All we have to do is give the announcement to the television networks and newspapers. Or rather, have the Locke Foundation do it, and the whole world will know within twenty minutes, I can guarantee it."

She had the good grace to laugh. "You're right. I sound like an imbecile, don't I?"

Paying no attention to this remark, I went on quickly, "There is one thing you can do for me, Belinda, and that's field any calls from newspapers for me today. I really don't feel like speaking to the press. I need a little quiet time by myself." I glanced at my watch. "Lila's supposed to come to clean today, isn't she?"

"Yes, she is. But not until one. She had a dental appointment at eleven. She called me yesterday to say she might be a bit later than usual."

"No problem."

"About the press, Vivienne, don't worry, I'll deal with them. If they insist on talking to you though, at some point, shall I have them call back tomorrow?"

"Yes. No, wait a minute, I have a much better idea! If Jack's still here, pass the press over to him. And if he's gone back to Laurel Creek Farm, give them the phone number there. He's as capable of dealing with them as I am."

With these words I escaped.

CHAPTER FIVE

Upstairs in my bedroom it was calm, tranquil, with sunlight filtering in through the many windows.

Opening the French doors I went outside onto the wide balcony, marveling at the mildness of the morning, wondering if this extraordinary Indian summer was nature's gift to us before we were beset by the violent winter weather typical of these parts. The Litchfield hills can be harsh, storm-swept and snow-laden from December through the spring; in fact there was frequently snow on the ground as late as April.

But I would not be here in winter. I would be in France at my property in Provence. For a long time now I have lived in an old mill that Sebastian and I remodeled some years before, and it is there that I write my books, mostly biographies and other works of nonfiction.

Sebastian and I found the property the first year we

were married, and because I fell madly in love with it he bought it for me as a wedding present.

The day we stumbled on it there was a piece of jagged wood nailed to the dilapidated old gate on which someone had scrawled, in black paint, *Vieux Moulin*—old mill—and we kept that name. A second primitive wooden board announced that the land and the mill were for sale, and it was those neglected acres of land that eventually became my beautiful gardens.

We enjoyed working on the mill together, Sebastian and I, and much of its restoration and renovation was inspired by his ideas as well as mine. *Vieux Moulin* and Ridgehill were my two real homes, one because it had been in my family for hundreds of years, the other because it was truly of my own creation. It didn't take much prompting for me to become quite lyrical about them both, since they were truly special to me. I divided my time between these two old houses; the one-room studio in New York was just a pied-à-terre, a convenient place to hang my hat and my typewriter whenever I needed to be in the city for work.

When I had arrived in Connecticut in August, on my annual visit, I had intended to return to Provence at the end of October. I still planned to do so. However, there was the matter of the autopsy report; I felt I couldn't leave without knowing the facts. On the other hand, the police would be dealing with Jack and Luciana, Sebastian's next of kin, and not with me. There was no real reason for me to hang around, other than my own anxiousness, my desire to know the truth about his death.

I wondered what the autopsy would turn up, what the Chief Medical Examiner's verdict would be. An involuntary shiver ran through me despite the warmth of the day, and determinedly I tried to cling to the belief that Sebastian had died of natural causes.

Pushing my troubling thoughts aside, I went and leaned against the wooden railings and glanced around. The trees in the gardens below, and sweeping down the hillsides to the waters of Lake Waramaug, seemed more brilliant than ever, fiery-bright plumage silhouetted against a clear cerulean sky. Some leaves had already started to fall earlier than usual, I noticed, and I knew that by the fifteenth of the month the branches would begin to look bare and bereft.

Bereft. That was exactly how I felt.

I wondered dismally if I were the only person mourning Sebastian. Certainly his children weren't grieving, and who could really know what an old man like Cyrus felt. He was, after all, ninety years old and in his dotage, with one foot in the grave himself. He had survived three of his progeny; now the last one was dead. How terrible it must be to outlive your own children, to have to bury them.

For a long time Sebastian had been the only remaining offspring of Cyrus Locke. As far as we knew, he was the only one living. There was a sister who had disappeared years ago, and what had happened to her was a genuine mystery, baffling to us all. She might be dead or alive.

Sebastian was the eldest child of Cyrus by his first wife, who had not survived the birth. There had been three other children by his second wife Hildegarde Orbach Locke, two girls and another boy.

Glenda, Sebastian's half sister and the closest in age to him, had committed suicide years before. His half brother Malcolm had drowned in a boating accident on Lake Como in Switzerland, in questionable circumstances. And Fiona, the youngest sibling, was the one who had vanished into thin air seven years ago, lost somewhere in that nether world of drugs peopled by the addicted, the depraved, the pitiful, and the homeless. The walking dead, Sebastian had called them.

Ever since her disappearance, Sebastian had been searching for Fiona and, as far as I knew, detectives in the employ of Locke Industries continued to look for the vanished woman.

The ancient patriarch Cyrus Locke aside, there were only Jack and Luciana left. And neither of them had children. How tragic it was that the Locke dynasty had so badly disintegrated into such a sorry state over the years; this great American family was almost finished, defunct. Malcolm Lyon Locke, the founding father, would turn over in his grave if he knew. I couldn't help wondering what he would think of his descendants if he were alive. That canny Scotsman from Arbroath, who had set sail for America from Dundee in 1830 and had been a millionaire by the time he was twenty-eight, would most likely be disappointed. And I, for one, wouldn't blame him.

If Luciana continued to hate the idea of children and would not permit herself to conceive, and if Jack did not remarry and beget a child, then the Lockes truly would be extinct. Well, not quite. There were some cousins, grandchildren of Cyrus's brothers Trevor and James, but they were somewhat ineffectual, nonentities really, who kept in the background and lived off their unearned incomes.

There was a knock on my bedroom door and I heard Jack's voice calling, "Can I come in, Viv?"

"Yes," I answered and as I went through into my bedroom the door opened and he rushed in, looking triumphant.

"I've done it!" he exclaimed. "I talked to the pastor over in Cornwall. Funeral's set for eleven. Burial forty-five minutes later. At Cornwall Cemetery. Up the road from the church."

"I know where it is," I murmured. "I was thinking, Jack, maybe we ought to ask a few people back to the farm for lunch—"

"A *wake*? Is that what you mean?" He looked at me curiously.

"No, of course not," I replied, shaking my head swiftly. "Not a wake. Just a simple lunch for a few close friends and family."

He guffawed. "That's a belly laugh! What family?"

"There's you and Luciana. And me. And your grand-father and Madeleine. You can't very well send *them* back to Maine without feeding them. Also, I'm sure some of your Locke cousins will want to come. And there will be a few of Sebastian's friends, people from Locke Industries and the Locke Foundation. His assistants, his secretaries, close colleagues."

"I suppose you're right," he admitted grudgingly, looking put out. "We'd better make lists. Compare notes later."

"What about the other wives that are still alive coming to the funeral? Betsy Bethune, for instance?"

"You can forget about Betsy," he muttered. "She's

playing the piano in Sydney. She's apparently on some sort of world concert tour."

"And what about Christabelle?"

"Good God, Christa! What made you think of *her*? I don't know where *she* is. Neither does Luciana. She's probably dying. Of cirrhosis of the liver. Somewhere. Don't invite her. Luciana'll have your guts for garters. She can't stand her mother."

"What about the memorial service at St. John the Divine?" I asked, changing the subject.

"Luce is responsible for that. She promised to handle it. Today."

"Did she finally agree to have it there? You know how . . . how contrary she can be."

"You call me a flake, her contrary. You're being pretty damn tough."

"I am. It's about time somebody called it correctly."

"Brutally honest today, kid. Is that it?"

"Yes. And you've been callous, cruel, and cold-hearted about Sebastian. *Savage*, in fact. I find that hard to tolerate. You're impossible, Jack."

"Okay, okay. Let's call it quits. Put our gloves away. Shall we?"

"My pleasure."

He swung around and headed to the door, but paused on the threshold. "Let's just get him buried. And memorialized. Then I can beat it. Go back to Paris."

Instantly, a nasty retort sprang to my lips, but I bit my tongue, and I said in a cool, businesslike tone, "You'd better have the public relations people at Locke Industries prepare the various announcements, and then we'll go over the material together. Just to make sure they strike the right note. That is, if you wish me to help you."

"I do. I've just spoken to Millicent Underwood. At the foundation. She's already working."

"*Amazing.*"

"What is?"

"Your sudden and inexplicable efficiency."

"I want to get this out of the way. Over and done with," he answered. Then he smiled at me.

I stared at him.

I took in that wide, genial smile, noted the complete lack of concern in his eyes, registered yet again the absence of sorrow, and I knew. He was glad. Jack was *glad* that Sebastian was dead.

This clarity of vision on my part, this sudden rush of knowledge stunned me. I could only incline my head before I turned away from him, walked across the floor to the small writing table in the seating area of the bedroom.

I stood with my back to him, composing myself. "I'll start making my list," I mumbled without turning around. I could not bear to look at him.

"See ya, Viv." Jack slammed the door behind him and was gone.

I remained standing with my hands resting on the writing table, trembling, endeavoring to calm myself. And with growing horror I could not help wondering if Jack Locke had come back to America to commit a crime. Had he returned to murder his father? The mere thought of this sent a chill trickling through me.

*   *   *

I felt chilled to the bone for the rest of the day as I went about my chores, trying to keep busy. I put my papers in order, filed my notes, and labeled the tapes from my tape recorder. The moment I finished a story I categorized all of the relevant research material and put it away for safety, and now I welcomed doing this. It kept my mind occupied.

At the end of the afternoon, not long after Belinda had gone home, I lit the fire in the den, made myself a large mug of tea, and settled down in front of the blazing logs.

Not unnaturally, my mind was on Jack and that terrible thought I had had about him earlier in the day. I turned this over in my mind now. It was one thing not to care very much that your father was dead, but quite another to actually be *joyful* about it. Was Jack happy because he had detested Sebastian so much? Or was it because he was going to inherit all that money, all that power? I seriously doubted that power meant anything to him but certainly the money did. And people did kill for money.

I sat staring into the flames, endeavoring to squash my disturbing thoughts without much success. My mind kept turning on Sebastian's death and Jack's possible involvement in it. *Patricide.* There was nothing new about that. It was an old story, as old as time itself.

Suddenly I had the need to talk to someone about my worries; the problem was there really wasn't anyone I thought I could trust. Perhaps Christopher Tremain. Certainly he was the only person who I felt absolutely sure about. Kit was kind and wise, and he had proved to be a good friend to me.

I was nothing if not decisive, and so I reached for the phone on a nearby table, lifted the receiver, began to punch in the numbers for France. Then I stopped, reflecting for a minute, and finally put the receiver back in the cradle. My natural caution had taken over.

There was no way I could call Kit. That would not be right, not fair to Jack, who had been my lifelong friend. We had grown up together and he was like a brother to me. And after all, it was only a suspicion on my part, nothing else. There was another consideration. Kit was not particularly kindly disposed toward the Lockes. He had taken an instant dislike to Jack the first time he had met him, and he frequently spoke of Sebastian in scathing tones.

I sighed under my breath, thinking of Kit. He was an American painter of some renown, and about two years ago he had bought a property in the area where I lived in Provence. As we got to know each other better, we realized we had a lot in common and there was also a strong physical attraction between us. About a year ago we had become quite seriously involved with each other, and for some time now he had wanted me to marry him. I kept stalling. I loved Kit and we were compatible, but I wasn't sure I could make the kind of commitment to him he needed and wanted. I suppose I balked at marriage: I had had my share of wedded bliss. Of course he was disappointed, but this did not alter our relationship.

On several occasions, just before I had left for New York, Kit had made a couple of snide remarks about Sebastian, and he had even gone so far as to suggest that I was still in love with him. Foolish idea that was.

Now, on further reflection, I realized I could never talk to Kit about Jack. He was a good man, and very fair, and I was confident he would keep an open mind. But unburdening my worries to him was not a solution to my dilemma, and it would be a rank betrayal of Jack. Nor could I take anyone else into my confidence.

Better to keep my own counsel.

Chapter Six

The night before the funeral I was restless. Sleep proved to be elusive. I tossed and turned for several hours before I finally got up in desperation and went downstairs.

Glancing at the hall clock, I saw that it was already three in the morning. Nine o'clock in France, and for a split second I thought of calling Kit. Not to confide my worries, since I had decided against doing that, but simply to hear a friendly voice.

In a way, I was a bit surprised he had not called me. He must have heard of Sebastian's death, and it struck me that the least he could have done was pick up the phone to say a few kind words to me. After all, Sebastian had not only been my husband for five years but my guardian as well, and surely it was obvious to my friends that his passing would have a distressing effect on me.

Marie-Laure de Roussillon, my closest girl friend in France, had phoned me yesterday to express her sympathy and ask if there was anything she could do, as had several other good friends in Paris and Provence.

On the other hand, to be fair and to give Kit the benefit of the doubt, perhaps he did not know.

Right now he was painting day and night in preparation for his next show, to be held in Paris in November. The last time we talked, about ten days ago, he had been hell-bent on finishing a huge canvas that was the last of his works for the current exhibition.

When Kit painted in this singleminded and dedicated way, he did so in total isolation. The only people he saw were the French couple who looked after him and his house. He never read a newspaper, watched television, or listened to the radio. He followed a simple but extremely disciplined routine: paint, eat, sleep; eat, paint, sleep, paint. Sometimes he painted eighteen hours a day, almost nonstop, and he continued like this for as long as it was necessary, until he had put the very last brushstroke on the canvas.

I suppose I could have phoned, given him the news myself, but I was reluctant to interrupt him. I was also conscious of his mild dislike of the Lockes. I didn't want to get a flea in my ear for intruding, disturbing his routine; nor did I wish to expose myself to some of his sarcastic remarks.

For a moment I toyed with the idea of calling Marie-Laure, just to chat for a while, and then decided against it. She ran the family château and vast estate near Ansouis, and early mornings were generally excessively busy for her.

Meandering through into the kitchen, I boiled a pan of hot milk, filled a mug with it, added a spoonful of sugar, and went into the library.

Turning on a lamp, I sat down on the sofa and slowly sipped the hot beverage. It had been Gran Rosalie's cure-all for almost everything when I was growing up, and now I took great comfort from this childhood remedy. Perhaps it would help me fall asleep when I went back upstairs to bed.

I knew why I was restless, filled with such unprecedented unease. It was the thought of tomorrow. I was dreading the funeral; dealing with Jack and Luciana was not going to be easy, nor did I look forward to coping with Cyrus Locke and Madeleine Connors.

In my experience, families seemed to behave badly at large gatherings like funerals and weddings; I was absolutely certain Sebastian's funeral was not going to be an exception to this rule.

In an effort to relax I purposefully shifted my thoughts away from tomorrow, focused on my own immediate plans. And after only a few minutes I made a sudden decision. I was not going to hang around here any longer than was necessary. There was no real reason for me to do so. Once the memorial service had taken place in New York next Wednesday, I would leave. I would book myself a flight to Paris for that night.

I longed to be back in France, back at my quaint old olive mill situated between the ancient villages of Lourmarin and Ansouis in the Vaucluse. There, under the shadows of the Lubéron mountains, amidst my gardens, olive trees, and endless fields of lavender I knew peace and tranquility. It was a world apart.

Certainly I am my happiest there. It was the one spot where I worked best over long periods of time, where I could truly concentrate on my writing. For some weeks I had wanted to get back to the biography of the Brontë sisters I was writing. Actually, it was vital that I did so; the manuscript was due at my publishers at the beginning of March, and I had only four months to finish it.

The thought of a long stretch of work over an unbroken period of time was suddenly rather appealing to me, and I found myself filling with that special kind of excitement which usually precedes a creative period for me.

As I settled back against the antique needlepoint cushions, feeling happier, thinking lovingly of my home in Provence, my eye caught the large photograph album on a bookshelf next to the fireplace. There were pictures of *Vieux Moulin* in it, and I had a sudden desire to look at them.

I rose and went to get it. Returning to the sofa, I opened the album, but instead of seeing the mill in Lourmarin, as I had expected, I found myself staring at photographs of my twenty-first birthday party in 1979.

I studied them for a brief moment.

How revealing it was to examine photographs after a long time had passed. How different we look, in reality, than we remember ourselves looking then, years ago. Whenever I cast my mind back to that particular birthday party, I think of myself as being so grown up at twenty-one. But of course I wasn't. My image, captured here on celluloid, told me how innocent and young I was in my off-the-shoulder white lace dress and string of pearls. My dark brown hair was brushed back, fell around my face in a soft, unsophisticated pageboy style, and my high cheekbones

were not as prominent as they are now. My wide
mouth looked tender, vulnerable, and a very serious
pair of green eyes looked out at me from the album,
expectant and trusting.

I peered at my face more closely. Not a line, not a
mark. I smiled to myself. Why would there be? I was
very young, just a girl, inexperienced and untouched
by life.

Sebastian was with me, smiling and debonair in his
flawlessly tailored Savile Row dinner jacket, his gleaming
white shirt punctuated down the front with those deep-
blue sapphire studs which he had had such trouble
removing later that night.

Here was Luciana, a bit plumpish in her pale pink
taffeta, looking as if a pound of butter wouldn't melt
in her mouth, her short curly hair a golden halo
around her radiant face.

Even at thirteen there had been a certain lusciousness about her, despite the puppy fat. How much
older she actually appeared to be in this particular
shot, certainly much older than the little girl she really
was at the time. And she had had the mouth of a
thirty-year-old on her. I knew that only too well.

I regarded the picture of Jack for a long moment. I
couldn't help thinking he looked like a little old man.
His hair was untidy and his dinner jacket was rumpled; his whole appearance was decidedly unkempt.
The expression on his face was surly, disgruntled, and
with a start I realized he had not actually changed
much. He was exactly the same as he had been at fifteen. Jack had never grown up, more's the pity.

Flipping the pages, I came to a series of photographs of Sebastian, which I had taken that summer,

when we had been on vacation in Nantucket. My favorite was a shot of him standing nonchalantly on the deck of a sailboat belonging to his friend Leonard Marsden. It was called the *Rascal*, and at the time we had joked about the name being so appropriate for Leonard, who was something of a playboy.

Sebastian's white opened-necked shirt emphasized his deep tan, and he was so boyish, so carefree in his appearance the snap took my breath away for a minute. His hair was tousled by the wind, his eyes very blue beneath the dark brows; he had been forty-one years old that year, but he certainly didn't look it. Not at all.

Nor had he looked fifty-six at lunch last week.

I had told him this at one point during the meal, and he had laughed delightedly, obviously pleased and flattered by my comment. And then he had told me I didn't look my age either, going on to remark that I appeared to be ten years younger.

A bit of a mutual admiration society it had been that day. And I had reached out, squeezed his hand resting on top of the table, told him that we both seemed to be defying time.

My comment had amused him even more. "You've always been my favorite, Vivi. I suddenly realized how much I've missed you. We've got to see each other more often, my darling girl. Life's too short not to spend some time with those one genuinely cares about."

I had reminded him that he was the one who was con-stantly traveling the world nonstop, whilst I was either sitting in New Preston or Lourmarin, and was therefore extremely easy to find. "Don't worry, Vivi, I'll come and find you," he had promised, smiling into my eyes. And I knew he meant it. But that could never be. Not now. It was too late.

Sighing sadly, I moved on, turning the pages, skipping over our winter holiday in Sun Valley, Idaho, that same year, ignoring the photographs of my graduation from Wellesley the following summer.

But I did pause for a second when I came to the section I had filled with our wedding photographs. Here I was in all my young glory, the sweet little bride in a short, white-silk dress holding a posy of white roses, gazing up at her handsome groom through eyes that saw no one but him.

My adoration of Sebastian was so patently obvious, and so touching, I felt my throat tighten with the remembrance of our years together as husband and wife.

I leaned back, staring into space, thinking.

We were married in July of 1980. The summer of my twenty-second year. This was just after I had graduated from Wellesley.

Once Sebastian and I had become lovers the previous year, I had not wanted to go back to college. Instead I had wished to stay with him, to travel with him, to be at his side all the time.

He would not hear of my dropping out. In no uncertain terms, he had told me I must complete my education and graduate. That was when we had had our first really major row. Naturally, we had patched things up in no time, since neither of us ever harbored a grudge.

Still, I have no trouble recollecting the way we had locked horns about that particular issue, and with such ferocity we had both been shaken by my head-strong stubbornness, forceful manner, and dogged determination to get my own way. He won. I lost. But Sebastian conceded that he had met his match. As for me, I was astounded at myself. I had not known I could be such a hellion.

Ever since our affair had started I had hoped he would ask me to marry him. Nonetheless, I was caught off guard and surprised when he did so. He had always gone on so alarmingly about the age difference of twenty years. This was something which had never bothered me in the slightest; he was young and boyish in so many different ways, I never thought of him as being older than I.

"Who are we going to get to give you away?" he had asked a few weeks before the wedding.

In the end we had decided that Jack should do it. We had grown up together, he and I, and he was the next best thing I had to a brother.

The marriage took place at Laurel Creek Farm, in front of a local judge who was a long-standing acquaintance of Sebastian's. The ceremony was held in the beautiful walled rose garden. It was simple and short, and once it was over there was a luncheon in the marquee on the lawn for the friends and family who had attended. Later that afternoon Sebastian and I had driven into New York City for dinner, glad to escape, to be alone, and married at last.

The following morning we set out for Africa, where we were to spend most of our honeymoon.

Our first stop was London and Claridge's Hotel. Sebastian had booked a suite for us there, and we were staying for two weeks. He had certain business matters

to attend to, and he had also wanted to get me rigged-
out properly for our impending African sojourn. "You
must have the right clothes, Vivi, you must be comfortable. We have to combat the heat, the sun, the constant
travel, and the cold at night," he had explained to me.

I had only been to London twice, both times with
my mother and Gran Rosalie, and it was a special treat
for me to be back there again with my husband.

I met many of Sebastian's friends; we went to smart
luncheons and elegant dinners; we attended the opera
in Covent Garden, and saw several plays in the West
End. I relished every minute of it. I was madly in love,
and so it seemed was he. We spent a lot of time in bed
giving pleasure to each other. He made love to me
most expertly, spoiled me outrageously, dressed me
fashionably, and showed me off proudly.

At one point, during the first week of our stay,
Sebastian took me on our special shopping expedition
for the appropriate clothing for East Africa, our next
destination. He bought me lightweight cotton pants,
cotton safari jackets, short-sleeved cotton shirts, as
well as four pairs of really good soft leather boots and
several large-brimmed felt bush hats for protection
against the sun.

At the end of the two weeks in London we flew to
Nairobi. This was to be our base for the three or four
months Sebastian had planned for us to stay. And as
long as I live I will never forget those months in
Kenya. I was besotted with my husband, thrilled to be
his wife, to share so many things with him, but I was
also captivated by Africa the moment I set foot there.
It was one of the most spectacularly beautiful places I
had ever been to in my life, and I was awestruck.

Sebastian knew Kenya extremely well, and it gave him a great deal of pleasure to show me his favorite spots, the areas he loved the most, and which had enticed him back time after time. And how truly magical they were.

Piloting a small plane owned by a friend in Nairobi, he flew me over the vast expanse of land that was the Great Rift Valley. This ran from the north to the south of the country, and was bounded by soaring escarpments so high and formidable they defied description. At times the Great Rift Valley, arid and desolate in parts, seemed to resemble a giant moonscape to me, and when I mentioned this to Sebastian he agreed and said he found it an apt description.

In contrast were the lush and verdant savannahs where we went on safari. It was here that we either drove or trekked, photographing the extraordinary wildlife—leopard, lion, elephant, buffalo, rhino, cheetah, gazelle, zebra, wildebeest, and giraffe.

It was from the savannahs that Sebastian took me into the Maasai Mara Reserve, and once more I was stunned and overwhelmed by the beauty of the land and the big game animals roaming across their natural habitat. I felt transported back to the beginning of time, when the earth was young.

Moving on, we drove down to Lake Victoria at a leisurely pace, spent a week relaxing on its fertile shores. When we were rested and refreshed we struck out again, heading south toward the Tanzania border and Mount Kilimanjaro.

What an awesome sight that massive volcanic mountain was, and its elevation was so high its twin peaks were lost in clouds and mists, only visible if one dared to venture upward, upward, and farther upward. Neither of us were mountain climbers, and so we hiked only a short distance up its easier, and much lower, slopes.

We camped in the foothills of Kilimanjaro, and explored the surrounding area, and at night we made love under its giant shadow. The night skies were incredible. We would lie beneath a sky so clear, so smooth it looked like a high-flung canopy of perfect, untouched black velvet.

"A sheltering sky," Sebastian would say to me time and again. One night, as we lay entwined in each other's arms, listening to the night sounds, staring up at the crystal-clear stars, he had explained: "It was here in this land, under this same sky, that human life began eons and eons ago. This is the Cradle of Mankind, Vivi." I listened attentively when he talked to me about Africa; I learned so much from him about that land, and about so many other things.

Following the sketchy, somewhat loose triangle Sebastian had mapped out, we moved slowly back up to Nairobi from Kilimanjaro, in order for him to show me the lakes and highlands of that particular area which he loved and knew intimately. Here too the land was extravagantly lush and spectacular, and I was more spellbound than ever. Oh those green hills of Africa . . . how they captured my imagination and my heart. I was forever in their thrall.

Poring over the album, my eyes settled on some snaps that had been taken of us on safari. Here were Sebastian and I, standing with our arms around one another, underneath a vivid flame tree in Thika. I thought I looked rather smart in my safari jacket, pants, and riding boots, my bush hat set at a jaunty angle.

Next to this I had placed an enlarged shot of the two of us flanking a Maasai herdsman. He was so proud and dignified, regal in his colorful, exotic tribal dress. The Maasai were tall and slender, a nomadic tribe who mostly herded cattle but were also renowned as fierce warriors.

And finally here we were, posing on the edge of Lake Nakura, one of the many soda lakes in Kenya, where the flamingo live. I stared hard at the pictures, marveling once more, thinking how amazing that scene was. The flamingos were a moving tidal wave of pink and flame, millions of wings spread across the vast dark waters of the lake. It was the most astonishing sight.

I have never forgotten those months in Africa with Sebastian . . . the memories are as fresh and vivid now as if I had been there only yesterday. In fact, it had been fourteen years ago.

Flipping the pages rapidly, not particularly interested in our other trips to other places at different times, I came at last to the old mill in Provence.

For a moment, I was quite startled at the images of the dilapidated, tumble-down structure which I had captured so carefully on film. I had completely forgotten what a dreadful ruin it had been, truly an eyesore when we first came across it by accident.

After leaving Kenya, Sebastian and I had made our way to France. We had spent several months at the Château d'Cose in Aix-en-Provence, which he had owned for a number of years. We had all gone there for the summers in the years when I was growing up,

when my mother was still alive, and they had been
memorable holidays. It was Jack's favorite place; he
felt at home there and because of his love for the
château he had made a strenuous effort to learn
French. And he had succeeded admirably.

During our travels around the provençal country-
side, Sebastian and I had stumbled upon the old mill.
It was situated near an olive grove amidst rolling
fields, just outside the centuries-old village of
Lourmarin. It was secluded enough to be absolutely
private, protected by plenty of acreage, yet it was not
too isolated from village life to make it boring.

Initially Sebastian purchased it for me as a wedding
gift, because I had fallen in love with it and the surrounding land, as well as with the picturesque village.
However, once we started work on the reconstruction
he began to recognize its great potential. He decided it
would make a perfect home for the two of us in
Europe, and he made the decision that we would live
there for part of every year.

For some time Sebastian had been losing interest in
château life and the winery, his charity work taking
precedence. More and more, he left the running of the
château and the land to an estate manager, and paid
only short annual visits. Since he was as enamored of
the mill as I was, he gave the château, its land and the
winery to Jack that year as part of his inheritance. Jack
had been thrilled, had spent every summer in Aix
thereafter, and had moved permanently to France
once he graduated from Yale.

In these early photographs of mine, *Vieux Moulin*
did resemble a heap of old gray stones, a formless relic
that would defeat anyone, even the most stoical, who

was hoping to resurrect it, to bring it back to life. As things turned out the project had gone well. Rebuilding and remodeling the original structure and adding two new wings had been one of the most satisfying endeavors I had ever undertaken. Sebastian had enjoyed it too, and we had spent some happy years there together until our divorce. And even afterward he occasionally came back to stay with me when he wanted to escape the world.

Moving through the album quickly, I came at last to the photographs I'd wanted to see in the first place, the finished shots of *Vieux Moulin*.

How splendid it was, its pink and beige stones turned to gold, gleaming in the sunlight under a pale-blue summer sky swept with recumbent white clouds. My favorite shot was of the house from a distance, viewed across the purple lavender fields at that hour in late afternoon when the sun is just about to set. It had an unearthly golden glow about it that was captivating. And next week, all being well, I would be going back there.

Holding this thought I closed the album and went upstairs to bed.

CHAPTER SEVEN

S ebastian's funeral was a distressing ordeal for me in a variety of ways, and I was sorrowful and forlorn as I sat in the front pew of the little church in Cornwall.

Jack and Luciana were on one side of me, Cyrus Locke and Madeleine Connors on the other, and I felt wedged in amongst alien beings, even though they were the nearest thing to family I had.

It was not that any of them had said anything unpleasant to me or behaved badly. Rather, it was their attitude that disturbed me. I detected a singular lack of grief in all of them and this made me angry inside. But I bit down on that anger, kept a calm demeanor, presented an inscrutable face to the world.

I sat perfectly still in the pew, my hands folded in my lap, wishing this day had never come into being. We all had to die at some time or other, none of us were immortal, but Sebastian had died too young, too soon. And how had he died? That was the thing that worried me.

Surreptitiously, I stole a look at Jack, who was seated next to me. He was pale, had dark rings under his eyes, and his expression was as inscrutable as mine. Only his hands betrayed his nervousness.

I closed my eyes, tried to concentrate on the service; after a moment I realized I was only half listening to the current president of Locke Industries who was giving one of the eulogies. My thoughts were on Sebastian's father who was sitting on my other side.

I had expected Cyrus to resemble a cadaver, to be at death's door. After all, he was ninety years old, but he looked surprisingly fit to me. His white hair was sparse, thinly combed across his mottled bald pate, and the skin of his face was almost transparent, stretched so tightly over his bones they were unusually prominent. Yet his eyes were bright, not a bit rheumy or vacant, and I'd noticed a spring in his step when he went up the path ahead of me earlier. A tall thin man with a mind like a steel trap, that's how I remembered him, and he didn't seem much different to me today. Older yes, and frail, but not quite as frail as Madeleine had made out to Jack. When he had spoken to me outside the church a short while ago he had sounded lively and sharp. It wouldn't surprise me if Cyrus Locke lived to be a hundred.

It was Luciana who had startled me the most when we had greeted each other as we had alighted from our cars. I had not seen her for a couple of years and her appearance was appalling. She was so bone thin she looked ill, and yet I was certain she had no real ailments. Her extreme thinness came from excessive dieting, I was convinced of that.

If Luciana ever did get pregnant she would probably have a hard time carrying the child. This was unlikely; pregnancy was not a priority with her, she had constantly proclaimed to the world that she did not want children.

The sad thing was she had lost her looks, lost the lusciousness that had sat so well on her when she was young, and had made her so pretty and appealing. Her head appeared to be too big for her wasted body and her legs were spindly. It didn't seem possible she was only twenty-eight. She looked much older.

At least she was wearing black, thank God. She was so contrary, so determined to be different, to flout the rules, I had half expected her to show up in a bright red ensemble. One thing was certain, she had obviously not managed to persuade her husband to come to the funeral; or maybe she had not invited him. Gerald Kamper was noticeably absent.

Jack coughed behind his hand, and began to fidget; I roused myself from my thoughts and focused my attention on the person speaking. It was Allan Farrell who had been Sebastian's assistant at the Locke Foundation. He spoke beautifully about Sebastian and with enormous sincerity. I was touched by his eloquence about a man he had been devoted to and with whom he had worked so closely for so many years.

About fifteen minutes later the service came to a close, and we all filed out of the little, white clapboard church with its red door and headed for the cemetery at the top of the hill in Cornwall.

* * *

The impact of seeing Sebastian's coffin being lowered into the ground was overwhelming. I began to weep, finally understanding that this was the end. I would never see him again. He really was dead—and almost buried.

I heard a strangled sob, and swiftly I glanced at Cyrus standing to my left. He turned to me helplessly and I saw the tears trickling down his ancient cheeks, saw the pain on his face. I knew then that he was suffering as much as I was.

Taking hold of his arm I helped to support him, as Madeleine was doing on his right. He and I huddled together under the trees, shivering in the cold, but drawing a measure of comfort from each other in our mutual grief.

A sharp wind had blown up, was scattering the leaves, whirling them around our feet as we walked away from the graveside and down the path to the cemetery gate.

I experienced an overwhelming feeling of sadness and a sense of finality as we left; a part of my life had come to an end. Nothing would ever be the same again.

At one moment I lifted my eyes, glanced up at the sky. It was clear and cloudless and a very bright blue, as his eyes had been.

Jack had heeded my advice and had invited everyone back to Laurel Creek Farm for lunch. Mrs. Crane, on duty again in full force, had had the good sense to cater the lunch, and she had hired plenty of local help to assist her. A splendid buffet table had been set up in the dining room, but I did not feel like eating.

Madeleine led Cyrus into the drawing room and I followed closely behind. The three of us sat down near the fire, the old man reaching out eagerly to warm his hands in front of the blazing logs once he was seated in a chair.

As a waiter approached with a tray of drinks, both Madeleine and I took a glass of sherry, and I turned to Cyrus and said, "Why don't you have one too? It'll warm the cockles of your heart."

He looked at me alertly, then nodded his acquiescence.

As I handed him my glass and took another one for myself, he murmured, "My mother used to say that . . . when I was a boy growing up. 'It'll warm the cockles of your heart, Cyrus,' she used to say." He looked off into space, and intently so, as if he saw something we could not see. Confronting ancient memories, perhaps, conjuring up long-dead faces, going back to his youth.   ·

"To be sure and it's an Irish expression," Madeleine volunteered, breaking the silence. "It was one I grew up with myself. Back in Dublin."

"I thought it was English," I said. "Gran Rosalie said it was, anyway."

"Sylvia. That was her name," Cyrus murmured. "My mother's name was Sylvia."

"Yes, I know," I replied. "I think I know every single name in the Locke dynasty. Sebastian told them to me, going all the way back to Malcolm from Arbroath."

"*Dynasty,*" he repeated, and stared at me over the

rim of his glass, his narrowed eyes flinty and sharp. "Are you mad, Vivienne? There is no dynasty. It's kaput, gone, finished, extinct." His glance sought out Jack and Luciana mingling with the guests at the far end of the room, and he added acidly, "And those two poor specimens are not likely to provide any future heirs in order to regenerate it."

"You never know, Cyrus, you never know," Madeleine soothed. "Don't be so negative."

"Who can help it," he muttered, tossed back his drink, handed me the empty glass, and went on, "Another sherry, please, Vivienne."

"Do you think you should?" Madeleine fussed and scowled at me. "You'll get tiddly," she warned, clucking to herself.

Giving her a scathing look, he said, "Nonsense, woman. And even if I do, so what? I'm ninety years old. What can happen to me now that's not happened to me in the past? I've seen it all, done it all, lived several life times already. Might as well get drunk. Nothing else to do."

"Of course I'll get you another sherry, Cyrus," I said, hurrying off with his empty glass.

When I returned with the refill, he thanked me, took a quick sip and said to Madeleine, "I'm hungry. Can you fetch me something to eat, please?"

"To be sure and that's a grand idea!" she exclaimed, looking pleased as she stood up.

I watched her walking across the floor in the direction of the dining room, a plumpish, handsome woman in her late sixties with a kind face and bright red hair that most obviously drew its color from a bottle these days. I thought it curious that after fifty years of living in America she still had a pronounced brogue.

Once we were alone, Cyrus tugged at my sleeve, pulled me closer and peering into my face, he said, "We loved him too much, you and I. Far too much. That was the trouble. He couldn't accept it. Frightened him."

I gaped at the old man, startled by his words. "Yes . . . yes," I said slowly, "maybe you're right."

"You were the only one, Vivienne. You were the best. The best of 'em all. The only one who was any good. Except for what's her name . . . Jack's mother? She might've measured up one day."

"Josephine," I said. "Jack's mother was called Josephine."

"Breeding was there, but no stamina," he muttered almost to himself, then drew himself up slightly and stared into my face again. "You were the best," he reiterated, nodding his head.

"Oh," I said, and hesitated, at a sudden loss. "Well, thank you for saying that. I'm not sure it's true, though. The—"

"Write a book," he interrupted, tugging at my sleeve again. "Write a book about him."

"Oh Cyrus, I don't know about that—" I began, and paused, shaking my head. "That's a hard one, a tough assignment for anyone. And he's certainly a tough subject to write about. There was always something so . . . so elusive about Sebastian, and I don't think I'm the right person anyway. I could never be objective."

"Do it!" he snapped and his eyes fastened on mine.

"Do what?" Madeleine asked, returning to the fireside with a plate of food for him.

"None of your business," he said, sounding irritated.

"Now, now, don't be cantankerous," she murmured, "Come along, let's eat, shall we?"

"Stop treating me like a child," Cyrus muttered, glaring at her.

I rose quickly. "I think I should go and talk to a couple of people . . . some of those I know from the Locke Foundation," I said. "Excuse me Madeleine, Cyrus, I'll be back in a few minutes."

I made my escape and headed toward Allan Farrell who stood talking to Jordan Nardish, a colleague from the foundation. I told Allan how moved I had been by his eulogy. Jordan agreed that it had been very touching, and the three of us stood talking about Sebastian for a few moments before I excused myself. Slowly I made my way around the room, acknowledging everyone I knew, talking to them for a moment or two, hoping to make them feel welcome. And we all shared our reminiscences of Sebastian, spoke sadly of his untimely passing.

I was on my way back to join Cyrus when suddenly Luciana was standing in front of me, blocking my way.

"You're something else," she said, her dark brown eyes hard, her expression frosty.

"I'm sorry, I don't understand what—"

"Don't give me that!" she exclaimed in a peremptory manner. "You know very well what I mean. Waltzing around here, playing the grand hostess, acting as if you're the grieving widow. You've been divorced from him for over seven years, for God's sake, and married to someone else in between. Enjoying it though, aren't you? Being the center of attention again."

"*Enjoying it,*" I sputtered in astonishment. "How can you say such a thing? Sebastian's *dead* and you think I'm *enjoying* this!"

"It's true, you are! I've been watching you. Sucking up to Cyrus, floating around, preening yourself," she shot back, her thin face twisted with dislike. "After all, it's not as if you cared anything about my father."

I was furious. Drawing in my breath in anger, I stepped closer to her, gripped her arm tightly, and stared hard at her. "Now you listen to me and listen very, very *carefully*," I said in a low, harsh voice. "Don't think you can pick a fight with me, because you can't! I won't allow it! And I won't permit you to create a scene at Sebastian's funeral, which is what you're trying to do. As for caring about him, I've loved him all my life, and you know it. I will always love him, and my life's that much poorer without him in it, the world a lesser place now that he's gone. Furthermore, you'd better start behaving in an appropriate manner as befits his daughter. You're only making a fool of yourself, starting in on me. Try to show a bit of dignity, Luciana. And grow up!"

I let go of her arm abruptly and walked away quickly, leaving her standing alone.

Crossing the long hall, I went up the staircase. I was shaking inside and close to tears. I needed a few moments alone to compose myself.

CHAPTER EIGHT

The door of Sebastian's upstairs study was ajar. I pushed it open and went in, glad to escape the crowd downstairs and wanting to recoup after my little skirmish with Luciana.

How hateful she was. She had not changed; when we were growing up she forever targeted me, tried to make my life miserable. Seemingly she still had that need.

Moving across the floor, I went to one of the windows, parted the lace curtains, stood looking out at the back gardens and the stables beyond. For a split second, in a flash of memory, I saw us out there in the stable yard—Jack, Luciana, and me.

We were all astride our horses, waiting for Sebastian, who was mounting his gelding. Without warning, my horse Firebrand had bolted, almost throwing me, and would have done so if I had not managed to hang on tenaciously. Sebastian had galloped after me and had helped me to reign in the horse.

Only later that day did Jack tell me that Luciana, then eight years old, had been responsible. He had seen her giving Firebrand several hard prods with her riding crop, which had caused my horse to take off like lightning. I might easily have been killed.

Even though we were both shocked that she had done such a wicked and dangerous thing and should be punished for it, we had not told Sebastian. We did not dare. He would have exploded, been harsh with her. It had been our secret, one of many we shared as children. Jack and I had been best friends, and he had never failed to stand up for me, or take my side. He too had suffered at Luciana's hands and, in consequence, he was forever wary of her.

Long ago I had come to understand that she had many problems when it came to her father, the chief ones being jealousy and extreme possessiveness. Even in death. That was quite apparent to me. Very simply, she had not wanted me to be present today. If the truth be known, she had probably not wanted Jack there either. Nor her husband.

Continuing to stare out of the window, I could not help thinking how sad and lifeless the stable yard looked. Once it had been full of bustle with horses, dogs, grooms, stable boys, and children milling around. But for years now it had been deserted.

After my mother died in 1976, Sebastian's passion for horses had lessened. A year later he had started to sell them off, and he had given away quite a number. By the time we were married his bloodstock had dwindled down to almost nothing, and the few horses he kept were for us to ride when we went to the farm at weekends.

Also around this time Sebastian's involvement with his charity work had increased to the point where it occupied him constantly. He had his hands full with Locke Industries and the foundation; we were traveling more and more, and doing good, helping others, had become his main passion.

Aldred, his major domo of many years, died in 1981. After that everything changed at the farm. By the time we were divorced, all of the horses had finally gone. What was once a thriving horse farm of some repute had become just another charming old farmhouse sitting in the midst of hundreds of magnificent acres.

In the last few years Mrs. Crane had been in charge, acting as housekeeper when Sebastian was in residence, caretaker in his absence. By the time she took over, all of the old outdoor staff had left, except for Harry Blakely, the aborist who looked after the trees. The gardens were tended by a team of part-time gardeners who came from a local nursery to keep them properly maintained.

Turning away from the window I thought: Nothing ever remains the same, everything changes. But then as I stood regarding the study I had to amend this thought slightly.

The room was exactly the same as it had been the day I finished decorating it eleven years ago. Nothing had changed here. Crimson-glazed walls, dark green plaid carpet, and English antiques that I had culled from different rooms in the farm still made the right statement, in my opinion. Sebastian must have thought the same thing, since he had left everything intact.

I walked through into the adjoining room, which had once been mine, and discovered that the little sitting room looked the way it had in my day. A melange of blues played against bright yellow walls, and the pieces of black-lacquered Chinoiserie furniture remained where I had placed them so long ago.

Curiosity truly getting the better of me, I wandered into the master bedroom. I was not in the least bit surprised to see that this, too, was unchanged. Shades of *Rebecca*, I muttered to myself, thinking of the old movie and wondered what Sebastian's last wife had had to say about my decorating skills.

If I remembered correctly, Betsy Bethune had not spent much time at Laurel Creek Farm. She was a famous concert pianist and was usually performing on a stage in some foreign capital, while Sebastian had been thousands of miles away in some Third World country. Which was why, in the end, they had divorced. They never saw each other, were never together, and Sebastian had told me at the time that it was pointless to continue the marriage.

I noticed a photograph of me in a silver frame, standing on an antique French chest of drawers between two windows. I went over, picked it up, and looked at it.

It was an enlargement of a snap he had taken on our honeymoon in Africa. There I was, in my safari gear and wide-brimmed bush hat, smiling at the camera. Sebastian had written across the bottom: *My darling Vivi at the foot of Kilimanjaro.*

I continued to gaze at it for a moment, and then I placed it back on the chest, surprised but also touched that he had kept it there for all these years.

"You can have that. If you want," Jack said, making me jump.

I swung around. "My God, don't creep up like that! You gave me such a start," I exclaimed.

He strolled into the bedroom, joined me in front of the chest. Lifting the photograph, he studied it for a moment, then handed it to me. "Take it. It's yours."

"Thank you. That's so nice of you, but are you sure?"

He nodded. "I'd keep it myself. But I have better pictures of you. And Luciana won't want it." As he spoke his mouth twitched, and he tried to suppress a laugh. He was unsuccessful and began to chuckle.

I laughed with him. "She came at me like a spitfire a few minutes ago."

"I noticed her angry stance. What was it all about?"

"She accused me of playing the grieving widow."

Jack shook his head slowly, looking bemused. "She's off the wall. Pay no attention to her."

"I don't. But she did make me terribly angry. I wanted to slap her. That's why I came upstairs, in order to get a hold of myself."

"Thought as much. That's why I came after you." He peered at me, looking concerned in the same way he had years ago. Clearing his throat, he added, "Are you okay, kid?"

"I'm all right, really. It takes more than Luciana to do me in, as you well know. I suppose I am a bit vulnerable, though. And I was absolutely furious the way she tried to make a scene, today of all days. She's as maddening as she ever was."

"You're right about that." Jack opened the top drawer of the chest. "There's another reason I followed you. Wanted to give you some of his stuff. It's in here. Choose anything."

Taken by surprise I said nothing. Returning the photograph to its place, I looked in the drawer with him.

"It's all mine. He left it to me." Jack took out a small black velvet case, showed me a pair of ruby cufflinks. "Would you like these?"

I shook my head. "But thanks anyway. However there is something I'd love to have . . . "

"Anything, Viv."

"His sapphire evening studs . . . if you don't want them . . . " I looked at him swiftly. "I'd understand if you didn't want to part with them."

"I don't want them." Jack began to open more of the small velvet boxes, finally found the studs, and handed them to me. "They're yours. There's a pair of cufflinks. Somewhere. They match. Ah, here they are."

"They're beautiful, thank you, Jack. It's so thoughtful of you to give me a few mementos in this way."

"I told you, take whatever you want. That goes for the farm too. It belongs to me now. Do you want his desk? Any furniture you had? When you were married?"

"No, no, and thanks again. It's lovely of you to offer, but the things you've given me are enough, and they really are so very meaningful to me."

"Change your mind, let me know."

We walked out of the bedroom through the main door, which led directly onto the upper landing. As we headed along the hall toward the staircase I paused, touched Jack's arm. "I suppose you haven't heard anything from the police, have you? About the autopsy, I mean?"

"You'd be the first to know."

"I don't understand it, Jack. Why is it taking so long to get the report?"

"The Chief Medical Examiner wants to make every possible test. To be absolutely sure. That's why he's taking his time. Nothing unusual. It's not even a week, Viv. Don't forget that."

"Believe me, Jack, I haven't," I said.

The following Wednesday morning, the memorial service for Sebastian was held at the Church of St. John the Divine in Manhattan. The whole world came— statesmen, senators, representatives of foreign governments, and all those who had personally known and loved him or had admired him from afar.

Luciana had done her work well. The church was filled with flowers; the eulogies were moving, touched me deeply. Beautiful things were said about this man who had done so much for the world. I sat with Jack, Luciana, and her husband Gerald, who had flown in from London.

The moment the service was over, I took a cab to Kennedy Airport and caught the night plane to France.

CHAPTER NINE

Whenever I returned to Provence I always felt a great sense of anticipation and excitement, and today was no exception. I could barely contain myself as I sat in the back of the chauffeur-driven car, watching the landscape slide by the windows.

We were traveling from Marseilles up through the Bouches du-Rhône, heading for Lourmarin in the Vaucluse, and *Vieux Moulin*. I could hardly wait to get there.

I had arrived in Paris from New York this morning, and taken a flight to Marseilles, where the driver from the car company I used was waiting for me at the airport.

His name was Michel, and I had known him for several years. Michel was a pleasant, friendly, and accommodating Provençal who was extremely well informed about the whole area. He could be relied upon to supply accurate information about local towns, villages, ancient chateaux and churches, antique shops, stores, and restaurants, although he only volunteered the information when asked. This was one of the reasons I liked him as a driver; he was never overly familiar or chatty, and therefore not in the least bit intrusive. I preferred to be quiet, to relax and think when I was being driven. I couldn't abide a constant stream of conversation.

I glanced out of the car window, thinking how extraordinary the landscape looked on this sunny and mild October afternoon. It seemed to be aglow in the legendary light of Provence that dazzles the year long, and which has captivated artists for centuries.

So many painters have come here to paint, attracted by this most spectacular light and the vibrant colors of the earth . . . terra-cotta running into burnt sienna and a mixture of browns, russets bleeding into gold, apricot and peach, bright marigolds, acid yellows, and every shade of green. These were the hues that came startlingly alive under the purest of blue skies.

Vincent van Gogh had splashed these brilliant colors across his canvases, thickly layered and richly textured. And in so doing he had created the first brightly colored paintings of the nineteenth century and at the same time immortalized the landscape of Provence and himself.

Sebastian had been an avid collector of Impressionist art at one point in his life. He had loved van Gogh's work, had owned a number of his paintings; now they would belong to Jack or Luciana. I could not help wondering to whom he had left them in his will, and then decided it would surely be Jack who would inherit them.

Michel was heading farther inland, and it was not long before we were skirting the town of Aix-en-Provence, which I knew well after years of spending vacations at the Château d'Cose. No doubt Jack would be arriving there next week; I suddenly realized I had no desire to see him. I had had enough of him for the time being.

The roads were virtually empty this afternoon and we were making good time. We were soon leaving the Bouches-du-Rhône behind and driving into the Vaucluse. This was the department of Provence I loved the most, and where I have lived, off and on, for the past fourteen years with both of my husbands.

One of the things which appealed to me about it was the diversity of its terrain. Fruit orchards, vineyards, and olive groves gave way to flat fields, rolling hills, and the mountain ranges of the Lubéron. Where I lived, just outside Lourmarin, the countryside was wonderfully colorful for the whole year. This was largely due to the enormous variety of trees, wildflowers, and fruit that flourished and benefited from the longest growing season in France.

Of course it had other attractions as well. The village was charming and picturesque and was known as the capital of the Lubéron. It was also considered to be a sort of cultural capital for the Vaucluse. Many painters, musicians, and writers like myself lived in the village and the surrounding area, and it was once the home of the great French writer Albert Camus, who is buried there. Music festivals, concerts, and art exhibitions were the norm the entire year.

As we drew closer to Lourmarin I opened the car window. The warm, sweet air wafted in, carrying with it the mingled scents of wildflowers, rosemary, fruit, lavender, and pine, familiar smells I loved and that always heralded home for me.

We were moving through open, pastoral country-side now, land filled with bountiful orchards and vines, olive groves, and my own lavender fields stretching almost all the way to the mill.

"Voila! Regardez, Madame Trent!" Michel suddenly exclaimed, breaking the silence.

As he spoke he slowed the car and just ahead of us, silhouetted in a jagged line against the pale blue sky, was the little medieval village perched high on top of the hill.

"It's good to be home, Michel," I said, my excitement increasing as he turned off the narrow dirt road we had been traveling and headed up the long drive-way leading to *Vieux Moulin*. Stately cypress trees, elongated, dark-green sentinels, flanked the drive on each side all the way to the paved courtyard that fronted the house.

The late afternoon sunlight was dappling the ancient stones of the sixteenth-century mill, and they looked as if they had been touched here and there with brushstrokes of gold. The many windows sparkled in the warm light, and the courtyard was filled with huge olive jars planted with vivid flowering plants that were cheerful and welcoming.

The big oak door stood wide open, and as we drew to a standstill in the courtyard, Phyllis and Alain Debrulle, the couple who worked for me, came rushing out.

Phyl, a transplanted Englishwoman married to a Provençal, gave me a warm smile and a hug, and said, "Welcome home, Mrs. Trent."

"Hello Phyl, and you can't possibly know how truly glad I am to be here."

"Oh, but I think I can," she replied.

Alain shook my hand, smiled broadly, and told me I had been missed, then he turned to Michel, who was taking my luggage out of the trunk, and spoke to him in rapid French.

"Ah oui, bien sûr," Michel said. "Merci beaucoup." Looking at me, he added, "Alain invite me to the kitchen for a coffee."

"Yes, I know," I said. "Come and see me before you leave, Michel."

"Oui, Madame. Merci."

I hardly had a chance to catch my breath before the phone started ringing. It occurred to me that the whole of Lourmarin must know I had returned from New York. Clearly the village had its own kind of tribal drums.

When I picked up the receiver for the umpteenth time in the space of ten minutes and said "Oui?" rather sharply, I discovered it was my close friend Marie-Laure on the line.

"I'm just calling to say a quick hello, Vivienne," she explained and then asked worriedly, "But is there something wrong?"

"No, of course not. Why?"

"You sound . . . how shall I put it . . . a bit rattled."

"I'm all right, really I am."

"You had a good journey, I hope."

"Yes, it was easy, Marie-Laure, after all these years I guess I've got it down pat. But can you believe it, the whole town seems to know I've arrived . . . I've already had a number of phone calls. I must be the big event of the day."

I heard the laughter and warmth in her voice as she said, "Yes, I think you are, chérie. It was Madame Creteau who told me, when I was at the boulangerie early this morning. She said Phyl had told her you were due around five o'clock this afternoon. I hope I am not calling at a bad time."

"No, no, it's lovely to hear your voice. Still, I must admit the village tomtoms never fail to surprise me. They're the equivalent of bush telegraph in darkest Africa."

"That's a unique way of describing it, yes," she exclaimed, laughing. "But you know how the locals love to gossip, to be into everybody's business, they just can't help it. They mean no harm. I'm glad you're back. I've really missed you."

"I've missed you too, Marie-Laure. How's Alexandre? And the girls?"

"We are all well, Vivienne." There was a moment's hesitation on her part, and then she said in a low, sympathetic tone, "I want to tell you again how sorry I am about Sebastian. It is such a loss for you. I do hope you are not suffering too much."

"I've been sad, of course, that's only natural. And in a way, I feel as if a door has been suddenly slammed on a period of my life that was very special to me," I murmured, sitting down on a nearby chair, glad to talk with her for a few minutes. "As you know, we didn't see that much of each other lately, because he was traveling constantly, but we kept in touch by phone. Obviously his death has been a great shock to me. It was something I never expected, Marie-Laure."

"How could you? He wasn't old, only in his fifties, and he always appeared to be so fit to me."

"Yes he was, and I think I'll feel much better when I know *how* he died. Unfortunately, Jack hasn't had the autopsy report from the police yet."

"*Really.* I thought you'd know everything by now," she said, sounding surprised. Then she went on rapidly, "There's been nothing more in the newspapers here. A few days ago they were filled with stories. The French press made his death sound most suspicious."

"So did the New York papers. But what can you do. . . . Anyway, to be honest the way he died is a bit of a mystery. I was glad to finally get away it was all so upsetting. Of course, I had to stay for the memorial service, it was very important to me that I attend."

"How did it go?"

"Very well. It was held yesterday, and the church was packed. A lot of dignitaries were there from our government and from foreign governments as well. And there were delegates from the UN, heads of charities, people from all over the world actually. The famous and the not-so-famous. It was very gratifying to me that so many people came to pay their last respects. But I crept away once it was over, picked up my luggage, and went straight to Kennedy. I couldn't wait to get back to my normal life."

"And I can't wait to see you. Can you come to dinner on Saturday night? It's just us, just the family. Perhaps you'd like to bring Kit?"

"Thanks, I'd love to come and I'll ask him later. I know he's been painting furiously, trying to finish the last big canvas for his show next month. I haven't called him yet. I just haven't had a chance," I explained.

"You'll come by yourself if he's not available, but I'm certain he will be. Oh yes, I'm very sure of that," Marie-Laure said knowingly, always the incurable romantic. "I had better go, Vivienne. I'm in the middle of paperwork for the antique show next weekend."

"And I must unpack. See you on Saturday, darling. Oh, about what time?"

"Around seven. Ciao."

"Bye, Marie-Laure."

We hung up and I went in search of Phyl.

Leaving my bedroom in one of the new wings, I walked along the hallway which linked this new part to the original structure. The latter was built entirely of large stones, ranging in color from soft sand and golden tones to various pale pinks and deep grays and all were exposed in the sixteenth-century manner.

Dating back to 1567, or thereabouts, the nucleus of the mill was a central area composed of four huge rooms that we had turned into the main living quarters. Virtually undamaged when Sebastian bought the mill for me, the interior rooms only needed repairs to their walls and ceilings. These were the rooms where the olives used to be pressed between gargantuan circular stones, and they were impressive. Immense vaults, several of which were thirty feet high, separated these massive spaces from each other and added to the grandeur.

A number of smaller rooms, forming the outer perime-

ter of the original structure, were in the worst tumble-
down state when we took possession of the property. All
needed to be rebuilt; this we did, turning them into a
series of storage rooms, pantries, and a laundry.

Throughout the mill we laid down new tile floors,
put in many additional windows, doors, and extra
beams to reinforce the ceilings. Sebastian had insisted
we use old wood and stones for our remodeling, either
culled from the mill's rubble or bought from local
builders; we also selected only those tiles and other
materials that had an aged look to them. It was impossible to distinguish the new from the old, and the finished effect was awe-inspiring in so many different
ways, but mostly because the infrastructure looked as
if it had been there forever.

The hallway led down three steps into the kitchen,
which was the crux of the central area of the mill and
part of an open floor plan. The dining and living
rooms flowed off it, as did the library. Although it was
full of the most up-to-date appliances, it had great
warmth and a rustic, country charm with its ceiling
beams, exposed stone walls, and terra-cotta floor.
Adding to the cheerful Provençal mood were the many
baskets, copper pots and pans, dried herbs, sausages,
and cheeses hanging from the beams.

An enormous stone fireplace was the focal point, its
generous hearth holding a giant-sized basket of logs, pol-
ished-brass fire tools, and tall wrought-iron candlesticks,
almost five feet high, topped with plump wax candles.

An old French farm table surrounded by wooden-
backed chairs stood in front of the fireplace, and I
went and sat down at it.

Phyl was standing near the stove and she glanced at

me as I did so. "A watched pot never boils," she said, nodding at the kettle on the stove. "I'm making you a cup of tea. I was going to bring it to you in the bedroom."

"I'll have it here, thanks, Phyl. And then I'd like you to help me unpack, if you wouldn't mind."

"'Course not," she answered, and glanced anxiously at the kettle again.

"By the way, Michel didn't leave, did he?" I asked. "I haven't paid him yet."

"No, he's still here, Mrs. Trent. He drank a coffee, then went out back with Alain. To have a cigarette, I suppose."

I nodded and said, "Phyl, the house looks wonderful. You've kept it up beautifully. Thank you."

She said nothing, but from the look on her face I knew she was pleased. Taking the kettle off the stove, she carried it to the nearby sink, poured some water out, and returned it to the gas stove.

"A watched pot," I reminded her, and reached for the telephone as it began to ring.

"Hello."

"I can't believe you're home and you haven't called me," Christopher Tremain said.

"Hi, Kit. Listen, I haven't called anyone yet. And you *are* at the top of my list. You just beat me to it by a few minutes."

"That's good to know. How are you? Did you have a good trip?"

"I'm well. And the trip was quick, easy."

"Then you're up to having dinner tonight? At least, I hope you are."

"I'd love to see you, I really would. But I need to

unpack, get settled in, get my papers organized, the usual stuff. You know what it's like. And after all, I have been away for almost three months."

"Don't I know it, darling. But all right, I'll let you off the hook tonight."

"Marie-Laure's invited us to dinner on Saturday."

"That's great, you've got a date. But what about tomorrow? Can we have supper?"

"Yes, that'll be nice. How's the painting going? Did you finish your last canvas?"

"I did. On Tuesday night, or rather, in the middle of Wednesday morning. I'm feeling a bit done in, but I'll be up and running by Saturday."

"Are you sure about supper tomorrow? Maybe you're too exhausted."

"I'm not going to cook it, just eat it. Listen, Vivienne . . . "

"Yes, Kit?"

"I just heard about Sebastian. His death. This morning on CNN. They had some coverage of his memorial service. I'm sorry. Are you holding up?"

"Yes, I'm fine, thanks."

"You must think I'm thoughtless, not calling you, but I didn't know. I've been leading an isolated existence."

"You don't have to explain, I realized you were probably holed up in your studio, going at it around the clock."

"Are you sure you're all right?"

"Yes, I'm positive. What time do want to have supper tomorrow?"

"You call it, Viv."

"About seven-thirty, is that okay with you?"

"Yes. I'll come and pick you up and you can give me a drink before I take you out on the town."

CHAPTER TEN

"Mrs. Trent, you have a phone call," Phyl said, walking down the steps that led out from the library to the swimming pool.

"Not another one," I groaned, pushing myself into a sitting position on the garden chaise. "I never knew I was so popular with so many people in Lourmarin."

"It's Mr. Locke," she said, coming to a stop next to me. "He's calling from New York, he said."

As she spoke I glanced at my watch. It was three-thirty on Friday afternoon and therefore nine-thirty in the States. Taking the cellular phone from her, I pressed line one. "Hello, Jack, I thought you'd be in Paris by now."

"Hi, Viv. I will be. Later today. I'm taking the French Concorde. At one-thirty. How is it there? Warm and sunny, yes?"

"Correct. I'm sitting near the pool relaxing."

"Viv, I've heard from the police. Detective Kennelly called me. Ten minutes ago. I just hung up from him. The autopsy report's in."

I sat bolt upright, swinging my legs off the chaise, gripping the phone that much tighter as I did. "What does it say? What's the conclusion?" I asked urgently.

"Suicide. Sebastian committed suicide. He died of barbiturate poisoning. Complicated by an excessive amount of booze."

For a fraction of a second I was stunned. Then I gasped, "I don't believe it! That can't be! Sebastian would never commit suicide. There must be some mistake."

"Afraid not. That's the Chief Medical Examiner's verdict. That he killed himself."

"But—but—couldn't it have been accidental?" I suggested, grasping at straws.

"No, Viv. It wasn't an accident. There was too much of everything in his system. The Medical Examiner did innumerable tests. They've ruled out everything else."

"What about the gash on his forehead?"

"That didn't kill him. I just told you. Barbiturates and alcohol did him in. That's what Kennelly said."

"How can the Medical Examiner be so sure it wasn't an accident?" I demanded, my voice rising in my anxiety.

"*I just told you.* There was far too much of everything in his bloodstream, brain, tissue, and organs. The stuff had to have been taken on purpose. You can't argue with a toxicology report. Facts are facts, they don't lie."

"But he'd never kill himself. Not Sebastian," I protested, truly convinced of this and therefore still disbelieving.

"How can you say that!" Jack snapped impatiently. "You've not been married to him for years, Vivienne. Nor spent much time with him lately. How could you know what was in his mind?"

"He was happy," I blurted out. "Very happy that day—"

I stopped short, suddenly realizing I did not wish to say any more than this.

"Sebastian happy!" Jack spluttered. "Come off it! He was never happy. Not in his entire life. He was always morose, somber. On the edge. He was a killjoy and a spoilsport. I ought to know. I lived through enough of his moods."

I felt a rush of cold anger sweep through me and I wanted to berate him, tell him he was wrong, tell him that he was being cruel, judgmental, and unfair. But I held myself in control, and said steadily, in a contained voice, "He seemed happy the day we had lunch at Le Refuge, that's all I'm trying to say, Jack."

"That was on Monday. By Saturday he'd taken his life."

"So that's when the Medical Examiner set the time of death?"

"Yes. Saturday night. And why Sebastian did it we'll never know. All *I* know for *sure* is that Chief Medical Examiners don't make mistakes."

"I just can't believe it," I repeated.

Jack said, "Believe it. That's what happened. It was suicide."

"And so bang goes your theory about an intruder," I remarked.

"And yours about a heart attack or a stroke," he shot back.

"Jack, how do the police explain the mess in the library? The overturned lamp and chair, the scattered papers?"

"They don't. Because they can't. They weren't there."

"But they must have some sort of theory, surely? They're used to this kind of investigation."

"They don't speculate. They only deal in facts, Vivienne."

"He must have staggered around," I said, thinking out loud. "Before he went outside. I wonder why Sebastian went outside, went to the lake, Jack?"

"I've no idea. And these are imponderables. We'll never know more than we know now. Listen, I gotta go. I gotta call Luciana. Fill her in. Get to the airport. See ya, kid."

He was gone as usual, before I could even say goodbye. I clicked off the cellular phone, lay back on the chaise, and closed my eyes. My mind was racing.

I was furious with Jack. His attitude about his father appalled me. Since Sebastian's death he had not been able to speak about him without sounding critical or churlish. I found this disrespectful, insulting to Sebastian's memory, but there was no point taking Jack to task about it. My words would be falling on deaf ears.

Only a few minutes ago he had spoken to me about Sebastian's death as if referring to a stranger, without emotion or feeling. Or concern for my feelings either. He was cold and heartless, and this troubled me.

Back in Connecticut, just before the funeral, I had wondered if Jack had killed his father. But I had dismissed that idea. Now I wondered again if Jack *had* done it, after all. Had he given his father doctored drinks, alcohol laced with barbiturates? A deadly mix, we all knew that. Did doctored drinks equate the perfect murder?

I sat up with a jolt, impatient with myself, and squashed this horrendous thought. I doubted Jack had killed his father. He was difficult, even hateful at times, but he was not wicked.

I also doubted that Sebastian had committed suicide. He had no reason to do so; he had everything to live for. I knew this for a fact. I knew it because Sebastian had told me that himself, he had told me he had never been happier, that he was about to start a new life, begin his life all over again.

Lying back on the chaise, closing my eyes, I reconstructed our lunch together at Le Refuge, relived the last time I had seen Sebastian Locke alive.

I was early. It was only twenty minutes past twelve. Nevertheless I increased my pace as I hurried up Lexington Avenue, heading for Le Refuge on Eighty-Second Street. I was due to meet Sebastian at twelve-thirty and I wanted to get there before he did.

I succeeded, but only by a few minutes.

I just had time to sit down at the table and catch my breath before he walked in, as punctual as he always was.

A few heads turned to look at him discreetly as he headed toward me. And even if the other patrons didn't know who he was, they could not help noticing him. He was tall and distinguished and he had the most glamorous aura about him.

At fifty-six Sebastian was as slender and athletic-looking as he'd always been, and I thought he was more handsome now than ever, with his deep tan and the wings of white in his dark hair. He wore a gray pinstripe suit, his white shirt set off by a pale-gray silk tie, and as always he was immaculate from the top of his well-groomed head to the tips of his well-polished shoes.

His face was serious, but his bright-blue eyes were smiling as he arrived at the table. Bending over me, he squeezed my shoulder and kissed me on both cheeks before sitting down.

"Vivi, my darling girl, I'm so glad to see you."

"I am too," I said, smiling across the table at him.

Then we both started to talk at once, and stopped instantly, laughing at ourselves.

"It's been months, Vivi, I feel I have so much to tell you," he said, reaching out, grasping my hand, holding it tightly in his.

"Almost a year," I remarked.

"Is it that long?" A dark brow shot up in surprise. "Too long then, darling. We must rectify that at once, not let it happen in future. But thank God for the telephone."

"Yes, thank God for it, but you don't use it as often as you used to, or should," I murmured, and added swiftly, "However, that's not a reproach."

"I know it isn't. And you're right. You'll consider this is a poor excuse, but I have been in some out-of-the-way places. Not to mention trouble spots, and phoning can be difficult at times. As you well know, having been there with me on many occasions."

"You've been doing wonderful work, Sebastian, cutting through all that red tape in so many countries, getting so much done. You've worked miracles lately," I praised.

"I've had a lot of good help. And we've been able to bring aid to people directly, which has been a breakthrough. Getting food, medicine, and medical supplies to those who are truly in need is gratifying. We've also managed to move in qualified doctors and nurses. Mind you, I'm afraid I've been creating more ripples than usual, if not indeed waves, wherever I go. I've antagonized a lot of people, Vivi, by refusing to deal with disintegrating governments and bureaucratic nincompoops who are quite frequently corrupt."

"Nothing's changed," I said, shaking my head. "You're still a rebel at heart."

"Am I?" He threw me a swift glance then laughed lightly. "I like to think of myself as being merely practical and efficient, a good businessman, Vivi, even when doing my charity work. I want to get things done the easiest way, the fastest way, but then you know that."

The waiter came and Sebastian ordered a bottle of Veuve Cliquot, which is what he usually drank, and then he went on, "But enough of me. What's been happening with you since you came back? The last time we spoke was in July, when you were still at *Vieux Moulin*."

"Not much really. Work mostly. I've just completed a story on the shift to the right in American politics, for the London *Sunday Times*, and I've almost finished my book on the Brontë sisters. I was in Yorkshire in early August, visiting Haworth, where they lived, and then I made my way here, as I always do in summer. To escape the—"

"Tourists in Provence and to reacquaint myself with my roots," he finished for me, his eyes crinkling at the corners with hidden laughter.

"You do know me well," I murmured, thinking how accurately he had quoted me. But then how often had I said those words to him.

"Don't I just, darling. Your patterns don't change much, Vivienne."

"Neither do yours."

"I suppose not."

The champagne was brought to the table, the bottle shown to him, opened, and poured.

We clinked our glasses and Sebastian said, "Where are you going to be spending Christmas?"

"Provence, I think."

"Oh, that's a pity."

"Why?"

"It would have been nice to see you over the holidays. I'm planning to be at the farm in Connecticut."

"That's a change, you're usually traveling the world, doing good somewhere, not celebrating," I exclaimed, taken by surprise at his announcement.

"I felt like an old-fashioned Christmas," he said, smiling at me. "The kind we used to have years ago, when you and Jack and Luciana were still children." He shrugged his shoulders lightly, and went on, "Don't ask me why."

"Nostalgia, perhaps," I suggested, eyeing him thoughtfully. "We all suffer from that at different times."

"True. Let's order, shall we? Before we forget to do so. As we so often have in the past."

I laughed, remembering the times we had been so busy talking we had forgotten all about eating. After looking at the menus we both decided to have grilled sole, and once the food had been ordered, Sebastian started to talk to me about India and at great length. I had been there with him many years ago to visit Mother Teresa, but we had only stayed in Calcutta briefly.

As I listened to him, as usual intrigued by everything he had to say, I realized there was something different about him today. It came to me after a moment or two. *He was lighthearted.* In the past few years, since our divorce, he had always seemed morose and gloomy whenever we met. It had often struck me that he was burdened down with worry—about the state of the world, his charity work, the Locke Foundation, Locke Industries, his problematical children. *Heavyhearted.* Today he was exactly the opposite.

Without thinking twice and before I could stop myself, I blurted out, "You're happy! That's what it is, Sebastian. You're happier than I've seen you for years and years."

He sat back in the chair and gave me an appraising look. "You always were the most perceptive, Vivienne.

"And yes, I am happy. Very happy. Like I've never been—"

He broke off, and glanced away.

"What's the reason?" I asked.

He was silent for a few seconds and then he slowly turned his head and gave me the most penetrating of looks.

It was then he told me.

Slowly, he said, "I think I can explain without hurting you, or upsetting you, Vivi. I just said you are perceptive, you're also intelligent, understanding, and a compassionate woman. Yes . . . I know I can tell you this without causing you pain."

"We've always been able to tell each other anything and everything," I reminded him. "How often you used to say that to me when I was growing up. And afterward."

"You know, Vivi, when you were a child you touched my heart. And when you were twenty-one you captivated me . . . I was entranced by you. That's why I married you."

"I thought you married me because you loved me," I said so quietly my voice was hardly audible.

"I did love you, I do love you, Vivi, and I always will. You are the most special person to me. But when we married I think I was simply entranced by that child who had touched my heart and who had grown up to be the most lovely young woman. And who so adored *me*. Perhaps that's one of the reasons our marriage was always so explosive . . . you were too young really, far too inexperienced, and so very vulnerable. I was too old for you. But I wanted it to work, God knows I did."

"So did I. And although our marriage *was* fraught, it was very passionate, you can't deny that, can you?" I challenged.

"I don't! My God, of course I don't, you should know better than that."

"What are you trying to tell me, Sebastian? That you've fallen in love again?"

He leaned across the table and his face was suddenly so glowing, so alive, so youthful even, I was momentarily thrown off balance.

He said, "Yes, I've fallen in love, Vivi. With someone

who totally amazes me, astounds me. And I love her in a way I've never loved any other woman, or *anyone*, for that matter." There was a slight hesitation, and he added gently, "I loved you in a different way. The love I feel for this woman is something . . . something of another world, something that I can't explain. It's the most extraordinary experience of my life. I've never felt quite like this ever before and I know I won't feel this way ever again."

"She overwhelms you sexually," I murmured, believing this might well be the truth. He was a very sensual man.

"She does. Very much so. But it's more than that. Much more. I feel absolutely complete and whole when I'm with her. It's as if part of me was missing until she came into my life. She seems to balance me in so many ways." He paused and gazed at me, reached for my hand. "I'm sorry, Vivi, I don't mean to hurt you."

"You're not," I reassured him and I meant what I said. "I know you loved me, well, love me, in a *certain* way, I understand that. You love her *differently*, that's all. Nothing's ever the same with other people. I know. I was married to Michael and it was quite a different marriage than ours. I know our marriage didn't work out for many, many reasons. But at least we had those five years. On the other hand, your marriage to Betsy Bethune blew up in no time at all. Relationships are always different."

"That was no marriage! It was not like ours!" he exclaimed. "Betsy was no wife to me."

"I realize that."

"Have I upset you?"

I shook my head and asked, "Who is she?"

He smiled, and it was such a beatific smile I was startled again; his demeanor was so out of character today. And I couldn't help thinking that whomever she was she must be someone very unique.

"You'll meet her," he ventured. "And you'll like her, love her even. And she'll love you, I know that. You'll be great friends."

"But who is she?" I pressed.

"She's a doctor. A scientist, actually. Very brilliant."

"How old is she?"

"About your age. No, a bit younger, by a couple of years."

"American?"

"No . . . I met her in Africa."

"Is she African?" I asked.

"No, she's European. I'm going to be meeting her in Africa quite soon, she's working on a project there. We're going to India together, then we're coming here for Christmas. That's why I hoped you'd be here, to meet her. However, I hope we can get together in France in the new year. Can I bring her to meet you at *Vieux Moulin*?"

"Of course."

"And if it's not too much to ask of you, I hope you'll be present at our wedding. We want to be married in the spring. You will be there, won't you, darling? I want you there."

Flabbergasted though I was, I found myself agreeing. "Of course, Sebastian. You know I'll be there, if that's what you want."

"I do, Vivi, I do."

*   *   *

I sat up, blinking in the sunlight and pushing my hair out of my eyes. And I asked myself the most potent of questions: *Why would Sebastian Locke commit suicide when he was about to marry the love of his life?*

Chapter Eleven

Half an hour later I was sitting with my friend Marie-Laure on the terrace of her home, Château de Beauvais, telling her about the autopsy report.

She listened patiently, as attentive as she always was to my words, and when I had finished she said nothing, simply sat there, digesting what I had told her.

Finally, after a few minutes, she murmured softly, "Mon Dieu, how terribly sad. What a waste."

"Yes, it is. And I can't help wondering why Sebastian would commit suicide when he was about to marry the love of his life."

She stared at me in surprise. "*He was?* How do you know?"

"He told me," I answered, and proceeded to repeat the conversation Sebastian and I had the day we lunched together in New York.

"You say he was euphoric that Monday," Marie-

Laure murmured thoughtfully, "Yet five days later, on Saturday night, he killed himself. It is obvious, is it not, Vivienne? Something must have happened during the course of that week, and whatever it was caused him to do this most terrible thing to himself."

"Or he was murdered," I said.

"You don't mean that, do you?" She looked at me askance.

"Well, it's a possibility, isn't it? According to the autopsy report he was full of barbiturates and alcohol. But someone could have doctored his drinks—the way they make a Mickey Finn."

"What is that? A Mickey Finn?" she asked, sounding puzzled.

"It is a combination of alcohol and chloral hydrate, and it usually knocks people out, makes them unconscious. It can also be poisonous."

"So, you think Sebastian was given this . . . Mickey Finn?"

"No, no, you're misunderstanding me, Marie-Laure," I said quickly, and explained, "A Mickey Finn is not necessarily lethal, and anyway I was just using that as an example. What I'm trying to say is that he might have consumed a quantity of alcohol that had been tampered with, you know, laced with barbiturates."

"Now I see what you are getting at. But who would want to do that? Who would want to murder Sebastian?"

"That's the problem, I don't really know," I answered glumly. "Although he *has* antagonized a lot of people over the years, and even quite recently. He told me that himself the last time I saw him."

"Who did he antagonize?" she asked.

"Mainly foreign governments. Or rather, *members* of foreign governments, people whom he suspected of being overly bureaucratic, who were slowing down his aid programs with what he considered to be their unnecessary red tape. Or those whom he believed to be corrupt. He just swept them to one side in that imperious way of his and plunged ahead, doing his own thing. In the process he performed innumerable miracles, of course. He may have been a bit of a maverick, and stubborn, independent, willful, and domineering, but he did get things done. And unlike anyone else ever has."

"I understand what you're saying, chérie. But surely you don't *really* believe a foreign government would send somebody to *kill* Sebastian, do you?"

"I don't know . . . Maybe. More peculiar things happen every day of the week. We certainly read about them in the papers, see a variety of bizarre incidents on the television news."

"It would be a bit risky, I think," Marie-Laure replied, nodding to herself. "After all, he was the world's greatest philanthropist. One of the most prominent men alive today. His killer, or killers, would be condemned by the entire world."

"Terrorists are condemned, but that doesn't stop terrorism," I pointed out. "And besides, killers have to be caught to be condemned."

"Very true," Marie-Laure agreed, and rose. She walked up and down the terrace at the back of the château, deep in thought.

I sat watching her, thinking what a truly good friend she had always been to me. When I had phoned her earlier, to say I wanted to come over to discuss a problem, she had dropped everything she was doing in order to receive me, to listen to me.

She was a small woman, diminutive really, and although she was forty she was like a young girl with her slender figure, dark, bobbed hair with bangs, and an exceptionally pretty face. She was also one of the most capable people I knew, running the château and its lands, which she had inherited from her father, being a supportive wife to Alexandre and a devoted mother to her two children, François and Chloe.

She and I had met thirteen years ago, when Sebastian and I were first working on the old mill, and we had taken to each other at once. And there had been times, over the years, when I had wondered what I would have done without her friendship.

Marie-Laure stopped pacing finally, came and sat down on the garden seat next to me. Staring into my face, she took hold of my hand, and said carefully, "I don't believe Sebastian was murdered. I think you must accept the facts, accept the autopsy report, accept that he took his own life."

"But he didn't have any reason to do that," I persisted quietly.

"Perhaps he did. How do you or I know? How does anyone know about another person, Vivienne? How do we know what goes on in someone else's mind?" She shook her head, and went on, "We have no conception. There is one thing, Vivienne . . . "

"Yes?"

"Could it have had something to do with the woman he was in love with?"

"What do you mean exactly?"

"Maybe she broke off her engagement to him," Marie-Laure suggested, her dark-brown eyes intent and alert as they fastened on mine.

"That's a possibility, I suppose anything can happen in a relationship. But I don't think she did that, no, no, no," I answered.

"Don't be so emphatic, chérie. Women have been known to change their minds. They do it all the time."

"No woman in her right mind would dump Sebastian Locke!" I exclaimed.

"You did, Vivienne," she retorted, throwing me a wise and knowing look.

"No I didn't. We separated by mutual agreement . . . we loved each other, we just couldn't live together. We were tempermentally unsuited."

"Let us consider this," Marie-Laure began. "The woman, who was younger than you, apparently, finds herself growing more and more nervous about the age difference between them. She gets . . . how do you say it . . . the cold feet, no? And so she ends their relationship."

"All right, it could happen, I'll grant you that. But even if she did break it off with him, he wouldn't kill himself over it. Not Sebastian. I just know he wouldn't. Honestly, it's not a good enough reason for me, Marie-Laure, it really isn't. Sebastian was tough and resilient. He had a strong character, and he had many things in his life which were of vital importance to him. His work at Locke Industries, the Locke Foundation, and all of the charities he was involved with. He was constantly traveling the world, dispensing aid. So many people depended on him, and he *knew* they did."

"I was always aware that he took his responsibilities

seriously. It was one of the things I've always admired about him," she said.

I bit my lip, pondering, then endeavored to explain more fully to her. "Listen to me, Sebastian would never kill himself over a woman, no matter how much he loved her. He was far too sophisticated, too strong a man for that. Don't forget, he never had any problems getting a woman. He had five wives altogether, including me. My mother was his mistress, and God knows how many other mistresses he had over the years. Furthermore, there's no doubt in my mind that women were falling at his feet right up to the time of his death. That's the kind of man he was. Women couldn't resist him. And I can't begin to tell you how fantastic he looked the day we had lunch earlier this month, better than ever. He was full of vitality and that fatal charm of his was wholly intact. He was irresistible, in fact."

Marie-Laure nodded slowly. "What you say about him is true, I remember his charisma, his great sex appeal, and certainly you knew him better than anyone. So, I cannot argue, your reasoning is valid. Therefore it must have been something else which caused him to take that most fateful step."

"Correct. But what could have pushed him over the edge?" I asked.

"I cannot even attempt to make a guess," she answered. "I just do not know. However, what we both know is that it wasn't a health problem, because the autopsy would have revealed any fatal disease. The police have done a thorough investigation and ruled out foul play, so we know that it was not murder. Anyway, chérie, that is too far-fetched an idea for me to even contemplate."

"What you're saying is that you believe he actually did kill himself. Am I correct, Marie-Laure?"

"Yes, you are. What other conclusion is there? We just don't know *why* he did it, that's all."

Marie-Laure and I stared at each other. We were both at a loss.

Eventually, she said, "Let us admit it, chérie, we will never know the reason. The only person who could tell us is . . . dead."

Chapter Twelve

Driving back to *Vieux Moulin* from the château, I replayed everything Marie-Laure had said, and as I did I began to feel much calmer.

My dear old friend usually made great sense and this afternoon had been no exception. I realized she had helped me to adjust to the fact that Sebastian *must* have killed himself. Very simply, there was no other explanation for his death. In the beginning, murder had crossed my mind but only fleetingly really; I had attributed his fatal collapse to natural causes, either a heart attack or a stroke. This was the reason I had been so shocked by Jack's phone call. Suicide had been the farthest thing from my mind.

But Marie-Laure had reminded me that we never really knew anybody, however close to them we were, or knew what went on in their minds. People could do surprising things. In essence, she had helped me to put matters in a better perspective, and I began to relax for the first time since Sebastian's body had been found.

By the time I arrived at the mill it was almost six-thirty. The sun was sinking low behind the ragged line of dark hills, the pale blue sky of earlier fading into an iridescent pearly gray. As I swung off the dirt road and into my driveway, it was already dusk.

Once I'd parked the car, I went inside and raced straight to my bedroom without even letting Phyl know I was back. I didn't have much time to get ready before Kit arrived to pick me up for dinner.

In my bedroom I pulled off my blue jeans and sweater, slipped into my dressing gown, and refreshed my makeup. After brushing my hair and spraying on perfume, I dressed quickly in beige wool culottes, a cream silk shirt, and black and beige shoes. Taking a black blazer out of the wardrobe, I slipped this on and made my way to the kitchen.

Phyl was standing at the old farm table, filling a wine cooler with ice cubes, and she glanced up as I walked in.

"There you are, Mrs. Trent, I thought I heard you come in a short while ago. This is for the Sancerre. Should I open it now, do you think?"

"Hi, Phyl, and why not." I glanced at my watch. "Mr. Tremain will be here shortly, he's usually on time. You know, Phyl, it's turned quite coolish, I think it would be better if we had drinks inside tonight. In the library, I guess."

"Good idea. Shall I light a fire?"

"No, thanks anyway. It's hardly worth it. We'll be going out for dinner in half an hour."

"There're a couple of messages for you, over there on the dresser," she said.

I strolled across the floor, took the messages from underneath the small old-fashioned flat iron that served as a paperweight, and read them quickly. Renny Jackson, my book editor in London, had called to tell me she would be in Aix-en-Provence next weekend, and could we have lunch. She said she would ring me again on Monday to make the date. The other message was from Sandy Robertson, one of the editors I worked with at the London *Sunday Times*. Nothing important, Phyl had scribbled. He will phone you tomorrow.

"Are you sure Mr. Robertson doesn't want me to call him back now, Phyl?"

"Oh yes, quite positive. He said he was just leaving the office, that he'd only phoned up to have a social chat with you."

"I see." I crumpled the messages in a ball, gave them to her to throw away just as the door bell clanged loudly.

"That must be Mr. Tremain," Phyl said.

"I'll get it," I told her and hurried out.

When I opened the door and greeted Kit a split second later, I was surprised to see how fit and well he looked, despite his arduous painting schedule of the last few months.

"Aren't you a sight for sore eyes!" he exclaimed, beaming as he stepped into the hall.

He swept me into his arms and hugged me tightly, not giving me a chance to say anything.

When he finally released me, he kissed me lightly on the lips and held me at arm's length, his expression appraising. "You look great, just *great*, Vivienne."

"So do you." I smiled at him. "And you don't look a bit done in, as you claimed you were."

"I am, though. But just knowing you'd returned put the starch back in me and cheered me up no end," he replied, grinning at me. Slipping his arm around my shoulders, he walked me across the hall, and his happiness at being with me was palpable.

"Since it's turned cool tonight I thought we'd have drinks in the library," I said. Looking at him, I added, "It's lovely to see you, Kit."

"And you. I feel as if you've been gone forever. Now that you're finally here I hope you're going to stay, Viv."

"Yes, I am, thank God. I've got to dig into my book again, finish it by March."

We met Phyl in the doorway of the library; Kit greeted her in his usual breezy, friendly fashion, before ushering me inside the room. Its walls were lined with books from floor to ceiling, and I had used wonderful old Provençal furniture.

Turning to me he said, "This is my favorite spot in the whole house, you did such a wonderful job on it."

"Thanks," I said and went to the table where Phyl had placed the wine cooler holding the bottle of wine and two glasses. I poured.

"Cheers," Kit said, touching his glass to mine. "Welcome home, fair lady. You've been missed."

"I've missed you too, Kit."

"I hope so," he answered and lowered himself into a chair near the big picture window which overlooked the gardens.

I sat down on the sofa opposite, and as I leaned back against the soft leather and looked across at him,

I was surprised to discover how much I really *had* missed him. I had not realized it until this moment.

Christopher Tremain was an attractive man by anybody's standards. Of medium height, he was slender, wiry in build, with a shock of dark-blond hair above a surprisingly unlined college-boy face. Since the first day I met him I've always thought of him as looking like the all-American hero, racing across a football field clutching a ball. Forty-two years old, he was a New Yorker as I was. He had lived in France for eighteen years, where he was deified as one of the great modern impressionist painters of his generation, and had moved to Provence from Paris two years ago.

Intelligent and exacting gray eyes stared back at mine staring at him. He said, "What's wrong? Do I have a dirty mark on my face?"

I shook my head. "No, I was just thinking again how truly fit you look, in the best of health. Certainly much better than you did just before I left in July."

"I feel better. It's the work, I guess. All that painting, the supreme physical and mental effort seems to have regenerated me."

"I know what you mean, work is a great turn-on for me too."

"Viv . . . look, there's something I want to say—" He stopped.

"What?" I asked swiftly, detecting an odd note in his voice. "What is it?"

"I want to get this out of the way before we go to dinner. When I was getting ready a bit earlier I had the news on, and CNN had a flash about Sebastian. I guess the autopsy report's been released by the

Connecticut State Police—" Again he cut himself short and looked at me worriedly.

"It has. Jack called me from New York this afternoon as soon as he knew. The Chief Medical Examiner's verdict is suicide, barbiturate poisoning. You must know that though, surely they had it on CNN."

"Yes, they did." He hesitated, before adding, "It seemed odd to me."

"*I* thought so. In fact I drove over to see Marie-Laure earlier to discuss it with her. She knew Sebastian a long time, and knew him quite well." I let out a long sigh. "We tossed it around for ages, and there doesn't seem to be any other explanation for his death. We finally agreed on that, we'd no alternative."

"I know how upsetting his death must have been to you, and I'm sorry I wasn't there to comfort you," he expressed with genuine sincerity.

"I'm okay, Kit. It was a bit of a shock at first, and Jack's news today knocked me for a loop. But as Sebastian would have said, life has to go on."

"Life's pretty unpredictable," Kit said, putting his drink down on the coffee table in front of him. "One never knows what's in store, what terrible shocks there are around the next corner."

Rising, he came and joined me on the sofa, stretched one arm along the back, and drew closer to me. "I want to help you, Vivienne, help you to cope, to make things easier for you, if I can. I'm here if you need me."

"I know that. I'm fine, honestly I am."

"Is it all right, Viv? Between *us*, I mean."

"Of course it is, Kit."

"So I *can* assume we're picking up where we left off in July?"

"Oh yes," I answered quickly. I was beginning to realize that I not only wanted to resume our relationship, but needed it, needed him.

He leaned forward, took my face between his hands, and kissed me passionately. I returned his kisses with the same ardor.

"Oh God, Viv, I want you, I want to make love to you," he whispered against my hair, when we finally drew apart. "It's been so long since we were together, I can't stand it. Let's go to bed now, before we go out to dinner."

I touched his face gently. "Later, Kit. We've got all the time in the world, you and I."

He shook his head. "No we don't. Who knows what tomorrow will bring. We've got to grasp today, live it hard, take life with both hands. Oh darling, I want you so much."

"Later, Kit," I said again. Leaning closer to him, I kissed him quickly and added, "Let's go to dinner and afterward I'll come home with you."

He looked at me swiftly, his eyes suddenly intense as he asked, "Will you stay the night?"

I nodded. "I want to see the paintings for the exhibition, especially the last one, the big canvas."

"Oh, so it's my work that interests you, is it, and not me," he laughed.

"Both," I answered and laughed with him.

When we had made our date for tonight, Kit had promised to take me out on the town. And, true to his word, he did.

We went to the best four-star restaurant in the vicinity, Le Moulin de Lourmarin. He had ordered champagne in advance, and it was served the moment we were seated at the table.

With our dinner, a marvelous veal stew, we had one of the best of our local wines, a Châteauneuf-du-Pape from a nearby vineyard, Domaine de Mt-Redon.

Quite aside from the delicious food and wines, Kit himself was in top form. He was amusing and expansive throughout the meal, talking about his work, his exhibition in Paris, and then he filled me in on the local gossip, told what had been happening during my stay in Connecticut. He kept me laughing and highly entertained for several hours.

Later, over coffee, he suddenly said, "Will you come to Paris with me in November, Viv? Come to the opening of my show?"

"Oh, Kit, I've got such a lot of work to do yet on my book," I began and paused when I saw the look of genuine disappointment settling on his face.

"Please, Viv, it's important to me that you're there."

"Then I'll come," I said, making a sudden decision. "It's at the end of the month, isn't it?"

"Yes, it's Friday the twenty-fifth of November. Why?"

"It's just that the last part of the month is better for me. It gives me a chance to get back into the book. I'll work like crazy for the next few weeks, so that I can take a long weekend off to be with you in Paris."

The look of pleasure that crossed his face told me what my acceptance meant to him, and I was touched. I said, "Thanks for asking me, Kit, I know your show's going to be a huge success. And I can't wait for my private preview of the paintings tonight."

"And I can't wait for you," he said, leering at me wickedly, then grinning he added, "But I honestly think it's better to view the canvases tomorrow. In the daylight."

"Oh you do, do you?" I answered, raising a brow.

I stood at the bedroom window, looking out toward the ancient castle of Lourmarin, waiting for Kit. There was a full moon and it illuminated the castle's Renaissance bulk, its stark towers, and brought a silvery sheen to the time-weathered stones.

I had always loved the view from his bedroom and tonight there was something special about it, something different. Perhaps it was the play of brilliant moonlight on those ancient ramparts and the rolling fields where the castle stood. Or maybe it was the dark sky, littered with bright stars and fast-moving clouds that occasionally scudded across the face of the moon to obscure it.

Or perhaps it was because I was different tonight.

I was more relaxed and at ease with myself in a way I had not been for a very long time. *I was glad to be with Kit.* That had registered with me hours ago. I had forgotten how good he made me feel with his warmth and attentiveness and loving gestures. This was nothing new. He had always treated me well, beautifully really. I'd just forgotten in the three months I had been away.

Suddenly he was there, standing behind me, resting his hands on my shoulders. Lifting my hair, he kissed the nape of my neck. Then slowly he turned me around to face him.

He was wearing a white terry-cloth robe, and he

handed one to me. "Please, darling, get undressed, let's go to bed," he murmured.

But as I started to move away he pulled me back into his arms and kissed me. It was a long hard kiss and when he released me, he said in a low, urgent voice, "Hurry, I can hardly wait, Viv, I've missed you so much."

A few minutes later I returned wearing the terry-cloth robe and joined him on the bed. We lay side by side for a second, holding hands, watching the sky turning color, and I was happy to be next to him, to savor this moment of rare peace and intimacy. Then in a sudden movement Kit pushed himself up on one elbow, lay on his side, regarding me intently. "You're beautiful, Vivienne," he said and opened my robe, began to stroke my breasts, my stomach, and my thighs, his hands moving over me lightly. Finally settling into a kneeling position, he bent over my body, kissing every part of me, until he finally arrived at the core of me. And it was here that his mouth lingered. I relaxed and let him love me as he wanted to, in the way he always had.

PART TWO

JACK
DUTY

Chapter Thirteen

I first came to the Château d'Cose when I was seven years old. If a small boy of that age could fall in love with a house then I did.

In those days I did not understand why I loved it so much. All I knew was that I felt at home. Its vastness did not frighten me. Nor was I intimidated by its grandeur. I was at ease in the great rooms. Or roaming through the meadows and woods of the estate.

Deep in my soul, I knew that I *belonged* at the château. Forever. This was my place. I never wanted to leave. When I had to, I was sad for weeks afterward. I could not wait to return. We came back every summer. It was never long enough for me.

My father gave me the château and its lands just after he married Vivienne in 1980. I was stunned when he told me. I did not believe he meant to go through with it. I kept thinking he would back off at the last minute. To my surprise he did not.

Sebastian had grown bored with the château. He was no longer interested in the vineyards and the winery. But that was my father. He soon grew bored with things. And with wives.

After he and Vivienne split up, Luciana and I started to call him Henry behind his back. After Henry the Eighth who had six wives. The name quickly deteriorated into Hank.

Luciana and I had secret names for a lot of people when we were kids. Vivienne was VTG. This stood for Vivienne the Great. My father thought she was just that. So did I. But Luciana detested Vivienne. So VTG was a derogatory name to her. Never to me. I laughed up my sleeve.

My half sister also hated Vivienne's mother, Antoinette Delaney. I didn't. I loved her. I thought she was beautiful. Her hair was full of sunlight, her green eyes the same color as the emeralds my father constantly gave her. She had pale, pale skin. When she was angry it turned bright pink. In summer she got freckles on the bridge of her nose. I liked her freckles. They made her real, less ethereal.

Antoinette was always very kind to me. She loved me a lot. As much as she loved Vivienne. I knew this because she told me, told me I was like the son she had never had.

I wouldn't allow Luciana to give Antoinette a nickname. Not unless it was flattering. We never did agree on that. And so she was never called anything behind her back. She was only ever referred to as Antoinette.

But I had my own name for her. She was my Special Lady. And she was *exactly* that. Truly special. She worked wonders in my young life, turned it completely around. And she helped to make me feel whole.

Then she went and fell down the cellar steps at Laurel Creek Farm. She broke her neck and died.

I was twelve and it broke my heart. I'm not certain that I've ever recovered from her death. There has been a void in me since then. No one has been able to fill it.

My twelfth year was hell.

Antoinette died, and my father started to lecture me about Duty. It was my Duty to look after Luciana when he was away. It was my Duty to study hard. In order to go to Exeter and Yale. It was my Duty not to let the family down. It was my Duty to follow in his footsteps. My Duty to run Locke Industries and the Locke Foundation one day. And it was always Duty in a grand way. And with a capital D.

I was still only twelve when Cyrus joined the act.

Whenever we went to see him in Maine it was *Duty Duty Duty*. Not surprisingly, I began to hate that word. I determined that I would never do my Duty. Not ever. But of course I did. Like the Pavlov dog, I had been brainwashed. I submitted to their will. And I did their bidding. After a fashion.

The Inheritance, as I called the château in those days, was deeded to me when I was only sixteen and attending Exeter Preparatory School. It was merely a small part of my vast inheritance, my grandfather and father being billionaires.

I sometimes thought of the château as a consolation prize. My father had married Vivienne, the woman of my dreams. I had always planned on marrying her myself. Not unnaturally, I was devastated when they tied the knot.

I suspect Sebastian realized this. Hence the château. Of course, giving it to me when he did saved inheritance taxes as well.

Once the château was mine, I flew to France whenever Exeter broke for vacation. I was thrilled to be at d'Cose several times a year, instead of only in the summer months.

Sebastian and Vivienne were also there a lot in 1980 and 1981. They got on my nerves. They were forever billing and cooing. Luciana and I christened them the Lovebirds.

The Lovebirds were preoccupied with the pile of rubble Sebastian had bought for her in Lourmarin. They were transforming it into a house. Eventually it was finished and they called it *Vieux Moulin*. I thought it was an imprudent waste of money. But I said nothing. It was none of my business. And, after all, *I* now owned the château. The house of my dreams, if not the girl.

I never did understand the attraction that heap of old stones held for Sebastian. An old mill, for God's sake. But then I never did understand my father. Now it was too late. He had been dead and buried for five months.

When I graduated from Exeter at the age of eighteen I went to Yale. Just as I was supposed to. Doing my Duty. I was following in the footsteps of those other Lockes who had gone before me. The first was my great-great-grandfather, Ian Lyon Locke. I would probably be the last, since I had no son.

I considered Yale to be a nuisance. It was preventing me from getting on with my life. All I wanted was to live at my château in Aix-en-Provence. I had been learning about my vineyards and my winery from

Olivier Marchand, who had run everything for years. First for Sebastian. And then for me. It was my whole existence.

At twenty-two I became master of my own fate.

After graduating from Yale, I moved to the château permanently, where I worked alongside Olivier. I was passionately consumed by the land. My land.

I was also passionately in love.

When I was twenty-three I married her.

Everyone thought she was eminently suitable. She was, when it came to pedigree. Eleanor Jarvis Talbot had the right lineage. She was Boston Old Money. Except that they didn't have any. Not anymore. This didn't matter to me. I had more than enough for both of us. Millions. In trust from my mother.

Eleanor was a lovely pale blonde. Tall and willowy. And highly over-sexed. I slept with her on our first date and continued to do so all through the last year I was at Yale.

Her cool, refined looks belied her sizzling nature. She was hot. Perhaps this was part of the attraction. She looked like a lady, behaved like a whore. When I was with her I was forever turned on just thinking about what we would do later. Actually, all we ever did was screw. Day and night, whenever we could. I was in seventh heaven, as they say. I couldn't believe my luck.

The family thought she was Miss Right. So did I. We were confused. Eleanor turned out to be Miss Wrong. From the very beginning the marriage floundered. Maybe it was partly my fault for not making her understand how much the château, the winery, and the running of the estate meant to me.

We honeymooned in Morocco. I will never know what that country is really like. Not unless I make a return visit. I spent all of my time in bed. On top of Eleanor. Gazing down into her limpid gray-blue eyes. Or lying on my back. Staring up at hotel ceilings as she mounted me enthusiastically. She liked to do that. The dominant position appealed to her. "Let *me* fuck *you*," she would say and she did. Over and over and over again.

Then we came home to the château. And things changed. They had to change. I had a real life at the château. I had work to do. It was my Duty. But I cherished my Duty in this particular instance. I was bound to the land and the winery.

The endless screwing had to lessen. But it didn't stop entirely. Unfortunately, Eleanor was like a rabbit. She was inordinately miffed when she couldn't get it all the time. Whenever she felt like it. She said I didn't love her. I believed I did. But she wore me out. I was exhausted. I needed a rest from all that unimaginative mindless fucking. I soon realized I had very little to say to her. Almost nothing at all.

This aside, she had no idea how to run a great château. Being a chatelaine meant nothing to her. Nor was she interested in learning how to be one. Her curiosity about what I did all day was nil. Her involvement in my working life was nonexistent. Then, after a year of marriage, another problem developed. She became fixated on my father. She couldn't stop talking about him. His presence seemed to ignite her. She became overly animated, abnormally effervescent, almost raucous. In his absence, a despondency set in. She sulked. Threw tantrums.

Eleanor still wanted to screw me endlessly. But my

interest in her was waning with rapidity. Her preoccupation with Sebastian sent a message loud and clear. I knew she really wanted to screw my father instead of me. Or as well as me. Whichever. This knowledge proved disastrous for our sex life. It rendered me impotent.

We divorced.

It was costly. But worth it.

And fortunately, despite our sexual marathons, there were no children from this regrettable union.

A glutton for punishment, I married my second wife when I was twenty-six.

I met Jacqueline de Brossard in Aix-en-Provence. She was the daughter of a minor baron and lived in a nearby château. What attracted me to her initially was her familiarity with château life. And her knowledge of the land. Plus her gorgeous body. Her looks were plain. However, her splendid French chic and great style more than compensated for this inadequacy.

Jacqueline de Brossard appeared to be the perfect mate. Ideally suited to me. We shared similar tastes. In most things. We were compatible. Nevertheless, our marriage scarcely outlasted the year. She had two all-consuming interests in her life. Spending my money was one of them. Infidelity the other. My second wife apparently did not wish to bed my father. As far as I knew. Merely every other man that crossed her path.

We divorced.

I vowed never to marry again.

I was now living in sin.

My paramour was an Englishwoman. Her name was Catherine Smythe. She was educated. Brainy. A bit of an intellectual. Fifty years ago she would have been termed a bluestocking. Catherine was an Oxford graduate. An historian of some repute. She had taught history, written about it, lectured on it.

I thought she was outrageously good-looking. Red-haired, green-eyed, pale-complexioned.

There were moments when Catherine reminded me of my Special Lady. Like the Special Lady's daughter Vivienne, Catherine was older than me. By five years. That didn't matter. I've always preferred older women.

Catherine and I met in Paris in August of 1994. She was staying with an English journalist friend of mine, Dick Vickery. I assumed they were romantically involved. My assumption was incorrect. They were just good friends.

She and I became more than just good friends in a matter of days. I liked brainy women. They stimulated me. Turned me on. Catherine was much better than a mindless screw. She was the ultimate.

She came to stay with me for Christmas. It was then I asked her to move in with me. She agreed. We saw the old year out together, greeted the new one in. Drinking champagne on the château's ramparts. Toasting each other. Getting drunk together.

It seemed to me that 1995 held wonderful prospects. Especially with Catherine on the premises. Indefinitely.

"I can't promise you marriage," I'd said to her over Christmas.

"Marriage!" she had cried indignantly. "Who's interested in marriage? Certainly not I. I've no desire to be legally bound to any man, present company included. I love my independence. I don't aim to lose it."

So that was that.

I had met my match.

Seven months after our first encounter this clever woman still fascinated me. Apparently I still fascinated her.

I moved away from the trees. Striding out, I headed for the château looming up in the distance, a great mass of stone.

It gleamed palely on this February morning. Watery sunlight glanced off its many windows. The gray-tiled rooftops and turrets were dark smudges against the hazy blue sky.

I paused, looked toward the château across sweeping green lawns, a formal garden and, just beyond the garden, the wide stone terrace of the château.

It was the perfect spot from which to view the eighteenth-century edifice at any time of day. This morning it looked spectacular in the soft light, with the mist rising off the lawns.

I was filled with satisfaction, knowing it was mine.

I glanced at my watch. It was almost nine o'clock. Time for breakfast with Catherine.

I found her in the library. She had been working there since seven.

"Aren't you a love," she said, looking up as I came in. "Bringing me breakfast, no less. Spoiling me."

"Your turn tomorrow." I put the large wooden tray on the coffee table in front of the fire and sat down.

She joined me a moment later. We sat drinking large cups of café au lait and eating warm, freshly baked croissants spread with butter and homemade raspberry jam.

"Jack, these are lethal."

"You say that every day."

"Three minutes on the lips, six months on the hips," she muttered, shaking her head. "I simply must go on a diet tomorrow."

"I like you the way you are."

"I'm getting fat, living here with you, Jack."

"Want to leave?"

"No, of course not, you fool," she replied swiftly, affectionately, laughing as she spoke. "This place is compelling."

"I thought it was me."

"It is. You *and* the château. Jack, I've come across something really fascinating, in one of the old books I found. I think I know where the name Château d'Cose might have come from."

I pricked up my ears. Leaned forward. I was suddenly more alert. The origin of the château's name had always baffled Sebastian. Olivier Marchand had been unable to throw any light on it. Neither had any of the old-timers who had worked here for years. Documentation barely existed. It was a mystery.

"Speak," I said. "Tell me, Catherine."

"As I mentioned, the book is old. It carries a series of paintings of about thirty famous people from the fifteenth, sixteenth, and seventeenth centuries. The spelling of those periods, reproduced in the book, is quaint—"

"What do you mean by quaint?" I interrupted.

"For example, Rabelais is spelled *Rables*. Buckingham, as in the Duke of, is spelled *Boucquin can*. The Queen of Spain is *la Reine Despaigne*, instead of *D'Espagne*. And the Queen of Scotland, which correctly is *la Reine d'Écosse* shows up as *la Rene de Cose*. Therefore, I

think that d'Cose, the name of this château, is a bas-
tardization of *de* Cose, and somehow refers to
Scotland."

I stared at her. "That would be peculiar. An odd
coincidence. *If* you're right. Malcolm Lyon Locke, the
founding father of the dynasty, was a Scotsman. Is
there any reference to my château in the book?"

"No. None at all. As I just said, it's a picture book
really, showing different paintings of . . . well, shall we
call them celebrities of the day. Rabelais, the writer,
the Duke of Buckingham, Mary Queen of Scots,
etcetera, etcetera. And, of course, the spelling of the
latter's name caught my eye at once."

"Keep digging. Maybe you'll find something else
that makes reference to Scotland. Maybe this was her
place?"

Catherine shook her head. "I doubt it. Mary was
mostly in the Loire Valley when she was growing up.
And after she married the Dauphin of France, she was
at the legendary Chenonceaux, the home of the king.
She was with Henry II, his mistress Diane de Poitiers,
his wife Catherine de Medici, and their son Francis
II, who was the Dauphin. The p*etite Reinette d'Écosse*
she was usually called in those days, the little Queen
of Scotland. Poor sad thing she was in the end. And
she met such a grisly death. Had her head chopped
off—"

The ringing of the telephone next to Catherine's
elbow interrupted her. Reaching for it, she said,
"Château d'Cose. Bonjour."

There was a moment of silence before Catherine
went on, "Oh hello, Vivienne, how are you?"

CHAPTER FOURTEEN

I took the phone from Catherine, sat down in the
chair she had vacated.

"Hi, Viv," I said. "How're things?"

"Fine, thanks. Jack, I'd like to come over to see you."

"When?"

"This morning."

"That's impossible," I said quickly. I'd caught something in Vivienne's voice. I knew when to protect
myself from her.

"What about this afternoon then? Or this evening?"
Vivienne pressed. "It's very important. Really it is."

"Viv, I can't. Not today. I got problems. Stuff to deal
with."

"You can spare half an hour. Surely. For *me*."

"Can't, Viv. Olivier has people coming. We'll be tied
up. All day. Winery business," I lied, improvising as I
went along. I'd known her forever. Since I was six.
Something was troubling her. I could tell. It echoed in

her voice. Instinct made me keep her at arm's length. Otherwise she'd rope me in.

"I really need to talk to you, Jack," she murmured in a warmer, softer voice. "About something that concerns us both."

Viv could beguile when she wanted to, didn't I know that. Swiftly, I said, "It'll have to wait."

"Not necessarily. Perhaps we can talk on the phone."

"I don't know when."

"We can do it right now, Jack. Listen to me for a moment, please."

"But—"

"No buts, Jack. I've finished the Brontë book, as you know, and now that I'm not so concentrated on my writing, the matter of Sebastian's death has broken through into my consciousness. It does—"

"Oh God, Viv! Not that old turkey! *Again.* Let it drop!"

"I won't, I can't. Listen to me. Sebastian's death does not sit well with me, not at all."

"He committed suicide," I snapped.

"I accept that. But I need a reason *why* he did it. I need to know. Only then, when I have a resolution, will I be at peace about it. And at peace with myself."

"No one can give you a reason. Only Sebastian knows. He took that secret to the grave with him."

"Not necessarily," she said.

"What do you mean?"

"I've been thinking—"

"What about?" I cut in, groaning inside. How well I knew that tone of hers. It spelled trouble.

"About his life. What he was doing in the last six to eight months of it. Who he was with. And just as importantly, how he was behaving. You know, what frame of mind was he in? Was he troubled? Or happy?"

"He was happy. The day you had lunch. So you claim."

"He was."

"How can you be so sure?"

"That's a stupid question, Jack. I knew him intimately. He *was* happy. Look, I remember how I felt that day, truly I do. And I was pleased for him, pleased he was about to start a new life."

"He was?" I was startled. "What do you mean by a new life?"

"There was a woman, Jack, a new woman in his life. He was in love, and he was planning to marry her."

Flabbergasted, I exclaimed, "You gotta be kidding!"

"I'm not. He told me he was planning to marry in the spring. In fact, he wanted me to meet her and he invited me to the wedding."

"That's sick," I said.

"No, it's not. We were always close. Very, very close. Anyway, don't digress."

Ignoring this admonition, I asked, "Who was the woman?"

"I don't know. He didn't tell me her name. That's the problem. If I knew who she was, I could go and see her. Obviously *you* never met her, since you sounded so surprised when I mentioned her."

"I didn't even *know* about her."

"Did Luciana?"

"No. I'm sure. She would've told me."

"Someone must have met her, Jack, and that's what I'm leading up to. I want to talk to people who worked with Sebastian on the charities in Africa."

"Why the African charities?"

"Because Sebastian said he met her there," Vivienne explained. "He said she was a doctor. A scientist. I want to talk to a lot of people who were involved in his life and activities, in order to get a better perspective about him in that six-month period."

"People might resent that. They might clam up," I pointed out. "They *are* very loyal to him. To his memory."

"I know. But I have the perfect reason. I'm writing a profile about him for the *Sunday Times* Magazine. Sandy Robertson okayed it last night. I'm planning an in-depth profile about the world's greatest philanthropist . . . who was probably the last of the breed. That's one of the reasons I wanted to see you, Jack. I'd like to get your impressions of him during those last few months last year."

"Vivienne, that's ridiculous! Why can't you just let it drop."

"I can't. I wish I could. Rationally, intellectually, I do accept his suicide. Emotionally, I cannot. At least I can't accept that he would kill himself when he was so happy, so positive about the future. It just doesn't sit well with me, I keep telling you that. There's something wrong here, something terribly amiss. Something strange must have happened after we'd lunched on that Monday. I just know it in my bones."

"And you aim to find out? Is that it? Hey, Viv, I have the perfect reason. The lady dumped him."

"Perhaps she did. That's certainly a possibility, I won't argue with you there, Jack. But I don't believe Sebastian would take his life because of a woman, not the Sebastian I know."

"And I know nothing. I can't help. Not with the profile."

"You might think of something, if you wrack your brains. If you really think hard about it, think back to those months last summer."

"I doubt it."

"The day of the funeral, Cyrus suggested I should write a book. A biography of Sebastian."

"The keeper of the flame! Is that your new role, honey?"

"Don't be sarcastic, Jack, it doesn't become you. And I might do it. I just want to be sure I can be absolutely objective about Sebastian. Writing the profile will give me a good idea about that. It'll be a sort of test."

"Who are you planning to interview, Viv?" I asked.

"His colleagues at Locke Industries and at the foundation. One person will lead to another, that's how it usually works. I'll soon understand who knew him the best, knew certain sides to him. I hope to talk to Luciana too."

"Viv, you know better!" I exclaimed. "You'll only get a flea in your ear."

"We'll see."

"Take my word for it, honey."

"Jack?"

"Yes?"

"You were in New York last month for the board meeting at Locke Industries. I just wondered if anyone mentioned anything to you. About the new woman in his life."

"No."

"Mmmm. Interesting. Perhaps they didn't know about her."

"You got it, kid."

"Jack, you will help me with the profile about him, won't you? It's so important to me. Important that I write this, and I do believe it will help me to come to terms with his death."

"Okay," I agreed reluctantly. And against my better judgment. "But there's nothing I know. I hardly saw him last year."

"You might think of something that would give me a clue about his moods, his behavior in those final six months of this life."

"I gotta go. I'll call you. Next week."

"I won't be here. I'm leaving for New York in a couple of days, Jack. I want to start the interviews with some of my old friends at the foundation. It'll be a beginning."

"Have a good trip. Ciao."

"Bye, Jack. I'll be in touch, we'll talk soon."

"Merde!" I said as I slammed the phone down and sat back in my chair, scowling.

"What is it, Jack? What's wrong?" Catherine asked in that calm voice of hers. A voice I had grown accustomed to these past few months.

"It's Vivienne. She's off the wall."

"That's a curious statement to make about someone so balanced and as down-to-earth and rational as she is," Catherine countered.

"She's not rational. Not down-to-earth," I exclaimed heatedly. "Not when it comes to Sebastian. She's obsessed with him. He's been dead five months. She's still ranting and raving about his death. I wish she'd just shut the hell up. Let him rest in peace. I can't stand her when she's like this."

"Like what?"

"Playing the keeper of the flame." I laughed, added, "She's carrying a torch," and laughed again at my play on words.

Catherine did not appear to be amused. She wore a concerned expression.

"From what you've told me, she adored him and you hated him. Never the twain shall meet," Catherine murmured. "You're poles apart when it comes to Sebastian Locke. You'll never agree about him."

"True enough, sweetheart. Vivienne's got a problem. Not enough to do. Her book on the Brontës is finished. Delivered. Now it's Sebastian. She's focused on him. Again. Merde!"

Catherine regarded me thoughtfully for a second or two, then said slowly, "Do you mean she's going to write a book about your father, darling? Is that what you're trying to tell me?"

"Not a book. A profile. For the London *Sunday Times*. The magazine section. The editor she works with okayed it. But there might be a book. My grandfather, the old coot, suggested it. At the funeral. Can you beat that. Jeez! She might do it too. Bet she does. Merde! Merde! Merde!"

"Jack, for heaven's sake, why *are* you so upset? You're being quite childish. Irrational, actually."

"I'm not."

"Whenever your father is involved I'm afraid you are very irrational, darling."

"Vivienne wants to probe. Dig into his life. The last

year of it. *I need to know.* That's what she said. She also said, *I need to know what he was doing. Who he was with. What he was like. His moods. His demeanor. I have to understand him. I want to pinpoint the reason he killed himself.* That's what she just said to me."

"How does she propose to get this information?"

"She's going to talk to people. Interview them."

"Who exactly?"

"People who worked for him. With him. At Locke Industries. At the foundation. Me. Luciana. God knows who else."

"And she's going to write about her conclusions, is that it?"

"Not exactly. She won't dwell on the suicide. Not in the article. Knowing her, she won't mention it. If she does, it'll be one line. The way she felt about him, still feels, it'll be a glowing profile. Flattering. She'll only show his good side. Understanding him, understanding the last few months of his life. That's what's important to her. This is purely personal."

"I see. But I really can't quite understand why you're so upset."

"I wish she'd let it rest. I don't want constant reminders about him. He's dead. Buried. I don't want her digging him up."

"I do think you're being just a little bit silly, darling. You just said she won't write anything bad about him. And I agree with you. From what you've told me, Vivienne's extremely loyal to Sebastian and to his memory."

"She's still in love with him."

"Oh I don't think so, Jack, really I don't. Vivienne's too alive, too sexual, and too sensual a woman to be still hooked on a dead man, from what I've observed of her, at least. Good Lord, no. She believes that life is for the living. It seems to me that she's batty about Kit Tremain. He's her life now, you know, not Sebastian Locke. Trust me on this. I know what I'm talking about, and I know I'm right."

"I guess you are." I immediately changed the subject.

Chapter Fifteen

"There was another woman," I said, staring across the dinner table at Catherine.

She stared back at me and then said, with a light, amused smile, "I'm sure there were lots of women before me, Jack. Quite aside from your two wives. I wouldn't expect it to be otherwise. You're a very attractive man."

"No. No. I'm talking about Sebastian. There was another woman in his life. Just before he died. A new woman," I explained. "I knew nothing about her. No one did. But he told Viv. The day they had lunch. That fateful week he killed himself. He told Viv he was planning to marry her."

"Who was she?" asked Catherine, looking at me alertly.

I shrugged. "No idea. Viv never asked her name. He never gave it. Just said she was a doctor. Viv mentioned it this morning. On the phone. Not before. Don't know why she didn't. I forgot to tell you."

"Presumably he was happy then. How odd that he took his life when he did."

"That's what Viv thinks."

"On the other hand, the nameless woman could have terminated their relationship," Catherine remarked.

I smiled at her. "That's what *I* think."

"What did Vivienne say?"

"That he wouldn't have taken such a drastic step over a failed love affair."

Catherine seemed to mull this over before saying, "Well, I tend to agree with Vivienne."

"But you didn't know him," I protested.

"No, not personally, and you haven't told me much about him. Only odd snippets. But I was quite aware of him long before I met you, Jack," she pointed out. "All the money he gave away to charity. Those huge donations to Bosnia last year. *Everyone* was aware of him. And naturally I'd read a lot about him. A great deal of space was devoted to him in the press." She paused to take a sip of her red wine. "He had half a dozen wives, didn't he?"

"Five."

"Same thing, more or less. He was rich, handsome, famous, so he had a lot going for him. He was sophisticated, I assume? Worldly?"

"Very."

Catherine nodded her head. "I think Vivienne's right. He wouldn't kill himself over a woman. He was too experienced. Anyway, I'm quite sure he could have had any woman he wanted."

"True. Women were mesmerized by him. He and I didn't get on. I've told you that. But I've got to give the devil his due. He was a magnet to women. They fell over themselves. To meet him. Fell at his feet. He didn't encourage that. He was very off-hand with women. But he had *it*. Presence. Charisma. Glamour. Sex appeal. And a fatal charm. Look, he was lethal. As a man. And unpredictable. Even a little crazy, in some ways."

"Mad, bad, and dangerous to know," Catherine mused.

"That about sums it up. You've got a good turn of phrase, sweetheart."

"Oh, it's not *my* phrase, Jack. Another woman said it long before I was born. In the early part of the nineteenth century, to be exact."

"Who?"

"Lady Caroline Lamb. She wrote it in her diary, the first time she met Lord Byron, the poet. What she meant, of course, was that Byron was *emotionally* dangerous. He was already something of a legend in London. Great fame had come to him early, after *Childe Harold* was published in 1812. Women schemed to meet him, squabbled over him. Although he was more chased than the chaser. Later Lady Caroline Lamb completed the phrase when she added, 'That beautiful pale face is my fate.' When she met Byron he had acquired a reputation in the London social world. A reputation for being dangerous and irresistible. Legend and rumor played a big part in all of this, of course. They can be very potent stimulants."

"Mad, bad, and dangerous to know," I repeated. "Yes, that fits Sebastian to a T."

"And no one knew about Sebastian's most recent conquest?" Catherine asked.

"I don't think so. I didn't. Neither did Luciana. She would've told me. Curious that he kept it a secret."

Catherine merely nodded, said nothing.

There was a little silence between us.

Eventually I said, "Do you believe in good genes and bad genes?"

"I'm not sure." Catherine raised a brow. "What are you getting at?"

"Could the compulsion to commit suicide be *genetic*?"

"I just don't know. Why do you ask?"

"Sebastian's half sister Glenda killed herself years ago. His half brother Malcolm did the same, in my opinion. He was in a boating accident on Lake Como. Supposedly an accident. It wasn't, I'm sure. Aunt Fiona, Sebastian's other half sister, became a drug addict. Disappeared. Years ago. She could be alive. Most probably dead though. *Bad genes*?"

"I simply can't answer that, Jack. But how awful, how terribly tragic."

"Yeah. I'm the last. The last of the Mohicans."

Her brow lifted again. Her expression was quizzical.

I grinned. "I'm the last male of the dynasty. Unless I spawn an offspring. Which is unlikely. And Luciana won't ever have kids."

After a moment of looking thoughtful, Catherine asked, "Don't you find that sad, Jack?"

"What?"

"That you're the last of a great American family."

"Not particularly. And I don't think any of them were that great. Least of all Cyrus and Sebastian."

"Why do you hate *them* so much?"

"Do I?"

"That's the way it's sounded to me, whenever you've spoken about them these few months I've known you."

"Sebastian was never a father to me. He was incapable of it. Incapable of loving me. Or anyone else," I replied and realized my voice sounded shrill.

"Vivienne says he loved *her*."

"*She* likes to think that! But he *didn't*. He was nice to her. Nicer than he was to the other wives. But he didn't love her. He couldn't. It wasn't in him. Oh, yeah, he gave lip service to it. But it *was* only that. Trust me."

"Why couldn't Sebastian love anybody?"

"How the hell do I know." I swigged some of my wine, lolled back in the chair. "Something missing in his genes?"

She ignored my question, asked one of her own instead. "What sort of childhood did your father have?"

"God only knows. Awful, I suspect. His mother died giving birth to him. Cyrus brought him up. With a nanny. Then Cyrus remarried. He once told me his nanny *and* his stepmother were hard women."

"It could be disassociation," Catherine muttered, almost to herself.

"What does that mean?" I leaned over the table, my interest quickening.

"It's a psychiatric term. Let me try and put it very simply, as best I can, the way it was once described to me. When a child receives no love, no nurturing at birth and in the very first years of life, that child usually grows up removed from association with others. Thus, the child cannot love because it has not been loved. It doesn't know *how* to love anyone. You'd have to talk to a psychiatrist to get a proper medical explanation of it in detail. But in my opinion, disassociation could very well be the explanation for your father's behavior, his inability to love, if this was the case."

"It was. Take my word for it," I said.

CHAPTER SIXTEEN

Catherine and I lay together in my great four-poster bed, sipping cognac.

I was enjoying the closeness, the intimacy.

Earlier, I had turned off the lamps. The only light came from the fire burning in the hearth. It filled the room with a warm glow. The intermittent crackling of the logs was the only sound. Except for the faint ticking of the clock on the mantel. It was peaceful here.

I was relaxed. At ease with myself. I frequently was when I was alone with Catherine. I was glad I had found her. Glad she was here at the château.

She had lived with another man once. Years ago. She'd told me all about him. It hadn't worked out. Not in the end. When we met in Paris there was no one of importance in her life. That was lucky for me. We were well suited. I liked her braininess. The way her mind worked intrigued me. I couldn't stand dumb women. I'd known a few of those. Too many.

I closed my eyes. Drifting. Thinking. Mostly about Catherine. There was never any pressure with her. Or from her. She allowed me to be me. To be Jack. To her I was her friend. Her lover. I was not the son of the famous Sebastian Locke. I was not John Lyon Locke, the last of the line in a great American family, head of Locke Industries and the Locke Foundation. She did not know that side of me. Nor did she care about it.

Catherine often heard me on the phone with the president of Locke Industries. And with those others who ran the company for me. As they had done for my father. Sometimes I spoke to my assistants at the foundation in front of her. But she paid scant attention to my phone calls. Neither was she curious about my other business interests.

Fortunately she loved the château and the winery. This pleased me. I had started to share my thoughts with her about the wine business. She always listened attentively. She understood my love of the land. My land, my vineyards.

Another aspect of her character was her lack of interest in my wealth. Catherine seemed to be as disdainful of money as Sebastian had been. Material things did not matter to her. This did not trouble me. I only wished she would let me spoil her. Give her gifts occasionally. But she found it hard to accept things from me. Unless it was a book. Or something else that was inexpensive.

She interrupted my thoughts of her when she said softly, touching my shoulder, "Jack, are you asleep?"

"No. Only dozing. Well, half-dozing."

"I've just thought of something."

"What?"

"Did the mysterious woman in your father's life show up at his funeral?"

"No."

"I wonder why not? Don't you think that's peculiar?"

"Not really." I answered. "The funeral was small. A family affair. In Cornwall, Connecticut. It was strictly private. Verboten to anybody not close. Or closely connected to him."

"I see. I'll tell you something, though. If I were in love with a man and engaged to be married to him, and if that man died unexpectedly, I'd be in touch with his family immediately," she exclaimed. "Even if I hadn't met them, even if they didn't know about my existence. I would want to be with them, to share my grief. And I would certainly want to be at his funeral." Catherine paused, bit her lip. "It's strange, Jack, it really is when you think about it. I mean, that she hasn't been in touch with you or Luciana, if only to express her sympathy, give you her condolences."

"She hasn't," I said. "But she could have been at the memorial service for all I know. Hundreds of people were. It was held at the Church of St. John the Divine in Manhattan. Since a public announcement had been made, the world at large knew about it. And came."

Catherine sighed. "And because you never met her, you wouldn't have known whether she was present or not."

"Precisely."

"Do you mind if I ask you something else? Something a little more personal?"

"Shoot."

"Had your father changed his will?"

"No. Why?"

"I just wondered. Often people who are about to commit suicide put their affairs in order."

"His affairs *were* in order, Catherine. Already had been for years. He was made that way. Mr. Efficiency. That was Sebastian."

"No legacy left to a woman you'd never heard of?"

"No. His will was made three years ago. Nothing was changed in it. If there *had* been a legacy to a person I didn't know, I'd have made it my business to find out about her."

"Yes, of course you would, darling. I'm beginning to realize these are stupid questions. I can be such an imbecile at times. Oh dear."

She fell silent.

So did I.

She moved her head and the firelight danced in her long hair, turned it into a shimmering cascade of flame around her pale face. She moved again, turned her head the other way, exposed a long white neck. Catherine had a swanlike neck, as Antoinette Delaney had had.

In a rush of words, I said, "You've often reminded me of someone, of my Special Lady, but never more so than you do tonight, Catherine. It's uncanny."

"Your Special Lady? Who's that?" This was asked softly, but I noticed that her face had tightened.

"Her name was Antoinette Delaney. She was Vivienne's mother. I loved her from the first moment she came into my life. When I was six. She was like a mother to me. Kind, warm, adoring."

"And I remind you of her?" she asked, sounding slightly incredulous. "Am I motherly?"

I laughed. "She was very beautiful. Like you. You have her coloring. The same red hair, white skin, green eyes. She was as tall as you are. As willowy and graceful."

Catherine smiled.

I said, "I've not told you this before . . . but my own mother died when I was two. Of bone-marrow cancer. Sebastian married Christa about two years later. They had Luciana together. But Christa was an alcoholic. Sebastian put her in a clinic. To dry out. She never came back to live with us. He didn't want her around us. Or anywhere near him. I think he despised her."

"So Antoinette was a friend of your father's? Or was she his lover?"

"Yes, his mistress. We were together for six years. All of us. In Connecticut and here at the château. They were wonderful years. Whatever I am today, she helped to make me. Any good there is in me comes from her. From her influence. And her love."

"That's such a lovely thing to say. So touching. And she must have been quite unique. No wonder you call her your Special Lady. But why was she only with you for six years?"

"She died."

"Oh Jack, I'm sorry. How tragic. She can't have been very old. What did she die of?"

"She had an accident. At least everyone said it was an accident. She fell down the basement steps at Sebastian's farm. She died instantly. She broke her neck."

"Why do you say, *everyone said it was an accident* in that peculiar tone of voice, as if you don't think it was?" Catherine's eyes fastened on mine.

I didn't respond. I looked away.

"Do you think she was murdered?"

"I've never known what to think," I said at last, turning to her. "It seems odd that she was going into the basement. In the early hours of the morning. And if she was pushed, who could've done it? Who would've wanted to anyway? Sebastian was in Manhattan. On business. Aldred was at the farm. He was my father's major domo. We were there. Luciana and me. And her nanny. And the housekeeper. Sebastian arrived at about seven. From New York. He said he'd come up early to go riding with Antoinette. But I've often wondered about that."

"Are you suggesting that Sebastian pushed her?"

"I don't know." I'd never confided this to anyone else before. I took a deep breath. Then I plunged. "He might have," I muttered.

"But why?"

"I don't know."

Catherine shook her head slowly. "Shades of Amy Robsart."

"Who's Amy Robsart?" I asked.

"She was married to Lord Robert Dudley, and on September the eighth in the year 1560 her body was found at the foot of the staircase in Cumnor Hall, where she was then living. Her death caused a terrible flurry at the time, became something of a cause célèbre, and in fact, it rocked the whole of England. You see, Robert Dudley was the closest friend of Queen Elizabeth the First. They were actually childhood friends. He was her dearest and most beloved companion. Never far from her sight. After she became Queen of England she bestowed many honors on him. He had a very high rank at court, and he was her Master of the Horse—"

"And rumored to be the Queen's lover. If I remember my British history correctly," I volunteered.

Catherine nodded. "That's right. Amy's death was a mystery, and some people tried to implicate Robert Dudley. Even the Queen was under suspicion briefly. But since he was at court with Queen Elizabeth he couldn't have pushed her himself."

"But he might have hired someone to push her . . . is that what you're getting at?"

"More or less. Certainly the stakes were high enough."

"In what sense?"

"With his wife's death, Robert Dudley was a free man . . . free to marry Queen Elizabeth."

"Would that have been possible?"

"Constitutionally, yes. And she did love him. Just as he loved her. But Elizabeth Tudor didn't want to marry anyone. Not really. She didn't want to share her power. In any case, I don't think he was involved or implicated in his wife's death. Neither was the Queen. She was far too smart to be a party to that kind of thing. As you know, I earned a doctorate in English history. What you don't know is that I specialized in the Tudor period. It's my forte. And in my opinion, Amy Robsart Dudley killed herself. I've actually written about this."

"And she did it because of her husband's involvement with the Queen?"

"No. Amy was known to have cancer of the breast. She was ill, and she may have grown despondent. Anyway, that's my considered opinion. She did herself in by throwing herself down the stairs."

"Antoinette wasn't ill," I remarked, thinking out loud. "The autopsy would have brought that to light. If she had been. So I suppose her death *was* an accident."

"I think it must have been. I didn't know your father, but I doubt very much that he would commit such a crime. Or hire someone to do it for him. Why would he? What motive did he have? He wasn't married to Antoinette. If he'd wanted to break up with her, he could have done so easily enough. He could have left her. It's as simple as that. He didn't have to resort to murder."

"I guess you're right."

Catherine moved closer to me, put her arms around me, and held me tightly. "Don't let something like this haunt you, as I believe it has been doing for years and years."

"Off and on," I admitted.

After a moment Catherine got out of bed and went into the bathroom.

I lay there thinking about my father. I wished she had not brought him up. Certainly not tonight. Not now. The discussion had been going on half the day. Ever since Vivienne's phone call this morning.

I groaned under my breath. I was sick of it all. And I was relieved Vivienne was going to New York later this week. When she was pounding someone else about Sebastian Locke she was leaving me alone. Vivienne maddened me at times.

Catherine came back, gliding across the floor. She got into bed, curling up against me, kissing me lightly on the cheek.

"You don't want this, do you, darling?" she asked as

she took the brandy balloon out of my hands and put it on her bedside table.

"Well," I began, but she stopped the flow of words with her lips.

She began to kiss me, lightly at first, but then the kisses became hot, fervent, passionate. Her tongue grazed mine as she slid it into my mouth. I kissed her hard, wrapping my arms around her body, pulling her on top of me as I did.

We stayed locked together for several moments. Then I broke away, cupped a hand under one of her breasts, and brought my mouth down to the nipple. I heard the soft groan in the back of her throat as I kissed her breast.

Eventually Catherine pulled away and trailed her mouth across my chest and onto my stomach. Then she slithered down in the bed. She crouched over me, touching me everywhere. Caressing the most vulnerable parts of me. I heard my own groans as she began to make love to me. She was a versatile lover. The most imaginative I'd known. Mindless fucking was not her style. Thankfully.

Her long hair trailed across my thighs and her mouth was suddenly on me, encircling me. I closed my eyes. Her warmth and softness enveloped me. Usually I became a potent lover within seconds, whenever she did this. Tonight nothing happened. I remained flaccid.

The foreplay was going on far too long. I soon began to realize that. She was growing tired. Suddenly, mortified and angry with myself, I stopped her ministrations. Gently I pushed her away.

Catherine was startled. She gaped at me.

"Be back in a minute," I muttered and stumbled into the bathroom.

I locked the door and leaned against it.

I was breathing hard. That awful, familiar sick feeling was engulfing me. I knew it well. For a moment I thought I was going to vomit. Bring back the brandy. I felt nauseated, dizzy. I steadied myself. The feeling finally passed as I stood there in the darkened bathroom, gripping the door jamb.

I was impotent. *Again.* So far, until tonight, it had only happened twice with Catherine. At the beginning of our relationship. But not since. I had begun to believe that my problem had been cured. Apparently not. "Merde," I whispered. I snapped my eyes shut. "Merde," I said again.

Eventually the panic subsided. I grew calmer inside. Switching on the light, I crossed the room. I splashed cold water on my face, dried it, stood staring at myself in the mirror.

The image I saw reflected there was not Jack. It was a pale imitation of Sebastian Locke. I resembled him greatly. There was no denying whose son I was. Even though I had his features, mine were less distinct. They were not so well defined. Not so sculpted as his had been. True, my eyes were also blue. But diluted, watery. His had been blindingly blue. Brilliant in his tan face. My complexion was pale. I always looked washed out. His dark hair had been thick and wavy. Mine was dark too. And straight. I was not in the least bit dashing and dynamic. As he had been. Nor was I loaded with his kind of irresistible sex appeal.

I bet *he* was never impotent, I thought, continuing to stare at myself with a degree of disdain. I bet *he* had a permanent erection.

I hated being a faded carbon copy of that man. I hated being his son. I hated him. I hated the memory of him.

After gulping a glass of cold water, I steadied myself, pushed the anger down. Deep down inside. Buried it again. Taking total control of myself, I pushed open the door. Slowly I walked back into the bedroom.

Catherine had put on her robe. She was crouched in front of the fire. Staring into the flames. Looking pensive, lost. I took my silk robe from the bottom of the bed, slipped into it. Went to join her by the fireside. I sat down next to her on the rug.

"I'm sorry," I said quietly, taking hold of her hand. "Too much wine. Followed by too much cognac."

She was silent. She merely lifted her head and stared at me.

Again I said, "Sorry."

"It's *all right*, Jack, really it is," she murmured in her softest voice. She smiled and instantly the worried expression in her eyes evaporated. Lifting her shoulders in a slight shrug, she went on, "We've many more nights together, I hope . . . hundreds of nights. We do, don't we, Jack?"

"Yes. I won't drink so much in future. It won't happen again," I promised. I wondered if I was whistling in the dark.

Leaning forward, she kissed me lightly on the lips and touched my face. "Don't look so concerned, so upset. It's of no consequence."

But it is. To me, I thought. I said, "You're a beautiful woman, Catherine, a very desirable woman . . . "

Leaning back, Catherine looked into my face. Then she kissed me. I returned the kiss. When we drew apart she touched my mouth lightly, traced the line of my lips with her finger. Then she lay down with her head in my lap, gazing up at me unwaveringly.

Her eyes did not leave my face. I stared back at her intently. Wondering what was going on behind that lovely face.

After a moment or two, she said, "You're *very* special to me, Jack. You've given me so much in the last few months. Love, warmth, understanding, tenderness, and passion. You must know how much I love you," she continued, her voice low, vibrant. "You must know I'm in love with you, Jack."

"Yes," was all I dared to say.

I noticed a little smile playing around her mouth as she reached up with both arms. She placed them around my neck tightly and pulled me down to her. Kissing her swiftly, I broke free of her embrace. I was afraid. Afraid of being inadequate. I lay alongside her, resting on one elbow, staring into her face once more. She fascinated me.

"What is it, Catherine?" I whispered. "You look as if you have a big secret."

"I don't have one, though."

"But you're wearing a secretive sort of smile."

"Not secretive. Smug, perhaps."

"Why smug?"

"Because I have you. Because I'm with you. Because you're the best lover I've ever had. Oh Jack darling—" She did not finish. She broke off, sighing deeply, contentedly. "I've never felt like this before. It's never been like this for me. Never ever. Not with any other man. You excite me so much. I want you. I want you to make love to me. *Now*."

"Oh Catherine . . . sweetheart . . . "

"Make love to me, Jack. *Please*."

"Catherine, I don't know . . . "

"Don't be afraid," she whispered and took off her robe, sitting up to do so, turning to smile at me.

She looked more ethereal than ever in the light from the fire. Her hair was a burnished coppery mass shot through with red and gold, tumbling down over her smooth white shoulders.

"Come to me, Jack," she said, reaching out for me. "Take me. Make me yours again. I want to give myself to you. I want you. Only you, Jack."

I felt the heat slowly rising in me. Desire began to throb through me as she spoke. Shrugging off my robe, I almost fell into her outstretched arms. I pushed aside my fear of failing her. I was going to take her. Love her as I had never loved her. Or any other woman.

I lay on top of her long, lithe body, fitting mine to hers. I kissed her neck and her breasts. I pushed my eager, trembling hands into the cloud of her red hair.

And as I continued to kiss her neck, her shoulders, and her face, she began to whisper to me. Her whispered words were tantalizing, erotic. They drove me on. Filled me with excitement.

It was not long before I found myself fully aroused. I was able to slide into her swiftly. Catherine clung to me. Her fingers pressed into my shoulder blades. She wound her long legs around my back and locked her ankles. I slipped my hands under her buttocks. Brought her closer to me. Finally I was truly joined to her.

I forgot everything. Everyone. I could think only of Catherine.

CHAPTER SEVENTEEN

"I understand why you never want to leave this place," Catherine said, linking her arm through mine as she gazed out across the landscape. "It's extraordinary. Breathtaking really. And quite magical."

"Yes, it is," I agreed. I was pleased with her. She had expressed my sentiments exactly. Captured in a few choice words what I felt about the estate.

Catherine and I stood on top of a hill, the highest point on my land. We were above the vineyards which grew on the slopes of the hillsides. They stopped short at the château's gardens. To the right of the château were the woods; to the extreme left were the fields and the château's farm. The Home Farm it was called.

Just beyond the farm was the winery. There were many buildings clustered together, with vast cellars underground. It was here that the grapes were turned into wine.

I glanced around.

I saw the panoramic view as if through Catherine's eyes. And it *was* a magical sight. The sky was a pure, pale blue. Very clear, blameless, without cloud. It was a bright, sun-filled afternoon. Almost balmy. Hardly any wind. It was only the middle of March. But spring was already here in Provence.

The land had undergone a change lately. I had noticed its sudden metamorphosis. New grass sprouting on the lawns. Tender green sprigs bursting open on the trees. Spring flowers shooting up in the gardens, brightening the many borders. They were vivid rafts of color against the dark soil.

I took a deep breath. The air here was clean, pure, bracing.

Turning to Catherine, I said, "I promised to show you the vineyards. Weeks ago now. So come on. Let's go. I think there's finally something to see."

Taking hold of her hand, I led her along the narrow path that cut down through the first slope.

"Look!" I exclaimed. I was suddenly excited and bent down, hunkering close to the vines. "The buds are appearing. Here! And here!" I pointed them out to her.

Catherine crouched down to look. She said, in a surprised voice, "But they're so tiny, Jack. I can't believe they become grapes."

"They do."

"How does that happen? I know nothing about vineyards. Please explain to me."

"I'll give it a try. First let me tell you about the *cycle* of the vine. It begins with the winter rest. In February and March the sap rises. Now this—" I broke off, pointed to a bud. "*This* tiny thing is what we call a spring bud. In April the budbreak occurs. That means the bud opens more fully. A few weeks later the leaves appear. By May the leaves open and spread out more fully. In June the vines will have started to flower. Later these flowers turn into very, very small grapes. Through July and August we will see their growth. Late August, early September, they start ripening. Finally, in October, the grapes are mature. In November the leaves fall. The cycle starts all over again. The winter rest begins, etcetera."

"It all sounds very simple," Catherine said, looking at me. "But I'm quite certain it isn't, is it?"

"No, it's not. It's much more complex. Especially the tending of the vines. The nurturing of them. Through the winter months. And the rest of the year. I tried to make it easy for you to understand."

"Thank you, and presumably the grapes are picked when they are ripe."

I nodded. "That's when the *vendangeurs*, the grape harvesters, come to pick them. *Porteurs*, the grape carriers, take the grapes away in *bénatons*, those big baskets you've seen lying around. They move them to the end of each row in the vineyard. From there the *bénatons* are carried to the winery, and the grapes are put in the cellars ready for vinification."

"Is the picking done by hand?"

"Yes. Olivier and I prefer it to mechanized harvesting. That's become popular in some parts in France. But it would be difficult here. On these slopes. Also, there's less chance of damage when the grapes are hand picked."

"What happens next in the process?"

"The wine is made, of course. It's stored in huge vats and casks in the *cuverie*. The vat room. I think I showed it to you. When I took you down into the *cave*, the big wine cellars, at Christmas."

She nodded. "I remember." She tilted her head to one side. "How do you know so much about wine making?"

"I don't know *that* much," I said. "I've still got a lot to learn. But it was mostly Olivier. He taught me. He started me out. When I was sixteen. When Sebastian gave me the château. Fourteen years later I don't know half he does. Even though I went to the University of Toulouse. To study the science of wine and wine making. Oenological training in France lasts for four years.

"I did get my diploma. But I'm not up to Olivier's standards. Not yet. He's one of the best oenologists around. Considered to be a great wine scientist and wine maker."

"He seems very dedicated from what I've observed," Catherine remarked.

"Over the years he's been improving everything. From the vintage of our red wines to the bottling of it. He's made immense progress in the last ten years. Because of Olivier Marchand our label, Côtes de Château d'Cose, is now considered to be a superior appellation."

"And he's your partner you said the other day."

"Not my partner. I've given him a piece of the business. He deserves it. All the years he's devoted to the winery. To the château. The running of the entire estate."

We began to walk down the slopes, heading toward the château.

After a moment or two, Catherine said, "What made your father buy the estate in the first place? I'm very curious about that. Was he interested in wine?"

"He liked it. Especially champagne. Veuve Cliquot. But he was just doing a good turn. For somebody. As usual."

"What kind of good turn?"

"A good turn for a widow woman. The widow of the man who owned Château d'Cose. About thirty years ago Sebastian was in Africa. Kenya. He met a Frenchman. In Nairobi. A man called Pierre Peyfrette. Through a mutual friend. Over the years they became close. Sebastian often stayed here. About twenty-three years ago Pierre was killed. In a car crash. Driving down here. From Paris. His widow Gabriella was at a loss. Didn't know what to do about the winery. The running of it. They had no sons to inherit. Just a young daughter. About my age. Gabriella wanted to sell the property, but there were no takers. Nobody was interested. It wasn't making money. Not in those days, anyway. So Sebastian took it off her hands. Bought it from Gabriella. Paid her very well. Maybe even too much. But it helped her start her life over. She moved to Paris with her little girl."

"I see. Did he ever run it? I mean the way you're running it now, Jack?"

"Good God, no! Not Sebastian! He found Olivier Marchand. Put him in charge. What a wise move that was. I was seven when I first came here. And I fell in love with the château."

"It's your home," she said very simply, in a quiet voice, her expression full of understanding. "You belong here. You love the winery and the vineyards.

You're very, very lucky, you know. You've found your true place in the world, found the work you want to do, your vocation. Found the life you want to lead. So many people don't. Not ever."

"But you have, Catherine. You know what you want," I said. "Know where you're going. You're like Vivienne in certain ways. You both have tunnel vision. Immense focus. You're a very functioning woman. And hardworking, thank God. I can't abide idle women."

"Neither can I. It's impossible for me to relate to them. I've nothing in common, nothing to say. I always knew I wanted to read history at Oxford, and later lecture and write about it after I earned my doctorate. I was fortunate in that I had a flair for writing as well as a studious nature."

"How's the book coming along? You've certainly been hard at it these past few weeks. Working like a regular little eager beaver."

She laughed, her face lighting up. "I find this place so conducive to work. And actually, in some ways, the book's proving easier to write than I thought." She shook her head. "Except that I'm not sure who's going to read it."

"A lot of people," I asserted. "Take my word for it."

Catherine laughed again. "I can't. I don't believe there is anyone around who is interested in Fulk Nerra, Count of Anjou, war lord and predator, known as the Black Hawk, founder of the Angevin dynasty and the Plantagenet line. Perhaps it only matters to me that the house of Anjou continued on its unrelenting course for well over a century, culminating in 1154 when Fulk's descendant Henry Plantagenet, Count of Anjou, was crowned King of England, married Eleanor of Aquitaine, and sired a son who became the famous Richard *Coeur de Lion*.

"I'm interested," I reassured her. I meant what I said. "You're a good storyteller. Even though you're dealing with facts not fiction. You've intrigued *me* when you've talked about the French-English connection.

"It sounds as if Henry and Eleanor had a real soap opera going. All their lives."

"That's one way of putting it," Catherine replied with a loud guffaw, looking amused. "And I suppose their lives together did have sort of . . . operatic overtones, what with their competitive, quarrelsome sons, Eleanor's scheming and meddling, Henry's philandering, and his constant banishment of her. He was always shoving her off to one of their many castles."

"It would make a helluva good film," I pointed out.

"Somebody beat me to it. A screenwriter. James Goldman. He wrote *The Lion in Winter*, which was all about Henry Plantagenet and Eleanor of Aquitaine."

"Peter O'Toole and Katherine Hepburn! That's right! I saw it. And it *was* a nutty family. Dysfunctional. Just like the royals today. I guess it's all in the genes."

"Not in this instance. The Windsors are not descended from the Plantagenets," Catherine replied. "They are of German descent through Queen Victoria and her consort Prince Albert. He was her cousin and all German. So was she, as a matter of fact. Her mother was a German princess and her father the Duke of Kent. He was descended from the Hanoverian kings who were invited to rule England because of their Stuart connection. In a way, Victoria was born because of the scramble by the brothers of George the Fourth to produce an heir. But going back to the

Plantagenets, they were eventually eclipsed by the Tudors. When Elizabeth the First died, the throne of England went to her distant relative, James Stuart, King of Scotland."

I laughed. "Whatever you say, Catherine. But I bet a lot of people *will* read your book. Because you tell it all so well. Make it sound so . . . modern."

"I guess human nature doesn't change much, Jack. Anyway, the Plantagenets were very colorful. But don't forget, I'm not really writing about them, but about Fulk Nerra. Nobody's interested in him. Except for me and my editor."

"Don't be so sure. Listen, far be it from me to tell you what to write. But get more of the Plantagenets into the story. I guarantee it'll be a best-seller."

"From your mouth to God's ears, darling," she said, still laughing.

We had reached the bottom of the slopes where the vineyards grew, all thirty-three acres. I paused, took hold of Catherine's arm affectionately. "I've got to work for a few hours. With Olivier. What about you? Are you going back to do more on your book?"

"For a while, and then I thought I would go riding. I think a good gallop across the fields will do me good. Blow a few cobwebs away. Would you mind awfully if I rode Black Jack? He's quite easy for me to handle."

"I told you before, you can ride any horse in the stable. Of course you can take Black Jack."

Leaning into me, she gave me a resounding kiss on the cheek. "Thank you. Have a good afternoon. Don't work too hard."

I smiled at her. "Nor you."

She was walking away, walking toward the château when I called after her, "Catherine!"

She swung around. "Yes? What is it?"

"How about dinner in Aix tonight? We've been cooped up here far too long."

"That's a lovely idea, darling."

"I'll make a reservation at Clos de la Violette. Is that okay?"

"Only perfect." She waved and went on her way.

I strolled toward the winery. As I passed the Home Farm I slowed. I almost went in to see Madame Clothilde. She ran the farm. As her mother had done before her. I had known her since I was a little boy. She had been a teenager then. Her husband Maurice was one of our vignerons, who worked in the vineyards. But he also helped out on the farm, along with their daughter, Hélène, and son, Vincent.

She always made me very welcome, whipped up a café au lait in an instant. Brought out a warm brioche, or a slice of tarte tatin.

My mouth watered. But I hurried on. Olivier was waiting for me. He wanted me to take a look at some bottles of wine. Quite a lot of bottles. He thought there might be something wrong with them. I wondered if they were bottle sick. I hoped it was only that. Wine that was bottle sick usually rectified itself if left to its own devices.

Chapter Eighteen

"There's a thin veil on the surface of this batch of wine," Olivier said when I found him in the bottling plant.

"*Maladie de la fleur*," I exclaimed as I walked over to join him. I was referring to the flower disease which was the most frequent form of spoilage in wine. It was the yeasts that created the scum, or veil, on top of the wine.

"You're right, Jacques," Olivier responded. "But fortunately it is only the young wine which we made last year. Not so bad after all. And not too much of it either, only a couple of casks. Hardly a great tragedy."

I nodded and said, "On my way over here I wondered if the wine might just be bottle sick."

"No, more than that. And this spoilage is only minor."

"We'll have to ditch the wine," I asserted.

"Probably. However, let us not dwell on it, since we

rarely have any spoilage. There's another reason I wanted to see you, Jacques, about something much more important. I want you to come with me to the *cave*."

"Okay, let's go." Turning on my heels I led the way. I knew he had a pleasant surprise for me. I could tell from his face.

Together we went down into the cellars.

These covered an immense area underground. It was here that the wine was brought to maturation and also sorted in casks, vats, and bottles.

There was a small wine-tasting area at one end of the red wine maturation cellar, and this was where Olivier was heading. Racks of wine had been arranged to create a two-sided corner. There were several chairs grouped around a small table. On this stood the mandatory white candle in its holder, a box of matches, various implements, and a fresh white linen napkin neatly folded.

Olivier had already placed a bottle of wine and two glasses on the table. The first thing he did was light the candle.

I stood watching him. He was tall, and he stooped over the table slightly as he began to open the wine. Olivier was my mentor, teacher, and friend. He was a good-looking man in a quiet, understated way. At sixty he was twice my age. But he looked much younger than his years. Maybe because he was a happy man. He loved his wife, his children, his work, and the bastide where he lived with his family. This charming old country house, part of my property, was situated across the fields near the orchards. He and his wife, Claudette, had made it a warm, welcoming home.

I watched Olivier opening the bottle. As usual I was struck by the way he worked on it. Delicately. Carefully. Like a surgeon. After cutting the red metal capsule around the neck of the bottle he removed it. This was so that he could see the wine in the bottle neck later. He then removed the cork, his movements smooth, gentle. I knew he did not want to disturb the sediment. Once the cork was out, he smelled both ends. Next he wiped the neck of the bottle inside and out with the white napkin. Finally, holding the bottle above the candle's flame, he peered at the color of the wine in the neck and nodded to himself.

A smile of pleasure came to his face. "Ah, Jacques, you are going to be pleased with this. I know you are."

After pouring two glasses, he handed one to me.

We raised our glasses to each other.

"Santé, Jacques," he said.

"Santé, Olivier."

We both sipped.

I rolled the wine around in my mouth, savoring it. How delicious it was. Soft, velvety, yet full-bodied. I held the glass up to the light. The wine was a deep red color. A beautiful red. Bringing the glass to my nose, I sniffed. Immediately I detected the perfume of violets. And something else, something not quite discernable.

"It's the red you put down in 1986," I said, grinning at him. "You used three grapes to make it. The Mourvèdre, the Syrah, and the Cinsaut. The first two for their deep red color and hint of violets in the taste. The Cinsaut also for its depth of color as well as the softness it brings to the other two."

Olivier beamed at me. "Correct. Well done, Jacques. It has aged well, don't you think?"

"You bet. You've created a wonderful wine. A *great* wine. Looking back, I remember how good the weather was that year. You said the wine would have a wonderful life span because of that."

"Thankfully, I was right. I think, though, that we must start shipping," he said. "The wine is ready. It must go out."

"I'm in favor. So let's do that. And let's have another glass of it. I'm sorry I didn't bring Catherine with me. She'd have enjoyed tasting this."

Olivier filled my glass.

I raised it to him. "Here's to you, Olivier. Congratulations."

"Ah, Jacques, do not congratulate me in this manner. We both worked on the wine."

I laughed, shook my head. "Oh no, we didn't. I was all of twenty-one. Knew nothing. Green behind the ears. I was still at Yale nine years ago. This is *your* wine. You created it, made it. You deserve all the credit for it, Olivier."

"Merci, Jacques. You are very generous, as usual."

For the next couple of hours I worked at my desk in my office in the winery.

There were accounts to study, figures to go over. I had been putting the job off for days. But I knew I had to get the paperwork out of the way. Today was as good a time as any. Gritting my teeth, I buckled down to it.

I worked until four o'clock. Finally it was all done.

After putting the account books away, I picked up the phone, dialed the restaurant in Aix. I made a reservation for dinner.

When I left the office a few minutes later I took with me the half-finished bottle of wine Olivier had given me. I wanted Catherine to taste it. I was proud of this wine. Proud of Olivier for having created it.

I walked out of the front door and into the sunshine, into the most glorious afternoon. I strolled along slowly, glancing about as I did. Everything looked so well kept. This pleased me. I wanted the estate to be in good order.

The château ahead of me stood on flat ground. It was surrounded on three sides by gently sloping hillsides clad in vineyards. They rose up behind the vineyards like a giant flaring collar. Or, as Catherine said the other day, a huge Elizabethan ruff. The gardens and the fields were spread out in front of the château, splendid now in the golden light of the fading day.

To me this was the most idyllic spot in the world. I had always been happy here. Even when I was married, my difficult wives had not been able to ruin it for me. I had simply tuned them out. Tuned into the land and the vineyards. Gone my own way. And I never wanted to be any place but here.

Out of the corner of my eye I saw a sudden flash of color. I veered to my left, made for the wooden fence at the side of the narrow road where I was standing.

Leaning against the fence, I scanned the horizon. Then I saw it again. That flash of bright blue. Suddenly I could see Catherine in the distance, saw the flowing red hair, vivid against the blue sweater she was wearing.

Catherine was galloping across one of the fields, her hair streaming out behind her. She was a good horse-woman. I knew that. But for a reason I didn't immediately understand I held my breath. When she took the first hedge I cringed. I was worried she was going to be thrown. Just as Antoinette had been thrown that day at Laurel Creek Farm.

I gripped the edge of the fence tightly, losing my grip on the bottle as I did. It fell on the grass. I left it there. I simply stood numbly staring at the figure in the distance. Waiting for her to fall off her horse . . .

The clock stopped. Its hands rolled back. I was pulled into my childhood.

A terrible memory I had kept locked inside me for twenty-two years broke free. It rose at last to the surface of my mind.

I was eight years old again. I was back at Laurel Creek Farm.

I was playing in the field with my red ball and bat when it happened. Antoinette was riding toward me, taking the hedge. And then she was off the horse, sailing through the air, falling, falling.

I dropped my bat and ball and ran as fast as I could. "Antoinette! Antoinette!" I cried. I was afraid. Afraid she was dead. Or badly hurt.

She had been thrown by Tyger Bright just as she jumped the hedge. Now she lay there in a crumpled heap. Her face was the color of chalk. Her hair, spread out around her face, looked more firey than ever against those pale cheeks.

Her eyes were closed. My fear spiraled. My teeth

began to chatter. *I thought she really was dead.* I knelt down next to her. Touched her face with my hand. She didn't stir. Yes, she *was* dead. Tears came into my eyes.

"Antoinette. Oh Antoinette. Speak to me," I whispered, bringing my face close to hers. But I knew she wouldn't speak again.

"Get out of the way, Jack!" Sebastian shouted, bringing his horse to a shuddering standstill, jumping down onto the grass. "You can't do anything. You're just a little boy." Pushing me to one side, he knelt next to her, touched her face, as I had done.

"Run, Jack," he said urgently, looking up at me. "Run to the kitchen. Ask Bridget to bring a damp face-cloth. And find Aldred. Tell him to come here."

I was immobilized. I stood there staring at Antoinette.

"What's wrong with you? Do as I say!" my father screamed. "Are you an imbecile? Go to the house, boy. Get Aldred. I need a man here to help me, not a child."

I ran. All the way back to the farm. I was panting when I found Bridget in the kitchen. "Antoinette fell. Off her horse. Wet cloth. My father wants a wet face-cloth. Take it to him please, Bridget."

Before Bridget could say anything to me, Aldred appeared. "What's wrong, Jack?" he asked quietly. "It's not like you to cry. Speak to me, child. What's wrong?"

Bridget said, "Mrs. Delaney's had an accident. Her horse threw her. Jack says Mr. Locke wants a damp facecloth."

"He wants *you* to go," I said, tugging at Aldred's

sleeve. "He needs a man to help. Not a child. That's what he said."

Aldred stared at me for a moment, frowning, but made no comment. He turned and raced out of the kitchen. Bridget followed him. I ran out of the house after them.

"I'm afraid to move her," I heard my father say to Aldred as I staggered up to them a few moments later. "That could be dangerous. Something might be broken."

"Here, Mr. Locke, let's put this damp cloth on her face," Bridget said. "It'll revive her. Yes, she's sure to come around in a few minutes."

"Thank you, Bridget," Sebastian said, taking the cloth from her. He placed it on Antoinette's forehead.

Aldred and my father spoke softly together. I couldn't hear them. I knew they didn't want me to know what they were saying.

She was dead. And they didn't want to tell me. I began to cry again. I pressed my balled fists to my streaming eyes.

"Stop that at once, Jack!" Sebastian said sharply, in a harsh tone. "Don't be such a big baby."

"She's dead," I said and began to sob.

"No, she's not," Sebastian snapped. "She's just unconscious."

"I don't believe you," I wailed.

"It's all right, Jack," Antoinette murmured, finally opening her eyes at last, looking straight at me. And only at me. "Don't cry, my darling. It was just a little tumble. Really, I'm fine, angel."

I was so relieved I sat down hard on the grass.

"Where do you hurt, Antoinette?" my father asked,

searching her face. "Can you straighten out your legs?"

"I think so," Antoinette said and did so as she spoke.

"Are you in any kind of pain, Mrs. Delaney?" Aldred asked.

"None whatsoever. I just feel rather shaken up, that's all."

"Let's get you upright, darling," Sebastian said. "Do you think you can sit?" he asked, looking at her in concern.

"I'm sure I can. Help me, please, Sebastian, would you?"

He did so. Once she was upright, she moved her head from side to side, stretched out her arms somewhat tentatively. Then she stretched her legs again.

"I'm sure there's nothing broken. I'm not really hurt, perhaps just a bit bruised," Antoinette remarked with a light laugh. "Although as I say that I think I might have sprained my ankle. I suddenly feel a twinge or two, can you help me to my feet, Sebastian?"

A moment later my beloved Antoinette, my Special Lady, was standing in front of me. She was alive. Not dead. My tears ceased instantly when she looked down at me, rumpled my hair, and smiled. "You see, Jack darling, I'm as good as new."

However, she had sprained her ankle. At least she said it felt funny. So my father lifted her in his arms and carried her all the way back to the farm.

He took her up to her bedroom and came out after a few minutes. Bridget was sent in to help her undress. Later Doctor Simpson came to examine Antoinette's ankle. "Just to be sure it's not broken," my father told

Luce and me. "And also to be sure she hasn't hurt herself in any other way."

After supper I went to Antoinette's room and tapped on the door. My father opened it. He refused to let me in to say good night to her. "Antoinette's resting," he said. "You can see her tomorrow, Jack." Without another word he closed the door in my face.

I slumped down on the floor next to the grandfather clock in the corner of the upstairs hall. I would wait until he left. Wait until he went to bed. Then I could creep in to kiss her cheek, to say good night.

I must have fallen asleep in the darkened hall. It was the sounds that woke me. The groaning. The moaning. And then the strangled cry. A split second later I heard Antoinette's voice. "Oh God! Oh God!" she exclaimed. There was a little cry again. "Don't—" The rest of her sentence was muffled.

I scrambled to my feet, ran across the hall. I burst into her bedroom. It was dim, shadowy. But I could see my father in the light from the bedside lamp. He was naked. He was on top of Antoinette. Holding her face in his hands. He was hurting her. I knew it.

"Stop it! Stop it!" I screamed. I flew at him, grabbed hold of his leg.

My father was strong, very athletic. He moved swiftly. Jumping off the bed he grabbed hold of me, lifted me up, and carried me across the floor. As he marched out of the room with me I looked back. Antoinette was covering her naked body with the sheet.

She saw me staring and blew me a kiss. "Go to bed, darling, that's a good boy," she said and smiled at me lovingly. "Sweet dreams."

I cried myself to sleep. I was just a little boy. Only

eight. And so I couldn't help her. I couldn't protect her from my father. He was back in her room hurting her. I couldn't do anything about it.

The next morning Antoinette was present at breakfast as she usually was. It seemed to me that she had never looked so beautiful. She was quiet. Lost in her thoughts. Whenever I looked at her she smiled at me in that special way she had. My father glowered at me over the rim of his coffee cup. I waited for him to chastise me about my behavior the night before but he did not. He didn't even mention it.

Later when we were alone, Antoinette gave me lots of hugs. And she kissed the top of my head and told me I was the best boy in the whole world, her boy, and that she loved me very much. She asked me to help her cut flowers for the vases, and we went out to the garden and spent the morning together.

I blinked several times and took a deep breath as Catherine came cantering up to the fence.

"Are you all right?" she asked, leaning forward, peering at me over Black Jack's head.

"Yes. Why?"

"You look a bit strange, that's all."

"I'm okay." I bent down, retrieved the bottle of wine from the grass. I regretted that I had dropped it so clumsily.

"Olivier has produced a remarkable wine," I confided. "Possibly a *great* one. The weather was excellent in 1986. The grapes were good. I wanted you to taste it. But I've probably ruined it. Dropping the bottle the way I did."

"Let's try it anyway," she answered. She gave me a wide smile, saluted, and added as she rode off, "See you in a couple of minutes."

I walked up to the château, my mind still focused on Antoinette and Sebastian. I had not thought of that awful incident since it happened. It had lain dormant for twenty-two years. But now that I had finally remembered it I understood everything. Understood that this was when I had first begun to hate my father.

Chapter Nineteen

A week later I got the shock of my life.
After my usual morning walk through the woods, I returned to the château. In the kitchen I found Simone, my housekeeper. She was preparing the breakfast tray for Catherine and myself. After exchanging a few words with her I carried the tray to the library.

Since the advent of Catherine in my life, I always ate breakfast there these days. I didn't mind. It was a pleasant room overlooking the woods. Catherine loved it. She invariably worked on her book at the big library table under the window.

Catherine had not come down yet. I poured myself a café au lait, took a warm croissant out of the basket, spread butter and homemade strawberry jam on it.

I was munching on the croissant when Catherine came in, apologizing as she did.

"Sorry I'm late. Oh good, I see you've started," she said, joining me in front of the fire. Sitting down on the sofa opposite, she poured coffee for herself.

After a moment, she went on, "Did you have a good walk, darling?"

"Yes."

"What's it like out today?"

"Sunny. As you can see. Not as mild as yesterday. But a nice day. For a good gallop."

"Oh I don't think I'll go riding," she responded. "I don't think riding would be good for the baby, do you?" Putting the cup down, she looked at me.

"*Baby!* What baby?"

"Our baby, Jack." She tossed back her flowing red hair and beamed at me. "I was going to tell you tonight, tell you properly over dinner. It just popped out now. I've suspected I was pregnant for the past week. And the doctor in Aix-en-Provence confirmed it yesterday."

I sat frozen in the chair, gaping at her.

At last I managed in a strangled voice, "*You're having a baby?*" I was not only shocked but incredulous.

All smiles, she nodded. "Yes. Isn't it wonderful?"

I was speechless. Words failed me.

She went on quickly, "I never realized I would feel this way, not that I ever thought much about children. I didn't care whether I had a child or not. But now that I *am* pregnant I'm just thrilled to bits. Terribly excited. It's really wonderful news, isn't—" Her voice faltered and abruptly she stopped. She stared hard at me. After a moment she said, "You don't think it's good news, do you?"

"No, I certainly don't. It's horrendous. A baby was never part of our plan."

"But Jack—"

"You were supposed to be taking care of yourself. You said you were using a diaphragm," I rasped. I glared at her. "What happened? Did you suddenly stop?"

"Of course I didn't!" she cried. She was irate. "Something must have gone wrong."

"Merde!"

"It can, you know."

"It shouldn't have, though. Marriage was never part of our deal. I told you I would never get married again."

"Who wants to get married?" she shot back angrily. "Not I, Jack. *I've* always told *you* that. I cherish my independence. And this is not about marriage. It's about a baby. Our child. Unexpectedly, I find myself pregnant, and I'm pleased about it . . . I'm looking forward to having the baby."

"You can't have it! Do you understand me? *You can't have it!*"

"Are you trying to tell me I should have an abortion?" she demanded. Her face had gone deathly white.

"You've no alternative!" I snapped.

"Oh but I do. I can have the baby."

"I don't want it, Catherine."

"I do, Jack. And I have no intentions of terminating my pregnancy. I thought you'd be as happy as I am."

"*Happy!* Don't be such a fool! This is a disaster."

"It needn't be. We don't have to get married, darling," she began in a softer voice. "We can live together, just as we have been doing these past few months. And we can bring up our baby together, here at the château. It's a wonderful place to raise a child, Jack. And honestly, matrimony doesn't have to figure in it, not at all."

"No way! Absolutely no way!"

"A lot of people do it, Jack. They—"

"I'm not a lot of people. I don't want this child. Don't you understand that? I'm not interested in this baby," I spluttered.

"I'm going to have it, whatever *you* say. You can't stop me," Catherine said, her voice hardening. There was a sudden change in her. She had acquired a defiance that brought a tautness to her face, and her body had stiffened. Her resoluteness took my breath away.

"If you have this baby we can't be together," I threatened. "It's the end of our relationship."

"That's fine by me!" she cried and jumped up. Her eyes blazed in her white face. "I will not get rid of my baby. And if you don't want to live with me and bring it up, then I'll live alone. I'll have the baby and bring it up myself. I don't need you. Or your bloody money, Jack Locke! I have enough of my own. And I'm quite self-sufficient. In every way!"

"So be it," I said coldly, also standing.

She glared at me, her fury apparent.

I stared her down.

Neither of us spoke.

"I'd better leave," she exclaimed in a curt, clipped tone. "I can be packed in half an hour, an hour at the most. Please be kind enough to order a cab for me. To take me to Marseilles. There are plenty of planes to London daily. I don't want to hang around here for longer than is necessary."

"Consider it done!" I answered angrily. I was rasping again. My voice sounded harsh to me.

Catherine walked across the room. She turned at the door. In a voice that dripped ice, she said, "You're afraid to be a father. You're afraid because you believe you can't love a child. And all because your father couldn't love you."

I opened my mouth. No words came out.

She threw me one last pitying look. Swinging on her heels she left, slamming the door behind her.

The chandelier rattled.

Then there was silence.

I was completely alone.

I did as she asked and ordered a car for her. Then I went to my office in the winery. I had work to do. But I also wanted to avoid Catherine. I didn't want to say good-bye. I didn't want to see her again. Not ever. Not as long as I lived.

Anger was fulminating inside me. I tried to shake it off. Work was the answer. I sat poring over the papers that had arrived by courier from Locke Industries in New York yesterday. Concentration eluded me. I pushed them away from me, sat back in my chair, and closed my eyes.

Endeavoring to calm myself, I made an effort to focus on my business affairs. I was not particularly successful. Emotions were crowding in, getting in the way.

I was angry. And hurt. I felt betrayed by Catherine. She had let me down by getting pregnant. It was irresponsible on her part. We'd had more than one conversation about birth control. She knew my feelings about children. I'd never wanted any when I was married. So why would I want them out of wedlock?

Suddenly her last words echoed in my mind. Had she spoken the truth? Did I really believe that I couldn't love a child because my father had never loved me? I had no answer for myself. How could I have an answer to an unanswerable question?

Catherine had said I was irrational about my father.

But this was not the case. I was very rational when it came to Sebastian. I knew where my feelings of antipathy sprang from. My childhood. He had never tried to help me when I was growing up. Never ventured to teach me anything. He had never made an effort to be a real father. Like other boys' fathers did. He had always left me to my own devices. Left me with Luciana and Vivienne. We had never indulged in any masculine pursuits. Or exchanged confidences. All he had ever talked about was my duty. And he had never loved me.

At least Catherine hadn't tried to convince me I was wrong about that. Instead she had given me a psychological explanation. *Disassociation.* That is what she had called it. She said it sprang from lack of bonding in the first years of a child's life. She ascribed Sebastian's inability to love to this condition. It made sense. His mother had died in childbirth. He had never bonded with Cyrus. He had said as much once. I knew he had hated my grandfather.

But *I* didn't suffer from disassociation. I had known mother love for two years. Those crucial years of a child's life. Then Christa had come along. She had been there to love me. And after Christa went away there was my Special Lady, Antoinette Delaney.

I sighed under my breath. Catherine might be right about my father. But she was totally wrong about me. Wasn't she?

Oh what the hell did it matter what she thought or said or did. She was out of my life. Or would be within the space of the next hour. It was regrettable really. I had cared about her. We had been good together. Built a good relationship. She had gone and ruined it. But then women usually did. In my life at least.

Chapter Twenty

"**G**ood God, where did you spring from?" I exclaimed. I stared at the door, startled to see my unexpected visitor. Her sudden arrival was a mixed blessing. Part of me was glad. The other part mad.

"New York," Vivienne said, laughing. She stepped into my office and closed the door behind her. "I got back to *Vieux Moulin* yesterday. I was going to phone you, but then I decided to surprise you instead."

"You succeeded." I got up, went to hug her. We strolled across the floor together. She sat down in the chair next to my desk and went on, "You do look busy. All those papers. Oh, dear, I do hope I haven't interrupted you."

"It's okay, Viv. I'd just about finished anyway. I've been hard at it all day. Locke Industries can be very demanding at times. Even long distance." I glanced at my watch. "It's almost five. I might as well pack it in now. Let's go and have a drink."

"It's a bit early, isn't it?" she demurred.

"Not necessarily. Depending on how you look at it. Here in Aix it's five. But in Rome it's already six. The cocktail hour. Anyway, I'm not offering you any old drink. But a very special one. So you can make an exception. Start drinking early for once. I want you to taste our new wine. Created by Olivier. In 1986. It's just matured. Come on, kid. Let's go down to the *cave*."

"I'd love to," Vivienne agreed, suddenly enthusiastic. She followed me out of the office.

Within minutes we were standing in the wine-tasting corner of the red wine maturation cellar. I ushered Vivienne to a chair. Then I took a bottle of the vintage 1986 red out of a wine rack and showed it to her.

"It was good weather that summer and fall. If you remember, Viv," I explained. "And the wine is excellent. It's aged well. Olivier mixed three different grapes. It has a wonderful taste. Very soft on the palette."

"I can't wait to try it," she replied and smiled up at me. "Go on then, open it. Let me taste your triumph."

"Olivier's triumph," I said.

I felt her eyes on me as I handled the bottle. I did so carefully. Slowly. I followed the steps taught to me by Olivier years ago.

Once I had poured a glass for each of us, I raised mine. "Here's to you, Viv."

"And you, Jack."

She took a sip and then another. After a moment she nodded. "It's wonderful. Like velvet on the tongue. And there's just the right hint of violets. Congratulations."

"Thanks. But I told you, it's Olivier's wine. Not mine."

Vivienne drank a little more, pronounced it the best wine ever created at the château, and said, "I'd like to order some of it, if I may."

"Sure. I'll give you a couple of cases. Tonight. Before you leave."

"I want to pay for them, Jack."

"No way. What's mine is yours. You should know that by now."

"Thank you. That's sweet of you. Anyway, don't stand there, come and sit down with me."

I did as she asked. Groaning under my breath. I knew her so well. Better than I knew myself, at times. And I could tell from her expression what was on her mind. She was about to launch into a long recital. About her trip to New York. About Sebastian. About the damned profile.

Wanting to get it over with, I broached the subject. "How's the profile on Sebastian coming along?"

"Very well, in certain respects. I talked to a lot of people at Locke Industries. To the president and his vice president."

"What did Jonas and Peter have to say?"

"Only good things, of course. I spent a lot of time with Madge Hitchens at the foundation. In all the years she went to Africa with Sebastian she never met any women with him. And certainly not last year. At least none that he might have been romantically involved with."

"She actually said that?"

Vivienne nodded. "Yes, she did, and, in fact, no one knows anything at all about a new woman in his life.

Nor did they know he was planning to get married this spring."

"Except you."

"That's right."

I laughed out loud.

Vivienne stared at me. "Why're you laughing like that?"

"Maybe she didn't exist. Doesn't exist."

"What do you mean?"

I laughed again. I knew I sounded cynical. I couldn't help myself. I said slowly, "Maybe this woman was an invention on his part."

"That's ridiculous. Why would he invent a new woman, tell me he was in love, say he was getting married this spring?"

"To light a fire under you, Viv. Get you going."

"Now why on earth would he want to do that?" she exclaimed.

"To make you jealous. That's what I'm trying to say."

"That's preposterous. Very far-fetched indeed."

"Not necessarily. Not when I really think about it." I gave her a knowing look. "Sebastian always cared about you the most. More than the other wives. You meant more to him than your mother ever did. Also—"

"I really find that hard to believe," Vivienne cut in. "He loved my mother very much."

Ignoring her comment, I said, "He could have wanted to start up with you again. Why not? Once you were very special to him. His favorite. Yep, that's it." I laughed more loudly than before. "He wanted to get you back. So he made himself look highly desirable. By inventing a new woman in his life."

"That's a ridiculous premise on your part—"

"I bet I'm right," I interrupted. "He *did* make you jealous that day. Admit it."

"No, he didn't," she protested indignantly.

"It's me you're talking to, Vivienne."

She was silent.

I sat drinking my wine for a few minutes. Neither of us spoke. I realized that I had hit the mark. He *had* made her jealous. When they had lunch at Le Refuge. That was typical of him. He had always been very clever when it came to women. And at pushing the right buttons.

After pouring more wine for us both, I murmured, "Why don't you fly to Africa? Go to every place he visited without Madge. The last year of his life. You'll discover he was there alone. I mean without a lover. Without a new woman. And *of course* Madge Hitchens was his only companion in the places he usually went to. Madge and some of the others from the charities."

Vivienne said, "During lunch at Le Refuge, when I asked Sebastian questions about his new girlfriend, his fiancée, because that's what she was, he said she worked in Africa. That she was a doctor. A scientist. It's more than likely that she was working in a laboratory somewhere. Maybe even somewhere isolated. I'm quite certain she didn't travel around with him. Why would she when she had a job? And *that* is the explanation, in my opinion."

"So you do believe she existed?" I asserted.

"Exists," Vivienne corrected.

I shrugged. "Who's to know. I still think it's odd that no one met this woman with him. It's not at all in character."

"What do you mean exactly?"

"Sebastian liked to show his women off. You should know that better than anyone. He loved a beautiful woman on his arm. Certainly, you were the prime example, Viv."

"If that's a back-handed compliment, thank you," she responded, and smiled at me.

"You're welcome, honey."

"Jack?"

"Yes?"

"Do you trust me?

"You know I do, Viv."

"And my judgment?"

"Sometimes," I hedged.

"Look, you must trust me now. I know *instinctively* that Sebastian meant every word he said to me. He wasn't trying to make me jealous, so that he could get me interested in him again. He *knew* me, and he certainly knew that would be the wrong way to go about it," she explained quietly. "Let me put it to you very simply. He *was* telling me the truth that day over lunch. He *had* met a young woman in Africa, had fallen in love with her. He loved her in a way he had never loved before. He said that in those exact words. He was going back to Africa to meet her. They were traveling on to India together. They were going to spend Christmas in Connecticut. At the farm. And then he was bringing her to France. To *Vieux Moulin*. To meet me. And you, I'm sure. They were going to be married here in France. This spring. I honestly and truly believe that this is exactly the way it was."

I realized how serious Vivienne was. I said, "Okay. Let's just say you're right. But why does it matter?

You don't need this woman to write your profile. You knew him better than anyone. She can't add anything."

"That's true, yes. I could start writing the piece tomorrow. But you've forgotten something. I want to know *why* he killed himself."

"Oh, Viv, *honey*. You're never going to know."

"I'm going to make a damned good try at finding out."

"How?"

"I'm going to find the woman."

"*How?*"

"I'm not sure. But I will. Believe me, I will."

"Why?"

"I want to talk to her. Interview her."

"*Why?*" I asked again.

"Because in my opinion she's got something to do with his death."

I stared at her. "You gotta be kidding."

"No, Jack, I'm not. I think that she's somehow connected to his suicide. And before you say it, not because she might have jilted him either."

"Then what?"

"I don't know. Not yet."

"Why are you suddenly so focused on this woman?"

"Because in his very predictable life she was the only thing that was different."

I nodded slowly. "That's true. But you'll never find her," I remarked. I meant this. I thought Viv was wasting her time.

"We'll see. In the meantime, wrack your brains for me, darling, and maybe you'll remember something, even a small thing could be pertinent."

"I'll try. But I already told you. I didn't see much of him last year."

Vivienne finished her wine without further comment. A bit later she said, "I'm getting tiddily here. Drinking on an empty stomach. And I've got to drive back to Lourmarin."

"I'll feed you," I said. "Stay to dinner."

"Why not? And thanks, I'd love to see Catherine. How is she?"

I cleared my throat. "She's not here, Viv."

"Oh. Where's she gone?"

"I don't know."

Vivienne frowned. "I'm not following you, Jack."

"She's left me. Gone back to England. At least she went to Marseilles. Early this morning. To catch a plane home to London."

"Oh, Jack, darling, I am sorry," Vivienne commiserated. "You two seemed so well suited. Perfect together. I thought you'd found the right woman at last. Whatever happened?"

"She got pregnant."

"So?" Vivienne asked, raising a brow.

"We disagreed. About the baby. She wanted it. I didn't. She dug her heels in. We argued. She said she was going to have it. No matter what I thought or said. In the end we had a screaming row. She left."

"And you let her go?"

"Yes."

"How could you be so stupid! So dense!" Vivienne cried, staring at me aghast. "How could you let that marvelous woman escape?"

I flinched under her critical gaze. "Look, Viv, I don't want to get married," I said finally. "And I certainly

don't want to have kids. She fully intends to have this
baby. Against my wishes. When she said she was leaving I didn't stop her. Anyway, it's for the best. It
wouldn't have worked. Not in the long run."

Vivienne regarded me for a prolonged moment.
Then she said in a low but vehement voice, "You're a
damn fool, Jack Locke. You've just made the biggest
mistake of your life."

PART THREE

LUCIANA
PRIDE

Chapter Twenty-one

I once heard my brother Jack tell Vivienne I was fragile, and I was astonished to hear him say such a thing. How totally wrong he was in his assessment of me.

I am not a fragile woman.

On the contrary, I'm one of the strongest people I know, mentally and physically. Certainly my father always understood this; that's why he called me a true Locke born and bred.

Sebastian saw in me the personification of the Lyon Locke character, and even said I was a genuine throwback to Malcolm Lyon Locke, that great Scotsman who was the founding father of our dynasty.

It is true, I have inherited many of the traits that made our family great. I have an iron will, determination, dedication, discipline, immense stamina, and a proclivity for hard work.

I am also unrelenting and ruthless in business, and

my husband Gerald says I'm a born trader with ice water in my veins when it comes to wheeling and dealing.

My father called me an accomplished dissembler and one of the cleverest liars he had ever met. He assessed me as being rather better at prevarication than his father Cyrus. Sebastian had been laughing when he said this to me, and I know he had meant it as a compliment. Although when he told Vivienne I was a liar he probably made it sound derogatory, and there is no doubt in my mind that he *did* tell her. He had always confided everything in her, ever since she had come into our lives when she was twelve and I was only four.

Nevertheless, he *was* proud of me, proud of my talents and skills, especially my negotiating skills. I had come to understand, early on, that he wished I had been born a boy. He would have much preferred to have had two sons to carry on in his footsteps, rather than just one.

However, in the end, the fact that I was a girl did not deter him when it came to the family business. As soon as I was old enough he steered me into Locke Industries in New York.

For several years now I have been running the British division of Locke in London, and the last time I spoke to my father, just before he died, he told me I had done a superlative job. He was very proud of me. "You're a chip off the old block, Luce. Well done, darling!"

In the course of this discussion, over dinner at his townhouse in Manhattan, he suggested that I might enjoy coming back to the New York office. It was there that I had started my business career after graduating from Yale. He said he had a special position for me: executive vice president in charge of all the women's divisions of the company.

I had been toying with the idea ever since. I still toyed with it. Certainly it was very tempting. All I had to do was tell Jack and he would arrange it. He had been at dinner that night, had noticed Sebastian's enthusiasm and mine and had commented about it. My husband had no objection; in fact, Gerald rather fancied the idea of moving to New York where he would be able to work at the U.S. branch of his family's investment bank.

If the truth be known, I should be head of the company, not Jack. My brother was supervising the business long distance, as my father had done for many years of his life. It wasn't very satisfactory, in my opinion, even though the CEO was competent, and had been handpicked by Sebastian ten years ago.

I was a hands-on manager and therefore I believed I would be better for the company. I longed to run Locke Industries instead of Jack, and there was no doubt in my mind that he would welcome this change.

My brother genuinely loved the château and the vineyards more than anything else in his life. Certainly he was good at running the estate. I was proud that he had made such a huge success of the winery, and that his label was now a superior appellation. He had done it by himself, with the help of Olivier Marchand, and chapeau to him.

No one could convince me that Jack was really interested in Locke Industries. He was chairman and did what he did only because it had been drilled into him for years that this was his chief role in life. Duty, Duty, Duty had been the eternal cry from Sebastian and Cyrus. Deep down within himself I think he probably hated Locke Industries. I loved the company; I lived for it.

An hour ago Jack had phoned from Aix-en-Provence. He had canceled the trip to London he had been planning to make this coming weekend. I was feeling somewhat put out with him because of this. I had been looking forward to talking to him about Locke Industries and business in general.

Now our chat would have to wait until next month, when he had promised to come to the birthday party I was planning for Gerald.

At this moment Gerald was in Hong Kong on business; he would be returning later this week. The thought of my husband prompted me to get up from my desk and walk across the office. I paused at the mirror hanging on the wall above a seating arrangement of sofa, chairs, and a coffee table.

I stood in front of the looking glass for several moments, regarding myself, wondering what Gerald would think of my new image.

At first he would be extremely angry because I had cut off all my blonde hair. He loved my long golden tresses. But he would eventually get used to this short, caplike cut that was more up to date. Also, the hairstyle made my head look neater, smaller, and therefore more balanced to my slender body.

Even my figure had changed, if only slightly, in the three weeks Gerald had been away. I had put on weight. Not much, only four pounds, but it was enough to make me look less emaciated. The weight gain had played havoc with my clothes and most of them were too small. They would have to go. I had ordered several new suits for work and they would be delivered to me next week.

I was pleased about my weight gain. Not only did I look better, I felt better. The pounds had started to come on quite naturally in December because unexpectedly I had started to eat properly again.

It was not that I had consciously dieted over the years; I never had. Very simply, I had never had much of an appetite. Not since I was twenty, when I lost my taste for food. That was when Sebastian had teased me about my weight and told me I was fat. "A regular little butterball," he had added a trifle scathingly, and the next day I had stopped eating correctly. In essence, I had brainwashed myself not to feel hunger, and in the process I had been starving myself for years.

For a long time Gerald had wanted a child. Now so did I. I felt the timing was right. After all, I was twenty-eight and Gerald was thirty-three. We were both the perfect age to start a family.

I wanted heirs. Sons and daughters who would rejuvenate the declining dynasty that the Locke family had become. I wanted *my* children to carry on, to lead the family into the twenty-first century, to expand our fortune and carry on the tradition started generations ago.

Turning away from the mirror, I hesitated, and then on an impulse I left my office and hurried down the corridor to the boardroom.

I went in and closed the door behind me, switching on the lights as I did. On the walls hung the portraits of the men who had made our family great.

In all truth, I did not need any reminders of my impressive heritage. This had been imprinted on my brain since I was a child, and I was filled with immense pride to be a Locke, to come from such a long line of brilliant entrepreneurs.

My father had forever termed them robber barons, and in the most derisive way, but I never thought of them as such. They were my idols, whether they were robber barons or not.

Occasionally I liked to study their portraits. These were copies of the originals that hung in the board-room in New York. I had had them copied for the London boardroom by a prominent artist, who had, in my opinion, painted portraits much superior to the originals. Their likenesses invariably inspired me to greater heights.

Viewing the images of my ancestors had now become something of a ritual with me. Each man fascinated me; I wished I had known them all.

I always started out with the founding father, Malcolm Trevor Lyon Locke. As I stood gazing up at his face now, I wondered, as I so often did, what kind of man he had really been, my great-great-great-grand-father.

Physically he looked like a nineteenth-century version of Sebastian. Or rather my father had resembled him, and it was easy to see where Sebastian's good looks had come from, and Jack's as well. Malcolm had the black hair, fresh complexion, and bright blue eyes of a typical Scotsman.

I knew all about him. He was a legend in the family. Born in Arbroath, a small fishing village and seaport on the east coast of Scotland near Dundee, he had sailed for America in 1830. He had been nineteen years old when he set forth to seek his fortune.

As the story goes, Malcolm soon discovered that the streets of New York were not paved with gold as he had been led to believe. And so he moved to Philadelphia.

A blacksmith by trade, Malcolm was enterprising and something of an inventor, always tinkering with bits of machinery and farm tools. Whilst he worked as a blacksmith, he started his own tool shop and small forge on the side, and operated them in his spare time.

It was in 1837 that the first steel plow with a self-scouring moldboard was invented. One year later, in 1838, Malcolm, who had himself been experimenting with plows, came up with an invention of his own.

Malcolm Locke created a moldboard of chilled cast iron that scours best with the least friction. It changed his life and set him on the road to becoming a millionaire. In fact, it was the beginning of the family fortune and Locke Industries, although in those days it was called the Locke Tool Company, so named by Malcolm.

From the portrait of Malcolm I moved on, stood in front of the painting of Ian. He was the eldest son of Malcolm and his wife Amy MacDonald, and Ian had been born in that propitious year of 1838.

When he was old enough, Ian went into the business with Malcolm, who by this time not only manufactured moldboards but all kinds of farm machinery and implements as well. The Locke Tool Company grew and prospered under Ian's steady if uninspired guidance.

Ian's first son Colin was born to him and his wife

Georgina Anson in 1866. I peered at his face. Colin did not look like Ian or Malcolm, but he had inherited the latter's genius for invention and his pioneering spirit.

When he was in his late twenties Colin went to Texas to drill for oil. He did not make a lucky strike and eventually returned to Philadelphia and the family business.

However, his experiences in the oil fields had prompted him to tinker around with drilling bits. Also, he worked on numerous other inventions in this tool shop. But mostly, when he had time, he tried to improve on the fishtail bit, which was most commonly used for drilling. He knew from experience that it constantly broke.

It was some years later, when he was in his early forties, that Colin came up with a drilling bit that would change the Locke Tool Company yet again.

After years of frustration and numerous different versions, he finally invented a bit that would drill through rock and quicksand. It was formed like two pine cones, one moving clockwise, the other counter-clockwise. These revolving cones, moving in opposite directions, had 170 cutting edges.

It was 1907 and Colin Locke's drilling bit was revolutionary. He was one year ahead of Bo Hughes, who invented a similar bit in 1908 and formed the Hughes-Sharp Tool Company.

I looked at Colin's portrait intently.

My great-grandfather was not as good looking as the other Locke men who had gone before him. He had blond hair and dark brown eyes, and it was obvious to me where my coloring had come from. Colin appeared quite dolorous in the painting. Sebastian had actively disliked him, and almost as much as he had disliked his father.

It was Colin Lyon Locke's invention that formed the basis of an even greater fortune for the family and the Locke Tool Company.

His famous drilling bit was sold all over the world, even as he continued to perfect it for several years. It is not possible to drill for oil today without using it, and the bit brings in hundreds of millions every year, just as it has since the day Colin invented it.

My grandfather's portrait hung next to that of his father. Cyrus, born in 1904, was the first child of Colin and his wife Sylvia Vale.

Grandfather was now in his ninety-first year. Whenever I thought of him I saw a white-haired old man in my mind's eye. Here, in this portrait, he was young, in his late thirties, and he had been attractive enough in a somber, glowering way. His hair had been a light brown and he had black eyes. He seemed out of place with his ancestors. To me he did not look like a Locke at all.

I thought again of the man I had seen at Sebastian's funeral and an involuntary shiver ran through me. How terrible old age was. Once Cyrus had been dominant, domineering, tough, and ruthless. He had run Locke Industries with an iron hand.

Now he was nothing. He had no power or influence in the company where he had once been king. He was just a frail, little old man who looked as if a wind would blow him over.

I moved on from the painting of my grandfather. The one next to it, the last one, was of Sebastian Lyon Locke.

My father.

And what a beautiful man he had been. So handsome. The eyes so brilliantly blue, the hair jet black.
And his features were as arresting as his coloring was,
finely sculpted and well defined. No wonder women
had dropped like flies at his feet. I couldn't blame
them. He had been a gorgeous specimen.

Five wives he had had. But only two children by
two of them. I wondered, as I had so often wondered
lately, why he had not had more offspring.

His first wife, Josephine Allyson, had been Main
Line Philadelphia and an heiress in her own right. She
was the mother of Jack and had died when he was
two. She had left him all of her money, millions,
which had been held in trust until he was twenty-one.

My father's second wife had been my mother
Christabelle Wilson. When he married Christa he had
been the grieving widower, or so I had been led to
believe.

I was the result of their brief union.

When I was small my mother was sent away to dry
out in a clinic in New Haven. She never came back to
live with us. I saw her from time to time, but it was
Sebastian who brought me up.

After he divorced my alcoholic mother, he took up
with Antoinette Delaney, Vivienne's mother. Their love
affair never became more than that, because she was
married to Liam Delaney who was wandering around
the South Seas.

Sebastian's relationship with Antoinette ended when
she fell down our cellar steps and broke her neck. If
she had lived I suppose she could have divorced Liam
for desertion at some point, and married my father. I

know he wanted to formalize their love affair. He told me this once. And he was certainly broken up about her death.

My father's third wife was Stephanie Jones, who had only a very short sojourn with us. She had worked with Sebastian as one of his assistants at the Locke Foundation. Jack and I both liked her. She had been an intellectual and rather quiet, but lovely looking, a cool, refined blonde who reminded me of Grace Kelly. Stephanie had always been kind to Jack and me, and we were sad when she was killed in a plane crash.

Then along came the great Vivienne.

My father was married to her the longest. Five years. It seemed like an eternity to me. I know he made her pregnant and that she had a miscarriage. Sebastian told me that himself. He was heartbroken about the loss of the baby.

I suppose it was inevitable that he would marry Vivienne. He had always favored her when she was growing up, and he became her guardian after her mother died. He paid her school fees and supported her financially, and she was always with us during school vacations and special holidays.

My dislike for Vivienne was quite intense. I couldn't stand her really, and I was glad when they finally split up. I always thought my father deserved better.

His fifth and last wife was Betsy Bethune, a career woman. To me she was the most unsuitable person he could have married. She was far too busy being a famous concert pianist to be a good wife to my father and I was not in the least surprised when he divorced her. I had never understood why he had married her in the first place. It was an enigma.

I stared hard at the painting of my father, and for
the longest time, studying his face intently.

Yet again I asked myself why he had killed himself.
It just didn't make sense to me. He had seemed perfectly all right when I was staying with him in New
York. In fact he had not been gloomy as he so often
was. He was much more relaxed, even happy, that
week before he took his life. I wished he hadn't done
it. I missed him so much.

I had always loved my father, even though he preferred Jack to me in many ways. He had always
devoted so much of his time and energy to Jack, but I
suppose that was natural, since Jack was his only son
and the heir apparent.

Vivienne had come between my father and me from
the moment she had arrived on the scene with her
unbearable mother. She stole my father from me when
I was a child, but I managed to get part of him back
when I was grown up.

After all, I was his real child, his biological child,
with genuine Locke blood running through my veins.
When I was a teenager he saw in me the second son
he had always wanted. That was one of the reasons he
had given me so much power in Locke Industries later
on. Of course he knew I was a good businesswoman,
practical and efficient like him; he knew, too, I would
not let him down. He was also aware of how much I
cared about the company.

Yes, my father had loved me. He had made that very
clear in his will.

"I give and bequeath to my dearest and most
beloved only daughter Luciana . . . " Those had been
his words before the bequests to me had been listed.

My father had left me half of his personal fortune and many of his prized possessions. Most of all, I cherished the priceless art collection of Impressionist paintings, especially all of those van Goghs, which he had given to me. That gesture in itself was another expression of his love.

I sighed to myself as I took one last, lingering look at the portrait of Sebastian. Then I walked out of the boardroom, turning off the lights and closing the door behind me.

CHAPTER TWENTY-TWO

My secretary Claire had placed a pile of faxes
on my desk in the short time I had been visiting with my ancestors in the boardroom.
They were mostly from Locke Industries in New York.

I read them all carefully, dealt with those that
needed a response, and made notations on the others.
After signing a batch of letters, I went into the adjoining office and gave everything to Claire.

Returning to my desk I made half a dozen calls to
Locke in New York, settled various bits of business,
and then looked over my appointments for the
remainder of the week.

Tomorrow I had a date for lunch at Claridge's with
Madge Hitchens from the Locke Foundation. She was
on her way to Africa on behalf of the foundation, and
she had stopped off in London for a few days to see
her daughter Melanie who was attending the Royal
College of Art.

Other than Madge I had no special engagements, just routine work all day, and that night Gerald would be arriving from Hong Kong.

Closing my appointment book, I put it away in my desk, then went in to say good night to Claire.

The London offices of Locke Industries were situated in Berkeley Square, and I paused for a moment when I came out of the building.

It was six o'clock and still light, a pleasant evening at the end of March, and I decided to walk home to Belgravia. I made for Charles Street, which would take me into Curzon, and from there I could head into Park Lane and Hyde Park Corner.

I liked walking in London, looking at the old buildings, enjoying a feeling of the past, and of history and tradition; also, it happened to be my favorite city. My father first brought me here with Jack when he was fourteen and I was twelve. Of course I fell in love with the place, the people and the culture, not to mention the manners of the British. They were so polite and civilized it was a pleasure to be around them.

It was the summer of 1979, and my father had come to London ostensibly to sell his apartment in Mayfair. But after he had put this on the market, he then turned around and bought a house in Eaton Square.

I was with him the day he viewed the house for the first time, and I'm not certain who liked it the most, Sebastian or me. Jack had absolutely no interest in it whatsoever. He was simply marking time until we left for the Château d'Cose in Aix-en-Provence, the only place he ever wanted to go. He had loved the château intensely for seven years. It was his grand passion.

In any event, the house was duly purchased, decorators were sent in, and we came back at the end of the year to spend Christmas at our new home in London. A great deal of care and money had been spent on it, and Colefax and Fowler had done a superb job, had created elegance, a warm ambiance, and great comfort. It was a real home, not a design statement, and Sebastian in particular was pleased with the finished result.

For me the trip was marred by Vivienne's presence, but I was so happy to be in London I managed to disguise my displeasure behind a fraudulent smile. This I affixed to my face permanently.

I also managed to make myself scarce that winter, rushing off to the Victoria and Albert, the British Museum, the Tower of London, Madame Tussaud's, and my favorite place of all, the Tate Gallery. I loved to wander around looking at the paintings, especially the Turners.

When we were growing up, Jack was always telling me that Sebastian was after Vivienne. He said it was a campaign, called it the Gradual Seduction of Vivienne, making this sound like the title of a play or movie. Jack insisted Sebastian was the fat cat waiting to pounce on the innocent virgin. But I didn't really agree with him; in my opinion, it was the other way around.

In fact, I had always believed that Vivienne was after my father even when she was a teenager, and when her awful mother was still alive. Her avid interest in Sebastian became more apparent than ever to me that Christmas of 1979, and she never let him out of her sight. She hung on his every word, and his arm, never gave me or Jack a moment alone with him.

At the time, I told Jack she was sleeping with Sebastian, but he pooh-poohed the idea. My brother had had a crush on Vivienne the Great for as long as I could remember, so I suppose he had not been able to support the thought that our father was where *he* wanted to be—in her arms.

I remember I wasn't too crazy about this thought myself, since she had long endeavored to drive a wedge between my father and me. As Sebastian's lover she would have a greater opportunity to do that, and knowing her she would take advantage of that situation.

I was smart enough to realize that I couldn't change the situation, if it did indeed exist. For this reason I involved myself in my own activities and let them get on with it. I advised Jack to do the same, but he persisted in hanging around the house. He called it "keeping an eye on things." I called it spying.

I came to know London well in those days, and the London house was my favorite place to be, after the Manhattan townhouse where I had grown up with Jack and Sebastian. Luckily for me, we spent quite a lot of time in England over the next few years. My father was becoming more and more involved with his African charities, and London made a good jumping off point to that continent for him.

After he married Vivienne he seemed to lose interest in London and in the house. In fact, they stayed at Claridge's when they were on their honeymoon, and later that year he bought the old mill in Lourmarin. I was glad my father had done this, because it prompted

him to give the château to Jack, and this made Jack so
happy he was almost delirious.

I was twenty-three when I moved to my favorite city
permanently. Sebastian gave me one of the top jobs at
the London office, and I was in my true element at
last, running some of the women's divisions.

Over the years Locke Industries had become a huge
conglomerate. We no longer made Malcolm's plows, at
least only a token number; instead we manufactured
tractors and other kinds of farm machinery, as well as
pickup trucks, jeeps, golf carts, and station wagons.

We had a building-materials division that produced
everything from doors and windows to floors and walls.
We made prefabricated houses, garages, and barns. Our
bathroom division manufactured a decorator-designed
line of tubs, showers, toilets, and all the accessories
used in a bathroom. We even had a shower-curtain division.

This diversification had been started by my great-
grandfather Colin and my grandfather Cyrus, long
before this was a popular trend in business. Then my
father had followed their lead when he was still running the company on a full time basis, quite some
time before he became so heavily involved with his
charity work.

Over the years Sebastian had bought a number of
corporations which he then proceeded to mold into
the women's divisions of Locke Industries. He had
purchased companies that manufactured well-known
brands of clothing, undergarments, hosiery, shoes,
swimwear, sports attire, and leisure wear.

When my father sent me to work in London, five
years ago now, one of the first things I did was to buy

a company specializing in cosmetics and body-care products. This led to several other acquisitions, but the first one quickly became a huge money earner, and I'm very proud of this particular purchase.

For years I had believed myself to be a dyed-in-the-wool career woman, and I had never really given much thought to marriage, even though I'd had plenty of boyfriends. But I had only been in London a few months when I fell in love.

It was Thomas Kamper, a business acquaintance, who introduced me to his brother Gerald, with whom he worked in the family's merchant bank in the City.

Gerald and I hit it off immediately, and our feelings were reciprocal. His lean, dark good looks and candid blue eyes struck a chord in me, and within six months of our first meeting we were married. I was twenty-four and he was twenty-nine.

I am still not sure whether Gerald's mother, Lady Fewston, was very happy about her youngest son acquiring an American for a wife, but Sebastian was all for the union. He liked Gerald, approved of the short engagement, and as a wedding gift he gave us the house in Eaton Square. I was particularly thrilled about this, as joyful as Jack had been when he got the château.

I loved Gerald for a number of reasons, not the least of which was his attitude about women. He did not have much time for the idle and the indolent who had nothing to occupy their days, much preferred women like me who were strong, independent, and had flourishing careers. He, like my brother Jack, was attracted to brainy women who had something to say for themselves.

Deep down I know that, despite my love for Gerald,

I would have hesitated about marrying him if he had
objected to my job. In fact, I would have probably had
only a few dates with him and let it go at that.

It was necessary for me to go to work every day,
necessary to my well-being and my sense of self. I
needed to be busy, to accomplish something, to make
a contribution in my own small way. And, after all,
Locke Industries was in my blood, a huge part of my
life. It always had been, and I wanted it for myself. I
hoped one day to get it.

Suddenly I realized I was almost home. I had been
walking so quickly I had reached Eaton Square in
record time. As I put my latchkey in the door and
turned it, the grandfather clock in the hall struck six-
thirty.

CHAPTER TWENTY-THREE

"When Vivienne said your father was planning to get married this year, I was completely taken aback," Madge Hitchens said, looking at me intently across the lunch table. "I didn't know anything about it, Luciana, did you?"

I stared at her without answering. I was stupefied to hear this.

Madge said, "I can tell by the expression on your face, and your silence, that you didn't. You look as surprised as I was when she told me."

Recovering my voice, I asked, "Who on earth was he going to marry?"

"Vivienne didn't know her name. That's why she was asking me."

I frowned and said quickly, "Vivienne thought you would know because you traveled with Sebastian constantly, spent so much time with him."

"Yes. But I wasn't aware of a fiancée. In fact, no one at the foundation was."

"How come Vivienne knew?" As I asked this question I realized it was stupid of me to even pose it. Vivienne had always been a kind of confidante to him.

"Sebastian told her," Madge replied, confirming my thought.

"But he didn't tell her the woman's name, Madge." I shook my head. "How like Sebastian that was. However, he must have told her something else, surely?"

"He did. He told Vivienne she was a doctor. A scientist. At least, so I gathered. He also said she lived and worked in Africa."

"What's Vivienne's interest in her now that my father's dead?"

"She's writing a profile about Sebastian and she wants to interview her."

"I see." I smiled faintly at Madge. "Well, at least we don't have to worry about the tone and content of the story, Madge dear. It's bound to be flattering, since Vivienne's writing it."

"Oh I'm sure it will be."

"Who's Vivienne writing it for? Did she tell you?"

"Yes," Madge said, nodding. "The magazine section of the London *Sunday Times*. As I told you earlier, she was in New York for several weeks, interviewing people at Locke Industries and the foundation. From what I gather, everyone spoke beautifully about Sebastian. But then why wouldn't they? He was a very unique man, and those who worked for him and with him revered him. They still do. I think Vivienne's premise for the profile is very accurate."

"And what is it?" I asked curiously.

"She's focusing on the idea that he was the world's last great philanthropist."

"The Last Great Philanthropist," I repeated. "Not a bad title, not bad at all, and you're correct; it is right on target."

"Your father was a great man, Luciana. In the eighteen years I knew him, a day didn't go by that I didn't marvel at him. He could win men's hearts by the sheer force of his personality, and he commanded energies beyond the average. And I've never known anyone with his strength of will. He was formidable in so many ways, and such a compassionate man as well."

"Yes, he was everything you say," I agreed. "And I've always believed that he could have been anything he wanted, even if he hadn't been born who he was. He was so brilliant, he would have succeeded at anything he did."

"He certainly had an extraordinary aura," Madge remarked. "It fared him well when he was dealing with some governments in Third World countries. They were awed, bowled over by him, and ultimately he brought them around to his way of thinking. Which brings *me* to another point, Luciana."

"Tell me, Madge."

"Even though Jack is now running the foundation and administering the money as your father did, he won't go on any field trips. I wonder if you could influence him to come to Africa with me later this year?"

"You must be joking! He won't listen to *me*, Madge! Or anyone else, for that matter. Jack's very stubborn, surely you know that after all these years. Why he grew up at your knee, as I did." I shook my head and finished, "He won't go to Africa. Or anywhere else, I'm afraid."

"Don't you think we could work on him, Luciana?"

I laughed hollowly. "We could try, but I'm not sure it would do any good. He never wants to leave that vineyard of his." I took a sip of water, and continued, "Madge, I think we ought to look at the menu and order lunch, don't you?"

"Of course." She eyed me for a long moment and then said, "I'm glad to see you've put on a bit of weight. You've been far too thin for far too long."

I smiled at her. "I know. I suddenly got my appetite back."

Once we had ordered, I took up the subject of Jack again, and his involvement with the foundation. "Jack doesn't mind giving away the money, Madge," I explained. "He's not a bit tight-fisted, and he knows it goes to help people in need. However, he doesn't want to be personally involved with the charities. He doesn't know how to deal with people the way Sebastian did. Don't ask me why, he just doesn't."

"Perhaps I could edge him into it," Madge began and stopped short, pursing her lips. "You know, I always felt that Jack hated living in your father's shadow. Maybe that's the problem."

"It could be," I agreed. "He's so much like Sebastian and in so many ways, but he does his damnedest to be completely different. It's as if he doesn't want to be my father's clone."

"I'm sure he doesn't." Madge gave me a hard stare, and asked, "Do you think Sebastian was *really* engaged to someone?"

"It's possible." I shrugged. "But he never told *me*."

"Or anyone else, except Vivienne. So if it was true, why *did* he keep it a secret?"

"Perhaps he didn't," I said thoughtfully. "Maybe she worked in a remote area. You know what *he* was like, jumping around all over the map. I could never keep track of him, could you?"

"Not all the time, no, and certainly he and I were often in different parts of Africa. Indeed in different parts of the world. But it is a mystery, isn't it? By the way, I think I ought to alert you. . . Vivienne plans to come to London to see you, Luciana, to interview you for the piece."

I merely nodded and stored this bit of information away.

At this moment the waiter arrived with our first course and I let the subject of Vivienne sink. To my astonishment I was hungry, and I even found my mouth watering as the waiter served me. I was about to eat Morecombe Bay potted shrimps for the first time in years, and I was actually salivating.

"Bon appetit," I said to Madge, picked up a thin slice of buttered brown bread and took a bite, then I dipped into the potted shrimps with relish. I'd first eaten them in 1979, here at Claridge's, where Sebastian had often brought us for lunch and occasionally for dinner. I had sworn off them years ago, because the shrimps were potted in pure butter, but I could enjoy them with impunity today since my aim was to actually put on weight.

"I hope I get a chance to see Gerald," Madge murmured, as she dug a fork underneath a Colchester oyster.

"He'll be back from Hong Kong tonight. Perhaps you'd like to have lunch with us in the country on Sunday."

"That would be great, Luciana, thank you. He's such a nice man, and he was very kind to me at the memorial service in New York, very comforting."

"That's Gerald, and I'm afraid he still feels badly that he wasn't able to come to Sebastian's funeral in Connecticut, but his father had just undergone surgery and he didn't want to leave him," I said.

"He told me all about it, and I could well understand his feelings."

"Would you like to bring Melanie with you?" I asked, smiling at her. "Or would it be too dull for her?"

"Of course it wouldn't. I'm sure she'd love it. Thank you."

"She's doing well at the Royal College of Art?"

"Spectacular. And loving every minute of it," Madge replied, and went on talking about her twenty-two-year-old daughter for the next few minutes.

As I listened to my father's former colleague and dear old friend of the family talking, I couldn't help thinking how well she looked. Madge had gone to work as Sebastian's administrative assistant when she was forty-two, when Melanie was just two years old. Eighteen years later she didn't look much different than she had then. Her hair, which came to a widow's peak on her forehead, was still as black as coal, her heart-shaped face smooth and unwrinkled. At sixty she looked much younger.

"You're staring at me, Luce," she said, regarding me with her head on one side. "Is something wrong?"

"How rude. I'm sorry. But I was actually admiring you, Madge, thinking how wonderful you look . . . the same as you did the first day I met you, when I was all of ten."

"Kind words will get you everywhere," she answered with a laugh. "And I feel wonderful."

"Sebastian always said you were very fit, the fittest person he knew. He even mentioned it the last time I was with him in New York. . . just before he died."

Madge stared at me, and then unexpectedly blurted out, "I miss him so much, Luce." Her fine gray eyes filled with tears, and she cleared her throat several times.

I reached out and took hold of her hand resting on the table. "I know you do. So do I."

There was a silence, and then finally recovering herself, she gave me one of her penetrating stares and said quietly, "I dwell on his suicide a lot. I can't imagine why he did it. I've racked my brains for a reason."

"Perhaps there isn't one, Madge," I said, squeezing her hand. "At least not one that we could understand."

Chapter Twenty-four

"Gerald, listen to me. Please don't go to sleep. *Please*," I said. "I want to talk to you about something and it's very important."

Stifling a yawn and rousing himself, my husband responded in an apologetic voice, "Sorry to be so sleepy, darling, I'm afraid I'm still suffering from the time change. But talk to me, please do, I'm all ears, I promise."

Pushing myself up on one elbow, I looked down at him and said, "I've stopped using birth control pills, so you may well have made me pregnant tonight. Isn't that an exciting thought?"

Gerald sat upright in bed and gaped at me. "Good Lord, darling, when on earth did this extraordinary change of heart occur?"

"I've been thinking about having a baby since December, Gerald. The time *is* right, don't you think?"

"I certainly do! I'm all for it, you know that. Good

Lord!" he exclaimed. "A *baby*. What a wonderful idea." He gave me a boyish grin. "Perhaps we *did* make one, we were certainly passionate enough, if that counts for ought."

He leaned back on the pillows, gave me a long penetrating look and added, "Well, well, well, so you want to be a mother, Luciana. What was it that actually wrought this unexpected change in you?"

"The fact that the Locke dynasty is on the wane has been bothering me for a long time," I said. "And the only way to rectify that is for us to have children. *Heirs*, Gerald. Heirs to follow in our footsteps. Mine and yours. I know you want children, and that your father wants grandchildren to go into Kamper Brothers. After all, your family business is one of the oldest merchant banks in England, just as the Locke family is one of the oldest dynasties in America. We can't let the Lockes and the Kampers become extinct, now can we?"

"Perish the thought," he said with a dry laugh. "And how many children are you planning for us to have, my sweet?"

"At least four," I answered. "Two for me, I mean two to go into Locke Industries, when they're old enough, and two for you for the bank."

"Sounds a bit cold-blooded when you put it that way, don't you think?" he murmured, giving me an odd look.

"It may sound it," I said. "But it isn't, not really, Gerald. I'm just being practical, that's all, and maybe we'll only have two or three. Perhaps we might have six, though. Who knows. There's some luck attached to it, I'm sure, but as far as I'm concerned, the more the merrier."

"Forgive me if I seem a trifle startled, but this is indeed something of a switch on your part. Quite a switch actually. You were always so much against having children."

"You've always led me to believe you wanted them. Don't tell me you've changed your mind. You haven't, have you?"

"No, no, not at all, Luce. I'm delighted about your decision, couldn't be more pleased if I tried. I suppose you'll want to continue working, and have a nanny for the baby?"

"The answer to both questions is a decided *yes*, and surely that doesn't matter to *you*, Gerald. You've always understood about my work."

"No, it doesn't bother me at all."

"And you *were* brought up by a nanny."

"Yes, thank heavens. My Nan was wonderful and I loved her very much when I was a child. I still love her. Pity she's retired, she would have been perfect for Bertie."

"Bertie?"

"Yes, Bertie the baby. Our baby. Sounds sweet, doesn't it?"

I laughed. "Not Bertie, darling. We're not going to call him that. He'll be named Sebastian after my father, Horatio after yours. So, in fact, his full name will be Sebastian Horatio Lyon Locke Kamper."

"Good Lord, that's a hell of a mouthful for a little baby."

"But he's going to grow up and be a tycoon and run Locke Industries. And anyway, he'll be known as Sebastian Locke Kamper. That doesn't sound too bad, does it?"

"It seems you've got it all worked out," Gerald answered. "Well, there's one thing I do know for certain, poppet."

"What's that?" I asked gazing into his vivid blue eyes. I loved him a lot.

"We're going to have rather exciting times these next few years, trying to make all the babies you want."

I laughed, reached up, and kissed him on the cheek. "I'm sure that won't worry you."

"Of course it doesn't, I'm mad for you, Luce."

"You're the sexiest thing, Gerald."

"Thanks for the compliment, and let me return it. So are you."

"Thank you. Gerald?"

"Yes, darling?"

"There's something else I want to talk to you about."

"I'm wide awake now, so go ahead, I'm listening."

"It's about Locke Industries," I began and then hesitated. "Are you sure you're not too tired?"

"I'm all right, tell me what's troubling you?"

"I'm not really troubled," I answered quickly. "Just concerned about Locke Industries."

"In what sense?"

"Jack's not really interested in running the business. He does what he does because he has to, and he was brought up to understand that he had to do his *duty*. God knows, that was drilled into him all his life. But he doesn't *love* Locke Industries the way I do. And I feel I should be running the company in his place. He could still have the title of chairman."

"Are you trying to tell me that you want to be

CEO and president?" Gerald asked, his voice rising slightly.

"Well," I began and paused when I saw the concerned expression settle on his face. "Don't you think I could do the job?"

"Don't be silly, Luce, of course you could do it. But it's awfully demanding and all-consuming. Quite frankly, I think Jonas Winston is a wonderful businessman and a great CEO and he's done a fine job for ten years, performed extremely well. Don't forget, he was handpicked by Sebastian. And Peter Sampson is a darned good second in command. I—"

"Do you think I can't run Locke because I'm a woman?"

"That has nothing to do with it!"

"Then why are you looking so worried?"

"You're my wife. I want to spend time with you, Luciana. Obviously I don't mind if you have a career, in fact I'm proud of you, your achievements. You know that. But I'm not sure I'd want you spending eighteen hours a day at Locke headquarters in New York."

"I wouldn't be doing that."

"Of course you would. You're a hands-on person, that's your style of management. I doubt you'll change."

"Maybe Jack would be happy if I became chairman in his place," I said, thinking aloud. "That's a much less demanding job. And it would be much better for the company than having him making decisions from France. You wouldn't mind if I were chairman, would you, Gerald dear?"

"No. But Jack might." He threw me a knowing look.

I shrugged.

Gerald said softly, "And how many decisions do you think Jack really makes? Mostly he approves of what Jonas Winston thinks should be done, the decisions that Jonas has already made. They discuss them, of course, but Jack listens to Jonas, I'm positive of that. He'd be a fool not to listen when Jonas is sitting there in full command of the company. I absolutely believe this is exactly the way it is. Trust me on this, Luce, please."

"I'm not sure you're right," I began and paused. I knew he was correct in everything he'd said.

"Look here," Gerald exclaimed, "I'm going to give you a bit of advice. It's the same advice I give to friends and colleagues who come and discuss a problem with me, a problem they have with someone else. I always tell them they're talking to the wrong person. I point out that they should be talking to the person they're at odds with, not me, because that's the only way they'll get any satisfaction, resolve the problem."

"So you're telling me I should go and talk to Jack?"

"Yes, I am, darling, if you want to pursue this matter further."

"And what if Jack is relieved and happy that I want to take over from him? How would you feel about that? And also, Gerald, would you really move to New York?"

"In a shot! Of course I would. Move to New York, I mean. I'd be happy living there, I could run our Wall Street office, we could live in that magnificent townhouse of your father's that's now yours and is standing empty. And we could spend weekends at Laurel Creek

Farm. I'm sure your brother would be happy if we made use of it in his absence. As for you taking over the chairmanship from Jack, that would be perfectly all right with me as long as you were not killing yourself at Locke Industries."

"I wouldn't be doing that!" I exclaimed. "Not as chairman."

"No, I don't think you would. You have more sense than that." He grinned at me in that boyish way of his and added, "It's absolutely necessary that we have some free time together, in order to make all those babies you say you want."

"I do want them, don't doubt that, Gerald."

"I don't. Now if Jack's not amenable to giving up the chairmanship, which he may not be, then you could suggest something else to him. You could offer to become joint chairman, share the responsibility with him."

"Yes . . . I guess I could . . . "

"Let's just suppose that Jack agrees to your proposal. How do you think Jonas would feel about it?"

"I don't think he'd mind. He's always liked me, admired me even, and we got on well when I worked with him at Locke in New York. I don't think I'm wrong in saying that both he and Peter Sampson respect me."

"And certainly you don't have any shareholders to answer to, since Locke is a privately held company with all of the shares in the hands of the Locke family."

"Except for Vivienne Trent. She has some shares. Sebastian gave them to her years ago when they were married," I reminded him.

"Good Lord, Luce, that's not a problem! Vivienne would never fight you in any way."

"Want to bet?"

"No, I certainly do not. And in any case, it's not even a fair bet, since she doesn't own enough shares to make a bit of difference one way or the other."

"That's true."

Gerald yawned and stretched. "I'm frightfully sorry, poppet, but I think I do have to go to sleep now. I feel as if I've been awake for four or five days, I'm so tired. It's the Hong Kong time difference getting the better of me at last." He leaned over, kissed me lightly on the lips. "But at least I had strength enough earlier to make love."

"And perhaps make a baby," I murmured.

He smiled at me. "I hope so, I really do. Good night, sweet."

"Good night, darling," I said and turned out the light.

Within seconds Gerald was fast asleep, breathing deeply. Poor thing, he really was exhausted after the long flight from Hong Kong, plus the time difference. He had arrived last night, looked fatigued, and yet he had insisted on going to the bank this morning.

Not unnaturally, his jet lag had caught up with him later in the day. He had succumbed to it this afternoon, had fallen asleep in the car as I had driven us down here to our small country house in Aldington in Kent.

I lay next to Gerald in the darkness, trying to fall asleep, but my mind was racing, working overtime. Mostly it was focused on Jack. I cared about him and I knew he cared about me; he had looked after me when we were little, had always been my champion. And despite his ridiculous infatuation with Vivienne I

knew he was always on my side when it came to the
crunch. We may have had different mothers, but our
father had made sure we were close and caring.

We had been through a lot, seen a lot when we were
children. I had shared Jack's hurts, as he had shared
mine, and I suffered with him when Sebastian and
Cyrus were forever brainwashing him about doing his
duty at all times.

In the last few years I had felt sorry for him. My
brother had had such rotten luck with women. No
wonder he had turned to drink at one point. His first
wife had become obsessed with our father; his second
wife had turned out to be a nymphomaniac panting to
get into any man's trousers. And now he had quarrelled with his girlfriend Catherine Smythe. I had met
her with Jack twice, and I was not particularly enamored of her.

When Jack told me two weeks ago that he had broken up with her and sent her back to London I was
not in the least surprised. Those two were totally
unsuited to each other and I had predicted to Gerald
that they were bound to split up in the end. She was
far too intellectual and highbrow for my down-to-
earth Jack.

At least my brother had the vineyards to consume
him. They gave him immense pleasure, and he relished the success his label had become in recent years.
Earlier this week he had told me on the phone that he
would never get married again, and I believed him.
Furthermore, even if he changed his mind, and did tie
the knot again one day, he would never have children.
He disliked them far too much, found them irritating.

Therefore it really was up to me to provide a new

generation of Lockes, my own Lockes who would take the family into the twenty-first century. I fell asleep thinking about this.

The following morning after breakfast, I went into the den and telephoned Jack at the Château d'Cose. He seemed glad to hear my voice, and pleasantly surprised when I told him I wanted to visit him.

"Is Gerald coming with you, Luce?" he asked.

"No, I'm afraid he can't. As you know he's been away for three weeks, and he's got a lot of work to catch up on."

"How long can you stay?"

"Two days, that's all. I need to talk to you about a few business matters, quite aside from wanting to see you, Jack. I really was disappointed that you cancelled your trip to London this weekend."

Ignoring this, he said, "When are you coming?"

"On Wednesday morning. Is that all right?"

"It's fine."

We said good-bye and hung up.

Chapter Twenty-five

As planned, I left London very early on Wednesday morning.

Several hours later I was being driven out of the airport in Marseilles, the driver headed in the direction of Aix-en-Provence.

I had not visited the château for some time and I had forgotten how beautiful Provence was. Now as we drove up through the Bouches-du-Rhône I leaned back against the car seat, occasionally glancing out of the window, enjoying the scenery.

It was a pleasant spring day. Sunlit fields, vineyards, and olive groves under a fine blue sky brought back a rush of childhood memories, and for a few seconds I was transported to another time.

I had first come to Provence when I was five years old, and I recall how confused I had been by the foreign language and this strange new place full of voluble people and unfamiliar sights.

I had clung to Jack's hand tightly, my eyes as big as saucers as I had taken everything in. But I had not been afraid. Quite the contrary. I remember that, like Jack, I had been excited about seeing the castle my father had recently bought. And when we had finally arrived at the Château d'Cose, Jack and I had been impressed.

Together, hand-in-hand, we had wandered around the great house, peering into its vast rooms, traversing its endless corridors, and exploring its dusty attics. We had been awed by it all.

We had spent many happy times at the château for the next few years, even though Antoinette Delaney and Vivienne had invariably been with us on our vacations in France. My father had wanted them with us and who was I, a mere five-year-old, to protest.

Vivienne. I wondered what to do about her.

Madge Hitchens had warned me she wanted to interview me for the profile of my father she was writing. No doubt she knew I was coming to Aix. Jack wouldn't have been able to keep that to himself. He told her everything. Like my father he had made her his sole confidante, a role which went all the way back to their childhood in Connecticut.

There was no question in my mind that she would come bearing down on me whilst I was staying with Jack. I at once decided to beat her to the draw. I would call her and make a date before she had a chance to phone me. I didn't particularly relish the idea of seeing her, but knowing her as I did, she would persist in hounding me until I talked to her. I might as well get it out of the way. And on my own ground.

The last time I had seen Vivienne was at Sebastian's memorial service at the Church of St. John the Divine in Manhattan.

She was miffed with me after our run-in at the farm following my father's burial; I was angry with her. She had tried my patience, playing the grieving widow the way she had during the course of that morning. Divorced from Sebastian for a number of years, Vivienne had been another man's wife and then his widow. I had seen no reason for her to adopt the role of widow at Sebastian's funeral, since she was merely an ex-wife.

Jack had said I was wrong, pointing out that Vivienne was genuinely grieving, reminding me that Sebastian had been her guardian after her mother had died. I'd quarrelled with Jack that day too; we had all been on edge I decided later and immediately smoothed it over with Jack.

I made up my mind to be civil and cordial with Vivienne when I saw her at the château. For undoubtedly I *would* see her.

Simone, Jack's housekeeper, and Florian, his house-man, were hurrying down the front steps of the château even before the car had drawn to a standstill.

A second later, as I alighted, they came rushing forward to greet me, their faces all smiles.

"Bonjour, madame," they said in unison.

"Bonjour, Simone, Florian," I responded, smiling back.

The driver had now taken my small case out of the trunk and when she saw it, Simone exclaimed, "Monsieur Locke said you would be here only two days. I see that is so from your luggage. C'est dommage, Madame Kamper, c'est dommage."

"Next time I hope to stay longer, Simone," I murmured, following her up the steps into the château. She had worked here for fifteen years and I had always been a special favorite of hers.

Jack came striding into the hall at this moment, saying apologetically, "Sorry, honey. I was on the phone. Paris."

"Hello, Jack," I answered and smiled up at him.

He hugged me affectionately and then held me away from him. "Luce. You're different." After a sharp and appraising look, he went on, "Cut your hair. Put on weight. Great! You look great."

"Thank you, Jack, and you don't look so bad yourself."

Grinning at me, he put his arm around my shoulder and walked me into the small sitting room next to the library. It was a cozy room, full of big armchairs and a comfortable sofa arranged in front of the stone fireplace. Green velvet draperies hung at the windows, the color repeated in the antique savonerie on the floor.

He said, "Let's have a chat. And a drink. Before lunch. I have a new wine. Special. You must try it, Luce."

"I would love to, and tell me, darling, how've you been? I hope you're not too down in the mouth about the split with Catherine Smythe."

"Not at all. Good riddance." He walked over to the console table, where he kept a tray of drinks and glasses, and proceeded to open a bottle of wine. "We were not suited, not right together. I'm glad she's gone," he muttered dismissively.

Sitting down on a chair near the fire, I studied him for a moment.

I could not help thinking how much he resembled Sebastian this morning. He was wearing a vivid blue turtleneck sweater which emphasized the color of his eyes. With his head of thick dark hair and finely chiseled features he was the spitting image of our father.

I almost said this and then instantly bit back the words, knowing they would offend him. He hated me to tell him he looked like Sebastian, and he forever went out of his way to dress quite differently.

Our father had been such an elegant, fashionable, and impeccably tailored man; Jack was just the opposite, favoring old sweaters, frayed shirts, baggy corduroys, and worn jackets that he had Florian endlessly patch and repair. I was really quite ashamed of his clothes. That is why I usually gave him sweaters and shirts, ties and jackets for birthdays and Christmas. He never seemed to buy anything for himself.

Jack would never admit it, but I knew he dressed this way on purpose, and that he reveled in looking slightly rumpled. I had long ago discovered that comparisons to Sebastian infuriated him, and yet they were almost unavoidable. There was no question whose son he was, they looked so much alike.

Glancing at me across the room, Jack started to give me details about the new wine, how it had been put down nine summers ago, and how it had turned out to be a jewel of a red, probably the best ever produced at the château.

As I listened, I began to realize that Jack spoke more fluidly and in longer sentences as he discussed the wine and Olivier, and how the latter had created it.

It struck me suddenly that this was because he was relaxed and talking about something that he genuinely cared about. Usually words came out of my brother's mouth in short staccato bursts, an abrupt speech pattern that had developed when he was about eight or nine years old. In those days, he frequently stuttered, an affliction that had upset all of us, not only Jack. I think this was why he began to speak in those short bursts. To avoid stuttering. At least that was my theory.

Carefully, Jack carried my glass of wine over to me, then went back to get his own. A split second later, standing in front of the fire, he raised his glass and said, "Here's to that great man whose name is Luciana."

I stared at him, a brow lifting as I did.

"That's what Voltaire said to Catherine the Great. It's a compliment."

"I realize that," I said. "Thank you." I then took a sip of wine, and nodded. "It's lovely, Jack, and not too heavy. Congratulations."

Beaming at me, Jack sat down on the sofa and asked, "What did you want to talk to me about, Luce?"

I took a big swallow of wine and said, "Locke Industries."

"What about Locke?"

"The running of the company *specifically*, Jack."

"Jonas is a great CEO. No problem there. Sebastian handpicked him. Jonas handpicked Peter Sampson. Our profits are high. We've never done better. What's your problem?"

"I don't have a problem, I agree with you, I think

they're both terrific and Locke is in great shape. What I'm trying to say is that I'd like to be more involved in the running of it."

My brother stared at me. "Want to move, Luce? Run the women's divisions. In New York. Like Sebastian offered. Is that it?"

"I might want to move to the New York headquarters, and take up the offer Sebastian made before he died, yes. But what I'm talking about right now is being involved at a higher level, a corporate level."

"Not following you, kid." My brother eyed me.

"I'd like to have a hand in the running of Locke Industries, not just the women's divisions."

"That wouldn't work! It wouldn't sit well, Luce. Not with Jonas. Nor with Peter. Interference. That's how they'd see it. Wouldn't blame 'em." He shook his head vehemently. "No, no, it wouldn't work."

"Because I'm a woman, is that it, Jack?" I asked quietly, staring him down.

"You know better than that. For this reason: *You need more experience.* You're not old enough to handle a company like ours. It's too big."

"Oh come on, Jack, don't say that. You know very well that Sebastian thought a lot about my ability, my practicality, and my efficiency. He had great things planned for me at Locke."

"He did. That's true. But you're not experienced enough. Neither am I. Luce, *I* wouldn't know where to begin. Nor would you. Down the road a bit maybe. Not now, honey."

I sighed. "I don't want you to think I don't have faith in Jonas, because that's not so. I happen to believe he's a genius and so does Gerald."

"He's proved it to me. Look at the balance sheet," Jack said in a voice that sounded tough.

"Have *you* ever wanted to run Locke Industries, Jack?"

He shook his head. "No. But you know that. I just told you how I felt. I wouldn't know how. Not even Sebastian wanted to run it. Not full time. Not in the end. And he helped to make it what it is. Tough job, Luce, real tough."

"You don't really like being chairman, do you?" I gave my brother a penetrating stare. "Isn't it a bit of a bore having to go to New York every two months? Having to deal with Jonas on a daily basis?"

"I don't talk to him every day," Jack cut in, frowning. "What're you getting at?"

"If you want to step down, I wouldn't mind being chairman, Jack. Really I wouldn't. You've never been interested in the company, you much prefer to be here running the vineyards."

He threw back his head and roared, his laughter echoing around the small room. "I always knew you were ambitious. But Jesus, Luce! Trying to take the chairmanship! *From me.* That beats everything."

"I'd only take it if you didn't want it. Or share it with you, if you felt like doing that. You know, to ease your burdens."

My brother began to laugh again, shaking his head. "I gotta hand it to you, kid. You got chutzpah."

"I'm being realistic. I love the business. You don't. I'd make a terrific chairman."

"Maybe. But it's *my duty.* To be chairman. I was brought up to do the job. And I will. Remember Cyrus and Sebastian drilling it into me? Night and day. Duty.

Duty. Duty. That's all they talked about to me. Don't
let the family down. Run the business. Look after your
sister. Be a dutiful son. Dutiful grandson. Dutiful heir.
Dutiful Locke."

"Yes, I remember," I murmured. "They gave you a
hard time, Jack darling, I know that."

"So leave it alone. And don't forget something.
Sebastian laid it all out. In his will. In the division of
shares."

"I know he did. Drop it, Jack. Forget I brought it
up. But in case you ever do want to retire from the
chairmanship, I'm ready to take over."

"You'd have to, Luce. That's the way the will's laid
out. The way Sebastian wanted it. There's no one else.
But if you *do* want to go to New York to run the
women's divisions, then do it."

I nodded, and continued, "Jack, there's something I
want to say. Look, I promised to talk to you on
Madge's behalf. She wants you to go out on a few field
trips. To Africa, for the charities."

"No way! Absolutely not!" he exclaimed. "I've told
Madge that. Several times. I'm giving away the same
amount of money. As much as Sebastian did. I'm even
willing to fund more charities. New ones she brought
to me. But no traveling. Not for me. No trips to Zaire.
Or Zambia. Or Somalia. Or Angola. Or Rwanda. Or
India. Or Bosnia. Or any of the places Sebastian liked
to wander around. Indifferent to disease, bombs, bul-
lets. Indifferent to chaos, murder, revolution.
Whatever. Absolutely no bloody way! *I'm* not insane.
He *was*."

"All right, all right, don't get so excited. It was only
a suggestion on Madge's part, well, a request really.

And I already told her that I was quite sure you wouldn't do it."

"Damn right I won't."

"Jack, did you tell Vivienne I was coming to stay with you?"

"Yes. Why? Does it matter?"

"No, of course not. I understand from Madge that she wants to . . . sort of interview me for the profile she's writing about Sebastian."

"Yes, she does."

"Then I'm going to phone her later and invite her over to the château. How about tonight? Does that suit you?"

"Sure. Invite her to dinner. If you want."

"I will," I said.

CHAPTER TWENTY-SIX

My brother was amiable and affectionate with me for the remainder of the day.

After a pleasant lunch at the château we walked over to the winery, where we spent some time with Olivier Marchand, and then I was given a grand tour of the ancient *cave* by the two of them.

From there Jack and I strolled across to the Home Farm and visited with Madame Clothilde, who insisted on serving us coffee and cake as we reminisced about the past.

Later Jack took me through his vineyards, talking to me proudly about the wines he would make this year. We went down to the lake, had a long walk through the woods, and finally came back to the château.

Here we had a cup of tea together in the small sitting room, a ritual started by Antoinette Delaney that had continued over the years.

After this Jack went back to work for an hour or two, and I retreated to my room to rest for a while before getting ready for the evening.

Earlier in the day I had spoken to Vivienne. She had agreed to drive over from Lourmarin to talk to me about the profile of my father she was writing. She had accepted Jack's invitation to stay to dinner, had sounded so friendly, so cordial I made up my mind to be as pleasant as I could with her. Being mean to her, making snide remarks had become habitual, and now I was determined to hold myself in check.

Whenever I came to visit Jack at the château he gave me the room that had been mine as a child. It was large, filled with light from the many windows and I loved the view of the meadows and the Home Farm.

Now I walked over to one of the windows and stood looking out at this view, which was so familiar to me and had been ever since I was a little girl.

Together Jack and I had run in those fields filled with wildflowers, climbed the great trees in the woods, swum in the lake, picked fruit in the orchard, and had picnics under the vine-covered loggia at the Home Farm. In those carefree days of our childhood it had been Clothilde's mother Madame Paulette who had ruled the roost. She had fed us delicious food, bustled about, chastised us if we were naughty, and generally fussed over us like a mother hen. Jack and I genuinely grieved for her when she died. She had been like a favorite cuddly aunt.

When we were little Jack had always been in charge of me, and I had tagged along no matter what he was doing. Fortunately, he had never seemed to mind this, had always been the protective older brother looking out for my welfare, always kind and good-natured with me even when I was up to mischief.

I thought of the discussion I'd had with him about Locke Industries before lunch. Jack had not erupted angrily, as Gerald had predicted he would before I left London this morning. However, my husband had been right about one thing: Jack had no intention of giving up what was his birthright.

It was not often my judgment was flawed when it came either to business or my brother, but in this instance it had been. However, Jack had taken it well, and no harm had been done to our relationship. He knew I liked to take control, be in charge. Also, he no longer overreacted now that he'd stopped his heavy drinking.

After taking off my suit and putting on a dressing gown, I carried my laptop to the bed and spent the next hour working.

Vivienne arrived punctually a couple of minutes before six, and Florian led her into the small sitting room where I was waiting.

There had always been a certain amount of animosity between us, and since neither of us was a hypocrite we made no pretense of great friendship by hugging and kissing. Instead we greeted each other rather formally and shook hands.

I sat down in my usual chair near the fire.

Vivienne took the one opposite, and said, "You look very well, Luciana."

"Thank you, so do you," I replied, trying to be nice.

Then taking control of the situation in my usual way, I got straight to the point before she had a chance to say anything. "How can I help you? What do you want to know about Sebastian that you don't already know?"

She looked uncertain for a moment, then cleared her throat and said, "I was hoping you could tell me what he was like the last year of his life. You saw him more than Jack and I, didn't you?"

"Yes. He was in London around this time last year. Early April, actually, and I spent a few days with him at the office. He came back in May. It was a weekend and he drove down to Kent on the Sunday, to have lunch with us at Goldenbrooke. He was very much himself on those two visits; by that I mean low-key, slightly remote, even a bit melancholy. Still, that *was* par for the course, right? He was a moody man, Vivienne, as you well know. Certainly we witnessed his mood swings and temperament when we were growing up."

"He could be morose," Vivienne concurred. "Often on the edge. He seemed to be carrying the burdens of the world on his shoulders." She gave me a hard stare, asked, "Did he tell you if he had any special plans? For the future?"

I shook my head. "No, he didn't."

"Can I come in?" Jack asked from the doorway. "Or am I interrupting?"

Vivienne exclaimed, "Hello, Jack. And no you're not interrupting. Come and join us."

Jack strolled in, gave her a peck on the cheek, then went and opened the bottle of Veuve Cliquot that stood in a silver bucket on the console. "How about a glass of bubbly, you two? Or would you prefer something else?"

"Champagne's fine," I said.

"Thanks, Jack, I'll also have a glass." Vivienne turned back to me and went on, "So Sebastian was being Sebastian right to the end?"

"You're not going to dwell on his suicide in the profile, are you, Vivienne?" I demanded, my voice suddenly turning sharp.

"I'm devoting exactly *one line* to it, that's all, Luciana. I am only interested in writing a profile of him as he was. So there were no new ventures on the horizon? Either at Locke Industries or the Locke Foundation?"

"Not that I know of," I responded and glanced at my brother. "Did Sebastian tell you anything about his future?"

"Nope. It was business as usual with him. And there was nothing different on his agenda. I've already told Viv that."

Looking across at her, I said swiftly, "Just before Jack came in, I was about to mention that Sebastian was in good spirits when Jack and I were staying with him last October. This stuck in my mind, because I hadn't seen him happy very often in my life."

"I noticed that too," Vivienne murmured quietly.

"I didn't witness this happiness," Jack muttered as he brought us our flutes of champagne. "If you two agree he was, who am I to argue? There must be something to it."

We all said cheers and raised our glasses.

I said, "There's more to this than just the profile, isn't there? You could easily write it without talking to either of us or anyone else."

Vivienne sat back, crossed her legs, and nodded.

"Certainly. But I told you, I want to get an all-around picture of him. Sebastian as seen through many eyes."

"Vivienne, I'm not stupid. Madge told me about the so-called girlfriend. But you're wasting your time because I know nothing about her. No one does. You're the only one he confided in."

"If she exists," Jack murmured as he came to join us. He hovered in front of the fireplace, sipping his drink.

"Oh she exists all right." Vivienne sounded so confident, I stared at her swiftly.

Jack murmured, "Maybe you're right, Viv. But you'll never track her down. How can you? You don't have a name."

"Oh but I do have a name. Actually I just found it. I know who she is, Jack. I hope to interview her within the next couple of weeks, and perhaps she might be able to shed some light on Sebastian's suicide."

"What do you mean by *that* exactly?" I asked.

"She might have a clue *why* he did it," Vivienne answered.

"Oh for God's sake! Forget all that nonsense, Viv!" Jack exclaimed. "I want to know who the hell she is. And how you managed to find her. Jesus! Talk about a needle in a haystack!"

"Let me first tell you *how* I found her," Vivienne said. "This past weekend I was going through an old appointment book, checking a date for Kit Tremain, when the diary fell open to a day last July. Monday, July the eleventh, 1994. I'd made a notation that I'd spoken to Sebastian that morning. He'd called me from Paris. As I stared at the page I started to remember our conversation. He'd told me he was staying at

the Plaza-Athénee, that he was in Paris to attend a
special dinner with a friend of his. It was a medical
dinner. I asked him if he'd like to come to Lourmarin
for a few days, and he said no, he couldn't, that he had
to go to Zaire for the Locke Foundation. Anyway, once
I'd remembered this conversation, I realized I had
something to go on at last. A real *clue*. The medical
dinner. It was the key to me. Since Sebastian was a
very well-known figure, I was quite sure he would be
listed as one of the important guests attending the
dinner. In press reports, if there were any.

"Following this hunch of mine, I flew up to Paris
for the day on Monday morning. I went straight to *Le
Figaro* and asked an editor I knew there to arrange for
me to have access to their back-issue files for July
1994. He did. Unfortunately, there was nothing in the
newspaper about the medical dinner, so I grabbed a
cab and shot over to *Paris Match*. I have a friend on
the magazine, Patrick Brizzard, a photographer I've
worked with in the past. Patrick helped me to go
through last year's July issues, and I found what I was
looking for, a brief mention of the dinner in the news-
makers section. And there, staring at me as large as
life, was a photograph of Sebastian. He was accompanied by a couple of French doctors. Male. And a
French scientist. Female. His girlfriend, the one he
told me about."

"Not necessarily," Jack said. "She could've been anybody."

"Not the way she was looking at him and he was
looking at her!" Vivienne put down her glass and
stood up. "Excuse me a moment, I left my briefcase in
the hall."

Alone with my brother, I said, "Maybe Vivienne's stumbled onto the real thing."

Jack shrugged. "Could be."

Vivienne came back carrying her briefcase. She took out a copy of *Paris Match* and a black-and-white photograph. "I was able to get this back issue through Patrick, who also made me a print of the photo. If those two people are not involved with each other, then I don't know a thing about human emotions," she finished, handed them to me, and sat down.

I regarded the photograph first. There was my father, looking impossibly handsome in an immaculately tailored dinner jacket. He was flanked by a couple of men on his left; on his right, a woman stood next to him. She was gazing up at him, rather than at the camera, and he at her. They had eyes only for each other; it was perfectly obvious how they felt. Even though I hated to admit it to myself, Vivienne was correct about their feelings. They looked as if they were in love.

Jack, who was leaning over my shoulder, said, "She's a good-looking woman. She reminds me of somebody. I don't know who. So tell us, Viv. Who the hell *is* she?"

Before Vivienne could respond, I glanced at the caption in the magazine and read aloud, "Doctor Ariel de Grenaille of the Institut Pasteur."

"I called the institute yesterday when I got back to Lourmarin," Vivienne said. "And she does indeed work there. Except that she's not in Paris at the moment. She's involved in a special project. *In Africa.* Since yesterday I've been trying to arrange a meeting with her, through the institute. However, she is unavailable, according to the institute. She's heading up some sort of experiment with a highly infectious disease. Quite literally she is in a sort of. . . quarantine. They won't even say where she is exactly. For the last twenty-four hours I've been trying to get in touch with her family."

"I've always said you're like a dog with a bone. You just won't let go of something when you get your teeth into it," Jack remarked. "Or was it luck that you managed to find her?"

"Not luck. I'm a damned good journalist, Jack, and that's the reason I found her," Vivienne shot back.

"I agree," I said, glancing at Vivienne. Although I had disliked her most of my life I had to admit that she was a true professional. I had also come to understand how much she had really loved my father. Her unswerving pursuit of the truth about his death had convinced me.

PART FOUR

ZOË
TRUTH

CHAPTER TWENTY-SEVEN

I am an old woman.

I must admit that to myself today, for it is the truth. Until very recently I thought I had escaped it, thought old age had passed me by. I felt so strong, so vigorous, so full of zest. But lately I have grown decrepit and worn out. It is as if all the life has been drained out of me, leaving only a fragile shell of a woman.

When one is young one never thinks of growing old, pays no mind to age. Youth lies to us, blinds us, gives us a false sense of immortality, makes us believe we are supreme, unbeatable, everlasting. How frightening it is to learn that we are only too mortal, vulnerable, and that in the end we must die. To be no more, to cease to exist, boggles the mind.

Last week, on April the sixth, I celebrated my seventy-third birthday. That evening, when I sat looking at myself in the mirror of my dressing table, I saw myself objectively for a fleeting moment.

What I saw startled me, made me suck in my breath
in shock. Surely the image staring back could not be
me, was not me, surely not. No, this woman was
not *me*.

I was called the great Zoë, the beautiful Zoë, the
woman every man desired. I had been irresistible to
men all my life, with my chestnut hair and sky-blue
eyes, my height and lithesome grace, my hourglass figure and perfect breasts and my long, long legs.

Last Thursday the woman in the mirror had only
the remnants of her great beauty left—the fine
blue eyes and the high cheekbones. The chestnut
hair was no longer thick and luxuriant, owed its
rich color to the skill of the hairdresser. The height
and the legs and the elegance had not been diminished with the passing of time, but the figure had
thickened.

But oh how glorious I had been once, when I was in
my prime. I had reigned supreme. My beauty had
been extolled far and wide. Men had worshipped me,
fought over me.

Charles came to Paris last week for my birthday.
"You look so very, very beautiful," he said to me that
night, lifting his crystal flute of champagne to me,
toasting my birthday. Well, beauty *is* in the eye of the
beholder. *Charles*. My son. My pride. My joy. Ma rai-
son d'être.

He came from Normandy with his wife Marguerite
and they took me for a celebration dinner at Tour
d'Argent, my favorite restaurant. I have always been
entranced by the views from its many floor-to-ceiling
windows, breathtaking views of the River Seine and
the bateaux mouche, Notre Dame Cathedral and the

glittering sky, panoramic vistas of this city that I made my own long ago. Forty-five years ago this month.

I came to Paris in April of 1950.

The chestnuts were in bloom in the Bois de Boulogne, gaiety filled the air, and Paris was still rejoicing that the war was over. Love, laughter, life lived to the fullest—those were the things we cared about then.

Five years after I had chosen this city to be my home I met Édouard. I fell in love. I loved him so much, I loved him until the day he died. I would have done anything for him. Anything at all. And I did.

When we are grown old and horrendous things happen to destroy the fabric of one's existence, age makes it easier to cope in so many ways. We have acquired understanding, wisdom is ours, and we have life's experiences to draw on and sustain us.

But in our youth when trouble comes to plague us we have few weapons with which to combat it, no ready references, no old knowledge stored in our bones, no inner resources to see us through. It overwhelms; it can destroy us.

I know this and I know it well.

It was in my early life that great trouble came to me. My life was difficult, terrible. Unconscionable things were done to me when I was young, destructive acts were perpetrated against me.

I suffered alone. I had no one to help me. No one to rescue me. No one to ease the pain. No one to console me. I sank low in my despair. I did not want to live. I thought that death was my only means of escape. I wanted to end my pain. But I did not take my life. I found courage and strength within myself. I lived again. I came back up. Slowly. I rose higher. I soared.

And ultimately I became the incomparable Zoë.

The woman all men wanted. The woman with the world at her feet.

Édouard wanted me from the first moment he set eyes on me. He was not solely driven by lust, although he lusted after my beautiful body, that is the truth. He wanted love from me as well. Love and devotion. I gave them to him willingly. He accepted them and returned my feelings in full measure. He adored me. He placed me on a pedestal. He made me his wife.

He gave me dignity, my husband.

Édouard died nine years ago at the age of eighty-nine. He never looked his age, nor was he senile in his latter years, but quite strong and robust to the very end. He died peacefully in his sleep, went gently out into the dark night, as gently as he had lived.

The king is dead. Long live the king, the saying goes.

Charles inherited it all. The ancient title, the château and estates in Normandy, the bulk of the family fortune. Charles hardly seemed to care about these material trappings of life. Heartbroken, he long grieved for his father. They had been close, inseparable, the best of friends since he had been a small boy.

Charles had his own son now, my grandson Gerard, who was six and would one day inherit the title. I had ensured the line, at what great cost no one would ever know. Nor should they.

The morning after my birthday last week, we had taken breakfast together, my son and I. He had looked at me at one moment, and said, "Maman, you are a great lady. Une femme avec grand courage."

I had smiled faintly as I had thanked him for his compliment.

Yes, I was of good courage, he was correct in that, and if I was a great lady, une grande dame, then it was because I had made myself one. I had not been born great. Nor had I been born a lady. But I had been born with courage.

Life is hard. It is meant to be hard. To test us, to test our mettle, to break us, or make us. And the lessons of life are equally hard. Yet if we are astute and *quick* then we only have to learn those lessons once.

When I was first married to him, Édouard told me that I had the face of a madonna. I had smiled and thanked him and kissed his cheek.

Later, when I was alone, I had peered at myself in the looking glass, searching my face. There was not a line, not a blemish, not a sign of pain nor a mark of sorrow on that face. How could it be that all the anguish I had suffered did not show?

I could not answer that. Perhaps if they cut me open all the suffering I had endured would be visible on my heart.

It was Édouard who made my life livable. He gave me the greatest of all gifts, the gift of happiness. And slowly, and with infinite love, he erased much of my pain.

I missed him. I was lost without him. Alone. Lonely. Devastated by his death, I lived on because I had taught myself to survive years ago when I was a young girl. I knew no other way to be. But I was only marking time, waiting for the day I died, when we would be reunited in another life, the afterlife.

The antique ormolu clock on the white marble mantelpiece began to chime, startling me out of my reverie. I glanced across at it, saw that the golden hands were sitting at three o'clock on the white enamel face. Then I looked down at the document on the desk. I placed it in the envelope, put that in the small letter case, and locked it. I sighed to myself, returned the case to the drawer of the desk.

I had frequently wondered at different times if there was a grand design, as Édouard had believed, a preordained reason for all the things that happen to a person in the span of a life.

Was *I* part of some great cosmic pattern? Had Édouard been interwoven into it? Were he and I simply pawns of fate, pawns who fulfilled their destinies when they came together, were joined as man and wife?

Once Édouard had said that what must happen *will* happen. Nothing can stop it. "Fate rolls along inexorably," he had said to me. "And you, Zoë, are my fate. And I am yours, don't ever doubt that."

My eyes settled on his photograph in the gold frame on my desk. It had been taken forty years ago, the year we met and married. He had been fifty-eight then, twenty-five years older than I, but so vital and alive.

I looked into his eyes and my own filled. Oh Édouard, I said to him silently, help me, give me strength.

Chapter Twenty-eight

I have lived in this house for forty years. I came here as a bride, and when I leave it finally, for the last time, it will be in a coffin.

It is then that the house will pass to my son Charles. He will live in it when he visits Paris from Normandy, just as his father and his ancestors did, and one day it will pass to my grandson Gerard.

Our family home has always been regarded as one of the most beautiful houses in the city, the finest hôtel particulier, as this type of grand Parisian house was called. It is located on an elegant street, the Faubourg Saint-Germain, in the fashionable seventh arrondissement on the Left Bank, a district I have always liked.

Those many years ago when I came to live in Paris, I found myself drawn to the Left Bank, preferring it to the Right, for it seemed to have more gaiety and spirit, a marvelous sense of joie de vivre that made *me* feel buoyant and full of life.

And I am still captivated by its quaint streets and wide boulevards, the small, enticing tree-shaded squares, the little cafés, the antique shops, and the art galleries.

Now, as it was then, the area is a haven for writers, artists, and the students of the Sorbonne, who all roam around the quartier, gather at the Café Flore and the Café Deux Magots, to while away the time and watch the world go by, as I once did when I was young.

In contrast, the seventh arrondissement also has an historic façade, visible in the architecture of gracious old houses like mine, the museums, and the public buildings. Whenever I wish, I can easily walk to the Rodin Museum or the Hôtel des Invalides, which houses Napoleon's tomb.

It was Édouard who first took me there, who explained so much about the Emperor, and gave me my first lesson in French history. I constantly learned from him, and knowledge was yet another of the gifts he gave me.

Or if I feel like it, I can stroll leisurely across to the Luxembourg Palace, to meander for a while through its beautiful gardens, sifting through my memories as I walk. For it is here that I brought my children when they were young, to run and play and be with other children. Those were the truly joyous days of my life, the golden days of their youth.

There is so much life, so much excitement out there on the streets of the Rive Gauche. Yet here, behind the high garden walls, my house is quiet, grown still, now that I am widowed and my children are raised and gone.

When children are small, one never thinks about

the day they will spread their fledgling wings and try to fly. No mother ever thinks that day will really come. But it does, and they go with hardly a backward glance. There was no real surprise in this for me. I had always told Édouard that children are only ever lent to us. When the time comes they must be given to the world.

The lovely, gracious rooms in my house are still the same, filled with priceless antiques, paintings, and objets d'art, extraordinary possessions my husband's family accumulated over the centuries, and to which he added throughout his lifetime.

Once these rooms rang with voices and laughter, but they have now been silent for some years. I no longer entertain anymore as Édouard and I once did so brilliantly.

For many years I was considered to be one of the great Parisienne hostesses, renowned for my table and my distinguished guests.

Only the finest quality in food and wines were acceptable to Édouard, who was a perfectionist, and our guests were of the highest quality too—ministers from the French Assembly, politicians, and prizewinning writers. And the upper crust of Parisian society, le gratin, the most closed and impenetrable circle of the elite, a circle open only to those of the same ilk.

I was in mourning for Édouard for several years, but eventually I put away my widow's weeds and began to entertain once more but on a smaller scale.

Without him by my side I soon lost the taste for it. There was no purpose in it anymore. I had always done it for him, to please him. I brought the world to him, to entertain him, and he had applauded me for it, loved every moment of it. Once he was no longer here to share them, the luncheons and dinners palled on me, became meaningless, irrelevant.

The back of the house opened onto a large garden, one of the few left in Paris.

Now I stood in the small salon looking out toward that garden on this glorious April afternoon. The gardener had turned on the antique fountains, five of them in all, each one placed in a different part of the garden. From where I was standing I could see them all easily.

Jets of water spraying upward into the air caught the sunlight, and yet again I realized how clever Édouard had been to add those fountains years ago. They looked so cool, refreshing, and pretty in the bright air, and the sound of water was never far from my ears when I was outside.

He had kept the rest of the garden simple. Green lawns were edged by wide borders of perennials in the palest of colors, and encircling the entire garden were tall trees that stood just in front of the high stone walls.

The trees were very old, had been planted by Édouard's grandfather in 1850. They were mostly horse chestnuts. Their wide and spreading green canopies were cool and inviting on hot summer afternoons or sultry evenings.

Édouard had made the garden beautiful for me, because he knew what it meant to me. I enjoyed sitting out there under the chestnut trees reading. I was a voracious reader and it was Édouard who had encouraged in me the love of books, which I had harbored since being a child. But there were no books available to me in those grim days and no time at all to read. They had worked me too hard and taken away my privacy, and much else beside.

This afternoon there was no time either for reading or going out into the garden. I had a job to do; I must do it well, in order to protect those things that I held dear.

Turning away from the window, I moved back into the room. The small salon was decorated in the palest shade of watery green, with a marvelous Aubusson on the floor and eighteenth-century French furniture placed in intimate groupings.

There were two large, gilded mirrors above the console tables on either side of the fireplace. I caught sight of myself in one of them as I crossed the salon.

I paused to stare.

And to assess.

Earlier, I had changed into a tailored suit of navy blue wool and a white silk shirt. A pearl choker encircled my throat and pearl studs shone at my ears. My only other jewelry was my plain gold wedding ring and a watch.

I decided that I looked rather austere but businesslike, which was exactly how I wished to appear.

I nodded, satisfied.

There was a light tap on the door and Hubert came in quickly. Inclining his head, he said, "Comtesse?"

"Yes, Hubert, what is it?"

"Do you wish tea to be served in here, Madame? Or in the grand salon?"

"I think in here would be preferable, Hubert. Thank you."

He nodded again and disappeared as quickly as he had arrived, gliding off on silent feet. Édouard had hired him as a junior houseman twenty-five years ago and he was still here. But now he was the senior butler and in charge of my household.

I sat down on a straight-backed chair to wait for my guest, who was due to arrive momentarily. And as I waited I asked myself how properly to deal with a loose cannon. I had no idea. I pondered this.

Suddenly I had no further time for thought. I heard the sound of footsteps on the marble floor of the foyer, and a moment later Hubert was opening the door of the salon.

I rose and turned to face the door expectantly.

"Madame," he said, "your guest is here." He ushered her into the salon, and went on, "Madame Trent, I would like to present you to the Comtesse de Grenaille."

I stepped forward, arranged a polite smile on my face, and stretched out my hand. "Good afternoon, I'm very pleased to meet you, Mrs. Trent."

The young woman smiled at me and grasped my hand firmly in hers. "And I am pleased to meet you, Countess. It is so very kind and gracious of you to see me."

I nodded, extracted my hand, and waved it in the direction of the seating arrangement near the French doors to the garden.

"Shall we go and sit over there? In a few moments, Hubert will serve tea, but we can chat whilst we're waiting, I think."

"Thank you," Vivienne Trent said, and followed me across the room.

She took a seat on the small sofa.

I sat down on the same straight-backed chair as before, which I preferred, and said, "When the Institut Pasteur telephoned me, they said you wished to talk to me about my daughter Ariel. Something to do with an article you are writing about the late Sebastian Locke."

"That's true, Countess, yes. I am writing a profile about him for the *Sunday Times*, the British newspaper. I am calling it 'The Last Great Philanthropist,' and it will deal with the essence of the man, what made him tick. I will touch on his great achievements, his compassion and generosity to the world's poor and suffering. It'll be a very positive story. Very upbeat, actually."

"I see," I murmured. "However, I am not quite sure how I can help you. My daughter is away, and I didn't know Mr. Locke."

"But your daughter did, Countess. Didn't she?"

I hesitated, but only fractionally, and then I nodded. "Yes, she did."

"I would like to talk to her about him, get her impressions of him as a man who set out to work miracles in the world."

"I don't believe she is available at the moment. In fact, I am quite certain she's not."

Vivienne Trent looked crestfallen, and then she leaned forward, rather urgently I thought, and said, "I want to be very open and straightforward with you, Countess. I am not only a journalist writing a story about him, but a member of the Locke family."

I merely nodded.

Mrs. Trent said, "If I may explain?"

"Of course, please do," I answered.

"I knew Sebastian from the age of twelve. My mother had a relationship with him for six years. When she died, when I was eighteen, he became my guardian. He sent me to college, to Wellesley actually, and looked after me in general. He and I were married when I was twenty-two and he was forty-two. We were married for five years and remained friends after our divorce. It was an amicable one." She paused and looked at me intently.

"I see," I murmured.

"Anyway, Countess, I'm telling you this because I want you to understand that my profile of him will be laudatory. It won't be critical of him, I'm not about to write a 'warts and all' portrait of him. Quite the opposite. And of course it would only be laudatory about your daughter, Dr. Ariel de Grenaille."

"I understand," I responded. "Thank you for explaining. But I don't know how much my daughter could contribute, even if she were available. And I did just tell you she's not."

"I think she could contribute quite a lot," Mrs. Trent said swiftly. "After all, she was the last woman he was involved with. Personally involved on an emotional level."

I stared at her but I said nothing. I just sat there, waiting, wondering what she would say next.

There was total silence in the room for several minutes. I knew Vivienne Trent was expecting me to make a remark, but I remained silent.

Finally, it was she who broke the silence. Clearing her throat, she said, "Countess de Grenaille, Sebastian told me he was going to marry your daughter."

"He said that?"

"Yes, he did."

"When did he tell you this?"

"Last October, early October. On the Monday of the week he died."

"You were his confidante, Mrs. Trent? Or did other members of his family know of his intentions?"

Vivienne Trent shook her head. "No one else knew, Countess, because I was his only confidante."

When I said nothing, she asked, with a slight frown, "Didn't you know they were planning to marry?"

"Oh yes, Ariel had told me. You must have been *extremely* close to him if he confided in you, Mrs. Trent, even after your divorce."

"I was. Sebastian trusted me implicitly."

"What did he tell you about Ariel?"

"Not a great deal *about* her, only that she was a doctor, a scientist, working in Africa. But he did speak to me about his feelings for her, the depth of his feelings."

"Did he now. How extraordinary. Unusual really, under the circumstances."

"I don't think so," she said.

"But you were once his wife. Was it not upsetting for you to hear that he loved another woman? To be told that he was going to marry her?"

"No, not at all!" she exclaimed rather fiercely. "I cared about him. I loved him. I wanted him to be happy, to have love and companionship in his life, just as he would have wanted that for me. Did want it, actually. As I've said, we were very, very close."

"I realize that you must have been."

"Countess de Grenaille, I know your daughter is

working in Africa. I would like to go and see her. Could you arrange this for me, please?"

"That is very doubtful, Mrs. Trent. She is unavailable."

"The Institut Pasteur said the same thing. The person I spoke to indicated she was working with infectious diseases. And explained that Dr. de Grenaille was in some kind of. . . *quarantine*."

"That is correct, she is."

"Could you explain what it is she is doing exactly?"

"I'll try," I answered. "Ariel is a virologist. Currently she is working with viruses that are known as hot viruses."

"In a laboratory in Africa?" Mrs. Trent asked, leaning forward eagerly, her expression alert, questioning.

I nodded. "Yes."

"Whereabouts in Africa?" she pressed.

"Central Africa."

"Could you be more precise, please, Countess?"

"Zaire. She is working in Zaire."

"With those hot viruses?"

"Yes, Mrs. Trent, I just said so. That is what she does. She has been working on them for the past seven years, especially the filoviruses."

"What are they?"

"Sometimes they are called thread viruses, because filo is the Latin word for thread. They are highly contagious and deadly. *Lethal*."

There was a knock on the door and Hubert came in, carrying the tea tray.

"Excuse me, Madame," he said placing the tray on the small antique table in the center of the seating arrangement, and glanced across at me. "Shall I pour the tea, Madame?"

"Oui, merci, Hubert."

"It sounds like very dangerous research," Vivienne Trent murmured.

"It is the most dangerous work in medical science today," I replied. "The slightest little mistake, the merest slip on her part, and she could infect herself. She would die, of course, if that happened. There are no known vaccines."

CHAPTER TWENTY-NINE

We were silent, she and I, as we sipped our lemon tea, but after a few seconds Vivienne Trent put down her cup and said, "I think I've read about the hot viruses. They're somewhat rare, aren't they?"

"Very, but so lethal I can hardly bear to think about them," I responded. "As I explained a moment ago, there are no vaccines against them, no known cures. They kill in a matter of a few days, and in the most devastating ways."

"How do they kill?"

"You don't want to know," I answered and drank a little tea.

Vivienne Trent did not press me. She asked quietly, "And they come out of Africa, am I correct?"

"Yes, you are."

"Where from exactly?"

"Various areas. I'm not really an expert, you know," I said giving her a slight smile.

"But surely your daughter has discussed her work with you? Told you about it?" she asserted, and a dark brow lifted.

"Yes, she has talked to me from time to time."

"Then you must know more than the average person, Countess, a person like me."

"I suppose I do."

"Countess de Grenaille, forgive me if I sound as if I'm prying. I'm not, really. I'm just trying to understand about your daughter's work. For my profile of Sebastian. Their emotional involvement aside, I can see that she must have had quite a lot in common with Sebastian, in that the foundation funded medical research there, fought disease. And, of course, he did love Africa, had so much knowledge about it. They must have got on very well—" She broke off, reached for her handbag. "Would you mind if I made a few notes? Just for background information."

Briefly, I hesitated, and then before I could stop myself I acquiesced. "No, I don't mind, that's perfectly all right, Mrs. Trent."

"Thank you so much." She offered me a warm and very winning smile, took out a notebook and pen, closed her bag, and went on. "You said the viruses come from various areas in Africa. Did your daughter ever tell you anything about their actual source?"

"Ariel and the other doctors and scientists working in this field of medicine believe that the viruses come out of the rain forests of Africa. According to Ariel, the viruses have probably been around for hundreds of millions of years. However, they've been undetected. Undiscovered. My daughter explained to me that because the tropical forests are now being destroyed in a very systematic way, the viruses are beginning to . . . come out. *Emerge*. And they've gone into the human population."

"But how does that happen?" she asked, her voice rising an octave, her intelligent eyes fixed more intently on mine than ever.

"Scientists have discovered that the monkey can act as a host for the viruses, other monkeys get infected and become carriers. Ariel told me that the viruses have somehow managed to mutate, have changed their genetic structure in order to jump from monkeys into humans."

"Oh, my God, that *is* frightening!" she exclaimed. Her voice was full of sympathy when she added, "It must be extremely worrying for you, Countess, knowing that your daughter is working with these deadly viruses, handling them constantly."

"It is," I answered, and then found myself unexpectedly confiding in her. "I'm afraid for Ariel. Always afraid. And afraid of the viruses. I try very hard not to think about her work, what she's doing. She's talented, you know, and very skilled. And she is careful, cautious—"

I broke off, reached for my cup of tea, reminding myself that I had not intended to have a long discussion with Vivienne Trent. But she was extraordinarily disarming. Her soft, sympathetic manner was effective, and I had begun to relax with her. I felt at ease. From the moment she had walked into the small salon I had detected something special in her, something fine and decent. Instinctively, I knew she was trustworthy, a good person. Besides which, we were only talking about Ariel's work. Not that there was much else to discuss anyway.

"That's quite a pressure on you, Countess de Grenaille," Mrs. Trent was saying. "Living with that kind of . . . *apprehension*. About someone you love, I mean. I know only too well. Years ago, when I was married to Sebastian, and he went off alone to places that were in turmoil, in the midst of revolution or upheaval, I could barely sleep for worrying about him. I was always quite certain he was going to catch a bullet or get blown up. Or be kidnapped by rebel troops. I also worried that he would catch some deadly disease. He used to wander around Africa quite unconcerned for himself, and my heart was very often in my mouth, the risks he took." She smiled and shrugged lightly. "But nothing ever did happen to him. I used to tell him that he had a guardian angel sitting on his shoulder."

I nodded but made no comment. I hoped my daughter had a guardian angel sitting on her shoulder when she was working in the laboratory. Night and day I lived with the knowledge that if she made the slightest error she would endanger her life.

Vivienne Trent cut into my thoughts, when she said, "There's been quite a lot written about hot viruses in the past few years, quite aside from the AIDS virus, I mean. Isn't one of the more deadly ones called Marburg virus?"

"Yes. It's from the filovirus family I told you about."

"Is she working on that?"

"Not anymore."

"What is she working on then?"

"A virus called Ebola Zaire. It's the deadliest, the worst. It kills in nine out of ten cases."

"Oh my God, how ghastly."

"It is."

"What are the symptoms?"

"A lot of bleeding . . . terrible bleeding . . . hemorrhagic fever—" I let my voice trail off. The horror of it was always too much to contemplate.

Vivienne Trent seemed to be digesting my words. Then she looked across at me and said, "What prompted Dr. de Grenaille to become a virologist?"

"Ariel was always interested in viruses and in Africa, and one day these two interests merged."

"So she always wanted to be a doctor, did she?"

"Not a doctor practicing medicine, but a scientist, and even when she was quite a young girl."

"I can certainly understand her interest in Africa," Mrs. Trent said and confided, "I went there with Sebastian on our honeymoon, to Kenya, and I fell in love with the place. I often went back to other parts of Africa with him, on foundation business, and it never ceased to fascinate me. Does your daughter feel that way?"

"Yes, I think she does. My husband's uncle had business interests and holdings in French Equatorial Africa, the French Congo, as it was known years ago. Ariel loved to sit and listen to his tales when he visited us. In 1973, when she was about twelve, he invited us all to the French Congo. We started out in Brazzaville and then traveled all over Africa. She too fell in love with its beauty and its mystery, its sense of timelessness."

Mrs. Trent nodded, remarked casually, "So your daughter must be about thirty-three?"

"Yes. Thirty-four at the end of April."

"I hope you don't mind me asking this, Countess, but was Dr. de Grenaille ever married before?"

"No, she wasn't. She's always been very dedicated to her work. She once told me that she had been so busy looking down the lens of a telescope all her life she hadn't had time to look up and find a man."

Vivienne Trent smiled. "I do wish I could meet her—"

"I told you earlier that's not possible," I cut in swiftly, sounding a little more sharp than I had intended. "She's in a laboratory that's been isolated, contained if you like, for safety. She's involved in a very special project at this moment. She and her team work long hours, and the work itself is very difficult, quite debilitating in a variety of different ways. For one thing, they wear special clothes. Biological suits—"

"Do you mean space suits, the kind astronauts wear?" she interrupted.

"Something like that. Plus helmets with windows, boots, and several pairs of gloves. Between the danger, the intensity of the work, and the complicated clothing, it's a very stressful environment, as I'm sure you can imagine."

"I can," Vivienne Trent said. There was a small silence. She leaned back against the sofa looking reflective. "Doctors like your daughter are the true heroes, Countess, so very selfless and in so many ways," she said at last. "You must be awfully proud of her and the contribution she is making. After all, she is endeavoring to create a safer world for us to live in."

"Thank you, Mrs. Trent, that's very kind of you to say so. And yes, it's true, I am proud of Ariel. Very proud." I paused, shook my head. "But I'm also very worried a great deal of the time," I finished with a pained smile.

"I can well appreciate why. Did your daughter meet Sebastian through her work? I imagine she must have."

"You're correct in that assumption. In actuality, she sought him out, went to see him. She wanted his foundation to fund a special project. A medical project some friends of hers were working on in Zaire."

"And did he?"

"Of course. Would you expect otherwise?" I looked at her pointedly.

She laughed. "No. He was always so generous, and especially when it came to medical research."

"From what I know of him . . . have learned about him, he was a very good man, I think." As I said this I realized Vivienne Trent's eyes were focused on a table at the other side of the room.

Following her gaze, I exclaimed, "Ah, I see you are interested in photographs of my family . . . of my husband Édouard, my son Charles, and my Ariel. She's the young woman in the photograph standing next to theirs."

Swinging her eyes back to mine, she said, "She's very lovely. May I go and take a closer look, Countess?"

"Please do."

She rose and walked across the room. I watched her staring at the photograph of Ariel, fully understanding her interest in my daughter. She then peered at the pictures of my husband and my son. It was at this moment that I felt the first stab of pain, a pain so fierce I closed my eyes and sucked in my breath, trying not to gasp out loud. I had not suffered from the pain for several weeks now and it took me by surprise.

"Countess, Countess, is there something wrong?" Vivienne Trent was saying.

I opened my eyes as she drew to a standstill next to my chair.

Taking a deep breath, I explained, "I'm afraid I'm in pain quite suddenly, Mrs. Trent."

"Can I help you? Perhaps I can get you something." Bending over me, her face taut with concern, she asked, "Are you ill? Do you need medication of some kind?"

I was moved by her consideration and reached out, touched her hand resting lightly on my arm. "I'll be all right, thank you. But I will have to bring our talk to a close now."

"Yes, of course, I do understand. You've been very generous with your time, Countess. In fact, I think I may have overstayed my welcome. When we spoke on the phone, you did say an hour and I think I've been here a bit longer than that."

"I enjoyed meeting you," I said. I was feeling faint, and when the stabbing pain attacked again I winced.

Vivienne Trent could not fail to notice this and exclaimed, "Oh, Countess! I know you're ill! I must go and fetch your butler. Don't you think I should do that?"

I could only nod. Then I managed to say, "There's a bell over there, near the console. You just have to push it, and Hubert will be here in an instant."

She did this and then returned to my side, hovering

over me. "I wish I could help you in some way, make you feel better, Countess."

"I'm afraid that's impossible, Mrs. Trent," I said. "You see, I have cancer. I'm dying."

Chapter Thirty

It is foolish for an old woman to fall under the spell of a younger one. Both women are bound to get hurt.

Inevitably the younger woman will grow bored, resentful of the older woman's wisdom and the burden of her age. And the old woman will feel hurt and abandoned when she is eventually rejected.

I suppose it is only natural that young feet want to keep running, doing, experiencing, while old feet have a tendency to slow.

I knew all this, had known it for a long time, and yet I had allowed myself to fall under the spell of Vivienne Trent. Fortunately, the negative aspects did not feature in the equation in our particular case. And for one simple reason: I was not going to be in this life very long. Therefore, there was no time for either of us to cause pain to the other.

My doctors had told me several months ago that

there was nothing more they could do for me. They had allowed me to leave the hospital so that I could spend what time I had left in my own home.

I had not told Charles or Ariel, or anyone else, how close the end was for me. There was no point. They could do nothing to help me. In one sense, I was being self-protective. I had long realized that I would not be capable of dealing with my children's emotions if they knew I was dying. I did not have the strength.

I yearned for peace and quiet, needed to spend what short time I had left leading as normal a life as possible. It was important for me to go about my business whenever I was able to do so with my dignity and pride intact.

Although I had not confided in my children, I had told Vivienne Trent the truth. I had done this one week ago today, the afternoon we were having tea. The words had been said without any thought on my part, nor did it matter that I had uttered them.

I felt quite comfortable that she knew I was facing imminent death. In part this was because she was a stranger. However, I had also witnessed her display of genuine concern for me, and she had shown me her compassionate side.

The fact was I trusted this young woman.

I had seen something fine and good and essentially honest in her that day. And in the past week she had proven that I was correct in my judgment of her.

A day hasn't gone by without her telephoning me to see how I was feeling. She has sent flowers and books she thought I might like. Two of the books were her own, books she had written herself.

One of them was about Napoleon and Josephine and the early years of their marriage, and the other was a biography of Catherine the Great of Russia. They had been most revealing of the author in so many different ways.

Every day for the past few days, Vivienne had come to tea at four o'clock, just to sit with me and keep me company. She had told me a great deal about herself, her life, her houses in Lourmarin and Connecticut, entertained me in such a delightful way she had managed to take my mind off my illness.

Thankfully I've come to feel much better in the last twenty-four hours. The pain has finally lessened. I'm almost free of it again.

Never once in this last week has Vivienne asked me a single question about Ariel and her relationship with Sebastian Locke. Nor did she mention the profile she is writing about him.

It is possible to know a person for a whole lifetime and not know them at all. Yet I knew Vivienne Trent the very first day we met, knew her as if we had been intimate friends for many years.

She was an endearing young woman, very beguiling, and crept under one's skin. I could understand why a man like Sebastian Locke had loved her as a young girl and later when she was a grown woman.

Vivienne was intelligent, sincere, warm, and loving, and she did not have a bad bone in her body. What is more, she seemed to be totally without cynicism.

In certain ways she reminded me of my daughter.

They were rather similar in character—responsible, caring, dedicated, and disciplined young women with good values and a sense of purpose.

But Vivienne was much more worldly, more sophisticated, and certainly more lighthearted than Ariel.

My daughter had always had an unusual aura about her, one that many mistook for aloofness. It was, in fact, an aura of isolation, something which is not uncommon in the truly gifted, who *are* different, who do seem somewhat removed from us lesser mortals. It is as though they live on another plane altogether.

Ariel's work had always dominated her life. She had had little time for anything else most of her adult years. Until Sebastian Locke came into her life. Now that he was dead I was thankful that she had her work as a virologist to fall back on. Dangerous work in so many ways, but it had always consumed her, was something she loved and was excited by. And it would get her through this difficult period in her life.

I longed to see her again before I died, my beautiful child of my heart. But I feared I would not. Unless she finished her current project sooner than expected and came home to Paris.

It was not possible for me to tell her how ill I really was. If I did, if I said I needed her, she would drop everything in Africa and come running to me. But that would be such a selfish act on my part.

She had been mine for thirty-three years and had given me so much pleasure and joy, fulfilled so many of my dreams and hopes for her. And she had been a good daughter. Therefore my impending death did not amount to much in the overall scheme of things.

I knew Ariel loved me, knew that I would live on in her heart and memory long after I was dead. Just as Édouard did. Like most girls she had been close to her father, and Édouard had adored her. She would have her memories to sustain her. She and her brother were also close. They would always be there for each other.

As for Charles, he would hurry to me when I finally told him the truth, and he and Marguerite would stay with me until the end.

But the pale rider on the pale horse had not come to take me yet. I believed I still had a few weeks left on this earth. I had felt so much better today. The medication had finally alleviated the severe pain that had attacked me so savagely last week. I was back on my feet again, able to cope.

I was determined that Vivienne and I would have tea outside in the garden today. I had told Hubert as much. He had agreed that it was warm enough, and I could see him now from my bedroom window. He was arranging cushions on a garden seat, and Josie, the maid, was covering a small table with a white linen cloth.

Glancing at my watch, I saw that it was 3:45. Vivienne would be here promptly at four. She was never late.

"Could I ask you something rather personal, Countess Zoë?" Vivienne said carefully, her head cocked to one side, her eyes smiling.

"You can ask me anything Vivienne," I said, "And I'll certainly answer you if I can."

"Are you French?"

"Yes, I am. Why?"

"You speak such perfect English, but I detect a slight accent. It's one I can't place. And you don't sound like most French people do when they're speaking English. I just wondered if you had been born somewhere else?"

"How clever of you to pick that up. You must have a good ear."

"So you're not French then," she asserted.

"Yes, I am, by nationality, Vivienne. I became a French citizen many, many years ago. But I was born in America. Of Irish parentage, actually. My mother and father emigrated to America with their parents when they were small children. They both grew up in New York. They met each other there and married."

"How amazing! You're an Irish-American, then."

I nodded and said, "Originally, yes. But why do you sound so surprised?"

"You're so French. You have such chic, such great style, what I call true French style, the way you look and dress, and yet you're not French at all—" She cut herself off and shook her head. "I shouldn't say that! Of course you're French. After years of living here, absorbing the culture, the mores and manners of the French, and being married to a Frenchman, how could you not be."

"Funnily enough I feel very French, Vivienne. And what you're hearing in my voice is a slight lilt I think. The Irish lilt I picked up from my mother when I was growing up. But do you know, I didn't even realize it was still in evidence when I spoke English."

"It's faint, but it's there," she answered.

"Let me explain. When I first came to Paris I fell in love with the city, long before I met Édouard and fell in love with him. I knew I wanted to live here, nowhere else would do for me, once I'd seen the city of light. So I immediately started to take French lessons, knowing that I must speak the language if I was going to settle in Paris. I'm glad I stayed. France has been good to me. I've never regretted moving here."

"Did you come to France from America?" Vivienne asked.

"No, from London. I had been living there through the war years." I picked up the teapot and filled her cup and then my own.

"Thank you," she said, sat back in the wrought-iron garden chair, and glanced around the garden. It seemed to me that she was lost in thought.

I studied her. She appeared to be preoccupied, as if she were troubled, and after a moment, I said, "Are you all right? Is everything all right with you, Vivienne?"

"Yes, of course, why are you asking?"

"You look so very preoccupied, even a little worried," I replied.

"Countess Zoë . . . there is something I feel I must say. I was going to mention it yesterday, but it was already getting late and I didn't want to tire you. I hesitate to bring it up even now."

"You can. I'm perfectly fine," I reassured her. "I told you earlier, the medicine has worked wonders for me in the last twenty-four hours. So why don't you tell me what's on your mind? Why don't you unburden yourself?"

"It's like this—" She stopped somewhat abruptly, sighed and looked away, but eventually she brought her gaze back to mine.

Her clear, green eyes were filled with such intelligence, candor, and honesty they almost took my breath away.

She said in a low, serious voice, "There's something I want to tell you, to explain."

I nodded.

"Last Tuesday, when I first met you, I was very drawn to you. In the hour I was here, I felt as if I knew you, as if I'd always known you. When you collapsed I wanted to help you. I couldn't bear to see you suffering. I've been coming to see you ever since because I cared. As we've talked these past few days, and come to know each other, it's seemed to me that there's a bond between us. It's hard to explain, because we did meet only a week ago. But I really mean what I say. I do feel close to you, Countess Zoë."

"I know you do, Vivienne, and I feel that way myself. There is a bond. As though something is pulling us closer together." I patted her hand. "I wish we'd met a long time ago. You're a very special young woman, Vivienne, and you've become quite dear to me in only a few days. I want you to know that you've been a comfort to me this past week. You have helped me to pull through that little crisis."

"I'm so glad!" she exclaimed, looking pleased, and took hold of my hand, held it tightly in hers for a moment.

"You remind me so much of Ariel," I confided, smiling at her. "I wish you had known each other. I think you would have been friends. Good friends."

"That's what Sebastian wanted, Countess Zoë. He said that last October when he told me he was going to marry her. He'd hoped I would be spending Christmas in Connecticut. He wanted me to meet Ariel then, and he was so disappointed when I explained I was going to be in France. He said he would bring her to Lourmarin in the new year, that he knew we would like each other, that we'd love each other when we met. He explained that he wanted me to be at their wedding in the spring. Actually, I had a strong suspicion he wanted to have it at *Vieux Moulin*."

"And how would you have really felt about that, if he had suggested it?" I asked, my eyes resting on her thoughtfully.

"I would have been pleased," she responded. "And I would have made them very welcome, given them a lovely wedding. I genuinely cared about him. He was my only family. But then you know that."

"Yes," I said softly. "I do."

"Countess Zoë?"

"Yes, Vivienne?" I looked at her alertly, detecting something different in her voice. I braced myself.

"I don't want to upset you, and I know *you* know that. I truly hope you don't think I've been coming to see you this past week because I have an ulterior motive. And, I'm quite certain you accept that I'm very sincere in all that I've just said to you. But I *have* to ask you something."

"Then ask me, my dear."

"I would still like to meet Ariel. Won't you arrange that for me, please, Countess Zoë?"

"Vivienne, I cannot."

"An hour, two at the most, that's all I need with her. I could fly to Zaire. Talk to her for a short while, and then leave. I'd leave immediately, you have my promise. *Please*," she pleaded.

"Vivienne, *no*. I cannot arrange it."

"What harm would it do?" she asked.

"More than you could possibly imagine!" I exclaimed and hated the fact that my voice had risen sharply, but I couldn't help myself.

Swiftly, I went on more softly, "When Ariel heard the news of Sebastian Locke's death she was devastated. She was ill for several weeks. A little later she even took herself out of her own research project, for her own safety. She was slow in recovering from the news of his death and she was afraid she might make an error in her experiments with the virus that could cost lives. His death affected her very deeply. And to have you go there *now*, only seven months later, to interrogate her, to ask questions about their relationship, about his demeanor, attitude, and mental state in the last few weeks of his life would only open up wounds. Wounds that have just begun to heal. The kind of work Ariel does is so stressful, so dangerous, I don't want her to be distracted by any emotional upsets."

I paused and looked at Vivienne intently. "Try to see it from my point of view, my dear. I want Ariel to be absolutely concentrated on her work, so that she doesn't make any fatal mistakes. In short, I want her left alone. By you. By anyone else who might cause her more grief. There's nothing she can tell you that you don't already know. You can write your profile without meeting her, please believe me you can."

"I understand how you feel, Countess Zoë, understand everything you're saying. I've only persisted about seeing her because I thought Ariel might have a clue."

"A *clue*?" I repeated.

"Yes, a clue why he killed himself."

"I doubt it very much. She can't give you an explanation about his death, Vivienne."

"She loved him, he loved her, and he was so *happy*

that last week of his life," Vivienne murmured. "Really happy, Countess Zoë." She looked at me and shook her head. Her expression was sad. "I knew him so well, and for so long, there was no way he could ever have fooled me. Not about anything. That awful gloominess, that moroseness of his, was absent. He was positively glowing. So why would he want to kill himself when he was on cloud nine and planning to marry your daughter?"

"Vivienne dear, listen to me. No one ever really knows why people do these awful, tragic things to themselves, take such terrible and irrevocable steps."

"His suicide has never made sense to me," Vivienne said softly, almost to herself. "The reason I wanted to see Ariel was because I had hoped she might be able to help me understand it."

"How would she have been able to do that?"

"I've always had an uncanny feeling that Ariel was somehow involved. Please don't misunderstand, Countess Zoë, I mean *indirectly* involved. I know she was in Africa when he took his life in Connecticut."

"But why do you think she would know anything?" I probed.

"Because his relationship with her was the only thing in his life that was *new, different*. His lifestyle was very predictable. His pattern didn't change very much. For years he had lived the same way."

"And how was that?" I asked curiously.

"He went from Manhattan to the farm in Connecticut, and then back to Africa. Or to some other part of the world where he felt he was needed. He did his work there, returned to the States, stayed a while, attended to business at the foundation and

Locke Industries, and went off again. But then he met Ariel in Zaire. He fell in love, made plans to marry her, but suddenly killed himself. To me there is something very strange at work here. I believe that something unusual occurred that week he was in New York. Between the Monday when we had lunch and the Saturday when he killed himself. But it's a mystery. I can't begin to imagine what it was."

"Maybe his life had simply become unbearable," I suggested quietly.

"What do you mean by that, Countess Zoë?"

"Isn't that why people kill themselves, Vivienne? Because their lives have become unbearable. They simply don't want to live any longer," I ventured.

Vivienne was silent. I could feel her pain.

After a moment she leaned forward, gave me a penetrating look, and said, "I want to explain something else to you, Countess Zoë. I loved Sebastian from the age of twelve. I will always love him, and part of me will always belong to him. But writing the profile of him is not very important to me in the long run. It was an excuse in a way. When I got the idea, I ran with it, thinking that it might help me to understand his death, even come to grips with it. Oh yes, it would be satisfying to write lovely things about him. But there is something much more pressing than my hero worship of him."

She paused, took a breath and went on, "I've always had the need to know *why* Sebastian Locke took his life. For myself. It was an act so out of character, so alien to his nature. And I won't have any peace of mind until I know. I think it will haunt me for the rest of my life. I needed to solve this terrible riddle right from the beginning, which is when I got the idea for doing the profile. I thought that talking to people who had known him might help, that I might eventually turn up the truth. And that's really why I wanted to see your daughter. Not to write about their relationship. But, selfishly, for my peace of mind."

"Thank you for your honesty, Vivienne. Ariel was just as perplexed as you, baffled by his suicide. And perhaps one day you *will* meet her, when her wounds have healed completely."

Vivienne nodded, let out a deep sigh, then she said in a low voice, "I just want to close this book and move forward, Countess Zoë, get on with my life."

"I understand your motivations and what drives you. And don't think for a moment that I'm angry, because I'm not. But I must say again that whatever you might think, my daughter couldn't possibly enlighten you."

"You sound so sure."

"I am."

Vivienne's tone was deflated when she said, "You were my only chance. I thought you were the one person who could help me get to the truth of it all through Ariel. I thought she held the key."

For a moment I could not think. My mind froze. I simply sat there in my beautiful garden, shivering slightly from the light breeze now blowing up, staring into those unflinching, honest green eyes that held mine.

And as I looked into the lovely face of this sincere young woman I made a momentous decision.

I knew she had integrity, that honor was an essential part of her character, and so I knew in my bones that I could trust her.

I rose. "Let us go inside, Vivienne dear. It's growing chilly," I said.

She nodded and stood up, took hold of my arm solicitously, and helped me into the house.

Once we were seated in the small salon, I leaned back against the soft cushions of the sofa and regarded her for the longest moment.

Finally, taking a deep breath, I said, "I am going to tell you a tale, a familiar tale that's as ancient as the hills . . . a tale of a man, a woman, and another man . . . "

CHAPTER THIRTY-ONE

"I was twenty-eight and a rich young widow when I visited Paris for the first time, Vivienne.

"Paris instantly captivated me and I decided to move permanently to France. For numerous reasons, I was determined to leave London for good. Suffice it to say that I believed it to be imperative for my well-being to do so.

"After several weeks in Paris I returned to London, put my house in Mayfair and its contents up for sale, gave my solicitors power of attorney to deal with my business affairs, and returned without delay to France.

"Within several weeks I had rented a furnished apartment on the rue Jacob on the Left Bank, hired a student to teach me the language, and begun my search for a proper dwelling place, one of charm, elegance, and permanence. My French teacher, a young

woman of good family, was instrumental in helping
me to find the perfect apartment on the Avenue de
Breteuil—large, airy, and light-filled. Whilst it was
being appropriately decorated and furnished I settled
down to my studies, and at the same time acclima-
tized myself to Paris and the French way of life.

"Even though I say this myself, I was quite beautiful
when I was young, Vivienne. I had great *allure*. I suppose that is the best word to use. My looks were glamorous, not so much exotic as lush. Men found me
irresistible. I did not lack male companionship in
Paris, and I had plenty of escorts to take me everywhere I wished to go.

"But I was well aware that women and not men
were the key to my success in local society. Only
women could propel me into the proper circles. Men
might admire me, flatter me, lust after me, wine
and dine me, and fall in love with me. However, it
was women who could open all the right doors; it has
always been women the world over who run the social
scene, make the decisions, and issue the invitations.
They can either make or break another woman, especially a newcomer to a city.

"I had no intention of allowing any doors to remain
shut or be slammed in my face. Nor did I plan to let
anyone break me. That had been done to me when I
was a child. *Almost*. I would never permit it to happen
again.

"Fortunately for me, I had a sponsor, a mentor, if
you will, someone I had met in London several years
earlier. She was a woman of a certain age and a
socialite of some standing, regarded as one of the
greatest hostesses in Paris, indeed in France.

"She was of fine lineage in her own right, had married into one of the grand titled families of France, and, like me, she was a widow.

"This accomplished and remarkable woman had been a friend of my first husband, the late Harry Robson. Because of his kindness to her during a most difficult time in her life, and their long-standing friendship, she took me under her wing when I moved to Paris in 1950.

"She was the Baronne Désirée de Marmont, attractive, elegant, charming, and very knowledgeable about everything. It was she who taught me about eighteenth-century fine French furniture, Aubusson and Savonerie rugs, tapestries, porcelain, and art.

"I had developed a good sense of clothes by the time I arrived in Paris, but it was the baroness who imbued in me her own brand of chic, her incomparable stylishness. What you admire in me, that sense of style you've commented on, Vivienne, I acquired from Désirée de Marmont.

"The first thing she did was take me to her favorite couturiers, milliners, and shoemakers, saw to it that I was dressed simply but elegantly in the height of fashion. It was her preferred interior designers who helped me to furnish and decorate the new apartment on the Avenue de Breteuil, again under her discerning eye. And it was she who found me the right butler, cook, and housekeeper to run things for me. In short, she supervised every aspect of my life.

"Thus Désirée turned me into a chic and polished young woman with unique style, grace, and sophistication, quite aside from my natural good looks. It was two years after my arrival in Paris that she decided I was 'finished' and, therefore, finally ready to be launched into Parisian society as her protégé from London.

"And so, Vivienne, I began my life again. It was my fourth life. I had had three others, two of which I had tried hard to forget, to obliterate entirely. No one knew of this, not even Désirée. She was aware of one only, my rather pleasant but dull life as the wife of the Honorable Harry Robson, third son of a minor English lord.

"Désirée had one child, her son Louis, with whom she was not on the best of terms. Although she was still in her early fifties I became a surrogate child to her in many ways, like the daughter she had never borne.

"There was a special bond between us, rather like the bond we share, Vivienne. She was not only my mentor in those days, but my inspiration. I aspired to be exactly like her and in some ways I believe I succeeded.

"A good woman, kind, loving, witty, amusing, and a wonderful companion, Désirée was part of that elite circle known as le gratin, the top crust. Yet despite this she was not in the least snobbish. I have observed in my long life that true aristocrats such as Désirée de Marmont and Édouard never are. In my experience it is the jumped-up no-accounts who tend to look down their noses at others.

"It was my dearest friend Désirée who introduced me to Monsieur le Comte, Édouard de Grenaille. The evening we met it was a coup de foudre as the French say, a thunderbolt. Or love at first sight, if you prefer. By this time I had already been living in France for five years. I was thirty-three and completely un-attached. He was a widower with no children, also uninvolved, and fifty-eight years old. However, Édouard did not look his age, nor did he seem it.

"He was a good-looking man, debonair and dashing, and was imbued with continental charm. He swept me off my feet. Within the year we were married. I became Madame la Comtesse, the mistress of this house and a wonderful old château in Normandy.

"We were sublimely happy for the first two years. Then a problem developed in the marriage. I did not conceive. Childless and longing for an heir to carry on the line, Édouard began to change. He became depressed, bad tempered, and critical of me. Oh, not all of the time, Vivienne, there were moments when he behaved like his old self, the Édouard of our courtship, and was kind, considerate. We had always enjoyed a good sex life, an active one, and we loved one another. But love and sex are not always enough. A marriage must be sustained by so much else besides.

"By the time our third wedding anniversary came around there was a genuine breakdown in our relationship. Édouard had grown more and more introverted, preoccupied as he was with his lineage and lack of an heir to carry on the family name. Somewhat irrationally he blamed me. Even though he loved me he took it out on me. For almost two years I ran to doctors and specialists in infertility, following Désirée's advice. The answer was always the same: There was nothing wrong with me.

"When I attempted to talk to Édouard about this, pass on the medical opinions I had received, he became angry and refused to listen. By now I was fully aware that he might not be able to face a simple fact: that he was sterile and unable to procreate.

"I feared for our marriage and I must admit I was profoundly relieved when he decided to go to Brazzaville in French Equatorial Africa. He had a long-standing invitation to visit with his uncle Jean-Pierre de Grenaille who owned vast estates there. I thought the break would do us both good. Édouard seemed to agree. He planned a long trip as he wanted to go on safari to hunt big game.

"It was the beginning of June in 1960 when he set off for Brazzaville. Before he left he expressed the hope that our three-month separation would have positive results. He said it might help to alleviate the strain between us.

"For the first two weeks Édouard was gone I spent my days undergoing further gynecological tests. Once more the results were exactly the same as before. Three new doctors confirmed to me that there was no reason why I could not have a baby.

"By the end of June I was feeling miserable, low in spirits, and overwhelmingly sad. I had had such a terrible childhood and youth. Suddenly it seemed to me that the past was repeating itself, albeit in a different way. I began to think that I was doomed to be unhappy, that life was not going to go right for me after all. I was also fearful that when Édouard returned from Africa our marriage would finally crumble completely, that we would end up either leading separate lives apart or divorcing. I was not sure which I thought was the worst scenario.

"The weather in Paris that summer was gruelling

hot and unbearable. Yet I had no wish to go to the château in Normandy by myself. Fitful, restless, anxiety-ridden, and constantly on the brink of tears, I went to see Désirée de Marmont, hoping that she might be able to both advise and console me. She knew why I had been troubled for so long and was also aware that Édouard had seen fit to blame me for depriving him of an heir.

"When I arrived at her country estate in Versailles to spend the weekend she took one look at me and threw up her hands in alarm. She told me I was too thin and exhausted, insisted that I must take a vacation immediately.

"Vivienne, even now I remember so well what she said to me all those years ago. 'Take yourself off to the Cote d'Azur, ma petite. Sunbathe, swim, relax, go for long walks, eat delicious food, shop for pretty things, and indulge in a romantic interlude with a nice young man if the possibility arises.' You can't imagine how shocked I was about her last suggestion. I was speechless.

"Then somewhat indignantly I told Désirée that I loved Édouard. She smiled. 'All the more reason to have a little lighthearted affair. It will make you feel more relaxed, instill confidence in you again, and when Édouard returns you will be in the right mood to work miracles. You can fuss over him, seduce him, make him feel virile, and believe me you will be able to put your marriage on a more even keel.' Naturally I insisted that an affair was out of the question.

"But on the Sunday afternoon, just before I returned to Paris, Désirée took me to one side, told me again that I needed a change of scenery for my own good.

'Go to Cannes, Zoë. Have some fun. And if there's a chance for a little flirtation, take it. What harm can it do? *None*. Providing no one knows about it. Just remember to be discreet, careful. And take the advice of an experienced woman, stay at one of the smaller hotels and use an assumed name.' On the way back to Paris I pondered her words.

"I never intended to go to Cannes, Vivienne. But during the course of the next week the idea of a holiday in the sun became more and more appealing. On the spur of the moment one morning I telephoned the Hôtel Gray d'Albion in Cannes and made a reservation under the invented name of Geneviève Brunot, booked myself a seat on the Blue Train, packed a few simple clothes, and left Paris for the south of France.

"Désirée had been correct about the change in scenery doing me good. After three days of sunbathing, swimming, long walks, and good food I was feeling much better and looking more like my old self.

"Cannes was busy that summer. The American Sixth Fleet stationed in the Mediterranean had just put into port. Hundreds of young ratings were on shore leave, mingling with the locals and the tourists. I managed to get lost in the crowds. There was a sense of jollity in the air, a feeling of festivity. Everyone seemed so young and gay and happy. I was infected with this spirit of joie de vivre. And of course I met a young man."

I stopped speaking and looked across at Vivienne. She was sitting on the edge of her chair, facing me. Her eyes were glued to my face, and I knew she had been listening attentively.

I said, "I'm afraid this is becoming rather a long

story, longer than I'd intended. Can I offer you some sort of refreshment, Vivienne? Tea? Coffee? Or would you like a drink perhaps?"

"If you're going to have something, Countess Zoë," she said with a small smile.

"I believe I will. I'm going to have a glass of champagne. Does that appeal to you, my dear?"

"That'd be lovely, thank you."

"Would you mind ringing the bell for Hubert, please?"

"Of course not," she answered getting up, crossing the room. After she'd done as I asked she glanced at the photograph on the console and said, "This one is of you, isn't it, Countess Zoë? When you were in your thirties?"

I nodded. "Yes, it is."

"How beautiful you were."

I merely smiled and glanced at the door as Hubert knocked and entered. "Madame?"

"Hubert, we would like to have some refreshment. Please bring us a bottle of Dom Pérignon and two glasses. Oh and perhaps you'd better retrieve the tea things from the garden."

Chapter Thirty-two

Vivienne put down her flute of champagne, leaned forward and said, "Please don't stop, Countess Zoë, please continue your story . . . you said you met a young man in Cannes . . . "

"I did, Vivienne. He was a nice young man, an American. For several mornings I had taken breakfast on the terrace of a small café not far from my hotel. He was usually there, drinking coffee and smoking a cigarette. He had always smiled at me or nodded politely, and on the fourth morning when I arrived he spoke to me. He said good morning in French. I responded with a smile.

"A short while later I paid my bill and left the café. I had not walked very far when the young man caught up with me. In rather halting French he asked me if I was going to the beach. When I said I was in English he grinned and asked if he could join me.

"I hesitated for a moment. But he was so clean-cut,

genial, and polite I asked myself what harm there was in it. Also, I had only ever seen him alone at the café, never with any companions. It struck me that he seemed lonely, which was the way I was feeling at that moment in my life.

"He must have noticed my hesitation because he excused himself for being rude, stretched out his hand, and said, 'Joe Anthony.' Taking hold of his hand I shook it. 'Geneviève Brunot,' I said, and added that he was welcome to accompany me to the beach.

"We spent the morning sunbathing, swimming, and talking in generalities. He was rather quiet and didn't say very much about himself. But then neither did I. That day I was reserved, somewhat uncommunicative. He invited me to lunch at one of the small cafés on the beach, and I remember thinking how young, healthy, and uncomplicated he looked as he ate his beefsteak, French fries, and green salad with such gusto, savored every mouthful of red wine.

"After lunch he walked me back to the Hôtel Gray d'Albion. On the way there he asked me to have dinner with him that night. Again I hesitated momentarily, and when I finally agreed to meet him later he looked so relieved and happy I was touched.

"And that is how it began, our little affair. The following morning we met at the café for breakfast and once again we went down to the beach together. That evening he took me to Chez Felix for dinner, then dancing afterward at La Chunga, a popular nightclub on the Croisette.

"By this time I had learned that Joe was only twenty-two years old. I was startled when he told me this because he appeared to be older and in fact was quite sophisticated. I did not dare tell him my age, admit to being thirty-eight. When he asked me how old I was I lied. I took off ten years and said I was twenty-eight. Joe believed me. It was true, I did look much younger than I actually was, everyone said that. I was slim and lithesome, and my face was virtually unlined. However, I *was* forthright with Joe about my status, and from the very beginning he knew I was a married woman with obligations.

"That night at La Chunga, as he led me around the dance floor, holding me tightly in his arms, kissing my cheek and my hair, I realized I could not stop the inevitable from happening. I knew we were going to end up in bed together. Joe knew it too. There had been something special between us from the start of our friendship.

"We spent the next four days and nights together, and then unexpectedly I panicked. As much as I liked Joe, thought he was attractive and engaging, I realized that I was risking far too much by continuing the relationship. It struck me most forcibly that I had no alternative but to bring our brief romantic liaison to an end.

"When I explained to Joe that I had been called home because of a sudden emergency, he said he understood. Nevertheless, he looked disappointed when I said we could never meet again, was saddened when we took our leave of each other.

"Later that day I boarded the Blue Train for Paris and my real life there. Almost immediately I began to regret the affair and wished it had not happened. The more I thought about it the more I believed I had been foolish and irresponsible. Constantly I chastised myself. On the other hand, there was no way I could turn back the clock. Nor could I eradicate my adultery. I kept telling myself I was not the first person to have had an extramarital affair. Hundreds of millions of people did it every day, and it was part of being human. But this knowledge did not make me feel any better.

"I tried hard not to dwell on those few illicit days I had spent with Joe in Cannes and to some extent I succeeded. But there were awful moments when those guilty feelings returned, usually in the middle of the night when I tossed and turned and wrestled with my demons.

"And then at the end of July I had something else to occupy my mind, rather serious worries in fact. I had missed my period. As the days passed I grew more and more convinced I was pregnant with Joe Anthony's child. In August my body started to undergo certain changes, in particular my breasts were tender and enlarged. I missed my second period at the end of August. By my calculations I was about five or six weeks into my pregnancy.

"I was panic-stricken, floundering, and did not know which way to turn. I thought of confiding in Désirée and then changed my mind, although I've never been sure why I did so. She was my dearest friend, I trusted her, and I knew she would never betray my confidence. And yet I could not bring myself to speak to her of my affair with Joe.

"Perhaps I was a little self-conscious, even a trifle ashamed of myself, although I knew that Désirée de Marmont was a wise woman of the world. She would never presume to pass judgment on me or anyone else. There was even one awful moment when I toyed with the idea of an abortion, but I dismissed this at once. It was far too repugnant to me.

"I am not a religious person. God was beaten out of me when I was young. When one suffers all kinds of abuse at the hands of adults it is hard for a child to keep her faith in God. As a young girl I used to ask myself why God was allowing such terrible things to happen to me, why God allowed such evil to thrive in this world. But I had no answers. I felt He had abandoned me. And I ceased to believe in God's existence.

"When I married Édouard I naturally had to give lip service to the idea of God because the de Grenailles were a devout Catholic family. However, it was only lip service. Imagine my surprise then, Vivienne, when one day at the end of August, when I was out walking, I found myself going into a church in the Latin Quarter. It was St. Etienne du Mont, a place of worship I had not frequented before.

"To this very day I don't know why I went into that particular church on that particular afternoon. I did not go inside to pray. I simply sat there letting the silence envelope me. The interior was very beautiful with its vaulted ceiling, soaring pillars, and stained glass windows. But it was the quiet, the absolute peace that made the greatest impression.

"I sat there for a long time. A kind of lassitude settled over me. My thoughts had been on the baby the entire morning, and I had been worrying, wondering what to do. But now I closed my eyes, let go of those worries, finally relaxing. Then without warning I experienced a rush of the most intense emotion, a feeling of such enormous love for the child growing inside me I was startled.

"Almost at once everything became crystal clear. With great clarity I saw right into the heart of things. I knew what I was going to do. When the baby was born it would be a de Grenaille. It would bring joy and happiness back into my marriage, and Édouard would love the baby as much as I already did. The baby was the solution to everything.

"A short while later I rose and walked slowly down the aisle, confident at last that everything was going to be all right. Just before leaving the church I paused to put money in the collection box. It was then that I discovered the church contained the reliquary of Saint Geneviève. I could not help thinking what a curious coincidence that was.

"Almost overnight my feelings of guilt and remorse disappeared and that wonderful sense of *rightness* remained with me. Édouard returned home from Brazzaville on the first day of September. From the moment he walked in I was convinced everything would work out. He was in such a wonderful frame of mind, Vivienne, my heart lifted even more than it had in church. He looked tan and fit, and he was full of good humor, gave the impression of being glad to be home. One of the first things he did was to apologize to me for his churlish behavior over those many, many months before.

"That weekend we drove to the château in Normandy, and in the tranquility of our lovely old bedroom we made passionate love. It was as if Édouard were trying to exonerate himself for his unfairness and unkindness to me during the past few years. His passion did not lessen that weekend and he kept avowing his love for me.

"Édouard made me radiantly happy that weekend, and my feelings for him were reinforced. I understood how deeply I loved my husband and how much he meant to me. A month later I was able to tell Édouard I was pregnant. Of course he was overjoyed. And for my entire pregnancy he was loving, tender, devoted, and considerate, and he could not do enough for me. I was completely content and happy as I carried the child to full term.

"Of course there were days when I had sudden misgivings, Vivienne. I am not devious by nature and occasionally my deception troubled me. But whenever I experienced a slight twinge of guilt, I focused all my thoughts on Édouard. I reminded myself I was about to give him the child he had wanted throughout his adult life.

"His first wife had failed him. I had not. I was going to present him with the heir he craved. I had ensured the family name and title. The de Grenaille line would continue. Édouard would never know that the child was not his. In any case he would be a good father, and thus would make the child his through his love, there was no doubt in my mind about that.

"I was certain that Joe Anthony was already back in the States, had disappeared into oblivion. Joe did not know my real name. I was Geneviève Brunot to him. Therefore I was safe. The baby was safe. I would never set eyes on Joe Anthony again. Or so I thought.

"My baby was born eight months after Édouard and I had enjoyed our passionate reunion at the family château. Édouard assumed the baby was premature and I did not contradict him. She was a dainty baby, small and delicate, and we named her Ariel. And indeed she did seem to be an airy spirit, a little sprite of a thing.

"For the first year of her life Édouard doted on Ariel, and then slowly that discontent I remembered so well took hold of him once again. He kept muttering that he wished she had been a boy and constantly expressed to me his need for a son. I knew that however much we made love I was not going to get pregnant by Édouard. He was sterile. I was filled with dismay. As time passed and his dissatisfaction with Ariel and with me only increased rather than lessened, I grew more nervous and depressed. And desperate.

"Under French law a daughter can inherit the title and estates, and naturally Édouard knew this. Very simply, Vivienne, he was a man obsessed. That overwhelming desire to have a son dominated him. The more he talked about it to me the more I understood that it was like a cancer gnawing at him inside.

"By the time Ariel's second birthday came around Édouard had become so difficult he was impossible to live with. He was temperamental, volatile, and extremely irritable with me. But then suddenly, later that summer, he had to go away unexpectedly and I welcomed this.

"His uncle Jean-Pierre had had a heart attack. Since Édouard was his only living relative, my husband felt he must go to Brazzaville to take charge of things. I encouraged him in this and when he left I breathed a sigh of relief. I was glad to be alone for a few weeks, to regain my equilibrium.

"Désirée de Marmont was leaving for Biarritz that same week and begged me to go with her. At first I refused but then at the last moment I accepted her invitation. I took Ariel and the nanny with me.

"As it happened, I met a man in Biarritz, Vivienne. He was a friend of Désirée's, and he proved to be a charming and considerate escort, taking me out to lunch, to tea, drives along the coast, and to the cinema. He and I became good friends very quickly. Patric Langalle was a local landowner, titled, and a married man. However, his wife never accompanied him when he visited Désirée's house, and I got the impression it was not a particularly happy marriage. I soon realized how attracted he was to me, and one day I made a decision. I would no longer resist his advances. I was going to have an affair with Patric. My husband was desperate for a son. I was going to give him one.

"And that is how Charles was conceived, Vivienne. Perhaps I have made my affair with Patric sound very cut and dried, even cold-blooded. But it wasn't, not really. Although I do admit it was a conscious decision on my part, desiring as I did to get pregnant.

"However, Patric was a kind and loving man, and he made me feel womanly again, and desirable, and my nervousness and despair soon fled. I felt better than I had in a long time. I admit it was different from my affair with Joe Anthony. Joe and I had stumbled into each other's arms unwittingly, almost by accident. This was more calculated, it's true, but I liked Patric and I knew how much he cared about me.

"Once Édouard had a son in his arms at long last he reverted to his old self, became the lovely man I originally married. He adored the children and he adored me. He became an exemplary father and husband, and we settled into domestic bliss.

"The next twenty years were the best years of my life, Vivienne. I never looked back. I never thought about Joe Anthony. Or Patric Langalle. Édouard and our children were my whole existence. I was content. At peace. The happiness I had dreamed of years ago was mine at last. I even forgot about my terrible childhood and the horrendous things that happened to me in my early life. I was a good wife, a good mother, and I reveled in these roles."

I paused and looked across at Vivienne. "I may have shocked you . . . admitting that I let Édouard think Ariel and Charles were his children."

"No, you haven't!" she exclaimed, shaking her head. "Not at all. You gave your husband everything he wanted, Countess Zoë, made him happy, brought joy into his life. He had those children from birth, so they *were* his. Besides, just because a man pumps sperm into a woman, gets her pregnant, doesn't mean he's a father. It's what a man does after the child is born that matters. From what you've told me, the count loved Ariel and Charles very much, and that's what is important, surely?"

"Thank you for saying that, Vivienne," I replied, and continued, "From the moment Charles was born there was never another cross word between Édouard and myself. We were so close, like one person, and our happiness was the thing I treasured the most. Yes, life was finally as I had dreamed it could be.

"Then out of the blue in the spring of 1983 my whole world fell apart." I stopped, took a sip of champagne.

Vivienne asked quickly, "What happened?"

"I received a letter from a man called Sam Loring, a stranger. He wrote that he was visiting Paris from Chicago, that he was a friend of Joe Anthony and Geneviève Brunot and wished to see me. I was stunned. I did nothing for two days, and then I finally phoned him at the Hôtel Scribe, as he had requested.

"We met that afternoon in the lounge of the hotel. He was a tall, lean, gray-haired man with a craggy face and looked as if he was in his early seventies. I had never seen him before.

"With no preamble I asked him what he wanted with me. He repeated what he had written in the letter, that he was a friend of Joe Anthony and knew about my affair with Joe twenty-three years earlier. He told me I had used the name Geneviève Brunot and that I had been a guest at the Hôtel Gray d'Albion in Cannes.

"Naturally I denied everything. His response was cold. He said he was sure I would not want my husband to know about my adulterous affair, nor would I want aspersions cast on Ariel's legitimacy. I took an indignant attitude, a haughty stance, and countered that he was talking nonsense. I got up to leave.

"Sam Loring pressed me to stay and brought out an old photograph. It was one of me and Joe Anthony taken at La Chunga all those years ago. Joe had his arm around me. I was looking up at him and smiling. I recognized at once that the photograph was definitely suggestive and therefore damaging. Sam Loring pointed out the date the photographer had stamped on the back of the picture. *July 1960*. I felt trapped.

"I asked Loring what he wanted exactly. But I knew

before he answered that he was after money. And, more than likely, a great deal of it. I also knew that if I paid him to be quiet now I was exposing myself to further blackmail later. On the other hand, what alternative did I have but to pay.

"Whilst Loring could never prove that Ariel was not Édouard's child, the date on the back of the picture was damning, and this frightened me. Furthermore, I did not want Édouard questioning anything about Ariel. Or about Charles, for that matter. I had to protect my children. And my husband as well. He was no youngster; he was twenty-five years older than I, and at eighty-six a fit and healthy man. Nonetheless, I did not want him unduly upset.

"Sam Loring shocked me when he asked for a hundred thousand dollars for his silence. I told him I had no intention of giving it to him. I pointed out that I had no guarantee that he wouldn't demand more from me later on. His answer was that I would have to trust him. 'Honor among thieves,' was his comment.

"I laughed in his face. I also asked him why he had waited so long to seek me out, to tell me this extraordinary story, which nobody would believe anyway, I said. Loring answered that he was retired, had serious family problems, great financial difficulties, and that if he hadn't been so desperate he would never have been in touch with me.

"I then demanded an explanation about Joe Anthony. I asked how Loring knew him, how he had come into possession of the photograph taken in La Chunga so long ago.

"It was a curious story that he told me, Vivienne. But

I believed him, I must admit that. Loring explained that twenty-three years ago he had been employed by an American businessman to run the security division of the man's company. In the summer of 1960 Loring was sent to Europe to follow his employer's son who was traveling through France and Italy alone. His assignment was to keep an eye on him, make sure he didn't get into trouble.

"The young man in question was Joe Anthony, of course. Loring confided that he had known about our affair from its very inception. He had seen us together on the beach, at the little café, at La Chunga, and entering and leaving my hotel. He also informed me that at the time he had hired a French detective to follow me, that the man had boarded the Blue Train when I did, that day I returned to Paris after saying good-bye to Joe.

"Apparently Loring knew within twenty-four hours who I really was and all about me. He even knew when Ariel was born and the hospital she was born in. Through the French detective, he had kept tabs on me for a few years thereafter, just in case Joe Anthony ever tried to get in touch with me again. As for the photograph, he had bought it from the photographer at La Chunga the day after it was taken and had kept it all these years.

"I told him I would get the money, arranged to meet him three days later, and left the Hôtel Scribe. In the taxi on the way home I told myself that Loring couldn't prove anything, that I would not succumb to blackmail, but the moment I walked into this house I knew that I would. I had far too much to lose.

"It took me several days to get the money together,

mostly because I wanted to pay Loring in cash. Fortunately, my late husband Harry Robson had left me a very wealthy woman, and I used some of his inheritance to pay the blackmailer.

"When I met Loring at the end of the week I demanded the photograph in exchange for the money. And I made him promise he would stay away from me. But even as I was speaking I knew there were no guarantees. Wanting to get rid of him, to be done with it, I took a great chance that day.

"Sam Loring did give me his word, for what it was worth, and vowed that I would never see him again. Then he handed me the photograph.

"As he did so he said, 'Good-looking guy, Joe Anthony was, wasn't he? Except that he wasn't Joe Anthony.' When I asked him what he meant, Loring said, 'Countess, you weren't the only one masquerading as another person, using an assumed name. So was Joe. His real name was Sebastian Locke.'"

Chapter Thirty-three

Vivienne was staring at me.

   She looked stunned and very pale. She exclaimed, "Oh my God! If Sebastian was Joe Anthony, then he was Ariel's father. Oh my God!" Sitting back in the chair, she shook her head as if denying this, and said again, "Oh my God! *Oh no!*"

I had anticipated this reaction from her and I merely nodded and said, "Yes," very quietly.

"Did Sebastian find out, Countess Zoë? Is that why he killed himself?" Vivienne demanded. "It must be so! Of course! He committed suicide because he discovered he was involved in an incestuous relationship, albeit unwittingly. That's it, isn't it?"

I did not answer her for a moment or two. There was a small pause before I said slowly, "For you to understand everything, Vivienne, I must begin at the beginning . . . the beginning of my life . . ."

"I was born on April the sixth in 1922. My parents

were Niall and Maureen Rafferty, and they christened me Mary Ellen. We lived in Queens, and the first few years of my life were happy. Things changed drastically for me and my mother when my father was killed in 1927. A construction worker by trade, he was hit by a steel girder on a construction site and died of head injuries.

"My mother struggled to support us for the next two years, but despite her valiant efforts she was not very successful at earning a living.

"However, she was a pretty if somewhat fragile-looking woman and when Tommy Reagan, an old friend of my father's, showed up one day she immediately set her cap at him. Tommy, known to be a hard-working, hard-drinking bachelor, fell for her and within a few months they were married.

"My stepfather had a steady job. He was one of the managers of a large and prosperous farm in Somerset County near Peapack, New Jersey. Along with a good salary he was provided with a house on the property, one he said was big enough for us, his new family.

"At first I thought everything was going to be wonderful, living in the country on a farm, having a man to look after us again. I soon discovered how wrong I was. Tommy Reagan resented me, detested having another man's child under his feet, and, looking back now, I believe he was insanely jealous of my mother's love for me, the special place I had in her heart.

"Certainly he took it out on me whenever things went wrong and sometimes when they didn't. He was a hard man who did not think twice about hitting me at the slightest provocation.

"When they were first married he was careful, never

struck me in my mother's presence, but as time went on and he recognized her dependency on him he grew careless. Or it could have been that what she thought no longer mattered to him. I've never been sure of that, Vivienne, although I do believe the gloss wore off their marriage rather swiftly.

"His attitude to me was unrelenting. His motto was spare the rod, spoil the child. I can assure you I was never spoiled if the number of beatings I received at his hands counted for anything.

"Tommy Reagan was an exceedingly strict disciplinarian, and the true example of a naturally vindictive man who turned into a tyrant when given a small amount of power. A bully and a coward, he only picked on the weak and defenseless, those who could not strike back.

"My mother and I were intimidated by him. I tried to keep out of his way as best I could. Almost always my mother had to back down whenever she attempted to defend me. I often heard her sobbing in bed at night, especially when he had been drinking.

"The fact was my stepfather made me his whipping post and years later, long after I had left the farm, I began to understand how sadistic he had been.

"It was sad and unfortunate that after only three years of marriage to Tommy my mother developed a heart condition and became a semi-invalid. She was bedridden half the time. Her poor health infuriated my stepfather, and my life became even more miserable. Aside from hitting me whenever he felt like it, he turned me into a drudge. I was made to clean the house and cook for him, for us, since my mother was too debilitated most of the time. I was ten years old.

"I grew up quickly, Vivienne. By the age of thirteen I was already well-developed and looked older than I was. Nubile is perhaps the best way to describe myself. My lush looks were in bud but had not yet flowered. However, my mother had already told me I was going to be a beautiful woman when I grew up.

"One day, during that summer of 1935, I caught the eye of the man who owned the farm. Suddenly, as I went about the property, he started to look at me more closely and longer than he usually had before.

"He became very friendly and invited me into the main house, mostly into his office, where he gave me candy and chocolates, ribbons for my long hair, old magazines, and, once, a book. And soon his hands were all over me, on my breasts and up my skirt, between my legs and anywhere else he felt like putting them.

"Thus began my real misery, Vivienne. It was not long before he was unbuttoning his trousers, showing himself to me and making me touch him. There were times when he even forced me to take off some of my clothes.

"Although I was terrified of him, there was nothing I could do to stop him from treating me in this way. My mother was ill; I did not want to upset her, make her feel worse by bringing my troubles to her. My stepfather was unapproachable and he would not have believed me anyway. Perhaps he even knew and turned a blind eye. He did not care about me, I was a nuisance. I endeavored to block everything out, made believe it never happened.

"The owner warned me that if I ever breathed a word to anyone about what he did in the privacy of his office he would get rid of us. He would fire my stepfather, turn us out without money or references.

"I blamed myself, thought it was my fault that he abused me the way he did, so freely, so wantonly. Just before he had started to waylay me, his mother had been visiting him and she told me that I was a lovely looking girl. But then she added in a spiteful voice that my looks were bound to get me into trouble one day. She said they would only lead me down the path to hell where Satan was waiting to devour me. As far as I was concerned her son was Satan incarnate.

"I was fourteen when he raped me in September of 1936. Naturally, I was a virgin and since he had been overly rough with me, forcing me, I bled profusely.

"There was a bit of a commotion about this matter. He had not properly locked the door in his haste to violate me. The housekeeper had walked in on us. Our disheveled state, plus the blood on the hooked rug, left little to her imagination. She knew what had taken place and told him so. But like everyone else on the farm she was afraid of losing her job. So he continued to do whatever he wanted with me.

"It was not until the winter of 1937 that he made me pregnant. I was fifteen and more frightened than ever when I realized I had conceived. But times were hard, he was my stepfather's boss, and we were dependent on him. Therefore, nothing much was said about my condition. My mother cried a lot. My stepfather blamed me.

"The owner of the farm was in his thirties and had never married. The idea of a child and a wife must have appealed to him. Much to Tommy Reagan's surprise, and mine, he married me because of the baby.

The wedding took place at the farm. It was conducted by a local judge, and it was a simple affair, rather hurried.

"The odd thing was he immediately went away and left me living in the house with my mother and stepfather. When he returned to the farm unexpectedly a few months later, he installed me in the main house with him. He continued to have sex with me until it was impossible for him to do so because of my condition. But he rarely spoke to me and there was no warmth between us, no kindness in him. I dreamed of running away, but I knew I could not.

"The first day of June my labor pains started. I was in labor for almost two days and when the baby was finally delivered on June the third I was totally depleted. They told me that the baby had died.

"I was very ill for several months. Weak, exhausted, and afraid, I did not want to get well. As long as I was sick in bed no one could hurt me. However, I knew I could not hide forever. When I was finally up on my feet my stepfather told me I was being sent away by my husband to recuperate. It had been decided that I would go to London to stay with my mother's sister Bronagh. Apparently it had been my mother's idea to send me there, and miraculously my husband had agreed.

"I cannot tell you how relieved I was to be leaving. I did not see my husband before I set out for New York to board the ship, since he was in Canada on business. However, I knew he was paying for my passage to England and a few new clothes, and that he had provided three hundred dollars for my expenses in London.

"The thing that stays in my mind is what my mother said to me, Vivienne, the day I left the farm. I've never forgotten her face, the way she looked at me, the sound of her voice. 'Don't come back to this place, mavourneen,' she had whispered to me when I bent down to kiss her. She told me she loved me, and I remember thinking how happy she looked that morning. I knew I was witnessing her profound relief that I was making my escape."

Lifting my glass, I took a sip of champagne and shifted on the sofa, making myself more comfortable.

Vivienne, who had been watching me alertly, exclaimed, "You're not going to stop, are you, Countess Zoë? I want to hear the rest of your story. Please."

"Then you shall, Vivienne," I said. "I am going to tell you everything . . . things no one else has ever heard."

CHAPTER THIRTY-FOUR

"It was in London that I started my second life, Vivienne. And it was much happier than my first, thanks in no small measure to my aunt Bronagh.

"She was my mother's younger sister and an actress. When she lived in New York she had worked with a small theater company in Greenwich Village. And it was there that she met a young English actor named Jonathan St. James. They had fallen in love, and when he returned to England in 1933 she had gone with him. They had been married for five years when I arrived to stay with them.

"The moment I walked into their little house in Pimlico my spirits lifted. It was a warm, cozy place, almost like a doll's house, and Jonathan St. James made me feel welcome and at home. Like Bronagh he was in his late twenties and the two of them were full of vitality, high spirits, and somewhat bohemian in their lifestyle. They were crazy about each other and the theater, and both were working in plays in the West End. Naturally, they were in their element. Their happiness and gaiety was infectious and I soon felt much better, better than I had since my early childhood when my father was still alive. They were loving with each other and with me.

"Slowly my health improved; my broken spirit began to heal. And Bronagh restored my soul. Sympathetic by nature, she had an understanding heart; gradually, I started to confide in her. Things came out slowly, little by little. Within three months she knew the whole story of my life, and she was enraged. 'You're not going back there, Mary Ellen. I swear to God it'll be over my dead body if you do. Mary, Mother of Jesus! It's criminal, what's been done to you, sure an' it is, mavourneen.' Jonathan, who by this time knew everything from Bronagh, agreed that I must not return to New Jersey under any circumstances.

"But no one seemed in much of a hurry to get me back, including my mother. Of course I knew that in her case she was protecting me, trying to keep me out of harm's way. She wrote to me regularly and never failed to tell me she loved me, and I did the same, sending her a letter once a week.

"At the end of six months in London I was a different person. Bronagh and Jonathan had truly worked miracles. They had cossetted and pampered me and it showed. I had put on weight; there was flesh on my bones at last. I had grown taller and my figure was willowy. The bloom was on the rose, as Bronagh kept saying to me.

"But most importantly, because of Bronagh and

Jonathan I felt safe, more secure than I had for years. I was no longer cowed and scared, fearful of being beaten or abused. The fear I had lived with for so long finally diminished and I came to understand that one day it would vanish completely.

"Once I had believed that the only way out of my torment was to die. I had been a mere child of thirteen when I had contemplated suicide, Vivienne, that was part of the tragedy. You see, I had had no childhood.

"But I turned a corner during those first few months in London. I was aware that I could become a whole new person, have a new identity, start again.

"That summer Bronagh found me a job through a friend of hers. I became a dancer in a cabaret in the West End. Because of my height and slender figure I made the perfect showgirl.

"I loved it all—the glamour, the costumes, the crowds, the glitter of the footlights. I had found my true métier. The stage was mine. It meant everything to me. It became my entire world. I put death and heartbreak behind me; I reached out for life.

"Since I was living in a brand-new world I needed a brand-new name. Discarding Mary Ellen Rafferty, which only reminded me of my pain and humiliation, I invented a new one for myself.

"*Zoë Lysle*. That is who I became. With this new name I acquired a different persona. Zoë had never been touched or damaged; she was clean, pure, whole. And every night when I stepped out onto the stage in my fine feathers I was reborn. I soared.

"I missed my mother, I worried about her, and I had moments of sadness when I thought about my baby who had died at birth. But these moments were fleeting. After all, I *was* only sixteen. I had started my life again . . . as Zoë. I looked forward always, never back.

"I did not hear from my husband and I was relieved he had remained silent for so long. When I had first arrived in London I had worried that he would eventually drag me back to America. But as the summer passed and there was no word from him I began to relax.

"Then on September the third, 1939, Britain declared war on Nazi Germany. The world turned upside down. The war years in London were extraordinary—full of hardships and danger because of the constant air raids. But I came through them relatively unscathed.

"After America entered the war in 1941, American troops started to flood into Britain. Every time I saw a GI I was scared to look at his face in case it was my stepfather. But he did not show up in London, although I knew from my mother that Tommy had joined the U.S. Army.

"As for my husband, I didn't know what had actually happened to him. He had sold the farm in Somerset County, divorced me, and had the legal papers sent to me in 1940, in care of Bronagh. I never heard from him again.

"Being a showgirl I had many admirers and went out with some of them. But I was forever wary, always on my guard, determined that I would not be exposed to the heartlessness of others ever again.

"However, in 1943 I met an English officer in the Coldstream Guards. He was the Honorable Harry Robson, a captain in the army and the son of an English lord. Harry's father had been married three times and his last wife, Harry's mother, had been an American heiress with a railroad fortune at her disposal. When she died in 1940 Harry had inherited everything.

"I was twenty-one when Harry and I started going out together. He was twenty-eight. Harry was bowled over by me the first time we met, and I was rather taken with him. He was pleasant to look at and in his demeanor, the first kind man I had met other than Jonathan St. James.

"Encouraged by Bronagh and Jonathan I accepted Harry's proposal. We were married in 1944. At the time he insisted I retire from the stage and I was happy to do so. I had grown accustomed to men ogling me. But in all truth, Vivienne, there was often a knot of fear inside when I sensed instinctively that I had attracted someone who might be difficult to handle. Curiously enough, loving the stage though I had, I never missed it.

"And so my third life began, Vivienne. Harry and I had five years together. They were good years. I was devoted to him. I know I made him happy; he gave me security and protection and a great deal of love.

"Harry was crossing Oxford Street in 1949 when he was knocked down by a double-decker bus. He died of massive internal injuries a week later. I was grief stricken. I had loved Harry, in my own way, and I knew I would miss this gentle, generous man who had been so good to me.

"After the funeral I went into mourning, kept to myself, and wondered what to do with the rest of my life. I was twenty-seven and Harry had made me a wealthy woman. I was his sole heir.

"I had no wish to return to America. There was nothing there for me. My mother had died not long after I had married Harry. It was a year after I was widowed that I decided to take a vacation in Paris. Almost at once I knew I would make it my permanent home. I did so and disappeared from the London scene forever.

"I began my fourth life when I married Édouard, but then you know a good deal about that life, Vivienne, and what happened to me in the intervening years. As I already told you, Sam Loring showed up in Paris in 1983 and blackmailed me to the tune of one hundred thousand dollars because of my affair with Joe Anthony, or rather, Sebastian Locke. I paid because I wanted to protect my family, even though I knew that it was risky to do so. Loring could come back at any time and demand more money.

"However, a few days after I had paid Loring I began to worry about another matter, one that had more serious implications than blackmail. I decided to go to America to check out something for myself. When I told Édouard that I had family business to attend to in the States he suggested I go alone. At eighty-six he did not feel like traveling anymore.

"I flew to New York and went straight to the Pierre Hotel, where I had booked a suite. The following day I hired a private investigator to do the work I required. It did not take him long. Within forty-eight hours he brought me the information I needed.

"What I had dreaded and feared was true. For several days I was in shock and incapable of thinking straight. But as the shock receded I filled with enormous rage. For the first time in my life I wanted to kill somebody . . . "

I realized that I could not continue.

A wave of emotion swept over me, and I was held in the grip of that terrible fury I had experienced twelve years ago. I was trembling inside.

"The rage has never really left me," I said at last, looking at Vivienne, holding her with my eyes. "Nor have I ever lost the desire to kill that man."

"Which man? Who do you mean, Countess Zoë?"

"Cyrus Locke."

"*Cyrus?* But why? Because of Loring? Because Cyrus sent Loring to follow Sebastian all those years ago, when you met him in Cannes?"

"No, Vivienne, this has nothing to do with Loring. In a way he was a godsend, coming to me when he did. He helped me without even realizing it, helped me to avert a great tragedy."

A puzzled expression crossed Vivienne's face. "I'm sorry Countess Zoë, but I'm afraid I'm not following you."

"Of course you're not," I said and stopped.

My throat suddenly constricted, I could feel the tears welling behind my eyes and I had begun to shake uncontrollably.

Taking a deep breath, I clasped my hands together to steady myself, but my voice quavered as I said, "Cyrus Locke was the owner of the farm in New Jersey. He was the man who abused me as a child and raped me when I was fifteen, the man who impregnated me, married me, and then discarded me like a piece of worthless garbage. And he stole my child. He told me my baby had died, but that was not the truth. My son lived. My son Sebastian."

As I said his name the tears crept out from under

my lids and slid down my cheeks. I brought my shaking hands up to my face and the tears continued to fall unchecked.

Vivienne came and sat next to me on the sofa. She took me in her arms and held me close, endeavoring to comfort me.

And I wept as I had wept in 1983, on the night I had discovered the shocking truth. And I felt as though my heart were breaking all over again, as it had done then.

CHAPTER Thirty-five

Eventually I drew away from Vivienne, found a handkerchief in my pocket, and blew my nose.

Then I looked at her.

She was white-faced, and I could see the pain in her eyes. Reaching out, I squeezed her hand. "Thank you," I said, and before she could ask any questions I went on, "I'd like to finish my story, tell you the rest of it, Vivienne."

She nodded. "You must."

"Armed with Sam Loring's information I grew suspicious when I began to focus on Joe Anthony's age—" I broke off. "I always think of him as Joe, never Sebastian. Anyway, he was twenty-two and I was thirty-eight when we met in Cannes. Sixteen years difference in age. My mind began to race. My baby had been born on June the third, 1938. He had died the same day, according to Cyrus Locke and the midwife who had delivered the child at the farm in New Jersey. Had my baby lived he, too, would have been twenty-two in 1960.

"It was hardly likely that Cyrus Locke had fathered *two* sons in 1938. No, only mine, I reasoned. Especially since he had not married again for several years.

"The unthinkable was staring me in the face. Was it possible that my child had lived? Was it possible that Sebastian was not Hildegarde Locke's son, but mine? And if he were, then I had given birth to a child by my own son. My daughter Ariel.

"I was horror-struck, and naturally I denied it to myself for some time. But in the end intelligence took over from emotion, and I was convinced that Cyrus Locke had lied to me all those years ago. I was haunted by the knowledge that we had committed incest, although we had done so unknowingly. I felt as though I were living in a nightmare. Ariel fathered by my own son. My mind shut down whenever I thought of this.

"After a great deal of soul-searching I realized there was only one thing to do. I must go to New York and start digging for the facts. I had to know the truth for my own sanity. As I explained to you, I hired a private investigator and asked him to obtain certain documents for me. I also told him I wanted him to provide me with information about Cyrus Locke. I was vaguely aware that, after divorcing me, he had eventually remarried and fathered children. I had noticed the occasional item about him in newspapers over the years, but wanting to forget that painful period in my life I had paid little attention.

"Several days later the private investigator reported to me at the Pierre Hotel. He brought with him various documents and a detailed summary of Cyrus Locke's life.

"The most important document was a copy of Sebastian's birth certificate. And there in black and white was the date of his birth: June the third, 1938. The father's name was given as Cyrus Lyon Locke. The mother's name was Mary Ellen Rafferty Locke. *Me*. The place of birth was shown as Reddington Farm, Somerset County, New Jersey. As I had requested, the private investigator had also obtained a copy of my marriage certificate.

"The report about Cyrus Locke explained additional things to me. Apparently he had moved to Maine after selling the farm in New Jersey and lived in a mansion he had owned since December of 1937. Obviously he had bought this immediately after marrying me. There was no doubt in my mind that he took the baby to Maine with a nurse, installed them in that house, and brought up the child himself until he remarried several years later.

"I think he always planned to do this, Vivienne. When he raped me he was thirty-three years old, unmarried, and childless. Once he discovered he had made me pregnant, he married me to get the child. He did not want me. I was of no further use to him. But he did want an heir. The more I pondered it the more convinced I became this was the only explanation. Otherwise why would he have stolen my baby?

"That night at the Pierre Hotel my world was shattered. I was so devastated I was unable to function properly for almost a week. Finally I managed to pull myself together and flew back to France. I had a life there, a husband and family who adored me.

"But it was not easy for me to go on, and for some months I was desperately ill. The doctors were baffled as was Édouard. I was not. I knew what was wrong with me. I carried a terrible secret in my heart. It was a secret I could not confide to anyone on this earth. It was the greatest burden I've ever had to bear, and I was concerned about Ariel. At twenty-two my daughter was beautiful and a brilliant student. Everyone predicted she would have an extraordinary career in medicine. I knew there had been no genetic damage; nonetheless, I fretted about her.

"It was Édouard who helped me to recover my health. He was no longer young, but he was a robust and active man, and he devoted all of his time to me. He was always at my side, always encouraging me. And he was full of love.

"Gradually, I began to feel better. I stopped blaming myself. I accepted that I could not change what had happened so long ago; therefore, I must live with it.

"Once I was finally on my feet I put every ounce of strength and energy into loving Édouard, Ariel, and Charles. I survived because I am a survivor by nature. In 1985 I received a letter postmarked Chicago. My heart missed a beat when I saw the name S. Loring on the back of the envelope. The letter was from Sam Loring's daughter Samantha. She had written to tell me her father had died. One of his last requests of her was that she write to let me know he had passed away. She told me that he thanked me for my aid in his time of need. So, my blackmailer was dead.

"When my beloved Édouard died in 1986 I felt that

my life had come to an end too. We had been very close for the last twenty-odd years of our marriage. He had been my great love and my cherished companion; he had been my whole life. Without him I believed there was no reason for me to exist. But I went on. I drew immense pleasure from Ariel and Charles, from my daughter-in-law Marguerite and grandson Gerard. As the years slid by I somehow managed to obliterate Joe Anthony from my mind and I put the past behind me.

"And then one night last September the past came back to hit me in the face. Ariel returned from Zaire, and she brought her fiancé to meet me. His name was Sebastian Locke.

"I will never forget that night, Vivienne. How I got through it I will never know. My mind was floundering, my senses swimming. Also, I saw what a wonderful man he was; I ached inside because I had been so cruelly deprived of my son."

I leaned back against the cushions, feeling depleted, then I finally finished, "And that is the story of my life. Now you know it all . . ."

Drawing closer, Vivienne took hold of my hand and held it in hers. "You have moved me so much, Countess Zoë. My heart aches for you when I think of what you've suffered. I don't know how you've lived through it."

"Very few people have an easy time in this world, Vivienne. What counts most is that we survive, endure."

Vivienne was silent for a few moments and then she said in a voice so low I could hardly hear it, "You told Sebastian, didn't you?"

"Yes, I did. What else could I do?"

"And that's why he killed himself, isn't it?" she whispered.

"Yes, Vivienne, I believe it is."

"You must have told him after he and I had lunch together on that Monday."

"Yes, that's so. I saw him on Wednesday."

"You came to New York?"

I nodded. "Ariel went back to Zaire. Sebastian flew to New York. I followed him. I telephoned him at the Locke Foundation, explained that I was in New York and had to see him urgently. He agreed. Why wouldn't he? I was the mother of the woman he was planning to marry."

"Where did you meet?"

"At his townhouse. I must admit, I was extremely distressed, in a turmoil inside. But I managed to hide it. I plunged right into my story. I told him I had once been married to Cyrus Locke, that he was my son who had been stolen from me by his father. And then I told him I was also Geneviève Brunot. He was stunned, reeling from shock. And of course he didn't believe a word of it. Not at first.

"However, I had the documents to bear me out. His birth certificate. And my own. My marriage license. Ariel's birth certificate. And the photograph of Joe Anthony and Geneviève Brunot, taken at La Chunga in July of 1960. The thing that baffled him was that this woman confronting him with a most horrifying story was Geneviève, the pretty young woman he had known in Cannes. I convinced him she and I were the same person. I explained that I lied about my age, had dropped ten years because he was so young. I had too many pertinent details about those four days we'd spent together. He had no option but to believe me. I also showed him some other photographs of me that had been taken that year. They helped to convince him that I *was* Geneviève Brunot.

"When he asked how I had found out about everything, I explained how Sam Loring had contacted me in Paris, blackmailed me, and told me of Joe Anthony's real identity. Before I could stop myself I confided some of the things I've told you today, Vivienne. About Cyrus Locke's abuse of me—"

I paused for a moment, then I said slowly, "I destroyed Sebastian, of course. I know that. But I had to prevent a great tragedy from occurring. I told him he must never again see Ariel."

Vivienne gave me a hard stare and shook her head. "And later that week Sebastian took his life. But he needn't have done that. He could have broken off his engagement to Ariel, and he didn't even have to explain why he was doing so."

"Yes, Vivienne, you're right." I let out a long sigh, clasped her hand all that much tighter. "All I knew that day was that I had to stop them from marrying. I never imagined he would kill himself. But I should have known, I should have guessed when he said, 'However am I going to live without her. She's the only person I've ever really loved.' I wept when he said that and so did he."

Vivienne was very still. Her eyes were brimming and slowly the tears ran down her cheeks. She could not speak. Neither could I. We just sat there holding each other's hands, caught up in our own thoughts.

After a while Vivienne roused herself. "You told me at the beginning that no one else knows any of this. Why did you tell me?"

"Because you had such a need to understand why Sebastian killed himself. I realized that if I didn't explain everything, you would be haunted by it for the rest of your days."

"Thank you, Countess Zoë, for confiding in me," she answered very softly.

"You know, Vivienne dear, I've never understood why it all happened . . . why I had to meet Joe Anthony in Cannes all those many years ago. Chance? Fate? I cannot explain . . . I don't think anyone could . . . "

"How tragic it is," Vivienne murmured. She looked at me closely. "I loved him so very much. Always."

"I know you did . . . and that's another reason why you had to know the truth. The truth sets us free, Vivienne."

PART FIVE

VIVIENNE
HONOR

Chapter Thirty-six

C ountess Zoë's house on the Faubourg Saint-Germain was very quiet when Hubert let me in. Quieter than usual, I thought as I followed him across the grand marble foyer.

"How is Countess de Grenaille?" I asked him as we went up the wide curving staircase together.

"A little better today," he said. "She has rallied again. She is a most remarkable woman, Madame Trent. And she is looking forward to seeing you."

"As I am her, Hubert."

He led the way down the corridor, opened the big double doors to her bedroom, ushered me in, excused himself, and disappeared, as always the perfect butler.

I glanced toward the antique bed and saw to my surprise that it was draped in its silk coverlets and was empty.

"I'm over here, Vivienne, sitting near the fire," Countess Zoë said in a voice that was stronger than I had expected. This morning, on the phone, she had sounded weak. I had been alarmed, worried for her health.

I turned to her, and, smiling, I walked across the room in the direction of the fireplace. And I could not help thinking how well she looked. Hubert was right, she *was* remarkable, extraordinary really. Her chestnut hair was stylishly coiffed and she wore makeup, expertly applied. I was again struck by the arresting looks of this seventy-three-year-old woman.

This afternoon she was wearing delphinium-blue silk lounging pajamas, most obviously couture, and sapphire earrings. The color of the silk outfit and the sapphires exactly matched her wonderful eyes. From the first moment I met her I had recognized her great beauty, and there had been odd moments when she had seemed very familiar to me. Puzzled, I had not been able to fathom why this was so. I knew now. She reminded me of Sebastian. It was her eyes, of course. Bits of sky, I thought, as his had been, and their mouths were identical. Sensitive, vulnerable mouths.

As I drew to a standstill at her side, she said, "I'm glad you're back in Paris, Vivienne, I've been longing to see you. Thank you for coming, my dear."

"I was planning to run over today," I answered bending down, kissing her on both cheeks. "I was just about to phone you and invite myself to tea, when you called the hotel."

Smiling at me, she patted my hand resting on her arm. "You've become very special to me, Vivienne."

"As you have to me, Countess Zoë." I was carrying

a shopping bag of books and I placed them next to her chair and went on, "These are for you, I hope you like them."

"I'm sure I will, you seem to know my tastes very well, and how kind you are, my dear. Thank you."

I went and sat down on the chair opposite and looked at her expectantly.

"I wanted to see you because I have something for you." As she was speaking she turned toward the Louis XV end table next to her chair and picked up a small package. Leaning forward slightly, she offered it to me and added, "This is for you, Vivienne."

I was surprised, and as I took it from her I exclaimed, "But Countess Zoë, you don't have to give me gifts!"

She laughed lightly. "I know I don't . . . come along, open it."

I did as she said, removing the ribbon and the gold wrapping paper. The small velvet box in my hands looked old, and when I lifted the lid I gasped, more surprised than ever. Lying on the dark red velvet was a heart-shaped brooch covered entirely with small diamonds and there was a slightly larger diamond set in the center. "Countess Zoë! It's beautiful! But I can't accept this, it's far too valuable!"

"I want you to have it. Harry Robson gave it to me when we were married in 1944 and I've always liked it. I think you will enjoy it too. It's a pendant as well as a brooch. If you look on the back you will see how it works. There's a little hook, so it can hang on a chain."

"But this is something you should give to Ariel or your daughter-in-law."

"Hasn't it occurred to you that you are my daughter-in-law? Or were, when you were married to Sebastian."

I simply stared at her without speaking. And of course she was correct. But the brooch was obviously extremely valuable and I was reluctant to take it.

She continued, "However, that is not the reason I am giving it to you. I want you to have a memento, something special to remember me by . . ."

"Oh Countess Zoë, I'll never forget you, how could I! You're the most extraordinary person I've ever met in my whole life."

"Please accept the brooch, Vivienne, you'll make me very happy if you do. It gladdens my heart to think that every time you put it on you'll be reminded of an old lady who has grown very attached to you."

"You sound as if you're not going to see me again. And you are! Every time I come to Paris!" I exclaimed.

"I sincerely hope so. But let us be realistic, my dear. I am an old woman and I am very ill. You know that, Vivienne. And I am not going to be on this earth forever. But enough! Let us not get maudlin today. Please accept the brooch. Do it for me."

"Well of course I accept it, Countess Zoë, and thank you very much. It's beautiful and you're very generous . . ."

I rose and went to kiss her. Then I looked down into her upturned face and said, "Just so long as you know that I don't need the brooch to be reminded of you."

"Yes, I do know that," she replied. Her vivid blue eyes were suddenly sparkling.

I could tell she was happy and this pleased me. I took out the diamond heart and pinned it on the jacket of my suit. "There, how does it look?"

"Dazzling," she said, glanced over at the desk near the window, and went on, "Would you please bring me the letter case on the desk, Vivienne?"

Nodding, I did as she asked. Then I went and sat down in my chair again. Leaning against the antique tapestry pillows, I watched her open the case and sort through the contents.

This woman had captivated me the moment I had entered her house and we had bonded almost instantly. I had fallen completely under her spell; there was something wholly unique about her. She had an understanding heart, was intelligent, wise, and brave. So very brave. When I thought of the painful things that had happened to her in her life, I wondered how she had ever stood it all, how she survived. It was miraculous that she had lived through those tragedies the way she had, so courageously. Zoë de Grenaille was indeed an indomitable woman. I was filled with admiration for her and I had grown to love her.

"Vivienne?"

"Yes, Countess Zoë?"

"This is Sebastian's birth certificate. Please burn it." Handing the document to me, she continued. "You can read it if you wish . . . "

I nodded, glanced down at the paper I was now holding. The facts were written there. They were exactly as she had told me. The names danced before my eyes. Cyrus Lyon Locke. Mary Ellen Rafferty Locke. Sebastian Lyon Locke. Reddington Farm,

Somerset County, New Jersey. And Sebastian's date of birth, June the third, 1938. How often I had celebrated his birthday with him on that date.

"This was the beginning . . . the beginning of a great tragedy," I whispered.

"Burn it, Vivienne. Please."

"Immediately." I went to the fire, knelt in front of it, and let the flames consume Sebastian's birth certificate.

"Now this one. My marriage license."

I held the piece of paper that had legalized the union between Mary Ellen Rafferty and Cyrus Lyon Locke and a wave of anger swept through me. He was at the root of it. Cyrus Locke. How evil he had been. I tore the marriage certificate in half and dropped the pieces into the fire.

"This is the photograph taken at La Chunga in 1960," Countess Zoë went on, handing it to me. "Consign this to the flames as well."

My eyes dropped to the picture. I was compelled to look at it, I could not help myself. It was a Sebastian I did not know who stared back at me. I recognized him immediately, there was no question who he was. But how different he looked from the Sebastian I had known. The older man. He was so young here, so untouched by life. And the Zoë next to him was the most glamorous of women. Her beauty was in full bloom. She looked glorious. No wonder she had been irresistible to men.

Conscious of her eyes on me, I placed the photograph on top of the logs and watched it curl and burn until it was no more, then I swung my head to look at her.

"You wished you could keep that, Vivienne," she said slowly. "And for a moment I almost told you that you could. But it's better to destroy everything. It's not that I don't trust you with the photograph, but—" Her voice faltered and she glanced away.

I said, "I know you trust me. And you're right, it's better this way. You'll feel easier in your own mind."

She sighed to herself and murmured, "Let me see what else is in here. Ah yes, my marriage license from Caxton Hall in Westminster where I married Harry Robson. No need to destroy that. However, here is my own birth certificate. Please burn it." Handing this to me, she settled back in her chair.

"Are you sure?" I asked. "I mean, there's no real reason to throw this away, is there?"

She was thoughtful. Eventually she said rather softly, "Ariel and Charles know that I was an actress when I was young, and that my name was Zoë Lysle. They're aware that I was widowed when I married Édouard, the widow of Harry Robson, supposedly my first husband. But they've never heard the name Mary Ellen Rafferty, and I want everything burned that could ever link me to the Locke family. Put it on the fire, my dear. Please."

I did as she asked and then pushed myself to my feet.

Countess Zoë said, "It was wise to get rid of the damning evidence. I wouldn't want Ariel or Charles to find it later. But I'm glad I told you everything, Vivienne. I think I've lifted a burden from you, taking you into my confidence, and it's lifted a burden from me, sharing my secret with you. That has weighed me down for twelve years, it's been a relief to speak of it with you."

I got up and went and crouched next to her chair. Looking deeply into those startlingly blue eyes, I said, "I will honor your confidence. I will never tell anyone as long as I live."

Leaning closer, Countess Zoë kissed my forehead, touched my cheek gently. "I know you won't reveal anything I've told you. You're such a fine person, so honest and loyal. And honor is bred in the bone with you. You could no more do a shoddy thing than Ariel could." She paused and looked at me intently when she said, "You've become like another daughter to me. I've grown to love you, Vivienne."

"Thank you for saying those lovely things, Countess Zoë, and I want you to know that I love you too."

A smile touched her mouth and was gone in an instant. A sudden sorrow seemed to settle over her and her eyes filled with tears. Reaching for my hands, she said, "It's as though I took a knife and plunged it into him. I'm responsible for Sebastian's death, Vivienne. I've lived with that ghastly knowledge for over seven months, and it's overwhelmed me. The sorrow is unendurable." Tears rolled down her cheeks.

"Please, please, don't blame yourself," I said. "You had to tell Sebastian the truth. There was nothing else you could do. You couldn't let him marry Ariel. That would have been unconscionable."

She fumbled in her pocket for a handkerchief. "His death is a shadow on my heart," she said.

I continued to console her and eventually she took hold of herself, became composed at last.

Hubert brought in the tea tray, poured for us, and left.

We sipped our tea in silence for a while. It was Countess Zoë who spoke first. She said, "Love is the only thing that's worthwhile in this terrible and incomprehensible world we live in. It's the only thing that makes any sense. Take the advice of an old woman who's seen almost everything and experienced much . . . don't make any compromises when it comes to marriage. Oh yes, you'll marry again, Vivienne, I'm absolutely certain of that. But you must only marry for love."

"I know, and there is no other reason, as far as I'm concerned."

"When the right man comes along, you'll know it. You'll be swept off your feet, but you'll be very sure of your feelings, I don't doubt that."

"I think I will, Countess Zoë."

There was a faint smile on her face, but I could see the tears glittering in her eyes when she said softly, "Oh, I don't doubt *you*, Vivienne. Not at all." There was a pause before she finished, "Your whole life is ahead of you. Live it well from this day forward."

Chapter Thirty-seven

I went straight from Countess Zoë's house to the restaurant where I was meeting Jack for dinner.

As I sat back in the cab, after giving the driver the address of Chez Voltaire, I wondered whether I should remove the diamond heart. It was still pinned to my jacket and looked wonderful against the black wool. I decided to leave it where it was.

Jack was already there when I arrived, and he rose as I was shown to the table. "Well, aren't you a sight for sore eyes," he said, kissing me on the cheek.

We both sat down. I looked across the table at him and said, "And so are you, darling."

He grinned at me. "You're looking very nifty this evening, Viv. Very chic. Great suit. Who gave you the pin?"

"I've had it for ages," I said evasively, now regretting that I had not taken it off in the cab after all.

"It looks very Sebastian to me," he said, motioned to a waiter, and went on, "What would you like to drink?"

"I'll have a glass of champagne, Jack, please."

"Good idea, I'll have that too. I'm really off the hard stuff these days." He ordered a bottle of Veuve Cliquot, the waiter went away to fetch it, and Jack continued, "So, have you tracked her down?"

"Who?" I asked, although I knew at once to whom he was referring. Ariel. She had been the subject of our last conversation at the Château d'Cose only a couple of weeks ago.

"The mystery woman in Sebastian's life. Ariel de Grenaille, of course," he said.

"No, I haven't," I replied. "And I don't think I'm going to either."

"Why not? You were so gung-ho about her . . . about speaking to her."

"Well, I've spoken to her mother and Ariel is in Africa. I'm not planning to go there, Jack, I don't think it's worth it."

"That's a change of tune! So what did you find out? From the mother, I mean?"

"Not a great deal. Ariel lives in Africa. That's where she was when Sebastian killed himself. So obviously she can't shed any light on the matter. She doesn't know any more than you or I do."

"*Is* she a doctor?"

"Yes."

"A scientist?"

"Yes, Jack, she works with hot viruses, such as Ebola and Marburg. That's what her mother told me."

"Jesus! That's dangerous work."

"Yes, it is."

The waiter came with the bucket of champagne and proceeded to open the bottle. This put a stop to Jack's questions. But the moment we were alone again he continued to press me about Ariel de Grenaille.

"*Was* she engaged to Sebastian?" he probed, his curiosity apparent.

I answered, "From what I understand, yes. They were planning to get married at some point this spring. About now. As he had told me, Jack. And that's it, there's nothing more to say. Except that you were always right. We'll never know why Sebastian killed himself. It's still a mystery."

"So you're not planning to interview her for the profile?"

"No, I'm not. Cheers." I touched my glass to his.

"Cheers," he said and went on, "Is it a work in progress? Or have you finished it?"

I laughed. "No, I haven't, not yet. But I'm going back to Lourmarin tomorrow, and I fully intend to add the final touches. All it needs is a good polish."

"I'd hoped you'd be staying in Paris for a few more days," he grumbled, sounding petulant. "I thought you could keep me company. I'm here on wine business until the end of the week."

"I'd like to, but I really must get back. I've such a lot to do, and my book on the Brontë sisters is coming out in the summer. I'll have to do a certain amount of promotion for it, travel a bit, and right now I need some time at *Vieux Moulin*. Quiet time. Alone."

"Are you going to Connecticut in August, as you usually do?" he asked.

"Yes, why?"

"I might be there at that time. At Laurel Creek Farm."

"I can't believe it! And I certainly can't believe you'd leave Château d'Cose!"

He began to laugh. "I'm thinking of spending a couple of weeks there, I'm not planning to move *permanently* to Cornwall, Vivienne."

I sat back in my chair and regarded him for a long moment. He looked well, thinner, and much better groomed than he usually was. I also realized he was in a good mood, almost benign, which was unusual for him. Taking a deep breath, I said, "Jack, I want to ask you something."

"Shoot."

"I want you to look me in the eye and tell me you don't love Catherine Smythe."

"Now you've gone and ruined the evening, Viv, and it's only just begun."

"Do you love her?" I pressed. When he was silent I went on relentlessly, "It's *me*, Viv, sitting here. Your oldest and dearest friend and you can't fool me. Look me right in the eye, Jack Lyon Locke and tell me that you don't love her."

"I do, but—"

"No, no, no, Jack. No buts."

"Who gave you that fabulous pin?"

"Don't change the subject."

"Okay, okay. I love her. So what?"

"I saw Catherine two days ago. When I was in London working with my publisher."

"You did!" He sat up straighter and stared at me intently. "How is she?"

"She looks fantastic. She's got a wonderful peachy bloom about her. I must say there are some women who really blossom during pregnancy, she's one of them. And she's in great spirits, happy about the baby, working hard on her book about Fulk

Nerra, and planning to move into a new apartment."

"When?"

"Well, she hasn't actually found one yet, Jack, but she's looking hard, and certainly she hopes to be settled in a new place before the baby's born." I stared at him, waiting for a comment or a question, but he said nothing. He gulped down his champagne and looked around for the waiter, who came in a flash to fill his glass.

Once we were alone, I said, "Catherine loves you very much, Jack."

"Go and tell that to the Marines," he muttered in a truculent voice.

I answered softly, "I know she does, and I also know that she'd like to be with you, with or without the benefit of marriage. In any case, she's very independent minded about matrimony, but then you know that."

"If she loves me as much as you say she does, then why did she betray me?" he asked in a sulky voice.

"How did she do that, Jack?" I murmured, frowning.

"She got pregnant when she knew I didn't want children."

"I don't believe that was on purpose. From what she said, it was an accident. Let me ask you something, just out of curiosity. Why are you so against children?"

"I'm not against kids. I just don't want any of my own."

"Catherine says you think you can't love a child. Because you believe Sebastian didn't love you."

He offered me a sardonic smile. "That was her parting shot to me, if I remember correctly. And she's off her rocker. Of course I can love a child . . ."

"Then why don't you go to London and get her,

bring her back to France? You could have a good life together, darling."

"No way, Viv. I'm better off alone."

"*I* don't think you are. She also told me something else, Jack. She said that you confided things about Sebastian and she thinks he was suffering from something called disassociation."

"Yeah. She spouted all that to me too! A lot of psychiatric mumbo-jumbo!"

"Not necessarily, Jack. There is such a condition, I've discussed it with a psychiatrist I know." I paused, then slowly I continued, "I think she's correct. Sebastian probably was afflicted with it."

"Well, well, well, so the worm turns."

"No, not at all. But I've thought a lot about him in the past few weeks, since I've been working on the profile of him for the *Sunday Times*, and I've come to see him differently."

"Tell me. I'm all ears."

"I believe Sebastian had a problem being intimate with us, loving us on a certain level. He just couldn't do it, the emotion wasn't there. Very simply, it was missing in him. And by *us* I mean you, me, and Luciana. My mother. And probably all the wives. You see, he never knew mother love, had never bonded with *anyone* during the first years of babyhood when that is essential. And yet, conversely, he was a caring human being, Jack. Look how concerned he was about the world, how he wanted to help those in desperate need. It was possible for him to do enormous charity work, to 'love' the world en masse, so to speak, because he didn't have to be *intimate* with all those people out there. He gave vast amounts of money, traveled the world making sure it was used properly. And gave the *impression* of being a 'loving' man.''

Jack was listening to me, taking in my words, and I could see that I had reached him. I went on, "Sebastian tried so hard, he did the best he could for us and he did care about us, Jack. In fact he always showed the three of us how much he cared, demonstrated it in so many different ways. He gave *you* the château because you loved it so much. It wasn't for tax benefits, as you've so often implied. He encouraged you to work with Olivier and learn the wine business. I know he expected you to run Locke Industries and the Locke Foundation one day, but he never said you couldn't do it long distance, the way he had always done. And he never once said you had to give up the winery. He spent time with you, he encouraged you to do so many things when you were young. Sebastian helped to make you what you are today."

Jack was staring at me in astonishment. "What do you mean, spent time with me? He never did that! He was forever traveling, always lumbering me with Luciana. And you, missy."

I laughed in his face. "Oh God, Jack, you sound like a maungy little boy. And for what it's worth, *I'm* the one who got lumbered with you and Luciana." I leaned forward and grabbed hold of his hand resting on the table. "Listen to me! Sebastian did the very best he could for you! *I know. I saw it.* And he did spend time with you. He taught you how to ride a horse, play tennis, row a boat and swim, and many other things. You've just blocked it out because you hate him for some unknown reason. Why, I'll never know. And I'll never know why you can't give him the benefit of the doubt."

"You have always viewed him from a different angle. You see him differently than I, Viv!" he shot back.

"That's true to some extent, I agree. But I think I'm beginning to see him more realistically. I know I always idolized him. And idealized him, as well. I've suffered from a complaint called hero worship for years. But I'm getting over that. He wasn't perfect, I realize this. He was moody and difficult, and one of the most agonized men in the world. That's why he was morose and gloomy so much of the time. And I believe his agony sprang from his awful childhood. Being brought up by Cyrus Locke and some hideous nanny, and then acquiring a dreadful stepmother like Hildegarde Orbach must have been perfectly horrible. Foul. Poor little boy. When I think about his childhood my heart bleeds. Actually, in my opinion, he turned out very well under the circumstances."

Jack was looking at me intently, digesting my words. He had an odd look on his face when he said, "You seem to have worked out his psychology very well . . . do you really believe he suffered from disassociation then?"

"Frankly, Jack, I do."

He nodded. "You said he couldn't love on a intimate level. Are you now telling me he couldn't love *you?*"

"Yes, I am. I don't think he loved me, not in the way you and I love people, Jack. Oh Sebastian said he loved me, gave me lip service. And I know he cared very deeply about me and my welfare, and that he was sexually involved with me. Very much so. But sexual passion can't be construed as love."

"The worm *has* turned," he said in such a soft voice he was barely audible.

"I see him in a new light," I replied, "I understand him better, that's all. And I don't love him any less than I ever did. My *view* of him has changed. Not my feelings for him. They're still exactly the same."

"I see."

"Try to give him the benefit of the doubt, Jack, can't you? I think you'd feel better if you did. You have no reason to hate him. He was a good father."

He said nothing. He sat there staring at me across the table, and suddenly I understood without him saying it that I had got through to him. And I realized he respected me more than ever for being so honest with him.

I sipped my champagne. I, too, was silent.

Unexpectedly Jack exclaimed, "But he always took what I wanted—"

"What do you mean?" I asked with a frown.

"My Special Lady, for one. Your mother. I loved Antoinette very much."

I was so taken aback I gaped at him and my jaw dropped. "Jack, my mother was a *mother* to you! She was a grown woman. They were heavily involved. She adored him. What on earth are you getting at?"

"I don't know . . . I always felt I was in some sort of competition with him . . . for her love and attention. And yours. I couldn't believe it when he married you. He took you away from me."

"Oh Jack, I'm sorry. So very sorry you've been harboring these awful feelings of . . . frustration and anger. And quite obviously for years. But Sebastian wasn't in competition with you, don't you see that? You were only a little boy. He was a man and one who was lethally attractive to women."

Jack sighed heavily. "I guess the shoe was on the other foot . . . I suppose *I* was competing with *him*. Is that what you're saying?"

"I think I am, Jack, yes." I leaned closer to him. "I want you to do something for me. And for yourself, and this is vitally important, so please pay attention, don't start looking around the restaurant in that way."

He brought his gaze back to mine. "I'm listening, Viv."

"I want you to go to London. *Immediately*. I don't want you to waste any time. I want you to get Catherine and bring her back to Aix-en-Provence. I want you to marry her at once so that the baby is legitimate when it's born."

"Why?"

"Because I want you to start your life all over again. I want a new beginning for you, a new beginning for the Locke dynasty. The baby Catherine is carrying is the future of the dynasty. And Catherine herself is your future, Jack. You'll never meet anyone more suited to you than she. And she loves you so much."

He sat very still, listening attentively to every word.

I smiled faintly. "It's odd, you know," I continued. "I've just suddenly realized that Catherine loves you in exactly the same way I loved Sebastian."

He lolled back in the chair, gave me a questioning look. And I couldn't help thinking that he looked so very much like his father at this moment. Leveling his blue eyes at me, he lifted a dark brow. "And how is that?" he asked finally.

"With all her heart and soul and mind," I answered.

Chapter Thirty-eight

The quietness of the old mill at Lourmarin had been restorative, just as I had known it would be. That was one of the reasons I loved to come back to Provence, to bask in the stillness of my house, to rediscover its beauty and the beauty of my gardens, to be at peace.

In the past two weeks the tranquility had been a godsend. I had sifted through my troubled thoughts, brought order to the chaos in my mind.

And now at last it was all so very clear to me. I understood everything and I had finally come to terms with myself.

I had changed.

I would never be the same again.

And I would never see the world in quite the same way, either.

Elements beyond my control had wrought these changes in me—Sebastian's suicide, Countess Zoë's confessions, Catherine's insights, my new-found knowledge of those I thought I knew, but had not known at all. And my new understanding of myself. I realized that at this moment in time I wanted to walk alone. For one thing, it had now become clear to me that I could not make a commitment to Kit Tremain. But I think I had always known that.

Jack and I had become closer than ever, perhaps because I had been so forthright about Sebastian and my revised perception of him. And somehow I had helped Jack to see the future more clearly than before.

Jack was at peace with himself at long last. He had resolved his hatred of his father; the turmoil in his heart had been vanquished. Jack had taken the advice I had given him in Paris. He had gone to see Catherine in London and brought her back with him to Aix-en-Provence. Between the two of us we had convinced her to become his wife.

They were married yesterday at the Château d'Cose.

It was an intimate wedding. We had all agreed this was the way it should be. Olivier Marchand and his wife Claudette were present, along with Madame Clothilde and her husband Maurice, and a few of the other old-timers from the estate, whom Jack, Luciana, and I had grown up with.

Luciana and Gerald had flown in from London, and Luciana was so cordial with me that I was amazed. She seemed happier and healthier. The change in her was so remarkable that I wondered if she were pregnant.

Afterward we had been served lunch in the garden. It had been such a lovely May day with the lilacs in full bloom and Catherine had made a beautiful bride in a pale pink dress and coat which set off her red hair. Jack had never been smarter in his life. He wore a dark blue suit, white shirt, and gray silk tie and looked more like Sebastian than ever. I had never seen him so happy. I was thrilled for him, thrilled for them both. They were going to be all right, those two. I had no fears.

Rising, I left my desk and walked across the library to the French doors overlooking the gardens. I stood for a moment staring out, thinking what a lovely evening it was. Then, pushing open the doors, I stepped onto the terrace.

My eyes turned toward the distant horizon.

The sky was changing as the sun sank low in the west. The colors along the rim of the horizon took my breath away: vermillion and orange running into peach and gold, violet bleeding into amethyst, and lilac striated with the palest pink. It was the most glorious sunset I had seen in a long time.

The radiant light streaming out from behind the darkening clouds looked supernatural, as if it were emanating from some hidden source below the line of somber hills.

Only the shrill ringing of the phone forced me to tear my eyes away from that extraordinary sky.

I stepped into the library and reached for the receiver. "*Vieux Moulin.* Hello?"

"Madame Trent, s'il vous plaît."

"This is she speaking. Hubert, is that you?"

"*C'est moi,* Madame. *Bon soir*—" He broke off, his voice trembling as he strived hard for control.

I knew what he was going to say, the news he had to impart before he spoke again. "Is it Countess Zoë, Hubert?" I asked quietly.

"Yes, Madame. She just died a few moments ago. She realized she was dying this afternoon. She asked me to let you know. 'Telephone Madame Trent immediately, Hubert. She must be told at once.' That is what she said to me. It was her last wish. She died gently, Madame. And she was at peace."

"Was her son Charles with her, Hubert?"

"Yes. Monsieur le Comte was at her bedside with his wife and little son. And Mademoiselle Ariel. Monsieur finally overruled his mother last week and brought his sister back from Africa."

"I'm so glad they were all with her," I said, my voice shaking. I brushed the tears off my cheeks. "Thank you, Hubert, for letting me know. Good night."

"Good night, Madame."

I replaced the receiver and went back to the terrace. I walked down the steps into the gardens Sebastian and I had planted so many years ago.

How beautiful they looked tonight. Many of the flowers had bloomed early this year. The borders were riotous with color and the early evening air was fragrant with their mingled scents.

I stood looking out toward my lavender fields and the meadows far beyond. Everything was a blur. I could not see anything through my tears.

My thoughts were of Countess Zoë. She had shown me that the past was immutable. My past was Sebastian and part of me would always belong to him. But I had let him go . . . I had exorcised his ghost at last. And now I could get on with my life. Like Jack, I could start anew.

Countess Zoë had set me free.